Please return on or before the latest date above.
You can renew online at *www.kent.gov.uk/libs*
or by telephone 08458 247 200

A PARALLEL LIFE

Harriet Compton-Milne can't remember a time when she wasn't worried. Just twenty-one, the qualified jeweller feels old before her time. She can match stones, make platinum shine but she can't leave Bolton because her brother Ben, an OCD-riddled genius, wouldn't be able to cope without her. Her eccentric parents aren't much help, but when big trouble arrives, the family – including Hermione, Harriet's acerbic, attic-dwelling grandmother – will have to act as a unit if they are to survive and keep their sanity.

A PARALLEL LIFE

A PARALLEL LIFE

by

Ruth Hamilton

Magna Large Print Books
Long Preston, North Yorkshire,
BD23 4ND, England.

British Library Cataloguing in Publication Data.

Hamilton, Ruth
   A parallel life.

      A catalogue record of this book is
      available from the British Library

      ISBN   978-0-7505-3465-9

First published in Great Britain 2010 by
Severn House Publishers Ltd

Cover illustration © Benjamin Harte by arrangement with
Arcangel Images

The moral right of the author has been asserted.

Published in Large Print 2011 by arrangement with
Severn House Publishers Ltd

Magna Large Print is an imprint of Library Magna Books Ltd.

Printed and bound in Great Britain by
T.J. (International) Ltd., Cornwall, PL28 8RW

Once Upon a Time...

...in a white room at the top of a tall tower, there dwelt a beautiful princess named Mathilda. She had long, nut-brown tresses, perfect features and skin of creamy alabaster. The princess did nothing for herself. Every day, she was bathed, perfumed and dressed in pretty gowns. Her nails were shaped, hands moisturized, and her face was treated with the finest creams available to human-kind.

She was fed by staff, massaged by physio-therapists, visited by servants. Mathilda did not even breathe for herself. Machinery dictated the rhythm of her life, delivering oxygen to lungs that stubbornly refused to inflate of their own accord. Her education was limited to the conductive type, which discipline involved two people work-ing in unison to discourage the wastage of muscle by moving limbs and spine in a pattern dictated by experts. Food arrived via a tube, while waste matter was collected in bags and removed efficiently by her faithful attendants. Music was played several times a day, and nuns read to her from Dickens and Austen, though no one was sure that she could hear or interpret sound.

This existence, dictated and paid for by her only visitor, had endured for many years. But she was easier than most other residents of Nazareth House, so lay staff vied for the privilege of serving

9

her. Nuns did as they were bidden by timetable, though a few admitted that the peace prevailing in Princess Mathilda's tower was a blessed relief. It was a calm place to be, a room in which rosaries could be said in quietude, an area that allowed contemplative moments often denied to members of a working sisterhood.

Sister Mary Magdalene sat next to the pristine bed. The white, bright room seemed to be an echo of an untouched soul, because Mathilda had never sinned. Most rights of Earth's superior species had been denied to this beautiful young woman because of a birth accident. It was a tragedy, but it was a fact. Mathilda, unlike several before and after her, had not been left to die in a side ward or a sluice room. She was here. She was here, and she deserved care.

Having taken her vows in seriousness, Magda allowed little space for suspicion that the patient was little more than a set of spare parts, an experiment, a guinea pig. The woman-child represented purity and, although she could make no choices, Mathilda was a physical embodiment of the primary rights of man – to life and to bodily integrity. Other choices would never be available to her, or so it appeared.

Magda finished her decade, placed the rosary in a pocket of her grey skirt, smoothed the bed, stroked a pale hand. 'When you first came, we wore white habits, Mathilda. There was a legend about some poor nun standing here in this very room. No one saw her, because she blended with the walls, so she was run over by a trolley. Nonsense, of course, but it's the nonsenses that get us

10

through our days. I pray God that you will wake.'

The girl had woken in her infancy, but fits had forced doctors to tranquillize her. Now, she simply slept, though her sleep was deep enough to be labelled coma. No longer tranquillized, the young woman remained in her state of suspended animation. For Mathilda, there was no happiness, no sadness, no depression, no joy. Seasons came and went, but she was not aware of sun, of wind or of rain. She simply existed and did no harm. None but the hardest heart could bear with equanimity the sight of such unfulfilled promise. What might she have become? Who was she?

'I'll take myself off now,' said the nun. 'A bit of Mozart later on, something nice and gentle, then...' Then what? The sound of a ventilator, sometimes a rush of air from a conditioning unit, footsteps in the corridor. This was a perfect environment in which to be not quite alive. God was good, Magda insisted inwardly as she left the room. He worked in mysterious ways, and no human was qualified to question Him. Nevertheless, a miracle was required. And there was no harm in asking, was there?

Mary Magdalene made her way across grounds towards the sisters' quarters. Both the main house and the convent were unattractive buildings spattered liberally in dull, grey pebble-dash. Across the acres, the eerie cries of peacocks seemed a perfect accompaniment to the nun's thoughts. She was sad today. The convent was no longer a convent. Housing just five sisters, it had been forced into commerce and was currently a bed and breakfast for people who came to the

North on business. Sometimes, it was used as a base for retreat, though the small chapel provided penitents with limited space for prayer and contemplation. 'God's will,' she muttered as she entered the convent's kitchen. Lay staff were chattering, peeling vegetables, basting meats.

'Hi, Magda,' cried the cook. 'How's your princess?'

'No change,' she replied. It was always the same answer, though people were kind enough to ask, at least. One of the better aspects of humanity was the tendency to care for a victim and to urge God Almighty to intervene.

'Pretty girl,' commented a peeler of potatoes. 'Bloody shame.' The woman blushed. 'Sorry, Sister. Shouldn't have said bloody.'

'No matter. I know how you feel.' Magda picked up a knife and attacked broccoli. It was a shame. The child should have died at birth. That was a sinful thought, so Mary Magdalene awarded herself another ten decades of the rosary for tonight. She must bow to the will of God...

One

Summer, 2006

Things were stirring in the roof.

Stirring was not the right word for the rumblings and stumblings of Hermione Compton-Milne. In a bedroom on the first floor, Harriet moaned and turned sideways, pulling a pillow over her head. Gran was on the loose. It was Tuesday, the loosest of all days, because Tuesday meant Family Breakfast. All residents of Weaver's Warp were required by law to put in an appearance in the breakfast room. Any refusers were debited like failed runners in some field event – back to the stables with several fleas in the ear and no treats for the foreseeable future. Escape was impossible. 'Oh God, oh God, oh God,' breathed Harrie. The Gestapo was on its way.

The first stairlift hummed. Harrie raised her pillow to listen.

'If he never smiled, he'd look better,' proclaimed the matriarch, from the other side of her bedroom door. 'What's his name?'

Gran's carer answered, 'Michael Jardine.'

'Yes, well, it was better when Taggart was alive. He'd a face like a bad knee, but he never looked like a pervert. When that Jardine smirks, you expect him to flash more than his teeth. He should wear a raincoat and frighten pigeons in the park. I've gone off that programme.'

Harrie grinned. Gran, a multiple sclerosis victim, had become a devotee of Sky Television and the many repeats on offer. Her favourite programme, *Last of the Summer Wine*, was praised frequently whenever she held court in her attic suite. No one was a patch on Bill Owen. Both the late John Thaw and Inspector Frost had also seemed to have gained her approval, as had some detective named Linley, who was judged to be 'a beautiful piece of furniture, and every home should have one'.

Harrie climbed out of bed and threw on some clothes. She had bathed before bed, and Gran did not approve of latecomers, so further ablutions must wait. She heard the second stairlift spring to life. Gran had moved to Mother's room, part-way down the second flight of stairs. After dragging a comb through wilful tresses, Harrie left her room and banged on a door. 'Ben?'

'What?'

'It's Tuesday, brother dear.'

'I know.'

'She's already on the rampage.'

'I know.'

'She'll go mad if you don't come down.'

'I know.'

'And if you say I know again, I'll bloody kill you.'

The door opened. 'I know.'

Harrie sighed. What was to be done about Ben? He was beautiful – far too beautiful for his own good. He was also an oddity and the cause of great worry for his sister. He lived apart, had no

14

friends and was abnormally keen on cleanliness. A genius IQ contributed little to his emotional well-being; in fact, Harrie believed that her younger brother's brain was a burden rather than an asset. 'Come on,' she demanded. 'Time for us to pretend to be human.'

In the downstairs hallway, Gustav Compton-Milne was patting his pockets and looking appropriately distracted, while his wife, on all fours beneath a coat stand, announced that she was searching for an earring. It was only a Butler and Wilson, but Butler and Wilson had been good enough for Princess Diana when it came to fun jewellery, so it was certainly good enough for... *I'll look later*, she advised herself.

Brother and sister walked into the breakfast room. Gran, who was not known for her patience, sniffed at the siblings. 'What on earth are your parents doing?'

Ben shrugged. His father had probably invented a system for running cars on hot water, but the theorem would be lost among his many pockets. Mother was... Mother was just being Mother. 'They've lost stuff,' he said as he took his seat.

'Gus?' yelled Gran. 'Come in here at once and eat.'

Gus wandered in. 'The address has gone missing,' he said to himself.

No one enquired about the address, so he took his position at the end of the table that faced his mother. 'Good morning, Mater,' he said absently. *'Exchange and Mart,'* he added softly. 'It was the right gauge and is very rare these days.'

15

'Toy trains,' scoffed Hermione. It was time for some people to grow up. Such a fuss Gus had made when the attics had been done over for her to live in. The man had almost wept when his railway layouts had been dismantled and removed.

Lisa sauntered in. 'Good morning,' she said to no one in particular. 'If anyone finds an earring, it's mine.' On any other morning, she would have been able to miss breakfast and locate her missing decoration, but Mother-in-law dictated that Tuesday was a family day. Butler and Wilson was expensive tat and deserved some respect. Perhaps the lost piece was outside the house?

Hermione glared at her small congregation. Benjamin, her grandson, had taken to living separately – his own kitchen and bathroom. Gus was... She sighed quietly. Gus was Gus. He was her only son and had been named, at his father's insistence, after Gustav Holst. Originally a doctor of medicine, Gus Compton-Milne had not related well to his fellow man, and he had wandered off into the bowels of medical research. His tracts on the subject of killer bacteria were renowned worldwide, and he had even managed to give the odd lecture at Yale and Harvard. Yes, his lectures would be very odd, Hermione judged.

Lisa. Poor Lisa. The mother of Hermione's grandchildren had been chosen at random, it seemed. Gus had married her within weeks of meeting her and had given her sparse attention once the two statutory offspring had been delivered. The neglected woman worked hard, supporting her family financially, and, in order to

16

keep some sanity, taking a series of lovers about whom no one was supposed to know.

Munching on toast, Hermione allowed her gaze to stray once again to her son. Gus had a woman. She was a common-or-garden type and she had enough room in her loft for all his bloody children's trains. Gus was a remarkably stupid man. He didn't deserve his wife. He certainly didn't deserve Harriet.

Harriet. Now, there was an almost perfect pearl. Harriet had given up her chance of university to stay at home and... And what? And sell jewellery in the second of the Compton-Milne shops? Why had the child taken upon herself the task of looking after Ben? Whether Harriet stayed or went, Ben would always be a bloody mess. Look at him! He was staring hard at his plate, was probably envisaging a million microbes clomping in clogs across its ceramic surface. He should work for his silly father.

'This family is a mess,' declared the grandmother. 'Harriet, you should not be here. Ben, you need some psychological help.' She grinned at Lisa. However naughty she became, Lisa would always be forgivable. As for Gus – what was the point? She could shout and bawl, but he would not hear. Gus marched to a different drummer. His children did not count. His wife was of no significance. His mother lived where his trains used to be. 'Multiple sclerosis is the least of my woes,' moaned Hermione. She would do better to conserve her limited energies...

The day still wouldn't make up its mind, mused

17

Harriet Compton-Milne as she dried the bench with a handkerchief. 'No guts,' she muttered under her breath. Light showers, the odd flash of sun, some mist earlier on. It was a half-hearted day. Heavier clouds had begun to drift in like late trains at Trinity Street. They rested on Harrie's shoulders with all the other stuff: the anger, the panic, the why-am-I-here business. Now, there was the why-was-Dad-standing-across-the-road stuff, but that probably wasn't worth thinking about. His woman must live in these parts, Harrie concluded absently. A spit of rain hit her arm.

She sat down and gazed at a park area that had once been pretty: flower beds, lawns, a bowling green. All gone now; all replaced by battered beer-cans and bottles from which liquid had been released into the stomachs of several errant teenagers. She was old before her time, could not remember feeling young. Bitter at twenty-one? Ridiculous. It was almost four o'clock. What the hell was she going to say this time? Should she help herself along with a few milligrams of diazepam? What about stepping in front of a bus? That would provide a solution of sorts, she supposed.

Raising her head, she stared into Bolton, noting that the day was not warm enough to show the blue rinse of pollution that inevitably wigged its busy streets. She could see all the way across to Bolton School, her old alma, the institution that had fitted her for Oxford. Why hadn't she taken her place among those spires and buttresses? Were there buttresses in Oxford? *She asks the questions*, Harrie advised herself before rising from the bench, leaving the park and crossing

Wigan Road. *I'm supposed to supply the answers to her queries. Bloody psychoanalysts.* There was, she believed, a Bridge of Sighs – one in Cambridge, too.

Rain began to fall properly. Well, the day, at least, had made up its mind. Thunder rumbled down the moors, while a fork of bright electricity warned the world that some ill-humoured deity was still in charge. She ran into the large terraced house and sat in a waiting room. It was beige, brown and cream. Abstract prints punctuated walls painted in magnolia over geriatric wallpaper. It was supposed to be a calm atmosphere, she believed. Outside, the storm raged noisily, seeming to echo her own inner turmoil. One of the gentler Beatles songs played in the background. 'Strawberry Fields'. She was unaccountably angry. Depression, she had been told, was self-loathing. Her own illness wanted to make her sleep all the time, but she resisted the urge. Life went on. It wasn't fair, but it went on. The woman was smiling and beckoning Harrie into the inner sanctum.

She rose. 'Here we go again,' she mumbled as she entered the consultation room. The doc was already seated – she was a fast mover. More magnolia in here, but with a bit of maroon thrown in as some kind of blessed relief; a few French Impressionist prints on the chimney breast. Oh, bugger it...

The door wouldn't slam. It owned one of those swing-slow contraptions at the top, and Harrie gave this item a baleful glance before focusing sternly on Miriam Goldberg. 'You should have a noisy door,' complained the new arrival. 'A heavy

19

slam is probably just what the doctor ordered for cases like mine.' The anger drifted away, because she could not be ill-behaved with so pleasant a woman.

Miriam shuffled some papers and tried not to smile. 'Sit down, please.'

'Have you nothing I can break?'

'Not today, no. Would you like a jelly baby?'

'Not unless it comes with a knuckleduster or a shotgun.'

'All right.' The doctor grinned. 'I could buy seconds from the market and you could smash crocks later in the backyard.' She shook the jar of sweets. 'There are black ones. I always think black ones taste best, don't you?'

'I'm not racist, so I'm not bothered.' Harrie chewed a nail instead. These visits were a waste of time. She had stuff to do. Waiting at the shop were two rings with suspect settings and some new stones to be sorted. 'Ben's at the dentist,' she murmured. 'This is his first time on his own, and he'll be terrified.'

'Where's your mother?'

'God knows. Or perhaps the devil does. She's having dinner and bridge tonight with some of her cronies. She can't play bridge for toffee.'

'Try her on jelly babies.'

Harrie flopped into the chair for clients. 'You should see someone about your fixation with those sweets.'

'Physician heal thyself?'

'Exactly. Go on, I'll have a yellow one.'

While Harrie chewed, Miriam Goldberg hung on to her exasperation. 'At eighteen,' she began eventually, 'your brother is old enough to cope with his own teeth.' Why should this poor girl take all the flak? 'And, if he can't manage by himself, shouldn't your mother go with him?'

Harrie raised her shoulders. 'I have no answer to that one.'

The psychologist reined herself in. She was here as a professional to listen to Harrie, to help her externalize her feelings and cope with daily disaster. 'How's your grandmother?'

The girl swallowed the remains of her sweet and smiled broadly. 'Utterly and dreadfully wonderful. She got Sky Plus, so she's happy. My grandmother is now self-crowned queen of UK Drama. She watches anything and everything, though I am slightly concerned regarding her new affiliation to the crime channels.'

'And your parents?'

Harrie sighed. 'What good is this doing, Doc? What am I to say? I don't know. I don't know how they feel about anything. Dad seldom shows emotion, because he's too busy trying to save the world from the little people. He says it will not be a neutron bomb, but a microbe that will see us all off. And as for Mother, after so much Botox, her face shows hardly any reaction, and she was never one for words.'

Miriam shook her head slowly. The Compton-Milnes were round the twist, and Harrie was paying the price for all of them. 'But she's a jeweller – she has to talk to people.'

The young client shook her head. 'But not to me – never in depth. Anyway, don't make the mistake of oversimplifying the dynamics within my family.

It's easy to say that my father is a boffin, my brother a genius, my mother a fool.' She leaned forward. 'Do you know how long it takes to make a diamond?'

'A million years?'

'And the rest.' Harrie picked up a pencil and twisted it in her fingers. 'To explain humanity would take the same period of evolution, and we don't have time to start planting trees.'

Miriam Goldberg frowned. 'Harrie, what about you?'

'Me?' She leaned back in her chair and stared at the ceiling. She was a qualified jeweller and was carrying on in the business created by her grand-father after the collapse of the cotton industry. She could match stones, mend a watch and make platinum shine like an item stolen from clear night skies. 'I'm just here,' she concluded. 'I'm just carrying on carrying on.'

'Still taking the don't-jump-off-the-roof pills?'

'Of course.'

Miriam shifted in her chair. This girl was stunning enough to be a fashion model, though she was no coat hanger. All curves were present and correct, so she wasn't sufficiently skeletal for a life of cocaine and catwalks. She had brains enough to have passed with flying colours every exam on her list, yet she had chosen to sell fripperies in the bigger of the family's two shops.

'When are you going to start thinking about yourself, Harriet?'

'Harrie.'

'You are brilliant, talented and beautiful.'

'Gee, thanks.'

22

The therapist stood and walked to the window. She knew Harrie's reasons for staying in Bolton, but they were as flawed as any impure diamond on a cutting bench. 'There are carbon deposits in your arguments.'

'Then I'll never be set in eighteen carat.'

'The flippancy hides a multitude of worries. When did you become a worrier?'

'Can't remember.'

'It's been always, hasn't it?'

Harrie indulged in a second jelly baby. She chewed thoughtfully, taking care to swallow before replying. 'I can't remember not being worried. Dad's never been there, Mum's always seemed an airhead, and no one ever took care of Ben. Woebetide has been the nearest thing to a parent since Gran lost the use of her legs.'

Miriam turned. 'Tell me about Woebetide.'

Oh, God. Harrie thought about the woman who had slipped easily into the position of Gran's carer. Woebetide was no oil painting. In fact, her exterior had frightened off a long line of Jehovah's Witnesses and double-glazing salesmen, yet she had intelligence to spare and an accent that had defied thirty years of exile from her beloved Mayo. She was kind, noisy, firm and loving. With no children of her own, she had been nanny and housekeeper for the whole of Harrie's lifetime.

'How did she get her name?'

Harrie laughed aloud. 'She woe-betided everything. It was, "Woe betide anyone who breaks one of the new plates," and, "Woe betide whoever took the cream off the top of me trifle," – except, of course, she says "troifle". The house has staircases, bedrooms, bathrooms and a Woebetide. She's part of the scenery that comes to life occasionally. If the house were sold, she'd be included in fixtures.'

'So she comes to "loife"?'

'Yup.'

'And you love her.' This was not a question.

'With all my heart. And Gran. She's always been a marvellous woman. Even with MS, she never complained. I remember when she first found out she had it – she came home and said that she would soon be able to sit down and forget all about jewellery. Sometimes, when she thought no one was watching, she would shed a tear. But she's brave and naughty. She's exactly how we should all be in old age. She certainly rages against the dying of the light.'

Miriam Goldberg smiled and returned to her seat. 'Harrie, the tablets are helping, but only you can climb out of the pit.'

'It's not a pit; it's a swamp. Quicksand.'

'Suicidal?'

'No. I'm not brave enough and not sufficiently cowardly.'

Miriam sat down and placed clasped hands on her desk. 'Stop being a martyr.'

'I can't leave him. Anyway, there's always the Open University, though they do seem to offer a whole bundle of Mickey Mouse subjects. But Ben needs me. He's the one who'll do really well at university.'

'No. I think Ben needs *me*.'

'You'd never get through to him. He's closed down.'

'Like your parents?'

Harrie nodded. 'He works hard, never plays, talks only to me. At school, he keeps his head down and carries on with his work, gets bullied, comes home, fears doctors, dentists, fears most people. He has me and only me. And I am forbidden to discuss him.'

'And you will dedicate the rest of your life to him?'

'I don't know.'

Miriam glanced at the wall clock. It was plain that Miss Harriet Compton-Milne had set herself in reinforced concrete. A clever and capable girl, she had denied herself the chance of a future because she dared not leave her brother in the care of his own parents. 'They'd still take you at Oxford.'

'I'm past it.'

'At twenty-one?'

Harrie shrugged. 'I may go yet, I suppose. But it would have to be–'

'It would have to be with Ben. You are your brother's keeper.'

No reply was forthcoming. No matter what, Harrie would keep the promise she had made to her brother. She was to tell 'them' nothing about him.

'Well?'

'No comment.'

Miriam sighed and settled back into her chair. This was promising to be a waste of tremendous talent, but the girl was fixed into her own claw setting, and the person whose talons held her there was a beloved brother. Harrie was clearly bent on hiding all that cried to be released from her troubled mind. 'You tell me nothing,' grumbled the therapist.

'It's stopped raining. There's a bit of information for you.' Harrie rose to her feet and walked to the door. Turning, she delivered a beaming smile that almost failed to reach her eyes. 'I'd try liquorice allsorts if I were you,' she pronounced before leaving the room. 'You might get somewhere with those.'

'In truth, you are not ill,' said Miriam. 'You have a difficult life – and that's different.'

Ben was wet through because of the recent downpour. He watched his sister as she descended steps cut into a hilly part of Wigan Road during the building of several terraces of Edwardian houses. She was beautiful and clever, and he was holding her back.

'You'll catch your death,' Harrie warned. 'Get into the bloody car.' She sat in the driving seat and hid her exasperation when he spread his own towel across the passenger side before climbing in. He was getting worse, and she was probably keeping pace with him. At three years of age, Harrie had fed Ben his bottle – under the watchful eye of Woebetide, of course. Even now, she remembered how he had stared at her, how he had chosen her as his sole ally before he could even sit up without cushions.

'I didn't go,' he said now.

She wasn't going to ask for a reason, as she already knew the answers. It wasn't the pain, wasn't the smell of mouthwash or the whirr of a

26

drill; he didn't like to be touched by anyone. Life, for Ben, was about not making contact. 'You'll have to phone and apologize.'

'Yes.'

'I can't always be there, Ben.' Terrified eyes. If she closed her own, she could still see fear burning in his; it had burnt for many years. But, as long as he could keep Harrie with him, he could manage within certain boundaries. Was he mentally ill, and were such diseases communicable? Had her poor little brother made her sick?

'What did your shrink have to say for herself?'

'Nothing much. Too interested in jelly babies and a calm atmosphere.' She started the car. 'What's going to be done about you? If you can't even get your teeth polished, what about uni?'

Ben shrugged. 'I'll go to Manchester and come home each evening. You didn't tell her about me, did you?'

'Of course not.' She turned a corner and headed for Chorley New Road. 'University is about getting away and broadening your horizons. You're expected to want to leave home. Leaving home is normal.'

'I'm not normal.'

Harrie dragged the car over to the pavement's edge, braked and turned off the engine. It was the same circle all the time – look after Ben, see to the shop, do the books, visit Gran upstairs, look after Ben, keep an eye on Mum's progress in the other shop, look after Ben, look after Ben...

'I'm sorry,' he whispered.

'So am I.' It wasn't his fault that his mother hadn't been well enough to want him. Gran had

27

seen to him in the night, while Woebetide had covered days. All the time, he had cried out for his sister. He screamed when she went to school, when she left a room, when his cot was moved into a separate bedroom. He never played with other children, was reading fluently by the age of four, and kicked up a fuss when forced into school, when left behind during Harrie's riding and dance lessons. 'You do need help, Ben.'

'Can't let anyone in. You know that.'

'At some stage in your life, you're going to have to trust someone other than me and Woebetide.'

'Gran's OK,' he muttered.

'Gran's moving towards a world of her own.'

'Lucky Gran.' Ben hugged his bag of books. 'Get me home, please.'

Home contained the strangest of Ben's many symptoms.

When Gran had invaded the roof, builders charged with the task of creating her suite of rooms were also bidden to do Ben's wishes. Two of five bedrooms on the first floor had been converted into a bed-sitting room, a kitchen and a bathroom for him. His living quarters lay behind a proper front door with several locks and bolts. Inside, the place was pristine at all times. The only visitor was Harrie, and she seldom failed to comment on the fact that Ben would make an excellent housewife, while she, untidy and disorganized, declared herself to be a slob. She dropped on to his brown leather sofa. 'I am knackered,' she announced. 'Put the kettle on.'

Through the open doorway between living

room and kitchen, Harrie watched her brother as he peeled back cling film from the hob of his cooker. He wiped the kettle before filling it, set it to boil and reached a tray from the top of his fridge-freezer. The cling film was a new development. He lined up two mugs on the tray, taken from a row of hooks beneath the cupboards. Every hanging item faced the same way, and all were graded according to size and colour. No one was allowed to use his personal cup. No one ever came, but even Harrie was not allowed to touch the stainless steel mug.

In the living room, where Harrie sat, floor-to-ceiling shelves flanked the chimney breast. Books were kept in sections, each stretch labelled with a piece of laminated card. He had trouble with books, Harrie knew, because authors allowed their work to be published by untidy characters with a tendency to make changes in the dimensions of their wares. The desk held two computers, one a normal size, the other a laptop. Wire cages contained disks in an order understood only by their owner – Harrie would never dream of touching anything in there.

A calendar on a wall served only to make the rest of the room bare and lifeless. He was a sad, sad boy. She cleared her throat. 'The lavatory thing, Ben.'

'What about it?' he called from the small kitchen.

'You can't bike home from Manchester at lunchtime – you'll have to use a public loo.'

He came in with the tray. 'I don't need to go to every lecture. Anyway, Gran promised me a car if

I passed my test, and I did.'

Harrie snapped her mouth shut so suddenly that she imagined toothache. 'What? You got in a car with a stranger? You went and did the theory without me to hold your hand?'

He nodded.

'You must be getting better.'

'I must, indeed.'

Ben was of the 'milk second' school. He poured tea, was dissatisfied with its colour, stirred the pot, poured again. When milk had been added, he passed a mug to Harrie. 'There you go, sis.'

'When did you do the test?'

'Yesterday. It was a piece of cake. Would you like a scone?'

She shook her head. 'Then why not go to Oxford or London? It's time to get away from here, you know.'

'Manchester will do. I have to do things an inch at a time – you know that. It won't be easy in Manchester, either, but at least I'll have this bolt-hole.'

She felt trapped, wondered when her own life might begin. Guilt moved in immediately, and a panic threatened. Miriam Goldberg had instructed her to go 'happily' into her panics, because they were proof that she was one of the truly alive. 'We live among zombies,' she had said. 'Let that surge of adrenalin remind you that you are one of the few thinkers left.'

Ben's eyes were asking questions, so Harrie told him about the so-called 'happy panics' she was meant to enjoy. 'The doc says that the world wears rose-tinted specs and sits at computers all

30

the time. I wonder if the glasses will reduce damage from the screens?'

He stood up. 'It's all my fault,' he began. 'If I could–'

'Neither of us was welcomed into the world,' she reminded him. 'Dad wanted a boy, a projection of himself, so he was satisfied when you were born. Not that he contributed to your development, of course. He and Mum scarcely speak, so we are bound to be odd.'

'What *is* normal?' Ben asked.

'How the bloody hell should I know? I'm too busy having happy panics. Anyway, congrats on passing your test, old fruit. What sort of car will you have?'

He smiled wryly. 'A van type of car with a chemical lavatory in the back.'

'You're joking.' But, as she left the room, Harrie wondered about that. It was just the sort of daft thing Ben might do.

Gran sat riveted to her TV. Christopher Timothy was trapped in snow on the less gentle slopes of the Pennines, the Siberian side. With no fear of hypothermia, he and his television crew made unsteady progress across a whited-out Yorkshire moor. Knowing when to be quiet, Harrie sat and waited for credits to roll. During Gran's favourite programmes, speech could be employed only if fire or war broke out.

But Gran was the one who fractured the silence. 'Have you been with that Jewish doctor again?'

'Yes.'

'Are you sane?'

31

Harrie laughed. 'Definitely not.'

The old woman laughed. 'Good – I like a bit of company of my own sort. That's not proper snow.' She waved a hand at her thirty-two inch plasma screen. 'It's just white stuff. They blow it out of a machine.'

Advertisements were helped along by Hermione's running commentary. 'Have you seen this one? They play make-yourself-at-home music, then show a household where one child's mislaid her shoes and the other's lost his scooter. In the middle of all that, the mother borrows thousands of pounds on the phone. What sort of a message is that?' She then proceeded to berate a shampoo that stuck split ends together and some ghastly Australian females who sang the praises of a car insurance firm. 'Nonsense,' pronounced Hermione before turning off the set.

Harrie grinned. There was no need to ask after Gran's health – she was clearly in fine fettle.

'What did she say?' asked Hermione.

'Who?'

'The Jewish woman, of course.'

'Ah. She seems to think I should run for the hills.'

'She's right.'

Harrie groaned. Here came another lecture. Words poured in a well-pronounced stream from her grandmother's mouth. It was all Grandad's fault for dying before his time, thereby denying Gus an example to follow. 'Your father has the answer to the world's problems on a piece of paper he has managed to lose, and he takes no interest in anything that isn't in a laboratory or on miniature rails.'

'Yes, Gran.'

'You should have gone to university.'

'Yes, Gran.'

'Where's the sense in it? Any of it? There's a danger that Ben will fail parlously because he can't fit into anything – even his own shoes. Shall we get him some new ones? But why should we? It doesn't all centre around Ben, child.'

'Yes, Gran.'

'And God knows what your mother is up to these days – not that I blame her completely. Mindless women have to find entertainment somewhere, I suppose.'

'She isn't mindless,' said Harrie. 'She may be undereducated, but that's a different matter.'

'Don't interrupt. You're the brains of this outfit, girl. Do something with yourself. Ben will survive.'

Would he? Harrie gazed out of a dormer window and watched a few birds squabbling at the top of an ancient tree. There was cling film on his hob and an outside lock on the bathroom door. He alone was allowed to use those facilities. Often, an overpowering smell of chlorine came under the door after one of his scrubbing sessions. He could not use public lavatories, would never be examined by a doctor unless his sister stood by, had to be accompanied on shopping trips for clothes and shoes. But he had passed his driving test, must have gone in a car belonging to some driving school, had used Harrie just to practise in Dad's aged Mini.

'Are you listening?'

'Of course.'

'Did he pass?'

'Yes.'

'Were you there?'

'No.'

Hermione beamed. 'There. I think he may be pulling out of his eighteen-year nosedive. Has he applied for a place at a university?'

'Manchester – possibly Liverpool, too.'

'Your father will spin in his test tube.'

Harrie laughed. 'Let him. I think Ben has to take baby steps, Gran. Better to have him settled on a course in the north than to have him do badly elsewhere. He'll be fine.'

'Will he?'

Harrie stood up and planted a kiss on the grey head. 'Of course he will.'

She left the room and went down to the middle floor. Music could be heard coming from Ben's suite. She placed an ear to the door and listened to some eerie Gregorian chant. Why couldn't he go for Eminem like everybody else? Even the odd joint would have been preferable to his obsession with cleanliness and order.

Harrie sat on the stairs. She was sandwiched between two levels that coexisted, no more than that. Dad and Mum used the downstairs rooms, though Dad did not socialize much. They had separate bedrooms and never visited the true head of the household, who had placed herself in the roof. Two stairlifts allowed her to come and go as she pleased, and she would sometimes put in an appearance at one of her daughter-in-law's soirées or coffee gatherings. Hyacinth Bucket was

34

the title Hermione had chosen as Lisa Compton-Milne's nickname. Lisa never got anything quite right.

The Gregorian chant got louder; some blackbirds fretted noisily outside, while the scent of Woebee's cooking drifted up the stair well. Just an ordinary house. With cling film on a hob.

Two

There's a mark on the kettle where I scrubbed too hard. Scouring pads are too harsh for brushed metal. When Harrie and I go for the shoes, I shall buy a new kettle, blue – just like the old one. Bananas are on their steel tree, apples and oranges in the bowl below, no dust on the Venetian blind. The kitchen will need a new coat of paint soon. Blue. I hope I can find the same shade. Checked for flies and ants, nothing found, no need for action. That bleach kills 99.9 per cent of household germs. Should I worry about the other zero point one? I am an idiot. When I read this diary, I know without a shadow of doubt that I am a cracked pot.

Essays done in under an hour, no challenge. Scrubbed the bathroom, left the bleach in there: must water it down before using again, have to be clean. Is the rug parallel with the hearth? Clock on my radio approximately thirty seconds slow, will rectify. Whilst over in the corner, might as well sort out the magazines – they are not properly aligned. Check global times: American zones, Australia, New Zealand. I am confined pro tem to Europe, but that's OK; my French is good, German adequate. Obsessive-Compulsive Disorder. A place for everything, everything in its place. Yet where do I belong?

Perhaps I should try to manage without the sites tonight. It's almost too easy. I have friends all over the world, and shared intimacies without true contact. It's

37

real, and it's unreal. Are we all pretenders? What did people like me do before the Internet?

I found out about OCD on the web when I was thirteen-ish. The obsessive rituals are embedded deep, yet I can seek no help because I allow no one near. Except Harrie, of course. She would hate what I do online, but would never hate me. Can I ever let her go? I suppose she will ultimately beggar off without my permission. Harrie is Harrie and I am a freak.

One of the sites is harmless. Myrightway is for OCD sufferers and we make light of each other's ridiculousness. But the others are a different kettle of fish – new kettle, blue kettle? Hell, I might join a poets' corner just for a laugh. In Myrightway, we have Chameleon, who must wear green on Mondays, yellow on Tuesdays and so forth. Barrit has to close all gates as he walks down a street, while The Counter needs to take a certain number of steps across a room, always right foot first. If he stumbles, he is forced by some inexplicable law to retrace his steps and begin again.

All, or some, of the above folk may well be members of my other sites, since the choosing of a handle under which to subscribe is the easiest part of the games. Dangerous games, especially in the place I found recently. Must not go there tonight. The first time, I was appalled; on my second visit, slightly shocked. Now? It is just part and parcel of my life.

Mother has the cronies in. She met them all in health clubs or BUPA hospitals, became their shepherd and now tries to improve all minds by pretending to play bridge. Bridge, like snap, is a game for children. We have never played Happy Families in this house. Chess is the great leveller, of course. I am champion at school, but have not allowed myself to be tempted by the possibility of Grand Mastership. Don't care enough. And Harrie would be bored by the whole business, so I'd be on my own. Managed the driving lessons, hated the instructor's aftershave. But passing that test in a Harrie-free zone was a massive achievement for me. I did that all by myself, yet I could not allow a dentist to touch my mouth.

The mask is in a box behind the locked door of my wardrobe. It is rubber, has holes for mouth and nose, a zip to strangle any sounds I might make in the throes of pain or passion. At school, they know I am different, yet they have no idea of how far I have travelled from the accepted norms. They call me Prof, Son of Prof, Boffin dot com, Brain of Britain. The physical attacks stopped when I produced that knife; they probably fear me now. I wonder what they would think of my rubber face-covering?

It will soon be time to begin tonight's adventure. I shall start on the safe site, then, if I need no sleep, move to the more adventurous areas of my not-quite-life.

In the meantime, I'll sort out the CD rack. Damp cloth, dry cloth, wipe and replace. What's Queen doing with Phil Collins? Better separate those two; the result of them breeding would be catastrophic. Shania Twain can stay with LeAnn Rimes – no danger there. And what happened to Sergeant Pepper? Mum bought most of these – she understands me sufficiently to know my taste in music, at least. I'll leave the classics to fend for themselves, set a scarred kettle to boil, make coffee. I can feel excitement breaking through my deliberately engendered reluctance. No harm will be done; I will be OK.

The Eckersley house was just a few strides away from Eileen's place of work. She was on call whenever needed, and she didn't mind in the least way because Hermione and Harriet were the lights of her life. Her husband, one Stanley Eckersley, was a lovely man, but the steadiness that was his forte could also have its downside; he was predictable. Stanley sat in the same chair every evening, newspaper open, feet resting on the fender, pipe by his side. After supper, he would fill the bowl and smoke in the back yard shed, as his wife did not enjoy the smell of tobacco.

She opened the door. 'Woebee's home, me laddo. Did you have a good day?'

His day had been satisfactory. He had done two gardens and had brought home a small gate to mend. 'How did you go on?' His accent was broad Lancashire, all vowels flattened to pancake level.

'God, Stanley, you should have seen the state of her. Acts like royalty, so she does. How-and-ever, I have some smoked salmon for our supper, so that's what you might call a plus.' She went through to her gleaming kitchen and set to work all over again. Herself Upstairs was very generous with unwanted food, though the salmon had been taken on this occasion from Herself Downstairs. Lisa wouldn't mind. Underneath her displays of silliness, the mother of Harrie and Ben owned a heart of gold.

Stanley opened the *Bolton Evening News*. 'How's the lad?'

Eileen appeared in the doorway. 'Never even went to the dentist. Shut himself away again, just as ever. God knows what he does in there. He doesn't need to go to school much because they have revision time in the sixth form, but he never steps out for a walk, won't eat with the family. I think he's daft in the head. Harriet makes ten of him, and that's the truth.'

Someone knocked at the front door and Eileen rushed to open it. 'Come in,' she cried. 'It's Harriet,' she informed her husband. 'Follow me into the kitchen,' said hostess to visitor. 'You can wash a bit of lettuce for me.'

When the salad was prepared, Harrie and Eileen sat over mugs of tea. 'What's the matter?' asked the Irishwoman.

Harrie sighed. 'Ben.'

'As if I didn't know. He's up all hours, you know. When I get up to go to the bathroom in the night, I can see from the landing window that he still has lights on. Mostly that angley-poised thing.'

'Anglepoise,' corrected Harrie absently. 'He's getting worse. Though he did pass his driving test after just five lessons from me – I didn't even know he was taking proper instruction. But I can't always do what needs doing, Woebee. I have the shop to run and my own stuff to do–'

'You never do anything.'

'Well, I–'

'You never do anything for yourself beyond visiting that psychiatrical person. You should be out having a high old time. Harrie, you owe no one anything. In fact, others are in debt to you,

41

because you could have been down Oxford mixing with the dans.'

'Dons.'

'Whoever – who cares? I do and your grandmother does, but we can't fix this for you. You have to go.'

'I don't want to go to uni. I sort of got past it.'

'So you're all right selling trinkets and the suchlike, is it? You're fine just making rings bigger for fat women and finding baubles for sugar daddies to give to their stupid bits of fluff on the side?'

Harrie burst out laughing. An indignant Woebee was a sight to behold because her eyebrows moved at least half an inch north, while her eyes seemed ready to jump out of their sockets. 'I came here for a break, not to be shouted at. But I'm keeping you from your supper.'

'Oh, beggar the supper – it'll not get cold, will it? Now. You know your grandmother has money a-plenty to spare and planning permission for a bungalow near the copse. You'd be grand, so. You'd be there, but not there. It's a good compromise.'

'Compromise.'

'That's what I said. Your brother has his own place in their place, so why shouldn't you have a house in the grounds? Stanley will help. He helped with Ben's doings, didn't he?'

'Yes, but–'

'Oh, away with your butting and iffing. He still walks past all the while, you know.'

'What?'

'Don't you mean who? The lad with the dog.

He's called Will. The boy, not the dog.'

'I know. He declared his undying love for me in 1996. We were both just about eleven and we shared an apple – very Adam and Eve. Ten years later, he just walks a dog. Hardly progress.'

'We've had some lovely talks, so we have.'

'About what?'

'Not about you, that's for certain sure. He looks a bit standoffish, but he's shy. That's why he needs the dog. It's you he's looking to bump into, missy.'

'Then why does he bump into trees when he sees me? He stares at me as if I'm from a different planet, all horns and green skin. Then he marches off with his dog and nothing happens.'

'Make it happen. I made Stanley happen. If I'd left it to him, I'd still be working in the laundry and he'd be sharpening the same pencil he was working on when I came across him. Women run the world, but pretend that the men have a hand in it. That's the secret of life.'

Harrie puffed out her cheeks. 'Bloody complicated.'

'Language, please.'

The young woman stood up. 'Get on with your supper. Thanks for being here. Thanks for letting me bore you silly.'

'Away with your bother.' Eileen Eckersley stood at the window and watched as Harrie disappeared into her parents' grounds. There'd be two bridge tables and eight tipsy women in the morning room. The dining room would remain cluttered until tomorrow. His Royal Professorship might be home, might be asleep on an army cot in his

43

laboratory. It was not a real home, had never been a home.

She became aware that Stanley was standing behind her. 'I remember when Harrie's mother had a bit of heart in her,' said Eileen quietly. 'I remember the light going out of her eyes once she had produced the son. I think she had that post-natal suppression thing. God, Stanley, I don't want to see that happening all over again to Harriet.'

'What?' He rattled the newspaper.

'It's no way for a young woman to live, tethered to a brother who can't set foot outside of his own pattern.'

'Is supper ready?'

She turned. 'Yes, Stanley. Supper is on the table, the sun's on Australia, the moon's on the wane. All's well with the world. Enjoy your smoked salmon.' She swallowed the desire to weep and found no appetite for food.

Harrie sat on the veranda of the gazebo. She could hear shrieks of laughter from the morning room, saw Mum sneaking a secret smoke outside the French window. She must be dummy in the current hand. In Harrie's book, Lisa Compton-Milne was a victim, not a perpetrator. All plastic surgeries and beauty treatments were compensations for a wasted life. Mum was not completely blameless, but she was confused at best. It wasn't her fault, was probably no one's fault. The twentieth century had been lived at a gallop and several people had fallen off the carousel. Lisa was one such person.

The woman who was Lisa's partner came and dragged her back inside. Harrie folded her arms, gazed at a navy blue sky and a million stars. A waning moon imitated an unfinished letter C with a small blot of cloud at its centre. Men had walked on that satellite owned by Earth. Well, they were supposed to have landed on it, though one of the many anti-America theories insisted that the whole business had been staged, possibly in some film studio. The moon versus Walt Disney? What a thought.

Something started to scramble about in the copse. Harrie turned and was assaulted by a huge creature with hot breath and a great deal of fur. She heard a man's voice: 'Milly? Where the hell are you?' The canine invader stopped licking her victim's face, then removed two feet from Harrie's shoulders.

'Sorry. Come here, Milly.'

Milly stayed exactly where she was.

'Milly?'

Harrie laughed. 'I could have had a heart attack just then. I was sitting here peaceably, thinking about the moon and Walt Disney, when–'

'I'm sorry. She got away.'

'She certainly did. I am the away she got to. You're Will Carpenter. We shared an apple and my first kiss.' She stroked the dog. 'Sit down, Will. She won't bite you, I promise. And neither will I.'

He sat down, taking care to leave a space between himself and Harriet Compton-Milne. With unsteady fingers, he leaned over and fastened the dog's lead to its collar. For almost a year, he had been imagining this moment, dreading it,

45

celebrating it, embracing it and her.

'She's a big dog,' commented Harrie. 'I am possibly scarred for life.'

The whole family was scarred. This beautiful girl, who seemed inseparable from her strange brother, had a mad father, an ill-behaved mother and a grandma who lived in the roof like one of the proverbial belfry bats. 'I'm sorry,' he repeated.

'I like dogs. Big ones, anyway. Small dogs are a bit yappy for my taste, and they get under your feet.'

'Yes.'

There followed a short, excruciating silence. Will sat with his Alsatian bitch in the company of a woman who had occupied his thoughts for many a year. Awake, he imagined being with her; asleep, he endured dreams in which she was almost always the central force. But the family was mad. He should have stayed in the south, ought not to have come back to Bolton. 'A lot of stars tonight.' As soon as the words were out, he cringed at his own stupidity. He was never going to be any good at this sort of thing, was he?

'The stars are hope,' she answered. 'Because, somewhere out there is infinity. In infinity, parallel lines meet.'

'What?'

Harrie smiled. 'It's just another of my many daft theories. Sometimes, I feel I am living a parallel life and that I shall be close to no one until I reach the great beyond. See? I am definitely daft.'

Will nodded. 'We all have our aberrations. Most of mine are in class Nine B.'

'Nine B?'

'Yup. They wear their convictions like medals of honour.'

'Good to know they have some convictions. Most of us believe in nothing these days.'

'*Criminal* convictions, Harrie.'

'Yes, I realized that. I was being deliberately obtuse. Or, in Woebee's words, opertuse. She has a language all her own.'

'I have talked to her.'

'Listened, more likely.'

He laughed nervously. Here he sat with the light of his life and a currently unbiddable dog. This was meant to be a beautiful moment filled by an invisible orchestra playing a quiet bit of Beethoven's sixth, but, in reality, he was in the garden of an insane family with a girl whose own brother was as loony as Milly. Milly would probably be trained in time, but Harrie carried the same genes as the rest of the Compton-Milnes. When would she crack? At thirty? After the birth of a child? In menopause? God, she was beautiful...

'You seem too shy for teaching,' she said.

'No. I wear a different hat at school. In fact, I have a whole rack of hats – depends which class I am taking.'

Harrie cringed when more hoots of laughter arrived from the morning room. 'Bridge,' she said. 'Mum and her friends. Bridge evening. Losers buy lunch next week.'

'Ah.'

'None of them plays well. In reality, it's probably a meeting of the planning department.'

47

'What?'

'They are laying foundations for new faces and flatter bellies. Some of them can't even laugh properly, since their faces are paralysed by Botox. Several won't laugh, as it encourages crows' feet.'

Will swallowed hard. 'You should walk with me and Milly sometimes. When you're not working, of course.'

'Of course.'

He hesitated. 'Walking is good exercise – better for the system than jogging. And chasing my mutt keeps the heart pounding.'

'Right.'

'Will you?'

'Will I what, Will? Chase your bloody dog?'

'Yes.'

'I might.' Harrie could hear his fear, could feel his desire. He was a good enough specimen, well-etched and defined as perfectly as only a dark-haired man could be. He was pleasant, educated and a very desirable property. But her antennae picked up every mixed feeling, every doubt and hope. Was this chemistry? 'You did chemistry at Cambridge?'

'Yes.'

Ah, well, he would know all about it, then. As a qualified chemist, did he sense her hopeful desperation? Or was it desperate hope? And was that organic or inorganic chemistry? 'I'll walk with you if and when I get the chance of it.'

'Good.' He was excited by the prospect, though not a little dismayed.

It happened then, just as the couple had taken the first tentative steps towards each other. A side

48

door burst open, and Ben ran out into the night. 'Harrie!' he screamed. 'Harrie? Where are you? I'm injured.'

Will leapt to his feet. 'Shall I go to him?'

'No. It has to be me.'

Will sat in the gazebo and listened while the MG's engine came to life, heard the swishing of displaced gravel, waited until the car could no longer be heard. Bridge-players had spilled on to the lawn, their arrival causing security lights to illuminate the scene. With a tightly tethered Milly, Will dragged himself away. The lunacy continued, it seemed. And he feared becoming a part of it, feared not becoming a part of her.

Ben refused to be abandoned by his sister. She was forced to hold his hand while he was examined, but to turn away while he was undressed. Feeling like an amateur contortionist, she managed not to scream when her metacarpals seemed in danger of becoming crushed. How would she manage jewellery with a broken hand?

An Asian doctor and two nurses were Ben's attendants. Harrie listened to the questions and opinion:

'How did this happen?'

'You used the wrong bottle of bleach? Human skin should never be exposed to bleach.'

Ben talked about Milton, a preparation used for the sterilization of infants' bottles. 'That's watered down bleach,' he insisted.

As time ticked on, Harrie came to realize that her brother had scrubbed his genitals with Domestos. She shivered, pictured that crease-

49

free cling film on the hob, cups perfectly aligned, books sectioned – would he be sectioned?

The doctor spoke. 'I want to talk to your sister alone.'

'She stays with me.'

Harrie decided to contribute. 'Is he decent?'

'Yes,' replied the nearest nurse.

Harrie turned and looked at her brother. In the hospital gown, he looked about nine years of age and scared out of his wits. 'I am going to talk to the doctor. No one will touch you. If anyone does touch you, I shall sue the bloody hospital. All right?'

'It's not all right.'

Anger bubbled in her chest, but she squashed it. Ben couldn't help it, couldn't help any of it, and she must not allow herself to become irritated with him. 'You managed a driving test, so you can manage to lie there for ten minutes.' She followed the doctor into the ward office.

Invited to sit, she perched nervously on the edge of her chair. 'Miss Compton-Milne,' he began, 'have you any idea of what your brother has done to himself?'

'I think so.'

'Do you know why he has done this thing?'

'No. He lives apart from me. In the same house, but he has his own rooms. Has he hurt himself badly?'

'Badly enough, though he did have sense enough to rinse himself with cold water. And I am about to send for a psychiatrist so that we can have him assessed.'

The room began to spin. What could she do?

What would Ben do if committed to a psychiatric unit?

'It has to happen,' said the doctor gently. 'For his own good.'

Harrie caught her breath and managed to keep her seat. 'Look, he has an IQ in the one-sixties. He isn't like other people. My father is Gustav Compton-Milne, and he, too, is gifted. They aren't... They aren't normal.'

The young man nodded. 'Please wait here. I'll get back to you as soon as I can. The nurse will bring you tea.'

After the third cup, Harrie felt as if she would drown in Tetley's. What were they doing, and how was Ben coping? And why the hell had he scalded his penis with neat bleach? It was all connected to the OCD, the rituals, the orderliness that dominated his life.

Another man came in. He had receding grey hair and twinkling blue eyes. 'Miss Compton-Milne?'

'Yes.'

'Don't get up, please.' He walked to the other side of the desk, sat down, placed joined hands on a copy of *Woman's Realm* that promised, in bright red capitals, to teach a reader how to improve her bust without surgery. 'Your brother is fine. Physically, at least, there is to be no lasting damage to his person. But he seems very childlike in the emotional sense.'

'I know.'

'With people like him, there is often a disparity in areas of development. He has galloped intellectually, yet is as confused as any twelve-year-old. Does he spend a lot of time alone?'

Harrie nodded.

'I should talk to his parents, really.'

'They can't do anything. Things are ... difficult at home. My father is seldom around and my mother maintains a position of neutrality – like Switzerland.'

'Ah.'

'You can't put him away. You mustn't. I am the only person he trusts, but he will grow out of this, won't he?'

The man sighed and shook his head. 'I can't in conscience section him this time. I have to take his story at face value and accept its content. But I warn you – this may well happen again. Or worse.'

Harrie looked him full in the face. 'Why did he do it? Why did he hurt himself?'

'That I can't say. I am bound by an oath, as you are probably aware. But I will go so far as to admit that I consider Ben to be a very disturbed young man. He is not steady, not confident. You tell me he seldom socializes?'

'Almost never.'

'And you?'

She shrugged. 'The same. I have a job in my family's business, Ben needs me from time to time, my grandmother is disabled and my father–'

'Is *the* Compton-Milne,' the doctor finished for her.

'Yes.'

'Ben needs to grow up.'

'He will. I'm sure he will.'

52

Harrie parked the car on a quiet stretch of Beaumont Road. She turned off the engine, sighed, then rested her weary head on the steering wheel. 'Why?' she asked. 'Why, and what's your next trick going to be?'

'Fuck off,' he mumbled.

She laughed mirthlessly. 'How can I fuck off? I have to hang around and look after you.' She raised her head. 'What the hell were you doing, Ben?'

'Thought it was shower gel.'

'Tripe,' she snapped. 'I'm not as daft as the doctors. What *is* this fixation with cleanliness of yours?'

'I hate dirt.'

'Then work with Dad. He's on a mission to clean up society. You'd be very useful to him.'

'I'd rather die.'

She couldn't say all of it, couldn't lay completely at his door the blame for her own intellectual arrest. For him, she had remained at home. She wasn't a coward, was she? Surely, she could have coped at Oxford, but she hadn't been able to leave this boy.

'I'm sorry,' he said. He put his head in his hands and began to weep.

Harrie tapped on the steering wheel and made a decision. 'Right. The self-pity isn't moving me any more, but I am moving – moving out.'

The tears dried up immediately. 'What?'

'The summer house, gazebo – whatever – will be dismantled and I'll have one of those American jobs. Foundations, drains, then a prefabricated house on top. It will be single storey, because that's all the planners will allow, but it will be all my own.' She turned and stared at him. 'If you want to see me, you'll have to come out of Celibate City and visit. I'm not coming to you any more. The place stinks.' She started the engine.

'You can't leave me,' he shouted. 'You're all I have.'

Harrie nodded. 'Sorry, bro. If I'm all you have, that's hardly my fault. But you are not all *I* am going to have.'

'You don't love me any more.'

'We aren't married,' she snapped. 'Yes, you're my brother; yes, it was a hard childhood. But I can't carry on beating up the demons you create. Stop making me feel as if I have to compensate for all you endured. I was there. I was alive. I suffered, too.'

'I'm sorry.'

'And if you say that again, you'll be left with nothing to bleach, because I'll cut it off. Don't worry, I'll use pinking shears – it won't fray and you'll never need a circumcision.'

The rest of the journey was completed in silence. Harrie informed an apparently only mildly interested Lisa that her son had accidentally dropped sharp-ended scissors into his thigh. The bridge eight had dispersed, so there was no other audience to bear witness to the lie.

Sleep eluded Harrie that night. When she did drift towards the edge of it, she saw a terrified child in a hospital bed, came to full wakefulness when the face on the pillow changed into that of a handsome young man with a panting, overgrown puppy by his side. 'He's afraid of me,' she whispered into blackness. 'Will's terrified of this whole damned family.'

Resolution remained intact. Tomorrow, Harrie would travel up into the gods, probably on Gran's stairlift – everyone needed some fun – and begin the process of ordering the wooden house that would contain the future of Ben's big sister. She had to stop being Ben's big sister; she must begin a new life as Harriet Compton-Milne, ready-and-willing spinster of this parish.

Ben turned off his eye on the world. For a moment or two, he considered smashing the webcam, but soon decided against such action. If Harrie installed a computer, he might be able to talk to her across the acreage without leaving his safe place. There was nothing to do. He played some music, medicated his injury, managed to pass water without losing consciousness.

Surely, having a partner had to be easier than this? Synchronized wretched masturbation with sickos all over the world was not ideal; nor was the need to cleanse the filth afterwards. But the thought of being touched by a human being whose standards of hygiene could scarcely be quantifiable was not attractive. The slightest rim of grey under a nail and he would head for the Pennines, wouldn't he? He wiped a smudge from a light switch, showered, prepared for bed.

Like a corpse, he lay flat, head slightly raised by a thin pillow. With arms on top of the duvet and hard by his sides, he endured the painful result of his earlier behaviour. He should suffer. It was only right that he should suffer. Because he wasn't normal.

Animals knew best. When one of their number became disabled or frail, he was left behind, sometimes killed by the rest. 'I should be culled,' he whispered. 'Because I don't belong. I can't make myself belong.' He didn't even want to belong.

Hermione seldom missed a thing. With dormer windows set into both sides of the roof, she needed only to wheel herself from room to room in order to have a panoramic opinion of all that happened around the house known as Weaver's Warp, a property handed down through generations of the Milne family. Before cotton had become Lancashire's staple factory industry, weavers had taken in spun thread and had worked it into cloth. The rooms she occupied had possibly been a sweat shop a couple of hundred years ago. When the builders had come to move out Gus's trains, they had found evidence of reinforcement in the beams; this had probably been put in place in order to support the weight of half a dozen looms. Now, it supported her.

The boy had been. He was a good-looking lad with a fine dog, and he had managed to talk to Harriet this time. Watching him had become a source of amusement and pleasure for Hermione; he clearly wanted to be with her granddaughter, yet was exquisitely shy in her presence. It was some kind of love, she supposed. Harriet deserved love. Hesitation on the part of a male was probably an asset in this age of bed-hopping, heartbreak, single parents and AIDS.

Ben. Hermione lit a cigarette and opened a window. Eileen Eckersley had the nose of an elephant when it came to residual nicotine. Harrie, Hermione's partner in crime, was the guilty party who smuggled in Benson and Hedges once a week. Ben. Such a kerfuffle tonight, all spinning car tyres and flying gravel. He wasn't right. Lisa's fault? Hardly. Lisa was, always had been, an excellent jeweller and a good saleswoman. Love had died in her. Hermione had watched the premature death of her own daughter-in-law. Gustav? She shook her head. Gustav was the creation of his own father, a good enough man who had pushed his son into Bolton School, into Oxford, into medicine. Later on, Gus had placed himself under the wings of the Universities of Manchester and Liverpool, together with the financial backing of pharmaceutical companies. It was hard to place all the blame at the feet of her only son.

'Was it me?' she asked herself aloud. 'Or Woebee? We did our best. If I could only get out of this damned chariot and walk, I'd march all the way to the root of the problem that is Ben.'

Tomorrow, she would talk to Harrie. Today, she reminded herself inwardly, because midnight was ages ago. Time to swing her senseless body into a prone position on the bed. Soon enough, she would need putting to bed before Eileen/Woebee's daily departure. Not yet. For as long as possible, Hermione Compton-Milne would wear purple with red, would rattle a metaphorical stick along life's railings, would wear slippers in the snow. Who wrote that poem?

Harrie, summoned into the Presence, placed her rear on Gran's padded footstool and waited for the inquisition to begin. Her second-in-command would open the shop and marshal the comings and goings of staff. 'I can't stay long,' she began. 'The clockmaker's due this morning. I have an early-nineteenth grandfather that needs attention.'

'Bring him here, then. He'll be more use than your real grandad, God rest him.'

Harrie smiled tentatively. 'No. He's all tick and no tock, Gran.'

'Even so. Eileen?'

A turbaned head poked itself through the kitchen doorway. 'I'm cupboards today.'

'Coffee, please. And don't fall off that step-ladder; I am not insured.'

Grumbling softly, the head disappeared into the kitchen. 'What's going on?' Hermione asked.

Harrie scratched her head. 'I'm not sure. I thought he was getting better, because he did the driving test without even telling me, but I may have been mistaken. He's still scrubbing everything. I found him last week making a terrible decision about double CDs. Should they stay with the singles in subdivisions of artistes, or should he make a new section for doubles?'

'His conclusion?'

Harrie shrugged. 'Don't know.' She lowered her voice. 'Ciggies bottom drawer, bedroom bureau. She won't find them while she's doing the kitchen.'

'What? Old X-ray eyes? Don't be too sure.'

The younger woman laughed softly. There was no point in hiding anything from either of these two. Between them, they would probably spot without hesitation an igloo in a white-out. And Gran had proved herself to be almost un-shockable. Any problem at all could be laid at the numbed feet of this eccentric, delightful creature.

'What happened last night, Harriet?'

Ah. 'Harriet' meant serious business. It had been the same at school. On normal days, she was Harrie, but when officialdom prescribed prize-giving day or some such formal occasion, it was Harriet. 'I'm not quite sure, Gran, but it was dealt with at the hospital.'

'I see. Which department?'

'A and E, swiftly followed by psychiatry.'

'Bugger.'

'Exactly.'

Hermione wheeled herself toward a front window. 'What has he done to himself?'

Harrie hesitated for a short beat of time.

'Well?'

'I think he bleached his manhood, Gran. If it wasn't Ben, that might even be funny in a Michael Jackson sort of way. He insisted he had mistaken Domestos for shower gel. I almost lost my temper with him.'

'You think he washes himself in bleach?'

'Weakened bleach, yes.'

'Why can't he use soap and water?'

'Gran, if I had answers, there would have been no visit to the hospital last night.' She sighed heavily. 'Time for me to become semi-detached –

if your offer still stands. One of those prefabricated jobs can be built within weeks. They do it all the time in America. I think they put cooking foil between the two layers as insulation.'

Hermione nodded absently. 'Of course.' She fiddled with a string of pearls. 'I should never have allowed Stanley to get those rooms done for him.'

Eileen appeared with a tray. 'Are you taking my husband's name in vain here? What's he done now? When last seen, he was innocently mending a gate. Yes, you should get your house built,' she advised Harrie. 'Time you had a life. Here, you pour the coffee while I carry on carrying on.' She returned to her task.

'She misses nothing,' smiled Hermione. 'I'll start the ball rolling out towards the copse as soon as possible.'

'Ben will have to be more self-reliant with me out of the house.'

Woebee's head made another brief appearance. 'You'll still be on top of him, but. You'd be better off taking one of those departments in Eagley Mills or such.'

'Apartments,' snapped Hermione with feigned annoyance. 'She'll do as she chooses, Eileen. Get the cupboards finished. It's time you did something to justify your existence.'

It was settled. Harrie was to have a posh shed in the grounds, and all of them would wait and watch. It reminded Harrie of a set of books she had read in childhood. *What Katie Did Next* would become *What Ben Did Next*. And the grandfather clock was waiting, too.

Three

Must get a new car soon. A new car is such a source of pleasure, especially for the first few weeks: clean and fresh, new number plate, sense of achievement. An automatic, I think. The roads are so busy now that gear-changing, especially during rush hour, is becoming a full-time occupation. Much better to crawl along without fiddling with a gear shift, and without worries on hill starts.

My supposed husband is an inverted snob – I think that's the term. He has used, over the years, a series of battered and bruised Minis into which he folds himself clumsily, knees almost under his chin. He's a fool. A clever fool, but he thinks he's so bloody special, too elevated for a decent car. What's a car after all? Why should he need any kind of status symbol? What's a car to a man who is going to be knighted one of these years?

Right. What's down for today? The shop, of course. Meeting with the accountant, lunch with Sadie Fisher, home, change of clothes, an evening with Alec. The thought of him makes me shiver with anticipation. If only les girls knew that I bed a man ten years my junior two or three times a week. They'd be crying in their soup; the resulting dilution might alleviate Sadie's weight problem, if nothing else...

A bottleneck here again at the top of Bank Street. I don't know what the hell the planners think they're doing, but this town is dying inch by inch. Soon, small

61

shops like mine will disappear altogether. My Milne's jewellers operates these days like a Lone Ranger at the centre of an almost empty block, businesses murdered, hope gone, lives ruined. Everyone shops at Middlebrook now.

I think I'll have a blue car. Blue is my colour, always has been. It accentuates my best feature, the large, long-lashed eyes that have been the envy of so many girlfriends over the years. Not bad for forty-four. My skin continues firm despite warnings on cigarette packets, the nose is perfect now – after a couple of small adjustments, of course, and my breasts can hold their own shape no matter what the situation, because they cost me an arm and a leg. Yes, I have excellent limbs, too, and men still turn in the street when I pass by. Any male would be happy to be seen out and about with me. With the exception of the Prof. Well, he got his money's worth: trained jeweller to carry on the family firm, pelvis wide enough to deliver naturally his two children. It wasn't easy, but I proved my worth.

There are ongoings at home. If I could call it home, that is. Better to say that the strangers among whom I live are at odds with one another and with life in general. The only person I talk to is my daughter, and that doesn't happen very often. Such a fuss last night when Ben had to be driven off to hospital. I pretended to follow my daughter's car while visitors watched, but I didn't bother, turned back when I thought everyone would have gone away. Harriet can cope. She always could.

Bridge ended prematurely, taxis ordered to take home my tired and emotional friends. Friends? Ha-bloody-ha. I am close to none of them. Alec is all I have and all I want. He is a closely-guarded secret, and he knows me better than anyone else in the world.

Park the car, enter my shop by the rear door, disable the alarm before it brings the house down. It's Alec's alarm. I met him when he fitted it. He's the last – I hope – in a line of lovers who have kept me sane throughout a lifeless, soulless marriage. Must make sure no one sees the latest packages – without Alec's constant flow of second-hand items that never touch the books, our bolting money would be a great deal less than I am going to need. I don't ask where he gets the stuff, almost don't care. I am out of here as soon as the shop gets its final condemnation from the powers that shouldn't be.

Coffee maker on, coat on a hanger, use the hand cream. What shall I wear today? Ah, yes, the sapphire and diamond earrings with the matching ring, a whopper almost as big as Princess Diana's was. I have been told more than once that I look like the princess, though I hope people notice that I have the better nose. She was unhappy, poor soul. God, how well I understand that!

My other shop is better placed and may survive. Well, let Harriet have it, because I shall be in Portugal with the love of my life. I'll put those pearls in the window, I think. Nice, fat, juicy pearls suitable for a nice, slender, firm throat. No, I mustn't wear them. The lily will be sufficiently gilded by the Diana furniture. Wedding season. I'll shove a few silver lockets in the display – they seem favourites as gifts for bridesmaids.

Half an hour till the shop opens. Check the main safe, make sure that all questionable items are in the floor safe. Only Alec and I know of the second safe's existence. We are well on the way to the quarter million mark. The books are clean and Alec's stuff is sold to people he chooses carefully. He swears it's not stolen, tells me he gets it from his second job – clearing houses. I have to believe... It won't be long now. We'll be gone, and no one will miss me. Not true. I believe Hermione will notice my absence.

Set up the earring stand. Creoles are so ugly, yet I sell more of these hideous items than of studs and sleepers. To Gus, sleepers are bits of wood beneath railway lines. Ha-bloody-ha again. When Harriet was born, Gus failed to hide his disappointment. He carried on "loving" me until I had produced a son, then buggered off faster than sugar off a shiny shovel into the world of research. Model trains filled his leisure hours. Occasionally, he would check on Ben's progress at school, though he seldom communicated with either of his offspring. That was supposed to be my job, I think. I don't like that jade, think I'll take it off display.

I know now that it was post-natal depression. Eileen and Hermione took over the rearing of Harriet and, by the time Benjamin was born, I was set in my pattern, because the first symptoms of Hermione's MS had begun to show shortly after the birth of my daughter. She is my daughter. Sometimes, I have to remind myself. However, Hermione stayed at home to help Eileen mind the children, while I ran the shops.

The Austrian crystal sells well. Glad I had those lights set into the display cabinet – see how the cute little hedgehog sparkles? From the age of three, Harriet has run to her grandmother, has known that Gran was ill, that Gran and Ben needed her. Am I jealous? I should pick up that phone, cancel Sadie and take

64

Harriet out to lunch. No, it would be awkward. Ah, I'll turn on the little fountain. When a customer sits next to that, they are soothed by water lapping over smooth stone. That, I worked out for myself. So I am not as daft as some might believe.

Right. Jewellery on, smile on, shoes shining, suit a miracle of understatement. A Renault, I think. Yes, I'll have a change. Alec says the Renaults are good. A blue Renault, a false smile, borrowed jewels, manmade boobs. But the whole is greater than the parts. Before I leave for Europe, I'll find myself. And Harriet. For some reason, it is suddenly important that she understands.

It was ten minutes after one by the time Lisa arrived at the restaurant. Sadie Fisher, already toying with a second glass of wine, hailed her friend enthusiastically. 'I'm booked in,' she whispered excitedly. 'Liposuction and a couple of tucks; soon be back to normal. Only a few weeks to wait.'

Lisa smiled and sat down. At the rate Sadie consumed carbs, she would never be anything approaching normal. 'Sorry I'm late – got a bit tied up at the shop. Have you ordered?'

'No.'

'I'll just have a green salad and a bit of chicken–' Lisa patted her flat stomach – 'or I could well be joining you in the liposuction stakes.' She smiled to herself while Sadie placed the order. Roast beef and all the trimmings? At lunchtime? No wonder the woman needed surgery. 'Did you have a good morning?'

Sadie shook her head. 'The boss is down with

65

irritable bowel syndrome again, so guess who had to run the department? Yours truly. It's all very well, but she'll turn purple if I order the wrong accessories. Some nice handbags in today. You must come and look.'

The food arrived. Lisa picked absently at lettuce and chicken, tried not to watch while Sadie stuffed herself. Still, near-starvation did pay off. Sadie was two years younger than Lisa, though she looked at least five older. That was the high price of indulging an over-healthy appetite.

Sadie was staring longingly at the pudding trolley when hell broke loose. Lisa, with a forkful of chicken halfway to her mouth, forced herself to clamp her lips closed when the whirlwind descended on her. A short, rounded woman, with dark curls and a toddler clutched to her chest, appeared at the side of their table. With her free hand, she grabbed a lock of Lisa's hair and pulled so hard that several strands were loosened. 'It's you,' she screamed.

Cutlery clattered on to plates, and a heavy silence hung over the small room. A waitress who had been pouring coffee gasped when she saw overspill gushing across a pristine cloth. That gasp sounded like the advent of an easterly gale, so quiet were the diners. A chef appeared in the kitchen doorway, cleaver held high in preparation for whatever he might find.

Lisa stood up. 'I beg your pardon?'

'It's you,' repeated the newcomer. 'You and my Jimmy.'

'I know no one named Jimmy,' Lisa said coldly.

Her hair had cost a fortune only yesterday. Oh God, the shame of it. The whole town was going to be buzzing with gossip within minutes.

'I saw you. So did the detective who works for me. You're meeting in Jimmy's mother's bungalow while she's in Eastbourne. Before that, you used the Pack Horse Hotel. You can't fool me, bitch.'

Lisa dropped back into her seat. 'I'm sorry. I don't understand.'

'Oh, really? Well, this is Daisy, mine and Jimmy's youngest. We have three of them. You are having an affair with Daisy's dad, my husband.'

Sadie Fisher forgot all about the puddings. She sat back and watched while Lisa Compton-Milne got dragged off her double-barrelled pedestal. The girls were going to love this one! As soon as it was over, she'd be on her Nokia mobile to Sandy, Mavis, Helen and... Wonderful. It seemed that the tiny intruder had more strength than most wrestlers.

'I know of no one named Jimmy,' Lisa repeated. 'Take your hand from my arm, please.'

'But you know the Pack Horse, eh? And that little bungalow halfway up Blackburn Road: roses in the garden, china figurines all over the living room? Eh? Don't sit there like butter wouldn't melt, you old bag. That's my husband you're messing around with, lady. *My* husband.'

Sadie noticed that Lisa blanched when the bungalow was described.

'Can't you get a man of your own?' the dark-haired woman continued, cheeks reddened by fury, baby beginning to grizzle because her

67

mother was shouting. 'Too old to find anybody that's still available?'

'I think we should go outside.' Lisa picked up her bag and asked Sadie to pay the bill. Outside on the pavement, the adversaries glared at one another. Lisa had the advantage of height, though a proportion of that was attributable to high heels on which she was suddenly less than steady. She walked away from the restaurant to avoid several dozen stares. 'Now, Mrs ... er...'

'Never mind who I am,' snapped the small woman. She balanced the child on a blue denim hip. 'I know who you are, Mrs Jewellery Shop. You're my Jimmy's sugar mummy and he's your toy boy. He's up to his old tricks again, but I am on to him.'

Lisa swallowed hard. She knew the bungalow well, had rolled about on a mock sheepskin rug under the watchful eyes of several cheap and ugly ladies in pastel crinolines. 'I honestly don't know a Jimmy. Or a James.'

'Right. Who do you know, then?'

'That cannot possibly be any business of yours.'

'Oh, really? Then I shall be wanting my money back off the private detective, because he's followed you from the shop to the Pack Horse, from your posh house to the bungalow – and I've got photos. I don't know what my fellow's told you, but his real name's Jimmy Nuttall, and we've been married nine years. You're not the first old dear he's been with, and I suppose you won't be the last. Just bugger off and leave him alone, or I'll make sure your husband and kids get to hear about it.' She marched off, her gait

68

made uneven by the weight of the child.

Lisa leaned against a wall. Within thirty seconds, her mechanism clicked back into gear, and she returned to the restaurant. The buzz of conversation ceased as soon as she entered. 'Mistaken identity,' she told Sadie, who quickly turned off her mobile phone. 'She seems to have confused me with some trollop who's having a good time with her husband. Ah, well–' she sat down – 'let's have coffee, shall we?'

Had anyone asked Lisa about the following five minutes, she would have been unable to remember the topic of conversation. Her mind raced, as did her pulse. How could he do this to her? They had been planning a new start abroad, somewhere warmer, sunnier. He swore undying devotion and ... and he held a large slice of her money in a place where the tax man would never reach.

'Are you all right?' Sadie asked.

Lisa returned to the present time. 'What? Yes, of course. I'm just thinking how terrible my hair must look. Do you think I should tell the police? It was assault, and there were many witnesses.'

'It's a thought,' Sadie agreed. 'It's coming to something when two old friends can't have lunch without one of them being attacked.' How was Lisa going to get out of this one? She wouldn't go for the law; of that, Sadie felt completely certain.

'There'd be bad publicity, I suppose,' Lisa said with a sigh.

Sadie squashed a smile. This gossip would feed the clan for weeks to come. 'Unavoidable, Lisa. Look, why don't you phone the shop and ask Simon to take over? Go home and rest.'

Lisa agreed. 'I feel a migraine coming on. I suppose half a day off wouldn't hurt. Do you mind if I go now?'

Sadie shook her head. Her fingers were dying to press a few more numbers on her mobile. She wanted to be the one to pass on the news, though she had possibly missed her chance, since Mavis would have texted all and sundry by now. Mavis was the only one Sadie had found time to reach. She should have left Mavis till last.

They both stood and each kissed the air at the side of the other's head. Sadie watched while her companion staggered out of the restaurant, then reached for her phone. Today, the air would be filled with music. Probably a dirge to accompany the social death of a certain jeweller who had long been too big for her hand-sewn Italian shoes.

It was cooler up on the open moors. Lisa parked her car and gazed, as if for the first time, at a landscape fit for any poet wanting to write about daffodils. Except, of course, that it wasn't daffodil season and the yellow fields were packed with burgeoning rape. Jesus Christ. How could a person's life change so drastically in the space of a few hours? This morning, she had been planning for a new car and a new life abroad, though the latter had been scheduled for the next year at the very earliest. He had played her like an ancient Stradivarius, hadn't he? Stupid woman whose sole aims in life were to look younger and ditch a husband who had all the charm of a dead rat.

'My reputation, such as it was, is destroyed,'

she told the windscreen. 'I've lost him and a load of money.' She had also mislaid several layers of self-respect. It had never been a thick cloak, but it had existed. Sadie Fisher would be buzzing with the tale. Mobile networks were possibly in meltdown already. 'Thank God I didn't change my mind and invite Harriet to lunch.' Yet a very small corner of Lisa's mind housed the suspicion that Harriet would have stood up to the woman, would have defended her mother. Because Harriet was always on the side of any underdog, wasn't she? Like her own brother...

Nowhere to turn now, Lisa supposed. Simon could run the shop indefinitely, while she would have to disappear very soon and for a considerable length of time. There was, of course, Hermione. Hermione, given half a chance, might orchestrate a G8 conference from her wheelchair. She couldn't do much for herself, but she wielded a long baton when it came to conducting the lives of others. Eileen, too, was a loyal servant of the family. 'Could I? Should I?'

She left the car and sat in a dip where a drystone wall had lost its capping stones. There were just three houses between here and the horizon. The rest of the landscape was a coat of many colours: several yellows, greens that ran from moss right through to emerald, shades that verged on blue. All these scraps of fields were sewn together with grey-brown stitches made of walls like the one upon which she sat. Lancashire was beautiful. She hadn't really noticed it before. Born in a back-street of Bolton, father unknown, mother a distant memory, Lisa had no one of her own. Alec had been her own...

Jimmy opened the door and stepped back a pace as she launched herself at him. Blood coursed down his left cheek, and he raised both hands in order to protect himself. She was mad; people must be right about the Compton-Milnes. Perhaps like married like – she was as insane as her legendary husband. Jesus, she packed a hard punch. But she had originated from the back-streets of the town, so perhaps she was reverting to type. 'What the bloody hell...?' he began as she hit him yet again.

'Jimmy bloody Nuttall,' she screamed. 'That nasty little wife of yours pulled some of my hair out in Antoine's this lunch time. Had your youngest brat with her, too. You lying, cheating, good-for-nothing toad.' Each adjective arrived in the company of a slap to his face.

He fled into the living room.

She followed, paused to take in the view of champagne in a bucket, flowers on a side table, strawberries in a bowl. 'You bastard,' she cursed.

'I'm leaving her,' he protested. 'I always meant to leave her for you, Lisa.'

She picked up the nearest ornament and threw it in his direction. It missed, but shattered another on the mantelpiece. 'So this is your friend's bungalow, is it? We're using it while he's in the bloody Seychelles? It's your mother's house. If I'd had any sense, I'd have noticed the absence of a resident man's clutter. Where's my money?'

He grabbed a large cushion and hugged it – any further missiles could be deflected, or so he hoped. 'What money?'

'My share. From the stuff in the floor safe. You said half of it was mine, but I haven't seen a penny piece of it.'

'It's OK. You'll get it when we leave – I promised you that, didn't I?'

'Just as you swore you were single after being heartbroken following the death of your fiancée. Get me my bloody money, or I'll...' She would what? What could she do? 'You and I are going nowhere, Jimmy.' She spat the name as if ridding her mouth of an unpleasant taste. 'No more goods in my safe from now on. The partnership is dissolved.'

'But–'

'But nothing. I want my cut. I'll settle for a hundred grand and your final exit from my life.'

'Lisa, I don't deserve this.'

'Neither do I. Neither does that furious little wife of yours. The child she had with her is called Daisy. I believe you have three in total.'

His top lip curled. 'I would have left everything behind for you.'

'You left honesty long, long ago, Jimmy. According to your better half, I am just the latest of your conquests. She might have been angry, but there was truth in her eyes. You're no good.'

'And you're a recycled virgin?'

'I have never lied. I have never pleaded a dead lover, just a decayed marriage. When does your mother return?'

He lowered his head. 'Sunday.'

'Then we meet here Saturday at two in the afternoon. Bring my cash. A hundred grand, and that is a mere fraction of the total accumulated these past few years. I mean it. Get me my money, or I'll have you dealt with.'

'Oh, yes? And whose army will you use?'

She smirked. 'If Hannibal could negotiate the Alps with a herd of elephants, I can certainly get past you. So bugger off back to the poor creature you're fastened to.' She turned, then looked over her shoulder. 'Saturday. And be prompt. I have no patience with latecomers.'

Outside, she found herself shaking with a mixture of fury and grief. Could she cope with this on her own? Beyond the odd grunt from behind *The Times* at breakfast, Gus hadn't spoken to her in months. And why should he help an adulterous partner? A man of narrowed vision, he probably imagined that no one really needed communication within marriage once the children had been born.

Lisa sat in her car and waited for the trembling to stop. When she finally managed to focus, she found herself staring into the dark eyes of Nuttall's wife. She was across the road in a parked Escort. Slowly, Lisa opened her door, stepped out and crossed the road.

The Escort's window was wound down. 'Well?' asked the occupant.

Lisa sighed. 'All yours, though he may weigh a little less because I relieved him of some blood. Don't worry – he'll live. There is a bit of business to be concluded here on Saturday afternoon. Beyond that, it is finished.'

A tiny hand touched Lisa's arm. 'Get in the car. Look, it's all right – I won't kidnap you, and I won't hurt you. I just need to talk to you, that's all.'

After hesitating for a few seconds, the older woman walked round the Escort, opened the passenger door and climbed in. There were small toys and sweet wrappers all over the place. Lisa's feet rested on a battered teddy bear in the footwell.

'Do you smoke?' asked the driver.

'I'd kill for one.'

They lit up, inhaled deeply, then both laughed nervously.

'I'm Annie Nuttall.'

'You know who I am.'

'Aye, I do. Now, don't say anything. If you don't tell me anything, then I don't know anything – OK?'

Lisa nodded.

'Saturday – is it about money?'

'Yes.'

'Right, set your ears on red alert because I'll say this only once.'

'As in *'Allo, 'Allo?*'

'Exactly. First, sorry I showed you up in that café. I lost my rag, and I'm not proud of myself, only I can't undo it. But I might be able to save you from more grief. Understand?'

Lisa inclined her head again.

'We have to work together on this. We need each other. He fits alarms – right? He knows the ins and outs of some pretty big houses and businesses. In plainer words, he knows how to be in and out like a bloody shadow. I think he leaves it a few months after fitting the alarms – he's clever like that. So first, get another firm to do your

75

shop – and your house, if he fitted that one.'

'OK.'

'Then–' Annie took another drag of nicotine – 'if he's done stuff like storing bits and pieces with you, get rid. Because, as sure as eggs are pointed at one end, he'll be in jail by the end of the year. I don't want you going down. You've suffered enough.'

Tears brimmed in Lisa's eyes. This, from her supposed greatest enemy, was a huge act of kindness. 'I don't know what to say to you.'

'Best say nowt, love. The less I know about what you know, the better, if you get my drift. I'll have to be off soon because my mother's got the kids and my twin lads are a caution.' The short neck stretched itself in a gesture of deliberately assumed pride. 'I'll be leaving him, going back to my mam. It won't be easy on me or her, but it has to be done. I don't want the boys turning out like him.'

'I understand.'

Annie smiled. 'Look, give us your phone number. I'll be careful – I'll call you from phone boxes. Bear in mind that the cops are on to him. Well, that's what the private dick says, any road. The less contact we have, the better. They'll find out that you knew him, of course, but you can avoid being his partner in crime, eh? He fitted your alarms and, if the worst comes to the worst, you stored stuff for him. Family heirlooms and the like.' She grinned impishly. 'Mind, have you seen his mother's ornaments? They don't need a safe, eh? Anyway, you should be OK.'

'Thanks to you, yes.'

Annie squeezed Lisa's hand after taking her card. 'When it's all over, maybe we can have a cuppa together, eh?'

Lisa blinked hard. 'He told me he was single, said his fiancée died. I suppose I needed to believe him, needed to be needed.'

Annie tutted and shook her head. 'Oh, and, by the way, you're not an old bag. You're the best-looking bird he's had so far.'

'Thank you.'

Annie's eyes, too, were wet. 'Go on. Bugger off and get sorted.' She turned the key, and the engine came to life. 'Er ... it might be an idea if you spoke to the cops yourself. Just say you're worried about a few things you've minded for him. Stay ahead of the game, and tell nobody else. Just me, you and the coppers. If you need help from your family, though, get it.'

Back in her own car, Lisa sat and waved as the Ford sped away. Her mind was in a whirl, but why should she be surprised? She hadn't questioned him about any of his 'house clearances' and 'special offers'; hadn't worried, because he and his ill-gotten gains were to have been her gateway out of a senseless life. She glanced to her left, saw him peering round his mother's net curtains. So, she would have to change the shop alarm and the one at home. Those things could wait a day or two because he would certainly not trespass further on her anger just yet. Harriet's shop would need to be dealt with, also. Lisa would have a word with Hermione, too, as soon as possible. It was time to come clean.

Her stomach threatened to rise to the occasion,

so she took a barley-sugar sweet from the glove compartment. There was no food in her, and that was the reason for digestive misbehaviour. *Sugar for shock*, she told herself as she pulled away from the bungalow. He had a few shocks coming, but he'd be needing more than sweets as a cure.

Gus was home – oh, joy. From behind a newspaper, he asked if she'd had a pleasant day. She told him it had been wonderful and that the shop had been razed to the ground in an arson attack. 'Good,' he replied, 'that's the ticket.'

Ticket to madness, she thought as she made herself a small meal of cheese and crackers. It was a warm evening, so she carried the food out to the garden and sat on the swing. She placed the glass of fresh orange on a small wooden table, picked at a cracker and a bit of Brie. Dusk was gathering, and the security lights blinked on and off each time she moved, but they were behind her, so they didn't interfere. She was halfway through her second cream cracker when she noticed her daughter sitting in the gazebo. After swallowing a mouthful of juice and a great deal of nervousness, she picked up plate and glass before walking towards Harriet.

'Hi,' said the girl when her mother arrived. 'Long day?'

'The longest ever,' Lisa replied. 'Total disaster.'

'Ah.' Harrie knew not to enquire further; if her mother wanted to talk, she would.

'Lunch with Sadie Fisher. She's going in for liposuction soon. I hope they have a strong machine – she's carrying more fat than a pork butcher.'

Harrie sighed quietly. Conversations with her mother could be a bit repetitive.

'And there was a scene in the restaurant, rather embarrassing. I need to think before I can talk about it, but I seem to be in a bit of a pickle.'

Again, Harrie offered neither question nor comment.

'I've been a terrible mother, haven't I?'

Harrie's spine was suddenly rigid. This was definitely not one of Lisa's usual topics. 'I don't know. You're the only mother I've had.'

'No. You had Hermione and Eileen. I wasn't needed, and I got used to that. Oh, and I'm a bit selfish.'

Harrie remained silent.

'It seemed easier if I worked and your gran looked after you. She'd just been diagnosed and decided to conserve her energies for her grandchild. I was sort of surplus to requirements. That just went on through my second pregnancy and Benjamin's birth. It became a habit.' She bit her lip. 'I have the feeling I owe you an apology.'

Now was the time for speech. 'Mum, I love you. I don't always like you, but I love you. And I am sick to the molars of the blame and compensation culture – it's mad. If a child is too thin, it's the parents' fault – if he's fat, ditto. Doesn't behave at school? Oh, that'll be because his dad thumped him once, ten years ago. It's a load of tripe and vinegar. Life's hard. End of.'

Tears threatened yet again. Lisa knew she was going to weep at some stage, but she needed the privacy of her own bedroom before indulging herself. 'I just wish I'd done things differently.'

'We can all say that.'

'Thank you, Harriet. Thank you very much.' Lisa took herself and her half-eaten supper back to the house. Leaving her dishes for Eileen to deal with in the morning, she dragged herself upstairs much earlier than usual, went through the exfoliation and oiling routine, held back her grief.

She was almost ready for bed when her phone rang. Digging deep in today's handbag, she responded to her over-loud ring tone – the sound track from Peter Kay's mockery of 'Amarillo'.

'Hello?'

'It's me. Annie Nuttall. Have to be quick, I'm in a call box and you're on mobile. I've left him. Still need to pick up some things, but I've made the break.'

'I'm sorry.'

'Don't be – he's a criminal. Now, listen.'

'You will say this only once?'

A nervous giggle was followed by: 'The woman you were eating with. Doesn't she sell handbags and stuff at Jenkinson's?'

'Yes.'

'I'll leave it a day or two, then I'll nip down to Jenky's and have a look round. I'll be very sur- prised to see her, and I'll apologize for disturbing your meal. You were the wrong woman. I can do nothing about the rest of the folk who were eating there, but I'll tell Antoine. Then, if it's talked about, he can nip it in the bud. You know my husband, but it's only through business, right?'

'Right.' She was going to sob very soon.

'You never had sex with that man.'

In spite of her deep unhappiness, Lisa grinned. 'I never had sex with that man. I'll tell Senate, Congress and the country, eh? Do a Clinton?'

'I don't care what you do, but be safe. I've got to go. The twins are thinking about having mumps.'

'I'm sorry.'

'So am I. Life's hard enough without having them two buggers making it worse. Ta-ra, Lise.'

'Bye, Annie. God bless you.'

Lisa sat in her lonely room and sobbed her heart out. She grieved for what she had lost, though she had never had it because it had been a lie. Another lie in a long series of untruths from men, including her husband. She mourned two neglected children, knowing all the time that for Ben it was too late. She wept because she feared tomorrow, its emptiness and hopelessness, and she was not looking forward to talking to Hermione. The wise old bird had to know. Lisa wasn't stupid, but her head was in a muddle just now. And she wept into a handkerchief because Annie Nuttall had been so kind. Annie Nuttall was in danger of becoming her first real friend.

'Why should she care?' she asked her tear-stained reflection. Why should anyone care for so neglectful a mother, so self-absorbed a woman? Why the bloody hell had her husband's oddness been a part of his attraction, all those years ago? He was odd, all right. *His son was even odder. At least Harriet talks to me sometimes,* she thought. *Ben won't even sit and eat with me on Christmas Day.*

81

Benjamin had been too heavy a burden for his sister. Harriet was biting her nails again. *I have to turn over a new leaf. It has to stop being about me, after I've protected myself from Alec/Jimmy. Bastard. He has to be dealt with. Hermione will know how to cope.* She climbed into her narrow bed and, amazingly, fell asleep almost immediately. Lisa Compton-Milne was thoroughly exhausted.

'Come in, Lisa – don't hover. Or do you want me to stagger across on my Zimmer to help you in? Eileen's gone shopping, so we are quite alone.'

Lisa didn't know where to start, and she said so.

'Beginning, middle, end – doesn't matter to me because I'll have it all mixed up by tomorrow. But I can see the red eyes and white knuckles, so get it off your chest before that changes colour as well.'

Lisa obeyed, perching nervously on the edge of a seat designed to be higher than most. It was an old lady's chair, and Lisa suddenly felt as aged as the hills surrounding her hometown.

Hermione studied her daughter-in-law. This was a tough businesswoman who fooled most people into perceiving her as a clown at worst – and at best as a woman who would not accept the passing years and age gracefully. 'You don't look pretty today, Lisa. Take your time, but hurry up.'

Lisa laughed out loud. 'You get worse.'

'I know. It's a gift. Come on – shoot.'

Lisa shot. Without malice or bitterness, she traced in words the pattern of her marriage, its disappointments, her love affairs and lesser dalli-

82

ances. Deducing from her companion's expression that no offence had been taken, she outlined the business with the man she had known as Alec.

'Is that it?' asked Hermione when Lisa had stopped speaking.

'Yes.'

'Good. Open this window wide and get us both a cigarette. I can't think without a smoke.'

They smoked in silence for a few minutes. 'How are you getting along with Harriet at the moment?' the old lady asked.

'There's never been a difficulty there, except she always ran to you when she was little so we still tend to be ships that pass in the night.'

'My fault.'

Lisa shook her head vehemently. 'No, no. Harriet is very clever, you know, and she says that it's not about fault and blame. It's a case of life being hard and having to cope with it. But I wish she could get away from Benjamin. God knows what he gets up to, but when I have caught sight of him recently, he's looked grim.'

Hermione stubbed out her cigarette, passing the evidence of her crime to Lisa. 'Get rid of that before the boss finds it,' she said, referring to her fierce Irish carer. 'I should have encouraged you to stay at home with those children – no more lectures on blame, thanks. As for my own son – I am thoroughly ashamed of him. His father was aloof, and he died young. I used to tell myself that Gus had no pattern to follow, but he overplays his part as mad scientist, you see. He has neglected those children dreadfully. As for you,

83

madam, I don't blame you for having lovers, though you might have chosen more carefully.'

'Sorry.'

'Yes, well, we all make mistakes. This one is a pearler, though. Would you really have gone?'

Lisa bowed her head. 'Yes, I would. No one needs me here.'

Hermione tapped her walking stick on the floor. 'You need us,' she said sharply. 'And need breeds need. This is the bridge you will build with your daughter. It won't be easy, but let's pull three members of this family together while we can. Go and rest – Simon will run the shop. I have to think and make notes. You know how forgetful I have become.'

Hermione lingered all day by her front window while Lisa slept. In spite of several tellings-off from Eileen, she refused to rest. 'Shut up, for God's sake,' she ordered when things came to a head. 'I'm thinking. Leave me alone – go and torment that poor man at home for a change.'

'You don't deserve me,' came the swift response.

'Nobody deserves you, with the possible exceptions of Pontius Pilate and Adolf Hitler. Go away.'

An elderly but pristine camper van insinuated itself through the double gates. Ben got out, locked the vehicle, then disappeared into the house. 'Good gracious,' whispered Hermione to herself. 'Perhaps he'll park that outside poor Harrie's bungalow. Stupid boy.' Thus she dismissed from immediate thought her only grandson.

A plate was slammed down on the small table in front of Hermione's chair. 'Liver,' snapped the deliverer of good tidings. 'With onions. Great for your blood, the both of them. I'll be back later.'

'Whatever for?'

'Because I will.' Woebetide Eileen Eckersley left the apartment and banged the door.

At last, the little red MG turned into the drive. Hermione watched while Harrie examined her brother's camper, waited until the girl was in the house, pressed a bell that would sound in the kitchen.

A pink-faced Harrie ran into the room. 'Are you all right, Gran?'

'Yes, thank you.'

Harrie stood, arms akimbo. 'Have you seen what he's done? Did you give him the money to buy that abomination?'

'I did not.'

'It's sparkling clean inside. I bet he had it valeted before picking it up.'

'You mean fumigated.' Hermione began to plod her unenthusiastic way through a small part of the liver and onions. 'Your mother's in trouble. I sent her to bed. Not a word to your father – if he turns up. Not that he'd hear you, of course. Can you put this disgusting food in a plastic bag and lose it for me? And if you'd kindly make me a sandwich, I'd be grateful.'

Harrie did her grandmother's bidding, taking care to keep the liver and onions with her so that she could dispose of the evidence elsewhere. 'There's your sandwich, Gran – ham and salad.'

'Thank you. Liver, indeed.' She bit into more

85

palatable food.

Harrie walked to the window and looked down at her brother's vehicle. What was he up to this time? Did he intend to go to university and live in that thing? Or was he up to something bigger? 'What was that about Mum?' she asked.

Hermione swallowed. Sandwiches were not easy because swallowing was not easy. 'Your mother has got herself into a great deal of difficulty. I'll tell you about it after I have eaten, then we must make a plan. She needs our help.'

Well, that was a novelty, Harrie pondered as she waited for her grandmother to finish eating. Her mother flittered about like a butterfly, hither, thither, seldom in the same place for more than a moment. Life still held some surprises, then. Though this hardly promised to be a happy one.

The camper van was to make for further distraction and experimentation. It was not only a means of travelling from A to B, but its very nature provided a situation in which a man might travel, yet live alone and separate from his fellows. Meals would have to be catch-as-catch-can, but he would manage. His intention was not only to discover a degree of independence in himself, but also to demonstrate to his sister that he could manage without her. The very thought of leaving his safety zone was daunting, but the time had come. Harrie, at twenty-one, was ready to move out and begin a life of her own. With summer stretching before him, Ben's intention was to explore the country as best he could once all exams were over. He would show her. He would show all of them.

She had kept her word, had not visited him since the evening of the accident. He steered clear of the sites. Soon, he would be out on the open road without his broadband connection, so he might as well prepare himself for that eventuality. A kind of excitement bubbled in him as he laid his plans. Scotland and Wales were well worth a look, as was the south of England. He could and would do this thing. He could and would make a life for himself away from all his self-imposed cleanliness and ritual.

After finishing revision for the day, he went out into the rear garden again. He had to get used to the great outdoors, to not having a shower, to getting dirty and remaining so for several hours at a time. He would need to use public facilities, would be forced to ignore the existence of germs and disease. A chemical lavatory could serve only a part of the purpose – there would be times when he would need to visit a proper, flushing loo. Perhaps this might be the first step towards a normal existence.

He entered the copse and stamped about, trying not to care about damage to shoes and trousers. It was a fine night, and he climbed his tree, sitting very still and studying a star-spattered sky. There were so many things he could be doing – swimming, go-carting, even skiing abroad. He could visit Manchester Airport, see the big jets taking off; he could try tennis or even golf. Chess wasn't enough. To gain a rounder, healthier attitude, he must go forth and mix with people.

'Milly?' It was Harrie's voice. Ben drew up his

legs and sat very still on the bough.

'Found her?' That was Will Carpenter.

'No sign,' shouted Harrie. 'She's probably discovered a rabbit hole.'

They passed right beneath Ben's feet before moving away to the old summer house. Harrie yelled, 'Here she is,' then all became quiet again.

Stealthily, Ben climbed down and moved in the direction taken by Harrie and her companion.

'I'll put her lead on,' said Will. 'Let's sit for a while, shall we?'

As silently as he could, Ben made his way along the side of the building. The dog sensed his presence and barked, but was ignored – they probably thought she was reacting to wildlife.

'Do you intend to stay in jewellery forever?' Will asked.

'No idea,' came the reply. 'I've decided to take life as it comes, see what happens and roll with the punches.'

'And your brother?'

'No idea. He isn't interested in jewellery. Unless he's bought that contraption as some kind of mobile shop, I'd say he intends to steer clear of retail. If he can steer the bloody thing at all. I wouldn't care to drive it.'

Ben backed away and took a circuitous route in the direction of home. A tear-stained Lisa sat at the kitchen table. He grunted, 'Hello, Mum,' and fled past her.

Lisa, her mouth still open in preparation for speech, clamped her jaw closed as he disappeared towards the stairs. No good would come to that lad, she told herself. There was an indefinable something in him that was wrong, out of tune and out of step. A different drummer? Did he walk through life to a rhythm no one else could hear?

Harrie was outside with Will Carpenter and that daft dog. It was an adorable item with attitude and beauty. It was also a thief – Lisa had seen it digging through the dustbins on more than one occasion.

Gus drifted in, patted his pockets, smiled absently at her, wandered off. She heard him rattling about in his study. Soon, he would find something and become engrossed in it, but the likelihood of him finding whatever he had been searching for was remote. He would forget his original target and set to work on something else. Wasn't he looking at honey? Hadn't she heard him talking on the phone about honey?

Alec/Jimmy remained at the front of her mind. She was also acutely grateful to his wife, the poor soul who had run back home to her mother. It was a grim life, but, with luck and a good following wind, Hermione and Harrie would come up with something regarding the money.

Police. Could she? Would she? Perhaps Annie Nuttall was right – bets should be hedged via the law before too much time elapsed. But Lisa would wait until Hermione had worn the thinking cap for a day or two. The old woman was a caution, but a rock when someone needed support.

Harrie came in. 'How are you now?' she asked. 'Gran told me.'

'Ashamed is how I am.'

'Don't be. Love makes fools of many people. You're hardly the first.'

'And won't be the last.' Lisa took a sip of tea. 'Thanks.'

'What for?'

'For being there. For not turning on me. Just ... thanks.'

'It's OK. Gran is on to it. Her mind is very sharp for her age, isn't it? Unless you want to know about the very recent past.'

'She's a good egg,' concluded Lisa. 'I owe her a lot.'

'Mum, we just get through. It isn't about mistakes and regrets and debts to people – it's about getting up every morning and doing what needs to be done.'

'Yes.' Lisa paused. 'How's Will?'

'Fine.'

'The dog?'

Harrie laughed. 'Terrible. Intelligent pups are always the worst. She ate Will's bike.'

'What?'

'Two tyres and a pedal.' Harrie stared hard at her mother. 'It'll be all right. And, if it isn't, it'll be all wrong, but we'll cope.'

Lisa sat for a while after Harrie had gone to bed. 'The daughter is the mother and the mother is the child,' she advised her teacup.

Gus returned. 'Have you seen a yellow-bound manuscript marked urgent?'

'No, sorry.'

He drifted off, and Lisa allowed herself a slight smile. He had lost his papers again; they were probably in the place where he had buried his feelings and half of his mind. If that was genius, she was better off in diamonds.

After watching rather too many of the documentary channels, Hermione did not trust the police unless they were Morse or Frost. The chances of encountering a real-life version of either of those two saints were remote at best. Crime programmes on Sky demonstrated only too clearly the shortcomings of forces on each side of the Atlantic, so the boys in blue – or in plain clothes – did not feature in her equation. Also, Lisa was guilty – there was no way of dressing up the fact. She had never questioned the source of the man's swag, so she was not going to be completely in the clear. He would condemn her, of course. He – whoever he was – was a blighter with a wife and children, so he would never take full blame for his crimes. Was Gus any better? Was Hermione's son less guilty because he was not a thief?

'And what if she gets into trouble?' asked Woebee, a feather duster held aloft. 'A fine mess that'll be, as Oliver Laurel used to say.'

'Hardy.'

'Whatever. But, if they come for her, how will she talk her way out of it? She handled goods that were stolen, didn't she?'

Hermione awarded her carer a long, hard stare. 'Sometimes, I think you know too much. This is too heavy a weight for your few brain cells. Just be quiet and do some cooking or cleaning or something.'

The Irishwoman bridled, arms folded beneath

a non-existent bosom, neck craning towards the ceiling, foot tapping on carpet, feather duster tucked under one arm. 'I'm the only one daft enough to put up with the shenanigans of this family, and well you know it. I care about what happens to you all, so I do. It's a mess, and I am praying all the time.'

'Then pick up your rosary and pray silently, please. There will be no police. Lisa is of a nervous disposition.' Gus had made her so. 'My son is as much to blame as anyone, Eileen.' He was a thief, yet his sins needed no safe in which they might be hidden, as he stole invisible and more important aspects of life.

The Jill-of-all-trades relaxed slightly. 'He was never a husband, never a daddy. My own daddy might have been a drunken old fool, but he loved us, came home with enough for us to eat, God rest him.' She sat down opposite her friend and employer. 'This isn't good for you, either.'

Hermione nodded. 'I know.'

'It'll play havoc with your shakes and your swallowing.'

'Yes.'

Eileen/Woebee got on with her dusting. The old lady needed time to think, and no one could help her just now.

Someone tapped at the door. 'Come in,' called Hermione.

Lisa entered. Even now, in one of her darker hours, she was perfectly dressed and manicured. She perched on the chair recently vacated by Eileen. 'I tried to handle it,' she began softly. 'Went to the police station, stood outside, went for a cup of coffee, looked in shop windows, returned to the police station. I wanted to keep you out of it, but I just drank a lot of coffee.'

Hermione frowned before asking Eileen to go out to the shops. When the two of them were alone, she sat and listened to Lisa's explanation. The police had not been told. Lisa had decided to come clean because a private detective hired by Nuttall's wife knew that Bolton police were interested in the man's movements. But she had failed. She was a coward.

'Would he involve you if he was arrested?' asked the older woman.

Lisa shrugged. She did not know the man she had so recently loved.

'And the newspapers would have plenty to say if you were involved.' Hermione bowed her head for a moment. 'Try to get hold of his wife. There must be a history of such behaviour – he is probably a seasoned blackguard.'

'Yes. I am not the first woman to be fooled by him.' Hermione studied her daughter-in-law. 'Even Gus will notice he's been cuckolded if it's in the *Daily Mirror*.'

Lisa straightened her spine. 'He won't care. As long as he has his trains in Sheila Barton's house, he'll weather the storm. Three years she has been his mistress. Mind, there's always a chance that sex isn't on the agenda for my dearly beloved husband, but his connection with her might stop his tantrums.'

Both women suddenly burst out laughing. The idea of Gus in a tantrum was too much, and it spilled out of them in loud chuckles. He would never shout, would never stamp and rage, because such actions were born of deep feelings, and he seldom displayed anything beyond mild displeasure.

'He won't throw his rattle out of the pram,' said Hermione as she dried her eyes with an unsteady hand. 'And he won't throw you out of my house, either. You are stronger than any of us, Lisa. I am pleased that you didn't involve the law, though goodness knows what might be the right way of handling this. Talk to the woman.'

Lisa nodded. Annie had promised to phone tonight. And Annie, unlike her husband, had a habit of keeping her word.

Four

They all thought Gus noticed nothing, laboured under the delusion that he was deaf, blind and lacking in common sense. But he wasn't. And he did notice things. The wife was in overdrive, Harrie was more worried than ever, while his son stayed out of the way as usual. Even Eileen Eckersley was in a state astutely described by Mother as 'worse than Russia'. Mother was herself, but that was typical as she took everything in her stride even now, when her stride had become dependent on walking frames. There was a plot on. It was big enough to send Harrie pacing about in the copse at night, sufficiently momentous to cause loud clattering of dishes and some Irish jabbering in the kitchen, and it had affected Gus, who usually maintained a position of silent neutrality.

His main concern continued to be the boy. There had been a degree of disappointment when Harriet had refused to attend university, but Benjamin was brilliant and could follow quite easily in the footsteps of Gus's much-respected father. If Benjamin wasted his life, that would be a sin, indeed. But the lad had managed school, just about, and was now in possession of a full driving licence, so surely there was hope? Perhaps the camper van would be a new beginning for him.

Things were coming to a head this morning. Wheels for Wheels had arrived. Part of a larger organization that owned limousines and wedding cars, Wheels for Wheels provided a private service for disabled people who wanted transferring from A to B. Today, 'A' was Weaver's Warp and 'B' was God alone knew where, but Hermione Compton-Milne's wheelchair was currently being bolted into the rear of a large, black van. Lisa fussed, just as she always did, while Harriet, in jeans and a ragged T-shirt that left her midriff bare, had clearly dressed with no intention of accompanying her mother and grandmother.

Gus stepped to one side of the open window and listened. 'Don't lose your temper, Gran,' Harriet was pleading.

'We'll be fine,' Lisa answered. 'Annie won't let us down. Perhaps I have known her for no more than five minutes, but I trust her. She's honourable – more than can be said for her husband.'

Doors slid into the closed position, and the engine started up. Gus looked at his watch. Wasn't he supposed to be somewhere? Doing something? He knew it wasn't bleach because he had done all of those tests – hadn't he? Yes, he had. Five of them this time. The public probably thought that the television advertisements were faked, but Gus earned a good living by analysing swabs from kitchens before and after the application of a certain product. It wasn't a swabs day, then.

Who was Annie? Why was Annie's husband not to be trusted? Mother was in pain. It had to be something big to drag her out of her penthouse.

Where was he supposed to be? Diary. Not on the desk, not on the bookshelves. Ah – it sat next to the clock on the mantelpiece. And Harriet had become a drug-dealer for her grandmother. She brought home skunk, a commodity that supposedly helped people with neurological disorders. It also made them paranoid... He opened the diary and smiled. Ah, yes. This was to be a special day.

It was trains. Excitement cut through him as he remembered a find in *Locomotion*, a magazine published and distributed for those who loved real trains. An aged replica of the Scotsman waited for him in Fallowfield. Only Sheila truly understood his anticipation. Her husband had loved trains. Gus smiled again. She was a good, plain woman with a big heart. He already owned two Scotsman models, but the one advertised was a beauty and the man was saving it for him. Being an internationally respected boffin certainly had its plus sides. For Professor Compton-Milne, the vendor had promised to keep the engine.

He wandered outside and stood by his Mini. Harriet was outside the gate, as if she followed Mother and Lisa in spirit if not in body. Whatever was occurring was enormous. Did he have the Fallowfield address? Yes. He opened the car door and placed his diary on the passenger seat. Should he talk to his daughter? Apart from daily pleasantries and meaningless quips, little of note ever passed between Gus and Harriet. He should try. But not yet, not now. Treasure awaited him in Manchester. With a quickening pulse, the man of the house folded himself into the tiny car, drove

97

towards the gate, nodded at his daughter, turned right and headed for the A666. Motorways were for speed freaks, and he was not one of that ever-increasing number.

'He has no idea,' Harrie muttered under her breath. Why was he like this? Other men had careers and projects, yet they found time for their children. Still, this was nothing new. Harrie had coped without a father for much of her life. There was no point in fretting now.

Sheila Barton described herself as adaptable, because she held down several jobs. She was lollipop lady, dinner supervisor and part-time classroom assistant at St Ethelbert's, the local primary school. Most importantly, she was a close friend to Gustav Compton-Milne, pioneer in the field of microbiology, leading authority on the subject of superbugs, man of standing and lover of model trains.

But he was not Sheila's lover.

After burying a husband thirty years her senior, Mrs Sheila Barton had heaved a sigh of relief and washed her metaphorical hands of the whole sordid business. No more sex. No more fumblings in the night, no danger of pregnancy, no worries.

This was a well-to-do widow, as she had inherited from the deceased man two mortgage-free properties – her own home and the house next door. She had opened up both lofts, and Gustav's trains occupied the whole attic area. The rest of the second house was rented out to a family, so Sheila had no real need to work. But work kept her sane. While supervising the local young, she congratulated herself repeatedly on her child-free state. Children were nasty, cruel, dirty little things, and she was better off without them. Yet, as she admitted begrudgingly on occasion, they did make her laugh. She had worked out that kids were OK as long as they were herded together well away from parents. School had rules, and children needed them. Kept in communes, they even managed to be mildly amusing.

In truth, Sheila did have a child. Some three years earlier, when clearing out her husband's belongings, she had found in a magazine an advertisement placed by a man who liked model trains. As her husband, too, had been a fan of miniature railways, she had replied, and Gus had been delighted. He took over the dead man's stock but never took advantage of the widow, didn't even try to kiss her, and he valued her company. His rent was seldom late, he contributed towards household bills, and she enjoyed taking care of him. Gustav Compton-Milne was a man in a million.

With her part-time lodger, Sheila Barton played the role of a public school matron-cum-cook. All he had wanted was space for his hobby, but he received much more than that. He was cared for, fed good, comforting foods including custards, sticky puddings and blancmange. Like a competent mother, Sheila heeded current laws on nutrition, so Gus also received his fair share of salads, fresh fruits and vegetables. Gus was her project, her hobby. He was going to save the world; therefore, she must save him from an ignorant wife who clearly didn't give two pence for his welfare.

Sheila cared.

She hung on his words, admired his cleverness, worshipped at the feet of the only truly intelligent man to have entered her life. With her, he was completely at home, speaking openly and with candour about his family and his work. Sheila was mother, sister, wife and friend to him, a safety valve that he could employ at will, allowing him relief and comfort in an atmosphere of tenderness and empathy. The fact that she understood little pertaining to microbiology was of no importance; she paid attention and warmed his slippers – that was enough for him. Home was here, on Wigan Road, because here he could be absentminded stationmaster, railway-building professor – whatever. He could be himself, and that was what mattered.

In her square, modern kitchen, Sheila peeled vegetables. She knew better than to expect him, so she kept ingredients prepared in order that a meal could be produced within half an hour at any time of day or night. If he failed to appear for a couple of days, she could consume the food herself. She was happy. For the first time in her adult life, Mrs Sheila Barton was completely contented.

She heard his key in the lock and, without thinking, dashed into the living room to check her appearance at the mirror. Whilst he neither expected nor wanted glamour, he probably noticed if she was untidy. 'Hello?' she called. 'Did you get it?'

'Yes, replied the disembodied voice. 'And it's a beauty. I'll go straight up. You can look at it later.'

Sheila smiled to herself. 'Have you eaten?

'I think not.'

'Half an hour?'

'Yes. Thank you.'

She heard him running up to the landing, listened as the metal ladder dropped at his feet. Time would hold no meaning for him now; she would need to coax him down with promises of onion gravy followed by spotted dick. But none of that mattered. Gustav was in his own little bit of heaven, and all was well with the world.

All was by no means well with Jimmy Nuttall's slice of the world. He waited in his mother's bungalow for two events, neither of which he anticipated with any degree of joy. His mother, due to return from holidays, would arrive to find her only begotten son in situ. She would not be pleased. Freda Nuttall did not like men in a house – they got in the way. Men were built for fields, factories and public hostelries, and they had no place in a single-bedroomed retirement bungalow with panic alarms and only one lavatory.

Jimmy also expected his wife. Annie, who could be dangerous when roused, had a tiny body that gave not the slightest hint of the strength in its limbs or the fury in its head. She was, and always had been, a force never to be ignored, especially at those times of her month when hormones bubbled in her blood. Although he had no idea of

101

the current state of her menstrual cycle, he knew she could be hell on legs even when on a supposedly level keel. She needed to talk about the children – that was the official line, anyway. In truth, the woman probably wanted to kill him, and he was fed up. Should he move the rest of Mam's pottery treasures in case they provided ammunition for Annie? Lisa had already caused a noticeable gap in the collection. Oh, to hell with it all.

There would be a divorce, he supposed. He hoped to persuade her otherwise, since the easiest option for him would be a return to the bosom of his family, but he held very little hope in that direction. Sighing deeply, he fussed about, tidying his mother's bedroom and kitchen before starting on himself. Unshaven and unwashed, he looked like a refugee from some terribly deprived quarter of a city under siege. God. He had as much chance of going home as George W. Bush had of being elected pope.

Reasonably tidy after his small efforts, he returned to the living room and sat down. Life with Lisa had been good. She was feisty and full of mischief. Older than he was, she had proved hard to keep up with, as her hunger for life had never been satisfied by that dry stick of a scientist she called husband. Well, she was out of the picture now, as was Annie, as were his three children. Fatherhood had never been his favourite game, but they were his kids and, at the end of the day, he had rights. Didn't he?

Annie's ageing car coughed to a halt outside the bungalow. Jimmy stiffened automatically. She would not be in the best of moods, would she? The door was on the latch, so she needed no key to reach her husband.

When she entered the room, he gulped nervously. 'Hi,' he managed when his throat settled.

'I need a new car,' came the quick reply. 'That one couldn't pass water, let alone an MOT.' She looked him up and down before asking the air why a person never had a baseball bat when it was needed most.

'Sweetie,' he began. 'I'm a twit. We both know I'm a twit, but can't we make some sort of effort here?'

She looked over her shoulder. 'Ooh, I thought somebody else had come in then. Were you talking to me? Listen, mate. If I'm a sweetie, I'll have to be one of them Smarties, because I'm too clever for you. Just wait. Just you wait, Jimmy Nuttall.'

'Wait for what?'

'Arma-bloody-geddon is what,' she shouted. 'Life is about to catch up with you, lad. I've stood by you through thick and thin, you thieving, good-for-nowt layabout. Well, I've had enough. I don't want my lads turning out to be criminals, do I? Following in Father's Footsteps? Isn't that a song? Aye, well, my sons will not be singing from the same hymn sheet as you, Nuttall. They'll be gradely folk, not gutter-muck.'

Jimmy looked up at the ceiling. Annie was off on one of her rants, and nothing short of an act of God would divert her. The chances of earthquake or hurricane were not strong, so he simply had to sit it out. Would she settle in a minute?

Would she calm down and allow him back into her life?

No, she was carrying on. He folded his arms and suffered the barrage of words that poured from her.

She threw herself into a chair near the window. 'So this is where you brought your bit of stuff while your mam was away, eh? I'm sure old Freda will be delighted to know you found a use for her bed. She never did like waste, your mam.'

'It's over,' he shouted. 'The affair, such as it was, is over.'

'I agree. It's definitely bloody over. I'm having the house – you can sign it over to me. It'll likely have to be sold, but me and the kids need money.'

Jimmy's jaw dropped. 'I was brought up in that house, Annie. Mam sold it to us cheap – it's my home.'

'We'll see.' Annie tapped an angry toe against floral carpet. 'Cops are after you for all the stuff that's gone missing from places where you put alarms in. The private detective told me that. He's a retired sergeant, and he still has mates in the force. You'd better make yourself scarce. In fact, you'd be safest going for total invisibility – try Alaska and wear white.'

He ran a hand through his hair. 'Bugger,' he cursed.

'You can add an "off" to that,' said Annie, her tone quieter. 'And then, you can take your own advice and bugger off for good.'

The front door swung inward, and a new voice reached their ears. 'Pull me in backwards,' ordered an off-stage woman. 'You'll have me spread out on this dreadful carpet like a sheepskin rug. We should have brought Eileen. She's adequate when it comes to the handling of a wheelchair.'

'Sorry, Mother,' came the reply.

Jimmy's skin blanched. Lisa was here, as was some female sergeant major in a bad mood. Wasn't Annie enough?

A wheelchair entered the arena. Jimmy saw a striking woman – grey hair, good clothes, severe expression. Lisa, in charge of steering, followed Hermione into the room. 'This is Annie Nuttall,' she announced. 'And that is Jimmy ... or Alec – depending on the day of the week, I suppose.' She parked the wheelchair next to Annie. 'Mrs Hermione Compton-Milne,' she added. 'My mother-in-law.'

A deafening silence followed. Hermione eyed the cluttered decor, sniffed, patted Annie's arm, then stared hard at the man. He had a weak chin and very nervous hands. He was plucking away at a folkweave throw on the arms of his mother's chair. Terror showed in the darting movements of eyes set rather too close together. Lisa had very poor taste in men, it seemed. 'Annie?'

'Yes?' Even Annie seemed slightly cowed by the visitor.

'Get your gun?'

Annie nodded. 'Yes, I got my gun, Mrs Compton-Milne.'

Jimmy sank lower in his mother's best armchair. Twin spots of colour glowed in ashen cheeks, and his heartbeat quickened, seeming to sound in his ears like the threatening drum of some Native-American tribe. Yes, this was a war dance, and he was the intended target.

Several seconds passed before Hermione went in for the kill. In clipped tones, she delivered his sentence. 'We know about Birmingham,' she stated plainly. 'Your wife has found a tidy sum in the eaves of your house. While searching, in order to pay bills and feed your children, Annie also discovered the weapon. Tax avoidance is one thing; the crippling of a security guard is another matter altogether.'

Jimmy opened his mouth, but delivered not a single syllable. He sat as still as stone, jaw hanging while he took in the implications of what he had just heard. He had hidden the damned thing well, had removed all ammunition and had given the item no thought in months. They held him by the throat, and they knew it.

'The gun is safe,' said the old woman. 'It is wiped of all fingerprints – exactly as the police would expect. But, if tested, it will doubtless deliver a missile very similar to the one taken from that poor man's spine. Wheelchair-bound, isn't he? Obviously, he has my complete sympathy.'

A battery-powered clock delivered a tinny account of the time. Lisa turned towards the window because she found herself incapable of looking at him. Armed robbery? She had been about to run away with a real criminal, and she cursed her own stupidity.

'Annie?'

Jimmy's wife gave her attention to Hermione. 'Yes?'

'You have always suspected that he was involved

in the Birmingham jewellery quarter robbery, haven't you?'

Annie nodded.

'But the way to be sure would be to have that gun tested?'

Annie inclined her head again.

At last, Jimmy managed to speak. 'I never shot him,' he cried. 'I wasn't even there – I kept that gun for a mate.'

'You were there.' Annie's tone was icy. 'You came back and locked yourself upstairs for days, said you had a cold. I saw it in the papers and on the telly. That poor man's life hung by a thread for weeks – even months. But I wanted to think the best of you, wanted it to be somebody else who did the robbery. I can tell now from your eyes that you were one of the gang that did it. You've never been able to lie to my face, have you?' She turned to Lisa. 'Don't worry – you've handled none of that stolen jewellery. It was years back, and it's all long gone – sold by the gang leader, I reckon.'

'It wasn't me.' The words arrived crippled by panic. 'I never did any of that–'

'Tell it to the judge,' Annie snapped. 'For now, you'd be best off just listening to what this lady has come to say.'

Hermione sniffed. 'He is guiltier than sin itself. Now, listen to me, Mr Nuttall. The ill-gotten gains you promised to share with Lisa are all yours, along with the stolen goods you hid in the floor safe. I have also placed a sum of money in here.' She tossed an enormous brown envelope on to a coffee table. 'Now, run, run, as fast as you can, because the law is on your tail. Breathe one word of your association with my family and the police get the gun.'

Lisa, who had remained silent throughout, finally managed to look at the man who had so recently been her lover. What had she seen in him? How desperate for love had she been? He was like a rabbit trapped in headlights, and the monster he faced was a Rolls Royce. When it came to putting people in their place, Hermione was the cream.

It was into this interesting tableau that Freda Nuttall stepped on her return from holiday. A taxi driver, having announced that he was leaving luggage in the hall, closed the front door in his wake. Freda stood dumbfounded in the entrance to her lounge. She saw Annie, two women who were unknown to her, and her son cowering in the best chair. 'What the bloody hell has he done now?' she asked.

Hermione glanced at Freda. 'Please sit down,' she invited regally.

Freda bridled instantly. 'In me own house?' she asked. 'I don't need telling to sit down in me own house.' Nevertheless, she sat, her eyes fixed on Jimmy's face. 'You may be my son, lad, but you've brought nothing but trouble to my door since you were knee-high to a standard lamp. I hope you've not been hitting her.' She waved a hand in the direction of her daughter-in-law. 'I'm used to your thieving ways – I've had to get used – but I'm not having her used as a punchbag.'

The punchbag spoke. 'Don't worry, Mam. He knows I'd have killed him in his sleep if he'd ever gone for me.'

'Good.' Freda surveyed her unwanted guests. 'And who the hell are you two? Leftovers from the Luton Girls' Choir?'

Hermione's mouth twitched. She found herself liking Freda Nuttall – because Freda did not fear truth, and she employed humour even when perplexed.

Freda waded on, addressing Hermione, who seemed to have placed herself in charge. 'I don't know what this has got to do with you, missus. Sitting there with a gob like a bagful of spanners, taking over me bungalow, and who broke me shepherdess?'

'I did,' replied Lisa. 'I'll get you another.'

Freda chewed her lip for a moment. 'Oh, aye? And who are you? His latest bit of fluff?'

For answer, Lisa lowered her head.

'Oh, I see,' said Freda, arms folding beneath an ample bosom. 'And did Annie catch you at it? She's no fool, is Annie. Though I have to say she were daft enough to get herself shackled to this bad bugger. He may be me son, but I can't say I'm proud.' She spoke now to Annie. 'And I wouldn't say no to a cuppa, love. I'm fair clemmed after all that travelling. And them Southerners couldn't make a decent brew to save their flaming lives. I'm going back to Morecambe next year. Continental bloody breakfasts – I ask you. Who wants bread and jam in a morning, eh?'

Annie stood. 'I'd better tell you now, Mam, that I'm divorcing him.'

Freda waited for further clarification, but none was forthcoming. 'Not before time, then. Don't forget me sweeteners and make sure you don't divorce *me*.' She swallowed. 'I think the world of you and them kids, girl, as well you know.'

Jimmy rose to his feet after Annie had left the room. 'I'll ... er...'

'Annie?' shouted Freda. 'Have a dekko in that there coronation mug. There should be forty pounds and ninety-seven pence for me lecky.'

Jimmy threw a note on to the coffee table before picking up Hermione's envelope. 'I borrowed a tenner from your electricity money,' he said. Without waiting for a reply, he fled from the scene.

Annie came in. 'You're a tenner down, Mam.'

'It's all right,' replied Freda wearily. 'I've got it here. Oh, see if we've any Bourbons. I fancy a nice biscuit with me tea.' She glanced at Hermione. 'Why are you in that wheelchair?'

While the visitor explained about multiple sclerosis, Jimmy started up his car and drove away. No one made any further comment about him. But, as the small-talk continued, Annie and Lisa glanced at each other. A shadow remained in their hearts. He would be back – of that, both felt certain.

Driving round the Lancashire countryside with his heart in his mouth and bundles of clothes stuffed into the back of his car was not Jimmy Nuttall's idea of fun. He didn't notice the lushness born of heavier than average rainfall, the pleats and folds at the edges of moors, swans on a reservoir, children taking chances by trespassing on acres dedicated to crops. No. All he could think of was bloody Birmingham. He hadn't even held the flipping gun, had he? He was just the soft swine who'd driven the car and found the weapon afterwards, when the other two had fled.

To conserve petrol, he parked in a country lane, ate a cold pasty and drank a can of lukewarm cola. 'I never killed anybody,' he told the windscreen, 'but I feel as if I could now.' Mind, he would probably need a wooden stake or some silver bullets to put a stop to those four witches – his own mam, Lisa, Mrs High-and-Mighty Compton-sodding-Milne and Annie. Almost drowning in self-pity, he lowered his head and rested it on hands that gripped the steering wheel.

He hadn't cried for years, but he wept now because his life was all but over. If the cops got their hands on that gun, he would be doomed. Every truly guilty party had disappeared like smoke dashed from a windswept chimney pot. 'I didn't even see a penny,' he wept. The handful of diamonds or whatever had been sold abroad, and the other two members of the gang had probably remained in Europe. Or South America, more like.

Where to go? He hadn't the money for Brazil, didn't know how to get a false passport, had no idea whether airport police had been alerted to look for him. Surely not? If they didn't know about Birmingham, they'd not be on standby for an installer of alarms, surely? Or would they? He'd nicked a fair amount of stuff just lately...

'Blood and stomach pills,' he cursed. Damn Annie. Private detective? What had been the blinking point of that? He'd never have left her for good – she knew that.

Women were strange creatures. They forgave each other too readily and never forgave men at all. His mother had sat there without a single good word for him; his wife and his mistress had joined forces, while the third Charlie's Angel, a hundred years old and in a wheelchair, remained close to a daughter-in-law who had cheated on her own scientist son. *I might as well not have existed,* he thought. *Not one of them looked at me. I bet they never even noticed I'd left.*

Tears drying on his face, Jimmy caught hold of a sudden brain-wave. Sally Potter. Farm cottage, father dead, lived by herself. *She's always fancied me, has old Sal,* he thought. Jimmy had taken Sally's virginity and her heart, and she had waited for over fifteen years for him to become a fixture in her life. She worked, didn't she? Yes. Sally had a bike, and she rode it all over the place – she cleaned houses. That farm she lived on was crumbling. The farmhouse and all outbuildings, left to rot quietly, would probably be acquired sooner or later by some builder with an eye for a bargain. But for now, Sally lived halfway up a path that led nowhere. And halfway to nowhere was precisely where Jimmy needed to be.

They'll think I've gone to London or somewhere down south, he *thought. But I'm too clever for them.* There had to be a way of getting that gun back. Going down for burglaries was one thing; attempted murder or manslaughter was another matter altogether. Yes, he had to stay here, in Lancashire. Yes, it had to be Sally Potter.

He swallowed audibly. Could he tolerate her?

She fawned and slobbered over him every time he visited – even after her dad's funeral, which had been attended by just him, her and the vicar. Sally wasn't completely ugly, but ... those craters in her face, large dents created by a morbid tendency to pick at teenage spots. And Sal's teenage spots had lasted well into her twenties. He wiped his forehead. Sal was a mess. But he had to go somewhere, wanted food and a bed. It was going to be Sally Potter. He needed her.

Gus polished off the last of his treacle sponge. 'That was wonderful,' he said.

Sheila Barton smiled. She felt truly blessed, because she had always wanted someone appreciative for whom she might cook. Her dead husband had been confined to a strict diet on account of some digestive diagnosis with a name longer than Wigan Road, so this relationship with Gus had been her first opportunity to shine at good, plain cooking.

He leaned back in his chair. 'I am very full,' he declared.

'Good.' Sheila began to gather dishes. 'I saw your daughter the other week,' she said, her tone deliberately casual.

'Really? Where?'

'Visiting that psychiatric person a few doors along. And I wouldn't be surprised if she saw you, because you'd forgotten your key again, and you waited for me at the bottom of Hawthorne Road. Remember?'

He nodded. 'Yes, I remember.'

'I've put a key under the middle-sized plant pot

on the top step. All right?'

He nodded. 'They know I keep my trains some-where and that they aren't likely to be in a laboratory. And there is nothing untoward about our friendship. Whereas my wife...' His voice died away.

Sheila, tray in hands, waited for him to continue. 'What about her?' she asked finally. Sometimes, Gus made her slightly impatient.

He shrugged. 'She leads an adventurous life, I believe.'

'Men?'

'Several. And not always savoury.'

In the kitchen, Sheila washed dishes noisily. She understood him very well. The conjoining of male and female flesh had been necessary, as Gus had needed children to whom he could bequeath his brilliance. But now that he was a father, he no longer needed to perform those ridiculous acts on which the survival of the species depended. Lisa Compton-Milne didn't know how lucky she was, it seemed. Also, she was clearly one of those cheap women who liked throwing herself all over the place to be prodded and pinched by lowlifes.

'There's something going on right now.'

Sheila looked over her shoulder; he was standing in the kitchen doorway. 'Really?'

He nodded. 'Even my mother is involved in it. I could be wrong, of course. If I were wrong, it would not be for the first time. But there is a new level of anxiety in the house. Because they think of me as some stereotypical mad professor, they believe I am impervious to atmosphere. I do notice things. Eventually.'

She dried her hands and set the percolator to perform its task. Gus liked Kenya blend, so she, too, had decided to prefer it above all other coffees. 'How's Benjamin?' she asked.

'As ill-informed as I am, I suppose. He's too busy keeping himself apart from the rest of us. I am hopeful that he will emerge in time to do something with his life.'

She poured the coffee and handed him a glass cup in a stainless steel holder. 'They don't deserve you, any of them,' she said.

Gus suspected that she was right, though the track along which she travelled led in the wrong direction. He should be the one to shift the points, wave the flag and take control of the journey – before it was too late. He did not know where to start, how to change himself into a parent. 'I have not been much of a father,' he said when they were seated in easy chairs. 'I can't remember their childhood, you see. One minute, they were babies, and the next – well – they were fully-grown strangers.'

'But you're a genius,' his companion cried.

Gus nodded. 'Perhaps – though that is hard for me to judge. But even a forgetful scientist should know his children. She – Harriet – is extremely beautiful and as bright as the sun. Yet she has dedicated her life to her little brother. Benjamin needs help, but so does she.'

Sheila felt her jaw slackening. For the first time ever, the most important person – the only person in her life – was admitting a fault in his make-up. Panic flooded through her veins. Would he give up his trains and dedicate his time to his

115

offspring? 'What are you going to do?' she asked tentatively.

'I haven't the foggiest,' he replied. And that was the absolute truth.

Will Carpenter was not making great strides in his effort to court Harrie. Although he had a first in chemistry and a postgraduate degree in education, he was not at all talented in the field of communication. No, that was hardly the case, as he was good at teaching, yet the one-to-one business between himself and his chosen one was not plain sailing. She was witty and inclined to deliver smart, double-edged answers to questions. Comments he made were similarly drowned beneath waves of humorous monologue. He adored her, feared her, was terrified by her family.

Their meeting place had been turned into a building site, so he was now forced to knock at the front door of Weaver's Warp in order to see her. Mrs Compton-Milne the Elder had always allowed people right of way through the copse, but builders had stemmed the easy flow of walkers, and there was a danger that the woods might become out of bounds once Harrie's chalet had been completed.

Now, the courtship had taken on a formal air. How could knocking on a door make a difference? It did, though. Their meetings were visibly engineered; the fact that he had often waited for hours in the copse to 'happen upon' her did not matter. He was knocking on a door, now, and was thereby declaring his intentions. Perhaps he had been born into the wrong era; perhaps he should wear a top hat and cutaway coat and raise a glass to Queen Victoria after meals.

They walked in silence along Weaver's Weft, the lane on which the Compton-Milne house stood. Milly, released from the restraints of a leash, bounded along like a practising young kangaroo.

Will cleared his throat. 'Your house seems to be making good progress.'

'Yes. It's just a shed with electricity and drains. Americans live in them all the time. It comes with all appliances built in, you know. Brilliant idea.'

'And it gets you away from Ben.'

Harrie nodded. 'Something has to shock him back to life. That apartment of his is a tomb. The camper van hasn't been used yet, but I live in hope. He couldn't have taken driving lessons and a test a year ago. He's working it out. I'm leaving him to it.'

Milly arrived with a large bough between her teeth. 'That's nearly half a tree,' Harrie chided. 'We are supposed to be saving the planet, you daft dog.'

Milly dumped her find before dashing off in search of further mischief.

'And ... erm ... how is your mother?'

Harrie stopped walking, causing him to go into reverse for a couple of paces. 'My mother is brilliant. Some people think she's so loose with her favours that her ankles have separate postcodes, but she's not like that. She's lonely and lively and she's forgotten more about precious minerals than I shall ever know.'

Will cleared his throat. 'Does your dad know about...?'

'About her dalliances? Of course he does. He has his own arrangements. I think I saw him waiting to meet his own arrangements a couple of weeks ago on Wigan Road. Plays the mad professor, but he's not as daft as he wants us to believe he is. They survive, both of them. Gran brought us up.' She touched his arm. 'You think we're all mad, don't you?'

He paused before replying. 'Eccentric, yes.'

'It's been an unusual childhood,' Harrie admitted, 'but I wouldn't change a moment for myself. Ben was more needful than I. All I wanted was Gran's awesome stories, something to read and the odd hour with Woebee.'

'Mrs Eckersley?'

Harrie nodded. 'She's amazing, a real-life Mrs Malaprop, every wrong word a winner. I remember her saying she was having mortal trouble with her cubicles. She meant cuticles. Childhood was a maze of guesswork and dragons. Gran gave us the dragons, knights and fairies, while Woebee provided us with a whole alternative thesaurus. Mother worked, Father worked, and Gran and Woebee were our carers. That's just the way it was. Why does this feel like some sort of job interview?' Without waiting for an answer, she dashed off in pursuit of the wayward dog.

Will followed her. He had a sudden feeling that it was now or never. She wouldn't tolerate any messing about. Harriet Compton-Milne was a pragmatic young woman, outspoken to the point of recklessness and as straight as any die. He grabbed her arm. 'Remember when I kissed you?' he asked, knowing that so stupid a question

118

would throw her straight into the role of comedienne.

'How could I forget?' she asked. 'Liquorice.'

'What?'

'You tasted of one of those terrible black Spanish sticks.'

'Did I?'

'You did. That was ten years ago, and I still get a whiff of it whenever you are around. Well, that and wet dog-hair. When it's raining, of course.'

His heart went into overdrive. There was no doubt in him – he loved her and wanted her and...

She kissed him. He pulled her close and hoped that his breath didn't smell of anything peculiar this time. She was reluctant to release him, so he was pleased about the new mouthwash he had acquired. Moments passed, and he forgot about liquorice and wet dog and mouthwash. How could one embrace mean so much? This was a match made in heaven or hell – certainly not on earth. 'God,' he whispered.

'Where?' she asked, her eyes mocking him gently. 'It was what you wanted, yes?'

'Yes.'

'And you were getting nowhere, yes?'

'Yes.'

Harrie stroked his face, one hand on each cheek. 'You're lovely, Will Carpenter. But you're afraid I might turn out as cracked as my brother. I won't. I am a totally unique kind of loony. God broke the mould when he invented me.'

'Are you ever serious?' he asked.

'Only when in love,' she answered before

marching off to find his dog.

Amazed, Will stayed where he was for several seconds. She loved him. She had almost said so – hadn't she? He wanted to run about punching the air, but he didn't. Teachers of maths, physics and chemistry didn't run about wild, but perhaps they should. His throat felt full, and he experienced a ridiculous need to shed tears. It was the happiest day of his life so far and here she came, dog behind her, the other half of some God-forsaken tree between its teeth. 'Thank you, Milly,' he said to himself. Because Milly had been a vital part of the whole equation.

The cottage looked derelict from the outside.

Jimmy pulled his car on to a dirt track at one side of the house, climbed out of the passenger seat and went to press his face against a window. Visibility was severely restricted by dirt and greying net curtains; it seemed that Sally's place had scarcely altered since the death of her father. She cleaned other people's houses, but not her own. Had she moved?

He tapped a coin against the window, banged on the door, walked round to the back of the cottage. The rear door was unlocked, so he let himself into a small, filthy kitchen and announced his presence by calling her name. There was no response. He walked through to the living room, shook his head when he saw the clutter and dust, lifted a pile of magazines and newspapers from a chair and sat down.

It was hell in here. Jimmy hoped he was mistaken, but he thought he caught a hint of an odour that had once been only too familiar when Sal's father had become incontinent. Surely not? Surely, she must have made some effort after the old man's death? The bed had been under the window. Good heavens – Mr Potter's medicines were still lined up on a plastic trolley – and were they his teeth in a jar? The television screen was clean enough. It was plain that Sal still enjoyed her soaps, then. But no detergents had been used on this place in many a month – could he really live here?

Just as he was about to beat a retreat, the back door swung inward. 'Jimmy?' Sal called. She entered the room, homely face glowing with anticipation. 'I recognized your car. How long have you been here?' she asked.

He cleared his throat. 'Not long, but long enough, Sal. This place is a bloody pigsty. When did you last clean up?'

The colour in her cheeks deepened further. 'I lost heart living on me own. Doctor gave me pills for depression, but they don't seem to help. All I've got is me telly. When I come home from work, I just sit and watch me programmes, then drag meself off to bed. I can't help it. Any road, why are you here?'

He sighed heavily. 'I've left her.'

'Left Annie?'

'Aye. Thought I'd shack up here with you, but I can't live like this. Nobody should live like this, Sal.'

She dropped into another chair, her position in the world remaining unnaturally high, as she was perched on a pile of clothing. 'I'll clean up. I promise. I'll go through top to bottom, honest. You know I'd do anything for you, Jimmy.'

'Well.' He pondered for a few seconds. 'I'll sleep in the car till you get straight. And we need a few bits of new furniture. You can sort that out – I'll give you some money.'

Sally beamed. 'Ooh, thanks, love.'

'Just one thing, though. Nobody must know I'm here. There's a good reason for that, so just trust me.'

'You know I trust you, Jimmy.'

He wondered when she had last taken a bath. Her navy cardigan was stained, and at least two buttons had parted company from the knitted item. A once-white blouse displayed a greasy mark where it stood away from her neck. He refused a cup of tea and returned to his car. If Sally wanted him, she had better get a move on.

At eight in the morning, she delivered tea and bacon sandwiches to him. He rubbed his eyes, grabbed the cup and surveyed his soon-to-be lover. She was sparkling clean in a new dressing gown, and her wild hair was anchored back into some sort of order.

'I've cleaned up,' she said proudly. 'Hours and hours, it took. I could do with a new three-piece and a bed as well. Can you afford it?'

He opened the car door and stepped out. 'Let's have a look first,' he said.

In spite of the shabby furniture, it was a different house. After inspecting every room like a sergeant major surveying ranks, he gave his opinion. 'You'll have to keep it up, though,' he warned. After all, she would be getting new furniture out of him.

She would never keep him, not permanently, but he would allow her some time while he worked out his next move. The furniture would be compensation for when he moved away and left her again.

He packed her off to Bolton with a shopping list, asked her to write down the date and times of delivery so that he could make himself scarce. Now, all he had to do was think hard. This could take months to work out, but there was just one goal in life.

He had to get the gun back...

Five

Sister Mary Magdalene was enjoying herself. The piecing together of a white altar cloth was one of the more pleasurable activities available to a bride of Christ. Around the edges of Irish linen, she was attaching lace made over fifty years earlier by French sisters in another order, so the work was taxing, delicate and absorbing. The joining of robust cloth to delicate fibre was difficult, and this altarpiece had to be taken apart every time it required cleaning. As it was used only on very high feast days, mending days were set well apart.

She threaded a needle, said a quiet prayer for survival of the lace – and stopped when she heard a strange sound.

It was one of the meters that recorded neurological and cardiac activity in the patient known as Princess Mathilda. Magda looked at the girl in the bed, glanced at the monitor, shrugged slightly. Electricity, and the machines via which it spoke, were not the most reliable of man's discoveries. The patient remained motionless, a perfect doll in a bed where she had spent many years.

Attacking the job in hand, Magda lowered her eyes and stitched. A second blip caused her to drop the needle. Surely not. Had the left hand quivered? Had she really caught a fleeting glimpse of movement just before looking down at her sewing? She folded the work and placed it on a trolley. God would not mind if one of his daughters ignored the ornamental aspect of service in order to do the work for which she had been trained.

Quietly, she walked to the bed and raised delicate lids from eyes that had never seen the beauty of this world. Pupils matched – neither one had blown, so there had been no nasty activity in the brain. 'Mathilda?' she whispered. 'Are you coming back to us, or is there a fault in our machinery?' The eyes did not shift.

In the good old-fashioned way, Magda took a pulse from the wrist. Mathilda's heart was as steady as a rock. There was no blood in the urine bag, no change in skin colour, nothing at all to put into the report. Nevertheless, the altar cloth was ignored for the rest of Magda's shift. Something odd was happening, and she did not know what to think, what to hope for.

'I never did have much of an imagination,' she told the still form. 'I'm not given to seeing things that aren't really there. Did you move that hand? Did you? And, if you did, does that mean you will wake? If you wake, how will you cope?'

These questions circled in Sister Mary Magdalene's head like a carousel at a funfair. Mathilda would have no language and insufficient strength to sit, let alone walk. She could be brain-damaged. Whilst technically alive, her mind had never functioned on its own, had never been employed since she was a very small girl. 'Even when you were a child, you had the fits. You don't want to

126

be going through life with the fits, do you?'

Magda sat and counted Hail Marys on her rosary. Scarcely daring to blink, she stared at the patient and wished... Wished for what? Hoped for what? That a beautiful young woman who was really a baby might wake and spend the rest of her time in a wheelchair? That death would provide a blessed release for someone who could well be severely epileptic or worse? 'God's will be done,' she begged at the end of five decades. 'Please, Jesus, do the best You can for her.'

Angelus was well under way when Magda reached the chapel. She prayed with her few sisters, continuing to concentrate on the princess in the tower. If anything else happened, the visitor would have to be contacted. Mathilda's real nightmare could begin if and when she woke from her long sleep. Life in a coma was no life at all; yet it was difficult to pray for improvement, as that would bring a minefield of difficulties.

As she dipped her finger into holy water on her way out of chapel, Magda was joined by Mother Benedict, matron of the convent. 'Are you all right, my dear?'

'Yes, Mother.'

'You seem a little distracted. Is there something on your mind?'

Magda thought for a second. 'Nothing real,' she replied. 'Nothing that requires reporting or confessing.'

Mother Benedict grinned. 'What a shame. I just fancied a bit of juicy gossip. Still, I'm hardly your Father Confessor, am I?'

There really was nothing to be said. Mathilda

showed no definite change. The hand hadn't moved, was incapable of moving. So there was nothing sensible to say. But, for the rest of the evening, Mary Magdalene remained on tenter-hooks. From now on, every time she was on duty, she would watch Mathilda like a hawk.

He ran out of the house as if the devil himself were pursuing him. The copse was no use – it was all cement mixers and sewage pipes. The van. That would have to do. He fumbled with keys, failed to open the door, tried again, dropped the keys, swore ... panic, panic.

Inside at last, he threw himself on to the bed in the back. Nothing would take away those terrible pictures. Breathing was difficult – there were no paper bags in here to help stop hyperventilation. *Slow down, slow down. It's happened and you can't change it.* Where is he? Where does he live? No, no, where *did* he live. Others had seen it, too. He hadn't been the only one on Blade tonight. Never again.

Sex and pain. It had all been about those factors and he ... he didn't belong any more, wasn't a part of all that, could not live any longer on the fringes of society. 'I can be ordinary,' he said aloud, the words fractured by quick, shallow breaths. 'I don't need ... that. I need Harrie's psycho woman.' There was help. Help involved people, invaded space, shared oxygen, a mix of words, feelings released, fears shot down in flames. 'I either get some help with this, or...' Or he might well end up crazy enough to copy what he had seen tonight.

When his breathing slowed, he left the van and

walked round the corner towards the nearest housing estate. It had to be done. Perhaps some of the others had already reported the event, but Ben still needed to do it. He found a phone box, breathed deeply for a few seconds, then dialled 999.

He gave the officer the web address of the site, then managed to approach the terrible truth. 'It was on a webcam,' he said. 'If you can get on the site, it may still be there. He wore a mask. A few of them have masks. Then he shoved an orange in his mouth and...'

'Go on, sir.'

'Hanged himself. I don't think he intended to die, but his camera was still filming him a few minutes ago. He wasn't moving.'

'And you are?'

'I don't matter. He spoke once, and he had a Midlands accent. He was Caucasian. I think I watched a man die tonight.' Ben slammed the receiver into its holder and ran back the way he had come, banging the door of the van in his wake before bursting into tears.

It had been a game at first, a lot of silly people typing ludicrous messages about sexual highs and how to achieve them. Several used drugs – he had always known about the cocaine that many of the group advocated. Then, suddenly, the discussion had taken on a darker hue. Someone famous had died this way, but he had used the wrong knot. With a bit of sense, a line of coke and a great deal of care with the rope, a man could reach nirvana without the help of a partner of either gender. And they had watched. All those separate people in widely spread geographical areas had witnessed the death of a man.

'Perhaps he's still alive,' Ben whispered. 'If the cops and ambulance can find him...' But would they? Sites like Blade were well-hidden, bounced all over the world: a server within a server, like an onion waiting to be peeled.

The man had hung the rope over a hook on his bedroom wall. It was a bedroom like many others. Aston Villa poster. Ben should have told the police about that. It had been over in seconds. The writhing might have been mistaken for pleasure, might have started as pleasure, but the stillness that followed was horrible.

Messages had come in:

Do you think he's dead?

What can we do if he is?

Anyone know where he lives?

I told him not to do it.

IT WAS HIS OWN CHOICE.

That final message, 'shouted' in upper case by Bladerunner, supposed leader of the gang, had sent Ben rushing out of the house. 'It was his own choice'. Sometimes, people needed saving from their own wrong choices. Sometimes, a man's sister had to take him to the hospital after a close encounter with bleach.

I am intelligent enough to know what's wrong with me, he thought. *And even if I don't fit squarely into society, I don't have to be completely weird. Maybe I will be some sort of hermit, but not like the Blades. Please, not like them.* Insight into his own condition had to count, had to mean that he could improve.

Obsessive-Compulsive Disorder was not a killer. Many people lived with it, managing to hold down jobs and hide their peculiarities from the rest of mankind. Lining up tins in a cupboard was one thing, but being unable to tolerate the untidiness of others had kept him in the margins. He didn't play football, cricket, rugby or tennis, had flatly refused to participate. He was different.

He was so different that he had sat and watched a man take his own life. That was nothing to do with OCD. Because he had known himself to be distant from and at odds with others, he had allowed himself to be dragged into areas that housed the truly unacceptable. Ben was not unacceptable – he was unaccepting. 'I am going to conquer this,' he told the ceiling of the camper van. 'And Harrie will have to help me. She will if I ask.'

He wiped his face with a tissue, sat up and stared through the windscreen at the dark house. In there, everything was normal. But somewhere, about a hundred miles away, an Aston Villa supporter of indeterminate age had put on a show for his fellow lunatics. That man would not see tomorrow, would never again hear birdsong or Brahms. It had been a terrible way to learn some sense, but Ben must heed his own reason now. It was time to make many changes. It was time to call himself to account.

Lisa was arranging some silver chains in a corner of her window when she noticed the small, tousle-haired woman with an infant in her arms.

It was Annie. Poor little Annie. Annie would probably be cross if she knew she was being described as 'poor', because she was feisty to the point of utter carelessness. She was straight. She had been loyal to her man until the final straw had broken the spine of her life. There had been many last straws, guessed Lisa. Annie deserved better.

Rushing out of the shop, Lisa called Annie's name. 'Coffee?' she shouted. 'In the back. We're not busy.'

Leaving her assistant to guard the shop, Lisa went into the office and set the kettle to boil. Instant would have to suffice. Annie wouldn't care. 'I shouldn't care, either,' muttered the manageress of Milne's Jewellery.

Daisy was a beautiful child. She sat on the floor with a marker and a pad while the adults talked. She coloured carpet as well as paper, but Lisa found herself past caring. What was a carpet at the end of the day? Floor covering, no more and no less. 'She's lovely,' Lisa commented.

'Aye,' agreed the child's mother. 'She's lovely till she wants her own road, then she does a fair imitation of Idi Amin, or whatever his name was. Our Daisy's what you might call wilful.'

This was motherhood, Lisa decided. The bond between parent and infant was strong and clear enough for all to see. 'I never knew my children,' she began. 'My mother-in-law brought them up, because she couldn't run a shop any more. And I...' She took a sip of coffee. 'I'm a very selfish woman.'

Annie nodded. 'We all have our faults, love. You

132

should see Billy and Craig – they're my twin boys. They have more faults than San Francisco.'

'Did they have mumps?'

'Did they buggery. They stuffed cotton wool in their cheeks and started talking like Marlon Brando. They don't like school. They thought mumps would be a good one, but they never knew their necks should swell up too. And they've had all them immunizations. They could start a war at Lourdes, I'm telling you.'

Lisa managed not to choke with laughter. 'Hard work, then?'

Annie nodded. 'And when the cash I found in the roof goes, I'm in queer street. I can't divorce him, because I can't serve papers – no idea where he is. So the house won't be sold, and I'll be cap in hand down the social. Have you seen the price of kiddies' shoes?'

Lisa shook her head.

'Criminal. Speaking of which, yes, I did know he came by his money dishonestly but, with mouths to feed and clothes to buy, I managed not to think about it.' She paused. 'Birmingham was the worst – a few years back now. Knowing he'd been there and yet hoping he hadn't was hell. The man in the wheelchair haunts me.'

Lisa touched her companion's hand. 'I'll look after you, I promise.'

The tiny woman raised her chin. 'No, you won't, missus. I don't mind being a charity case for this damned government – God knows they're throwing enough cash at immigrants – but I couldn't let you keep us.'

'Did I say I'd keep you?'

133

'No, but—'

'No, but I didn't. Can your mother look after the twins?'

Lisa shrugged. 'At a push with a steamroller. It'd be all right when they're at school, but she couldn't cope with holidays.'

'Could she manage Daisy?'

'Freda could. Freda worships my little madam. They sit on the floor with all the figurines and do fairy stories. She's all right, is my ma-in-law. I don't know how Jimmy managed to go so wrong, because his mother's a lovely woman.'

Lisa fell silent for a few moments. Had Ben been naughty as a child, had Harrie listened to fairy tales? Their mother had not been a lovely woman. Their mother had run around enjoying herself because home was boring. How many women tolerated a non-event of a marriage for the sake of their offspring? Probably thousands.

'What's going on in that head of yours?' asked Annie.

'Not a lot.' Lisa grinned. 'God knows there's plenty of room for not a lot to bounce around. If I get two thoughts at once, we call it a boxing match.' She tapped a temple. 'Work for me, Annie. Basic wage and a percentage of everything you sell. Hours to suit; a nice, clean job; learn about jewellery from me and Simon.'

Annie swallowed hard. 'I've no experience except in a chippy.'

'It's just the same, except for mushy peas, and you don't offer salt and vinegar.'

Annie laughed aloud. 'Would you like a plastic fork with that necklace, madam?' She stared hard at her husband's ex-mistress. 'That was lies about space in your brain, wasn't it? I reckon you're a very clever woman, Lisa. There's something about you, something that's held you back–'

'A husband,' Lisa whispered. Simon knew the score, yet she still didn't want him to hear how she really felt. 'He's a red-carpet job. America, Japan, Australia – wherever he goes, he is treated like a god.'

'Why?'

Lisa shrugged lightly. 'He's going to save the world.'

'That's nice for him, I'm sure.'

'Microbiology.'

'Ooh, what a big word.'

'He messes about with cultures in little glass dishes. Hospital superbugs. Flesh-eating bacteria; disease in the gut as well. And he earns a fortune testing products for big companies – medicines, household cleaners, stuff like that. Because the bugs are in our homes now, you see. He wanted the government to stop all hospital visiting, and he got really mad when they wouldn't. Can you imagine being in hospital for weeks and no one coming to see you?'

Annie shook her head. 'You don't like him, do you?'

'Not much. He's never done me any harm, but he's more selfish than I am.' She went on to talk about his fixation with model railways and his lady friend on Wigan Road. 'I don't know whether the relationship is close, but he's really happy when he's been there. She feeds him, I think. I've seen custard on his tie more than once.'

Annie placed her mug on a coaster. 'We've both been daft, then. Both married a bloke who was wrong for us. I suppose we got on with it the best way we could. But I wish I could divorce him, get rid – I'd feel tidier.'

Lisa tapped a manicured nail on the desk. 'The police would find him if they had the gun. Mention Birmingham and they'd build a three-ring circus on the M6.'

Annie agreed. 'But he'd drag your name into it, wouldn't he?'

'I suppose so.' It occurred to Lisa in that moment that she didn't particularly care. But she had to care, for the sake of Ben and Harriet. Was she a mother after all? Was she on the brink of some massive change in attitude? Probably not.

Annie picked up her daughter. 'Well, I'll go and ask the two mams about minding the twins and Daisy. Say bye-bye to the nice lady, love.'

Daisy twinkled. 'Bye-bye,' she said sweetly. 'Can I have ten pence for being good?'

Lisa laughed.

Annie shook her head. 'See? She's going to be one of them there dictators when she grows up. Like Tony Blair.'

When they had left, Lisa felt lonely. She thought about her circle of bridge-and-Botox pals, folk she had happened upon in her fruitless search for everlasting youth. They weren't real. Annie was real – terrifyingly so. Annie was prepared to do just about anything to keep her little family together. She would work hard, remain humorous in the face of any kind of threat, would never throw in the towel. *I think I have a friend,*

Lisa told herself after releasing Simon for his lunch break. *And I am going to keep her.*

It was like being in prison. Even with new furniture and clean windows, Sally Potter's cottage was dark. He hadn't stayed in all the time. Firstly, he had needed to get out for sanity's sake; on another occasion, he had bought clothes and something to read. He'd kept himself out of town so far, as he didn't want Annie or anyone who knew her spotting his vehicle in the area, but he took a chance, drove to Chorley and got himself a Bedford van.

Anger still bubbled when he thought about Lisa. She hadn't been born with a silver spoon in her gob; she had acquired her attitude from her mother-in-law and from a few certificates in gemmology or some such highly important subject connected to chips of diamond and bits of gold. He had been the love of her life, yet she had turned on him. He wondered who would be the next on her list, because she wasn't likely to cleave unto that dry old stick with his trains and his microbes.

Sally was getting on his nerves. She kept poring through acres of catalogue pages in her search for sexy clothing that would actually fit her larger than average frame. She wasn't exactly obese, but she sometimes looked like a heavyweight wrestler in drag – large arms, bootlace straps over the shoulders and a faint moustache on the upper lip if she hadn't done whatever she did to remove facial hair.

He leaned back in a new cream leather chair. If

he pressed a button, the back tilted and a footrest appeared from beneath the seat. But he couldn't be bothered. She was out scrubbing other people's floors, while he was stuck in with terrestrial channels, a crackly radio and today's *Daily Mail*. This was no life for a man of ambition. He needed to be out and about, putting bets on, scoping out the odd detached house in one of the better areas, sinking a pint in a town-centre pub.

It was time to venture forth again, he thought. With a baseball cap and some dark sunglasses, he would be unrecognizable and relatively safe. But if he stayed in this dump any longer, he might well become a candidate for the funny farm. She would be back soon, cooing and clucking and cooking his dinner. Stir craziness was not for him; he donned his disguise, left the house and set off over the moor towards Bolton's ring road.

In the town, he bought cigarettes, a *Bolton Evening News*, a couple of shirts and some shaving cream from the market. It was after he had left the news kiosk that he spotted Annie. She was talking to a woman in the doorway of a shop, and that shop was Milne's Jewellers. So. The scene in the bungalow hadn't been enough for them. They continued to meet, that was as plain as a pikestaff. As he was the only factor they had in common, they had to be talking about him. What was there to talk about? They had the gun from a robbery he had never committed, so he was already stymied. What the hell was going on? Could they do any more to him?

He rushed back to his newly-acquired Bedford, lit a cigarette and waited for his hands to become steadier. Perhaps they were going to give the gun to the police. Surely not – that old bird had said quite clearly that as long as he didn't mention Lisa's part in concealing loot, they would hang on to the gun. What else, then? Mrs Compton-Milne was not the type to break a promise. He had met her sort before, so did Annie still have the gun? Or was it in Lisa's shop?

He drove back to Sal's house, slamming the door after letting himself in. She wasn't back yet. At the tiny kitchen table, he made a list of possibilities. The gun could be at either of the Milne shops, or it might be in that rambling great house on the outskirts of town. There was a chance that Annie still had it, but he doubted that. Lisa's house. Weaver's something-or-other. It didn't matter. The lane, too, was Weaver's whatever, and he knew exactly where the Compton-Milnes lived. There was a small wood at the back of the house; there was also a great deal of land. He couldn't dig that lot up, not without a JCB. But he could get into the house. Even if she had changed the alarm, there was nothing he couldn't handle. They didn't own a dog. The old girl lived in the roof. The lad had a house within the house, but it was unlikely that the kids had been dragged into the gun business.

I'll have a quick shufti tonight, he promised himself. Without the gun, they had nothing. The police might still be looking for him, but as long as he wasn't connected to the Birmingham shooting he was reasonably safe. It all boiled down to a gun left in a car all those years ago. No. It was really his own stupidity, because he should have disposed of it. Furthermore, he should never have let Annie find out where he kept his hidden cash. Hindsight was always 20/20, wasn't it?

He heard Sal's bike creaking its way round to the back of the house. Jumping up, he shoved the list into his pocket and rushed to fill the kettle. 'Nice cup of tea in a minute, love,' he said. 'Oh, and I'll be out tonight,' he added as casually as he could manage.

'Where?' Sally asked.

'It's one of the houses I fitted with an alarm. It's gone faulty, and they've had burglars two nights on the trot. The cops will be there in case the robbers come back, and I said I'd go. Not to mend it, because they want to catch the buggers, but just to be there and see why it's not working.'

'Right. When will you be back?' She had soft eyes. They were almost bovine: gentle, unquestioning, accepting. Yes, she was like some pet calf that expected – and got – affection from its owner.

'Early hours. It could even be morning. But you'll be all right,' he assured her.

The sad brown eyes filled with tears. 'I don't like being on me own,' she said, bottom lip quivering. 'That was why I let meself go, Jimmy. See, it's very isolated round here for a woman by herself.'

'I know that, love.'

'I need you, Jimmy.'

He knew that, also. Although his conscience had seldom troubled him in the past, he suddenly felt guilty. She'd been dealt a bad hand, had poor Sal. And here she was with the ace of spades

140

cleverly disguised as her king of hearts. 'I'll be as quick as I can.'

'Promise?'

'Promise.'

He escaped upstairs for a wash and a shave, and found his camouflage jacket and some black shoe polish. This was going to be a massive task, and he needed not to be visible. Wire cutters and other tools were in the van, so he was ready for the off.

Sitting in the van, he thought about his twin boys, Billy and Craig, who were both little rascals, both up to their ears in trouble at school. He missed the boys, missed Daisy, missed Annie, kept missing his way. *I wish I was a good man,* he thought. *But I have to get that bloody gun back, fair means or foul. I have to.*

'I'm not leaving you.' Eileen Eckersley stood her ground, arms clasped across a flat, unforgiving chest. 'That was a bad one. You'll be sore in the night. What if you need the bathroom?' She shook her head. 'No, that was a really bad one.'

Hermione cleared her throat. 'They've all been bad ones. I've tried to have good ones, tried to fall upwards instead of downwards, but the chap who discovered gravity forbids it. I fall. I fall down. It happens.'

Eileen tutted. 'Two and a half hours in hospital. Two and a half hours just to see there was nothing broken.'

'Oh, well, I am sorry. I'd have arranged for a fractured femur if I'd known that was what you wanted. In fact, I might have gone for a broken

141

back if I'd realized you felt so strongly.'

'That isn't what I mean, and well you know it. How-and-ever, I am staying the night. You can shout from here to Limerick, and I'll still be here. Have your tantrums, but sit still while you're having them. I am off to make a cup of tea.'

Hermione grinned to herself ruefully, then grimaced when her legs began hurting again. It wasn't getting any easier. It had started all those years ago with blurred vision and a knee that didn't always bear her weight, but, lately, things were becoming intolerable. It was the beginning of June, and she'd had a headache since New Year.

'I remember when my left leg started running away with me,' she said to the open kitchen door.

'So do I. They thought you were shoplifting, didn't they?'

'They did, indeed. But what could I do? My left leg made decisions of its own, and the rest of me was forced to follow. And, were I to shoplift, it would be something a bit better than three pairs of cotton knickers.'

Eileen reappeared. 'No more remissions, eh?'

The older woman nodded. 'Just bad to worse from now on. And these painkillers don't do a thing beyond interfering with my digestion. All I ask is the occasional good day.'

'I know.'

The aspect that really annoyed Hermione was her deficient immune system. Other people got colds; she got pneumonia, antibiotics, steroids and lectures on smoking. Swallowing was difficult. She didn't want to end up with her head clamped to the wheelchair and a pipe into her stomach. Never to taste food again? What was the point of staying alive if and when that happened? She had her stash of tablets in case she decided she'd had enough, but what if she became too disabled to get them and to swallow them?

'Biscuit?' called Eileen from the kitchen.

'No, thanks.' It was a baby cup today, a plastic thing with a spout to guard against spillage. Eileen would never help her if it came to suicide. She was a good Catholic, and she believed in the sanctity of life, whatever the situation. Lisa might. But Lisa would have to answer to the law, and that would never do.

'There you go.' The tea was placed on a tray attached to the wheelchair.

'No,' snapped Hermione. 'Get me out of this contraption and into a chair. And I am a bone china woman. I want a cup and a saucer.'

'Oh, please – you're still shaking from the fall.'

Hermione glared. 'Walker, chair, cup – NOW!'

When the transfer of woman to easy chair and tea to china had been achieved, the old woman was breathless. Determined as ever, she slowed her breathing and lifted the cup to her lips. The tea was tepid, and she drank it in just a few seconds. 'There,' she gloated. 'I can do it. And I shall do it. We are not defeated, Eileen. Not yet, anyway.'

The carer had to dash a tear from her face when she ran briefly back across to her own house. She prepared a supper for her husband and explained to him that she would be away for the night. 'She's getting frail, so she is. Not in the

143

brain department – oh no – she's twenty-five in her head. But her poor old body is breaking down, Stanley.'

'Comes to all of us, love.'

Eileen stood by the table, a fork in her hand and tears on her cheeks. 'She's one of those things like the Blarney Stone – you think it'll be there for ever. But the water drips and the stone wears away. It's the tiredness that annoys her. And the nearly choking when she eats.'

Stanley Eckersley looked at his wife and felt his heart breaking. The Compton-Milnes had been her life, because she had been denied children of her own. She loved Hermione, loved all of them, but her devotion to the elder Mrs Compton-Milne was total. 'I think you were right, Eileen, what you told me the other day. You know – the day when she went out with Lisa. Something particular happened, and it's upset her. Her MS is always worse if something gets her goat.'

His wife nodded and wiped away her tears with the skirt of her apron. 'It was bad. She said she'd met a very amusing lady called Freda, but there was more to it than that. A lot more.'

'And she wouldn't let you go with them.'

'No. It's all tied up with Lisa, of course. There's always something afoot with that madam – another boyfriend or some such foolishness. Her husband pays her no heed, so she looks elsewhere for comfort.' Eileen sniffed. 'One man in a person's life is trouble enough.'

Stanley grinned. 'Aye, you've said that more than once.'

'You know I don't mean it.'

'Aye, true enough.'

'I'd never have put up with you all this long while if I meant half I said.'

He stood up and put his arms around her. 'Go on, lass. I can sort meself out and wash a few pots. She needs you.'

Stanley ate his meal and cleaned everything up. The Compton-Milnes had been good to the Eckersleys. If Eileen had to stay across the way for a while, it was no matter. Hermione deserved the best. And his Eileen was the best.

It was an enormous task, thought Jimmy Nuttall after parking the van. Having travelled on foot down Weaver's Weft, he found himself facing a house that must once have been four or five weavers' cottages. The needle in a haystack metaphor didn't apply – this would be like searching Blackpool beach for one particular grain of sand. It was hopeless. He could check his own house, but he could not bring himself to believe that Annie had been allowed to take the gun back home.

He stood behind a hedge and lit an Embassy. It wouldn't be in his mother's bungalow, either. And it certainly hadn't found its way into any of the shops' safes. After extinguishing his cigarette, he crept down the side of Weaver's Warp, saw the woods, looked at the recently erected bungalow. This was no place for a gun, either; not with builders milling around and digging holes for sewer pipes. It might be further into the copse, but again, where to start? It was hopeless. 'But I bet the old girl has it,' he whispered. 'She's the

145

sort to put herself in charge. Lives in the roof.' He turned and looked back at the house. 'It's in there,' he muttered. 'She'll be sitting on it, because she doesn't want Lisa dragged in.'

He could probably get inside, but he wasn't completely sure of the layout. The alarm he had installed for Lisa covered the ground and first floors only, so he had never been up into the dress circle. He remembered the second lot of stairs, but had no idea when it came to the apartment – which was the bedroom? Was there a safe? Where was the kitchen? Getting caught in the act would not be a good idea, as he was already a suspect in local burglaries, and an invasion of Weaver's Warp could well make the old girl change her mind and give the gun to police. It was a bloody mess.

There had to be a way of getting the gun back. Deep in thought, he turned away from the house and began the walk back to his van. It was in that moment that the ghost appeared. Dressed in white, it wielded a stick that was very real, while the words it spat emerged in a thick, Irish brogue. 'Get yourself on your way before I kill you. There's nothing here for the likes of you. We don't feed tramps.'

He stumbled in a rut on the unadopted lane, righted himself, then felt the weight of her weapon across his back. Turning, he growled at her, roaring like a tiger in a cage. She didn't budge an inch. Thanking God for the boot polish on his face, he raised a hand to grab the stick, but she was too quick for him. It whipped across his face, cutting into flesh, tearing as she dragged it away with a downward movement. 'Get yourself lost,' she screamed.

A light came on in a bedroom of a cottage opposite the big house. The sash window shot open. 'Eileen? Is that you? Are you all right?'

'There,' she snarled. 'My husband and my son will be here in half a second, so run. They have a gun.'

Gun? Was the gun in the cottage, then? Yet another bloody address to wonder about. His face was wet – he knew that he was bleeding. There was no ammo with the gun. Had they bought some? Jimmy ran as fast as his legs would carry him, turning right into the main road, jumping into the van, driving off with gears grinding and tyres screeching.

In the lane, Eileen fell to her knees. She suddenly realized in a small way how Hermione suffered, because a failure in the leg department was terribly frightening. It must be purely horrible to suffer like this all the time. She had stood up to the intruder, yet now, when he had gone, her nerves had gone into overdrive.

Stanley found her in a heap, slippered feet peeping out below the hem of a white nightdress. There was just a quarter moon, so the light was frugal. How had she seen the man in the dark? He posed that very question.

'He lit a cigarette,' she explained. 'I was on the landing listening to Hermione's breathing. She stops sometimes, you see, especially after one of her falls. And I saw through the hedge just a flicker of light. God alone knows what he was up to. He'd skin as black as a pot, but he was a white

147

man, I'm sure, because the black had patches showing through. Like a soldier, you know?'

'Camouflage.'

'Aye, that's the one. I frightened him, and I hit him twice because I didn't want us all smothercated in our beds by some burgling traveller.' With her husband's help, Eileen rose on unsteady feet and allowed herself to be led down the side of the house and into the family kitchen.

Lisa was there, face creamed, eye mask pushed up into her hair. 'What the devil's going on, Stan?'

'Nothing much,' he said grimly. 'My wife's just half-killed an intruder. He was out there in the bushes, and she saw him strike a match. So she tackled him.'

Lisa sank into a kitchen chair. 'You could have got yourself killed,' she chided gently. 'Why didn't you wake us?'

Eileen shrugged. 'I don't know. I just took Mr Gus's walking stick and clouted the tramp.'

Stanley raised said stick. It was bloodstained. 'She clouted him, all right. He ran like he had a snake clamped to his arse.' He blushed. 'Sorry,' he said to Lisa.

The stairlift buzzed. 'Oh, hell. She's on her way down.' Lisa filled the kettle and set it to boil. 'See? Even after a bad fall, she's got to be at the front of the queue if there's a performance on. My mother-in-law misses nothing.' She went to meet the miscreant. They heard her almost tender lecture. 'You should be in bed. There's nothing for you to worry about – have you seen the time? It's nearly two o'clock.'

Hermione entered, Lisa pushing the wheelchair. 'Well?' asked the matriarch. 'Has war broken out? Did Saddam's chaps find his misplaced weapons of mass destruction, or has Bush misinterpreted his satnav and bombed us instead?'

In spite of everything, Lisa found herself smiling. She might have married the wrong man, but she had no regrets about being related to this fierce, humorous woman. 'It was a tramp,' she said. 'And Eileen beat him about the face.'

'Why?' asked Hermione, whose philosophy tended to run on the lines of live-and-let-live.

'He was at the front, then he was at the back,' replied Eileen. 'Probably trying to pinch stuff. I waited till he went back to the front, then I hit him in the back with the walking stick. Then in the front as well – on his face.'

Hermione processed the information, separating backs of houses from backs of people – she was used to Eileen's meanderings. 'Is he dead?'

'He ran very fast for a dead man,' said Stan. 'I hope I'll be as lively when my time comes.'

Hermione was studying Lisa. 'What's the matter?'

Lisa swallowed. 'It was him,' she said. 'Don't ask me how I know – I just do. He's been here, near my family, in our garden, almost in our house. He'll not stop till he finds it.'

It was Eileen's turn to be confused. 'Till who finds what?' she asked, eyebrows almost disappearing into her hairline.

'Never mind.' Hermione's gaze remained fixed on Lisa's face. 'I thought he'd be long gone – down south or across the Pennines, at least.'

Lisa shook her head. 'He's not predictable, Mother. And, the more I hear about him from Annie, the more I am inclined to feel that he might very well be dangerous. He cares about no one but himself.'

Eileen glanced from one woman to the other. 'If someone's making tea, I'd like three sugars. I've just had an encountrance with somebody who's looking for something somewhere. And the somewhere this nobody-somebody is looking is right here, so I need treating for shock.'

They sat round the kitchen table drinking tea. Stanley dipped digestive biscuits into his cup until his wife reminded him that he was in company.

'Oh, leave the poor man alone,' advised Hermione. 'If dunking biscuits is his worst fault, he's not going far wrong in the world.'

Lisa, near to tears, tried to hide her fear behind a hand. She cupped her chin, slender fingers creeping up towards an eye. Poor Eileen. Poor old Woebee had just had a close encounter with a lying, cheating thief.

'Does Annie know where he's living?' asked Hermione.

'No.' Lisa sighed deeply. 'She says Freda has seen neither hide nor hair since the day we all met. He could be just about anywhere.'

'But you'd like his anywhere to be somewhere else,' remarked Eileen.

No one answered her.

Revived by sweet tea, the Irishwoman continued. 'There are folk here – me and him – who have been associated with this family since time memorial.'

'Immemorial,' interjected Hermione.

'Whatever. We even go out of our way to guard you all against danger, but we still sit here drowning in tea and Annies and Fredas and men with no names. Don't you think you should tell us what's happening?'

Hermione breathed deeply. 'Not at two o'clock in the morning, no. If we carry on, we'll have Harriet awake, and that will never do.'

Lisa cleared away the dishes and pushed Hermione back to the first stairlift. 'Go with her,' she told Eileen. 'And don't start asking questions, because she needs her sleep.'

In the kitchen, Stan asked if he could do anything to help.

Lisa smiled at him ruefully. 'Some days, I feel I am past help. You'd better ask God to come to my aid. I think He's the only one who can make a difference.'

'Good night, then.'

The door closed. Lisa allowed the flood to pour. She sobbed because she had been a fool, because she had been a poor mother, because she didn't deserve help from Hermione, Eileen and Stan. But most of all, she wept because she was afraid of Jimmy Nuttall. He was still in the area, and there was no way of guessing what he might do next.

He sat in the van, shaking with fury as he mopped blood from his cheek. A blinking old Irish witch had done this to him, and he wanted to sort her out. He knew who she was. Lisa had regaled him with tales of Eileen Eckersley, known by younger

151

members of the family as Woebee, because she always said, 'Woe betide anyone who...' He flinched. God, she packed a fair wallop for a thin, pale ghost.

What now? Home to poor Sal, he supposed. He could always say he'd stopped a robbery at the non-existent house he was supposed to be visiting. No, not yet. He didn't want to be any-where at the present time, so he parked in a country lane, took out a torch and looked through the Bolton newspaper. When he reached the small ads, he sat up and took notice. That was a phone number he recognized, though he had never used it.

'Bloody hell,' he murmured. Had they given him the main chance on a plate, delivered via the local press? Would he dare? Could he engineer a way of making a killing?

He folded the paper and sat for at least an hour – smoking, sipping pop from a can, reading and rereading the short message. 'Help wanted', it began. He was the one who needed the help. But he couldn't do this thing on his own. There was one person on earth who trusted him completely, and she was his current landlady. Sal. Could she do it? Should she be involved in this mess? How might he persuade her without telling her the whole truth?

Jimmy Nuttall closed his eyes and saw her face. She was smiling at him, adoration illuminating her face and making her almost lovable. Sally Potter would go to any length to secure her man. This was the way forward, then.

Six

Annie proved her worth within a fortnight. She watched Lisa and Simon for a few days, then leapt into action when a young couple approached the counter and asked to look at engagement rings. They were clearly short of money, and Annie knew only too well how that felt. 'Are you superstitious?' she asked the girl.

'Not particularly, no.' She glanced sideways at her fiancé. 'He's not, either.'

'Good. Stay there, and I'll be back in a minute.'

She left the shop, retrieved an item from the office, placed it on a little velvet tray and returned with a look of triumph in her eyes. 'What about that?' she asked. 'Second-hand, but who cares? It's the love that matters, eh? Now, it's not a huge stone, but it's nearly clear of carbon. And diamonds are carbon – they were trees, you know. Millions of years ago, that was a bit of wood. Then it went to peat, then coal, then, after ages and ages, it turned into a diamond. So the bit of carbon makes it natural – a tiny fleck of darkness that allows the rest to glitter.'

The female customer picked up the ring. 'It's lovely, is that,' she said.

'Right.' Annie picked up a sizer. 'Try it on.'

'It's a bit loose.'

'No problemo.' Annie sized the girl's finger. 'Now, if you decide to have this ring, not only is

153

it a bargain – look at that price tag – but we'll also resize it for free, and tell your families to buy sunglasses, because I'll make that baby shine like the North Star.'

'We'll take it,' said the man. 'And with the change, we can buy a bit of furniture.'

In the doorway to the office, Lisa stood and smiled. Annie had a gift that was not born of or improved by learning – she was excellent with people. That young couple would trust Milne's from this day on. If they did well, they'd be back for other items, because they would remember that they had been treated with fairness and sympathy. 'Well done,' she said to Annie when they had left. 'Shall we have a cuppa? Simon, you know where we are if we're needed.'

In the office, Lisa praised Annie and said she would make a fine jeweller as long as she carried on in the same vein. 'It's about trust, and you convinced them. You even convinced me, and I'm an old hand. Now, sit down and listen.'

Annie sat while the kettle boiled. She did as she had been bidden, her eyes widening with every sentence delivered. 'But you didn't actually see him?'

'No. No one did. Weaver's Weft is unadopted, and we haven't bothered with street lights or paving. We like it the way it is – it's more rural and natural. With a big housing estate just a few hundred yards away, it's nice to be a bit different from the usual.'

'Yes.' Annie tapped her nails on the desk. Since becoming an apprentice, she had started to take care of nails, hair and makeup, and she was, Lisa

154

had decided, quite a pretty young woman. 'What makes you think it's him, though?'

Lisa shrugged. 'Instinct. According to Eileen, he was in camouflage – well – cammy-flow is her word for it. He wore a combat jacket, and his face was blacked up. Baseball cap, too.'

'He does have a camouflage jacket and a black baseball cap. But so do a lot of folk.'

'Are you defending him?'

'Am I heck as like. I'm just trying to make you feel a bit safer, that's all.'

Lisa felt that she would never know security again until Jimmy Nuttall disappeared into the bowels of some jail, preferably one several hundred miles away from Bolton. 'It'll be the gun, Annie.'

'Aye, it will. If it is him, that's what it'll be about. He gets something fixed in his head, and there's no shifting him. If he used all that energy for something useful, he could do quite well in life. But no. He wants the easy way. Fit an alarm, go back months later and pinch the family silver. Or drive a couple of lunatics to Brum, get a few quid for it, end up holding the bloody gun.'

'You believe he didn't shoot the guard.'

Annie pondered. 'I can't see him hurting another bloke, not really, not with a gun. But he'd do the driving. And he prefers to work by himself. No, I don't think he put that man in hospital. He was dead scared, though. When he came downstairs the day after, he turned the news off. Guilty as sin, but not a killer, Lisa. Just a thief and a chancer.'

Lisa nodded in agreement.

'I didn't think he'd be your type,' Annie said. 'Too rough for you. What the bloody hell did you see in him? Something like Johnny Depp in *Pirates of the Caribbean?*'

'Not really. But Johnny Depp's a great improvement on Albert Einstein and his test tubes. I married a dry stick. Even his mother can't stand him. I mean, she loves him, but she prefers to love him from afar. Except on Tuesdays. Tuesdays, she loves him at family breakfast, though she hides it very well, keeps going on about his trains and his silences.'

Both women burst out laughing. 'We both married wrong 'uns,' said Annie, giggling, 'and neither of their mothers is right pleased with their kid. Where did we go wrong? I mean, what's Catherine Zeta Jones got that we haven't?'

'A wrinkly husband,' replied Lisa. 'Come on, we've stuff to do.'

It was as if they had been working together for years. There was an easiness between them, a lack of embarrassment, no need for the usual getting-to-know-you ritual. Annie had never had time for friends; Lisa's circle of acquaintances had been ill-chosen – all bridge-players, wine buffs and plastic-surgery addicts. Yet these two women, so different on the surface, were like sisters under the skin.

Annie looked up from her dusting. 'I'm glad I met you, Lisa,' she said.

Lisa felt exactly the same. It was an ill wind that brought no good at all with it. Annie was the good, but the ill wind was still blowing over the town.

Ben couldn't settle to anything. He didn't need to study, because the exams so far had been a walk in the park, but he wanted to calm down.

The suicide had been plastered all over national presses. Police were reputed to have a team of IT specialists working to discover the instigator of the website. If they succeeded, Ben could well be discovered as a member of the group and as a witness to the terrifying event. He found himself rocking on the edges of chairs, wanted to run, didn't know where to go. Obsessive-Compulsive Disorder closed down most avenues for him, so he made a momentous decision: he was going to get the hell out of this bloody house.

Tuesday's breakfast was the usual mix of accidental humour and gritty talk from Gran. Dad was excited about his third or fourth Flying Scotsman, and he had a great deal to say about honey from New Zealand. It seemed that bees limited to feeding from just one specific flower produced honey that helped greatly in the healing of stumps after limbs had been severed. While everyone else's stomach churned, Gus spoke about MRSA and the application of said honey to sites where flesh was being eaten away.

Harrie was giggling. Only someone as gaga as Professor Gustav Compton-Milne could chomp on toast while delivering a monologue on the benefits of maggots, leeches and honey.

Hermione glared at her son. 'Shut up,' she ordered for the second time. 'Some of us prefer not to suffer nausea before, during and after breakfast. Your strong stomach is to be commended, but please consider the rest of us.'

Lisa dug an elbow into her daughter's ribs. 'Behave yourself,' she whispered. It occurred to her that she had never before dug her daughter in the ribs. Suddenly, and at this very late stage, she was becoming interested in her children. Ben looked terrible, she noticed. He was pale and gaunt, was probably reacting to his sister's intention to move far away to the other end of the back garden. Lisa thought of Annie and her love-them-hate-them attitude to her three children. Annie adored her kids, no matter what they did. She worked just part time in order to look after her charges and to rescue her mother from Tweedledum and Tweedledee, as she had lately nominated the twin boys.

Harrie managed to stop chuckling, though her mouth twitched as she spread manuka and jelly-bush honey on her toast. The jar announced its origin as New Zealand, so her stomach should be healthy, at least.

'I've advertised for help,' Lisa announced.

Hermione glanced at her. 'Help? For whom?'

'For Woebee,' said Harrie. 'She isn't getting any younger, and this is a big house. Woebee needs to dedicate her time just to you.'

Hermione pursed her lips. 'Because I am now such a cumbersome burden.' She sighed. 'Yes, yes, it is getting worse. I suppose we should employ someone for the heavier work. Well done, Lisa.'

'Are you ill, Ben?' Lisa asked.

'Tired,' he snapped.

'Is it the exams?'

He shook his head.

Lisa continued. 'You should be out and about making friends. It isn't healthy, locking yourself into your own prison.' She addressed her daughter. 'And you, madam, should be finishing university by now. We can get someone else to run the shop.'

Harrie nodded. 'I've got a place for September. Manchester. I'm reading history, then I'll do a PGCE and teach.'

Ben dropped his knife, bent to retrieve it. He was so fed up with everything and everyone... He sat up, looked at all the people round the table, then jumped to his feet. 'You aren't real,' he began loudly.

'Sit down, dear,' said Hermione.

But the dam was crumbling. 'I watched a man die recently. On my computer. Live. I watched a live death. I lived his death. And you sit here and...' He ran a hand through his hair.

Pointing to Hermione, he continued, 'She orders us all to have breakfast together once a week. We do it because she holds the purse strings. Sorry, Gran – I have almost nothing against you, but Tuesday breakfast is a nightmare. Especially with him.' He pointed to his father.

Gus looked up from his newspaper. 'What?'

'Puffer trains and bacteria, Father. With the odd virus thrown in to flavour the mix. You don't listen. You've bored Mum to death for years, and she's turned into an advertisement for Harley Street–'

'Rodney Street,' interspersed Hermione.

Ben shook his head. 'See? I tell you someone

committed suicide, and Gran corrects my geography.'

'You said he died. I didn't realize he took his own life. I'm sorry,' Hermione said.

Close to despair, Ben turned on his sister. 'I apologize for having taken up so much of your time, Harrie. I mean that. But I needed to talk and you went all Al Anon on me. Leave him alone and he'll come to his senses, eh? I can't *find* my senses.'

'Then you should see someone about that.' Harrie's tone was soft.

'We are damaged,' he yelled, 'because of him.' An accusing finger stretched in the direction of Gus. 'You are the least real of all. You aren't a husband, you aren't a father – you're just a walking encyclopedia of irrelevances. Our mum did at least keep the family business ticking. You? Too important for us, aren't you? Did you know that your daughter sees a psychologist? You are to blame for that. Because it's all about how and who *you* are, isn't it?

Gus tilted his head to one side. 'What are you talking about?' he asked.

'Me and her,' came the swift reply. 'I am supposed to be proud to bear your name, am expected to go into medicine or research – did you know that I can't bear to be touched? That I have to live alone to make sure everything is germ-free? That I had to be treated in hospital after burning my body with bleach? Do you know anything about anyone at this table? No. Mostly because you don't want to know, but also because we've become the two-dimensional paper

160

puppets you need us to be so that your precious, sacred work will not suffer.'

Only Ben's laboured breathing and the chime of a clock interrupted the short silence that followed. Lisa looked down at her nails, while Hermione, clearly shocked, wiped her face with a napkin. Harrie kept her eyes fixed on her brother; Gus simply stared into the near-distance, his head nodding slightly as he processed what had been said.

'Well?' shouted Ben at last.

Gus steepled his fingers and rested his chin on them. 'I do know what goes on, Benjamin. I have disappointed your mother, you and your sister. My own mother, too, believes that I have been an inadequate father. For these and all my other sins, I beg forgiveness.' He stood up and left the room.

Ben pursued his father, screaming and cursing, the sound of his voice fading as the pair left the house.

Lisa rose from the table, but Harrie grabbed her arm. 'Don't go,' she pleaded. 'It needs to happen. Ben is working something out, and it's pretty horrible because I stepped aside and left him to it. If he has to take it out on Dad, so be it.'

Lisa shivered. 'But he won't kill him, will he?'

'Of course he won't.' This answer came from Hermione. 'Benjamin couldn't hurt anyone; it isn't in his nature.'

Lisa continued to tremble. What a mess. She and Annie spent their working hours worrying about Jimmy turning up, and now trouble that had simmered for years at home was about to cover everything in boiling magma. 'God, Harriet, I am so sorry.'

Hermione snorted. 'Never mind sorry, Lisa. You did your best within your own capabilities. He has not been an easy man to live with – nor was his father. My husband was an arrogant fool, and Gus has grown up to be very like him.'

Lisa burst into tears and ran from the room.

Harrie looked at her grandmother. 'I'll just ... er ... I'll be back soon.' She left the room and made her way to the front of the house. Ben was sitting in the driver's seat of that ridiculous camper van. He was weeping. Their father's Mini was just turning left into the lane. So, however close their encounter had become, each had survived it. She looked at her brother, saw that he was engrossed in his sorrow. 'I can do nothing,' she told herself. And she should do nothing. For now, it was best to leave the cauldron to cool.

Had Harrie been possessed of X-ray vision strong enough to penetrate walls and bushes, she might have beheld a mind-altering sight. Halfway along Weaver's Weft, a Mini was parked. The man inside the car suffered the usual discomfort that resulted from squeezing six feet of body into a space suitable for a much smaller man. This nuisance he had tolerated for years, as he was determined not to leave a large footprint on the planet.

He was sobbing into a handkerchief. The man who owned several half-answers to questions pertaining to life and death, the respected professor who used to be a doctor, the red-carpet visitor welcomed in all continents, had finally met his match. His own son had ripped away at him and laid him bare. If only Benjamin knew. If only any of them knew...

But they couldn't know. No one could know. Each man had an Achilles heel, and Gus's lay deep inside, buried beneath years of hope, despair, joy and sorrow. His secret. His burden. And he had a terrible pain in his stomach.

The welt on Jimmy's face looked as if it might take days to heal, and it threatened to leave a scar. Although Sal pleaded with him repeatedly, he would not see a doctor, and he refused point blank to go to outpatients.

Sal bathed it and treated it with antiseptics. He told her that he was undercover as a representative for Apollo alarms; that he was working with police to discover why some alarms did not do a proper job. She was angry with the police, but she believed every word that came out of her lover's mouth. At one point, she asked why the crime had never been reported in the papers, and he told her that everything had to remain a secret while the matter was investigated. 'And you're the one with the wound,' she concluded sadly. 'It's not fair. Still, I'll do my best to stop it turning into a scar.'

He needed to test her even further by manufacturing a story credible enough to push her in the direction he needed her to take, 'You have to help me, Sal,' he pleaded. 'I'm in a lot of trouble, but it's none of my doing. The wife is trying to control me.'

She put down the lint with which she had

bathed his face. 'She never deserved you, that Annie. You wanted looking after proper, didn't you? She didn't value you, love.'

He shrugged lightly. 'Aye, but my children needed me. That's why I stayed as long as I did. If it hadn't been for the boys and Daisy, I'd have slung my hook years back.'

Sal sat next to him on the sofa. 'So she's friends with this Compton-Milne lot?'

'Yes. Well, she knows them.'

'And you want to find out where a gun is, even though it's not your gun, like. How did all that come about?'

He wove her a tale about giving a lift to a couple of old school pals who had needed to get to Birmingham. 'I thought they were straight,' he said. 'Supposed to be fetching a man from Brum to come and work up here. Well, they didn't find him.'

'All lies?' Sal asked.

'Absolutely. Then, when we got home, I found out they'd robbed a jewellery depot and put a bloke in a wheelchair. And they'd left the flaming gun in my car. I hid it in case they came back for it – they were big lads who likely wouldn't take no for an answer. Annie only went and found it, didn't she? And she's given it to the Compton-Milnes to hide.'

'Why?' She dried his face with cotton wool. 'Why would she do a terrible thing like that?'

Jimmy raised his shoulders. 'Why do women do anything? It's for bargaining with. If I don't send money, if I try to see the kids, she's going to give that gun to the cops and I'll go down for something I didn't do. They'll load the gun and fire it, and you can bet your last halfpenny the bullet'll match the one that was lodged in that poor bloke's spine. I'd go down for years and years.'

'What about them that really did do it?'

He shook his head. 'South America, I should think. I'd forgotten I even had the bloody gun. Then, when I told her I was leaving her, she goes and gives the thing to the posh buggers.' He placed a hand on Sal's knee. 'But I do have a confession, babe.' Babe? With a moustache like that, she looked like somebody's grandad.

'Spit it out, then,' she answered.

He inhaled deeply. 'Lisa Compton-Milne. I had an affair with her. She tells everybody she dumped me, but I left her because I could never get you out of my head, Sal. So you'd have to go careful, give her loads of respect, pretend you like her. When the lies about me come out, keep quiet. Just try and find that gun for me.'

'I'd have to give up me other jobs, Jimmy. It says hours to suit, only I bet it's nearly every day. Did you say the old one's crippled?'

He nodded. 'I think they call it MS. But she's got some daft Irishwoman looking after her, so you'd not be hauling the old girl from pillar to post every five minutes.' He touched his scar, a mark made by said daft Irishwoman. 'Phone the number – you've nothing to lose. Phone from one of the houses you clean. Go on, Sal. Do it for me.'

As ever, Sal did exactly as she was told. She would go to the ends of the earth if Jimmy needed help. A few days later, having been awarded an interview, she rooted in the sideboard drawer for references. 'I can get a couple of more recent ones,' she told him. 'Only, the folk I work for won't want to lose me, none of them. I'm highly thought of as a housekeeper, you know.'

Jimmy smiled to himself. Housekeeper? She was a scrubber, and it showed. 'You'll be the best,' he said, his mind still racing. What if Annie went and visited the Compton-Milne house? No, she'd never seen Sal, didn't even know her name. And the Compton-Milnes were a bit on the grand side for Annie. No. Annie would stick out in that house like a boil on the face of a baby. It would be all right, he told himself repeatedly. It was the best thing to do, and he congratulated himself on his cleverness. He had found the advert; he had persuaded Sal to apply. It would all work out for the best. And if Sal located that gun, he'd be in the clear.

So this was how the other half lived.

Sal adjusted her dark green beret and tugged at the buttons of a matching raincoat that only just fitted her. She had wanted to wear her best mac, but Jimmy had advised her to be dowdy, but clean. The shoes were worn, though polished to a bright sheen, while her bag was a plain, canvas holdall. She hoped she looked homely enough for these posh people.

The house was massive and built from local stone. There were dormers in the roof, and Sal guessed that there must be eight or ten bed-rooms. She swallowed nervously, trying hard to remember all the coaching she had endured. She had to be polite, but not... What was the word? Subservient? She didn't really know what it meant, but she was ready for polite.

Lisa answered the door. Sal could tell it was Lisa because she was the wrong age for other women in the household. This was the woman Jimmy had slept with. She was beautiful – nails manicured, hair perfect, clothes understated and probably designer-labelled. But she didn't know how to hang on to her man, did she? Sal guessed that Lisa Compton-Milne had probably never cooked for him, comforted him, or bathed a wound. And beautiful women were often rubbish in bed because they thought beauty was enough. Well, it wasn't.

They went into a large family kitchen where Lisa sat and listed details of the job. 'It's a big house,' she explained, 'but my son has his own quarters on the first floor – he looks after himself – and my daughter and I work full-time. She will be going to university at the end of summer. She also has her own place – a bungalow at the end of the garden. If she wants anything done, you will be paid separately. Any questions?'

Sal swallowed. 'Er ... what's the hourly rate and will you pay bus fares? Only, I ride a bike to me jobs at the moment, but this would be a long way to pedal. It's two bus rides from where I live.' She had to start saying 'my' instead of 'me'. Jimmy had told her.

'Seven pounds and fifty pence, and yes, bus fares would be paid.'

Sal tried not to gasp. Seven fifty an hour? For twenty hours a week? That was ... that was a lot of money, especially if it was in cash.

'Do you have children?' Lisa asked.

'No. My husband died before we had any babies.' Jimmy had told her to be a widow. Widows, it seemed, were respectable and more likely to be offered a job. God, if she got this one, she hoped she would remember to carry on being a widow.

'When could you start?'

'Oh, in a week or two. I'll leave you them there photocopies of references, and, if you want letters of recommendation from my current employers, I will furnish you with them gladly.' She had remembered that bit of Jimmy's tutoring, at least. And she'd remembered the 'my', though she should never have said 'them there'. This was hard work already, but seven fifty? Brilliant.

'Good. Now, show yourself round the house – I am sure you can be trusted, Mrs Potter.'

'And you'll let me know?'

'Of course. I have your address here. Thank you for coming.'

When the woman had left the room, Lisa sat and pondered for a few moments. There had been three applicants in total. One was waiting to go into hospital for an operation, so she might well be out of action for a month or more; the second had three children at school, and children had a tendency to become ill at the most inconvenient times. It would have to be Mrs Potter. Lisa didn't know why Mrs Potter made her uncomfortable, but that shouldn't matter, as there would be minimal contact between the two women. Still, there'd been something odd about the way Mrs

Potter had looked at her prospective employer, as if she had been sizing her up. Perhaps that was a good thing, because an interview ought to be a two-way process.

Sal was walking around with her jaw hanging loose. These were good leather sofas, beautiful curtains with weights in the hems, excellent rugs on stripped-wood floors. There was real money in this place. Five bookcases, two sideboards, a couple of rooms big enough to need a fireplace at each end. Was there a gun, though?

She turned to leave the drawing room and almost collided with Lisa. 'Sorry,' she exclaimed. 'I didn't realize you were there.'

'Would you like a month's trial?'

'Ooh yes, please. I can't wait to get polishing that panelling. It's like something out of a film, isn't it?'

Lisa nodded absently. The applicant was almost too agreeable, too eager to please. 'Work notice for your current employers, then telephone me if you can get to a phone. Your references are more than adequate.'

Lisa stood at a window and watched Mrs Sally Potter as she made her way back towards the lane. She was just an ordinary female carrying a little too much weight, a woman with a plain face and lank hair. After serving the public for over two decades, Lisa knew she had good instincts when it came to people. Within two or three minutes of a customer entering the shop, Lisa had him or her assessed. Annie had the same instinct, it seemed.

The woman had stopped to look at some

bedding plants. Then she turned and surveyed the house like a prospective purchaser. Lisa was weighing up a woman who was weighing up everything else. *Let's just hope she's thorough,* she thought. *I don't have to fall in love with her, do I?*

'Is that to be the one, then?'

Lisa jumped, then turned to look at Eileen Eckersley's unlovely face. 'Month's trial,' she answered.

'She'll last a week,' foretold the oracle. 'The legs'll go from under her when she has to knuckle to for one of your bridge evenings with three courses and the caviass to start with.'

Lisa smiled. 'Caviar. I think I'm giving up bridge, Eileen.' She was giving up a lot of things. Bridge was one, fornication was another and, lower down the list, plastic surgery would also be given a miss.

'Why?' asked Eileen.

'I don't know.' That, at least, was the truth.

Love had opened Harrie's eyes. Bombarded all her life by songs and books about it, she'd been ill-prepared for the reality. Its power was immense, seemingly boundless. It was disturbing and wonderful and too much to cope with. Love made her see everything differently, though it had little to do with poetry or morning dew on flowers.

Love was staring into space while ignoring a customer; it was driving along in the wrong gear, smiling when there was nothing immediate to amuse her, feeling sorry for those who were not in love. It was also very annoying. She had given away a piece of herself. Her body didn't matter –

170

that could cope with itself – but she wasn't the person she used to be. She was sometimes vague, distracted and forgetful. She had better pull herself together before the shop went bankrupt. Was this an illness?

She told him off frequently 'I don't own me any more,' she said. 'Not completely. The Competition Commission should deal with this. There's been a takeover, and I wasn't even invited to the meeting.'

Will always had an answer to give the woman he loved. Someone else had done the bidding on the telephone, and he was just a figurehead standing in for some invisible foreign company with Swiss bank accounts and an urge to govern the whole world. Or he was an official receiver sent to pick up the pieces after the Harriet Compton-Milne meltdown. He adored her, and he wasn't even put off by her family any more. Even now, standing with her outside the central police station in Bolton, he was not particularly worried. He was concerned about Ben, yet he knew that his Harrie was perfect for him. She had her faults, but she made him laugh. Love and laughter were all he needed. He had been a serious boy born of a serious family, and Harrie had lifted him on to a different level.

She held his hand tightly. 'I'm encouraged,' she said quietly. 'He already phoned the police anonymously. He actually used a public telephone. And now he's in there.' She waved her other hand at the door. 'Terrible thing to say, Will, but the guy who killed himself did a lot for my bro.'

Will agreed. 'And he threw out all his bleach?'

171

In spite of the seriousness of the situation, Harrie grinned. 'Cognitive therapy does work. Only two sessions, and he's already dealing with the here and now rather than his past. He has OCD, but even that's going to be made easier.'

'Your woman did this for him?'

'No. She sent him to Manchester; Miriam knows her own limitations. Whoever is helping Ben is magic – he breaks down all Ben's problems and fixations into little bits. The bleach is just the beginning, Will.'

Will could not understand why the Compton-Milne parents had not dealt with this earlier, and he voiced that concern.

Harrie looked up to the sky as if seeking inspiration. 'Difficult one. He was allowed his genius – that's how my father excuses Ben's oddity. My mother – well – she just wasn't around much. I look at her now and I know why. She married the wrong man, handed over her children to Gran and grabbed life by the throat. But she was only strangling herself. I'm watching her recovery now. She is, you know, a very clever woman. Underneath the facelifts, there's a decent brain.'

Will looked at his watch, glanced at the Town Hall clock. 'Over half an hour, Harrie.'

'Oh, well. Ben will be thorough. He says he's hiding nothing, because he wants sites like that one to be closed. It took some guts for him to come here.'

'Especially with me.'

She laughed. 'He likes you. He's got over the don't-take-away-my-big-sister thing. It's like watching him come alive, you know. I hope the

172

improvement continues.'

Ben emerged at last. 'Bloody hell,' he cursed. 'That was some interview. But the good news is that my name will be kept out of it. After all, we can't have the Compton-Milnes dragged through the mud. Think of Father's wonderful reputation.'

They drove home in Ben's camper van to find a large rear sticking out of the under-sink cupboard in the kitchen. 'Erm ... do we know that face?' Harrie asked.

The rest of the woman backed into the room. 'Hello,' she said as she struggled to her feet, face the colour of beetroot. 'I'm Sal Potter, and I was looking at your U-bend.'

Harrie managed to contain her glee. 'I've never had my U-bend examined before. Have you?' she asked Will.

'Only under a general anaesthetic and by the best surgeons,' he replied gravely. 'What's the diagnosis?' he asked the stranger.

'Peelings,' she announced. 'And fat.'

Ben nodded. 'That would do it every time. Try Syrup of Figs.' He left the scene.

Harrie continued to play the game. 'Are you Corgi registered?'

'Eh?' Sal's face, though a lighter shade, was still very red.

'Plumbers are usually Corgi registered. Then they can do gas fires and boilers as well.'

'Ooh.' Sal wiped her damp forehead. 'No, love – I'm not a plumber. I'm your new home help.'

'It's all right,' said Will. 'She knows.' He pushed Harrie towards the outer door. 'Ben will be all right. Go and sell some diamonds. You need to keep me in the manner to which I am aspiring to become accustomed.'

Sal picked up her cleaning box and left the room hurriedly.

'We should be kinder to people,' said Harrie from the doorway.

'You're no fun at all.' He blew her a kiss and followed Ben upstairs. Today, he was going into Ben's rooms for the first time. He had been ordered by his girlfriend to make a small mess and see if Ben got flustered. 'How big is small?' he asked himself as he walked upstairs. Oh, well. He would make it up as he went along.

Sal was about as much use as a chocolate fireguard when it came to imagination. She had looked in drawers and cupboards, but had failed to search unusual places. 'Have you taken the books off the shelves?' he asked impatiently. There was no go in the woman, no zest. But he had better keep his temper, because he needed her.

'What books? There's books all over the place, thousands of them – it's like a blinking library. And his office is all piles of stuff – if I moved one thing, the whole bloody lot would come crashing down. It'd be like knocking rows of dominoes over. It's all right for you sitting here, Jimmy. I'm the one that could get caught. They found me under the sink – I said the pipe had been blocked. See, they come home at unusual times. That's why I have to do dinners that can be warmed up on separate plates in that microwave.'

'Oh, I know you're doing your best.'

'They both have help in them shops. They can

turn up whenever they want. Then there's that Irishwoman.'

He remembered her, all right. Even now, his face hurt when he yawned or smiled. Not that he had a lot to smile about... 'Sal, just keep looking. Pictures on the walls – see if they've got hinges. Could be a safe behind one of them. Same with mirrors.'

Sal, worn out and overheated, sank on to her new sofa. Leather was all very well and good, but it wasn't the right thing on a day as hot as this one. 'I'm too tired to make the tea,' she said crossly. 'If you want to eat, you'll have to help yourself, love.'

He wasn't used to this. So far, Sal had been compliant almost to the point of slavery, hadn't been able to do enough for him. But travelling from one end of Bolton to the other twice a day, then cleaning a large house and cooking for a family, was clearly too much for her.

'I'll make a pot of tea and some sandwiches,' he said.

'Even the professor comes home sometimes,' she moaned now. 'Then Her Upstairs keeps sending the Irishwoman down for stuff. I get no chance to have a proper look round.'

'You'll manage.' He tried to inject confidence into his words, but they sounded hollow. Sal wasn't the sharpest knife in the drawer. 'And you're on better money, aren't you?'

She stared mournfully into an empty grate. It was too hot for a fire, but there was nothing quite so miserable as a fireplace without a flame. Her house looked shabby, too, because she hadn't the strength to carry on cleaning after a day spent at

Weaver's Warp. Daft name for a house. Daft bloody housekeeper, too, that Eileen woman. She talked a load of rubbish, and she kept popping up unexpectedly all over the place like a bad penny.

'There you are, love.' He placed a cup on the coffee table and pushed a ham sandwich into her hand.

She looked at him. 'What do you do all day, Jimmy?'

He dropped into his chair. 'Well, I read the paper, go out if I get sent for, fit an alarm – whatever.'

'But you don't go out every day, do you?'

For answer, he shrugged his shoulders.

'Couldn't you run the Hoover round and do a bit of dusting?'

They were all the same, bloody women. They wanted everything on a plate. They demanded love, attention, clothes, conversation and, on top of all that, help in the house. 'I'm no good at housework,' he replied.

Sal stood up and dragged herself to the door. 'I'm going in the bath,' she announced. 'It'd be nice if you washed the pots while I'm up there – even the breakfast things are still on the table.' She left the room.

He snapped his mouth into the closed position because he needed not to react. After finding a duster, he dragged it round the room, then set off in search of the vacuum cleaner. It was under the stairs. As he cleaned, he cursed under his breath. She had to find that gun. Meanwhile, he'd better pull his socks up and become a nice, quiet housewife.

The nightmares were the worst part.

Sometimes, Ben managed to wake and stop the terror, only to experience it all over again as soon as he went back to sleep. Staying awake didn't work. Although the exams so far had been easy, he did not want to be falling into brain-dead mode in the middle of his last physics paper. Once he had finished his A-levels, he would get into that camper van and go somewhere – anywhere – in order to learn to live with himself.

The therapy he had started in Manchester was already helping. Intelligent enough to have insight into his own condition, Ben soon learned that his problems with contacting people on a face-to-face basis could be dealt with by himself, as long as he was open to suggestion. So the best part was that he began to accept Ben.

Often, when he slept, he was in the room with the man who hanged himself. Ben could see the Aston Villa poster, a shirt hanging from a picture rail, magazines about sadomasochism, even photographs of family on a chest of drawers. Once or twice, he saved the man, but, for the most part, he stood and heard him choking to death. On waking, he would find himself bathed in sweat and with tears on his cheeks. 'What the hell was I doing on that site?' he asked himself repeatedly. Teenage hormones were intrusive and caused odd behaviour, but Ben's behaviour had gone beyond odd. 'I am out of step,' he told his reflection as he prepared to go downstairs. 'And it stops now.'

Harrie had called a summit conference. Dress

was to be casual and everyone would be allowed to share a couple of bottles of good Crozes Hermitage. He had no idea what that was, but he was definitely going to have his share, as it might take the edge off whatever was about to happen.

Harrie called for him, banging on his door with a rhythm they had chosen in order that she might be identified. He let her in. 'Long time no see, sis,' he said with a smile.

'Yes, well it worked, didn't it?' She looked round his sitting room. Cushions were disordered, while CDs, usually kept behind bars, were lying on the floor. 'Deliberate disorder?' she enquired.

'Probably. I was thinking about that before you arrived. Even my disorder has a kind of orderliness to it, possibly symptomatic of something or other. But I could pick out Patsy Cline from that heap over in the corner within ten seconds.'

'Don't bother, can't stand the noise.'

'Shania Twain?' he asked with the air of a sommelier offering the best vintages.

'No, but I could be persuaded to go for George Clooney.'

'He doesn't sing.'

'Exactly. Right. Are you ready?'

He wasn't, and he said so. 'Why are you doing this?' he asked. 'What are you hoping to achieve? Do we interview our mother and decide whether or not to employ her? Or do I have to plead my case as a son, you as a daughter?'

Harrie smiled. 'We're going cognitive. We come clean – all of us – then draw a line and start again. You know the score – you've been practising in Manchester.'

'Can't we have Meatloaf instead?'

But Harrie was not in the mood for 'Bat Out Of Hell', so she pushed him out on to the landing and guided him downstairs. He did not go willingly, though Harrie had told him over and over that Father would probably not turn up, while Mother had more to confess than anyone else. She shoved him into the kitchen. 'Sit,' she ordered, 'and stay.'

Ben woofed politely.

Lisa was fiddling with a modern corkscrew with which she had never developed a good relationship. It was a wooden article with a skirt that sat over the bottle, arms sticking out of each side of the upper part, but no head. 'This decapitated doodah is the bane of my life,' she moaned.

'Drunk already,' whispered Harrie to her brother.

'Promising,' he replied from the corner of his mouth.

They sat. Ben dealt with the headless lady while Harrie placed herself at the top of the table. 'I can't read the minutes of the last meeting because we never had a last meeting.'

'Inaugural.' Ben smiled as cork and bottle separated company. He filled three glasses, drank half of his, declared it to be good, then sat back to await developments.

'Your father has scarcely been seen since that breakfast, Ben,' said Lisa. 'You scared the living daylights out of him. Still, at least you got a reaction.' She sat back in her chair. 'I've had two double vodkas,' she confessed. 'And no food. I want to tell you about your dad. I want to do it

179

now, right away, before I lose my thread completely.'

Brother and sister held their breath.

'I loved him.' Tears welled, but she carried on. 'He was kind and gentle, or so I thought. I think he was simply disinterested. The men I had known before him had been ... livelier, sometimes frightening. So, anyway, I married Gus. He was this clever man who gave me a job in his jewellery shop while he ran a general practice.' She took a mouthful of wine.

Harrie touched her mother's hand. 'It's all right to cry. It says so in the constitution of this committee.'

Lisa smiled wanly. 'When you get married, you expect joy, especially at the beginning. We were still on honeymoon when I heard him sobbing in a hotel bathroom. I asked him why, and he told me never to ask because the truth would hurt me. I felt as if a knife had gone through my chest.'

'Oh, Mum,' breathed. 'Do you know now?'

Lisa shook her head. 'No idea.'

'Have you asked?'

'I have abided by his wishes. There is a terrible, terrible sadness in your father.'

'Poor Dad,' Harrie whispered.

Lisa nodded. 'Your father is the biggest pain in my neck, but don't hate him. He's your father. I know he's Thomas the Effing Tank Engine; I know he went from stethoscope to microscope in one easy step. That was because he was no good with people.' She stared hard at Ben. 'Don't be like him, son. Don't get yourself tied up in misery.'

180

Ben blinked to shift water from his eyes and, as if clearing Becher's Brook, he rushed through his own confession. 'I just want to be normal,' he concluded, 'but I don't know what normal is. No one does.'

Lisa bit her lower lip. 'Ben, you can't shock me. I am really sad about what you went through, especially when the lad died, but life is one long learning experience. Look after yourself, be safe, be happy.'

'I'll try,' he whispered before addressing his sister. 'Right, Miss Chairperson, what do you have to say to this belated communion of three-quarters of a family?'

Harrie grinned. 'History at uni later this year, wedding next spring. We're not planning children immediately, because we already have Milly.'

'Are you sure?' Lisa asked.

'Oh yes. Milly is essentially noticeable. Sorry, sorry, yes, I am sure. We're going to live in my shed. At least the dog will have a nice, big kennel. Will and I could end up with just a kitchen. Big dog.'

The door flew inward. 'Oh,' exclaimed Eileen Eckersley. 'I didn't know you were in confluence.' She pointed to the ceiling. 'I am sent to fetch cocoa and to count the silver.'

'What?' Lisa stood, her gait unsteady. 'Why?'

'Because *she* ran out of cocoa and *I* am keeping an eye on Podgy Potter.'

Lisa, at a loss, shook her head and sat down again.

'Woebee?' asked Ben. 'What the heck are you talking about?'

181

'Cocoa,' she snapped. 'Brown stuff. In a tin.'

'Podgy Potter?'

'She's into everything everywhere. I am up and down those stairs like a rat in a drain, though I have to creep. I am not a natural creeper.'

'What happened to that nice Virginia creeper we had on the–?'

Lisa cut Ben off. 'Is Sal Potter taking stuff?'

'Not yet, but she even had the kickboards off under the kitchen cupboards. I asked her what she was doing, and she said she was being thorough. Very pleased, I was, when she told me we have no mice. There's something not right with her.'

The three of them started to giggle. That Woebee should find someone stranger than herself was a miracle.

'Well, I hope you think it's funny when all your Apods disappear.'

'Ipods,' Harrie managed.

Eileen grabbed the cocoa, stamped out of the kitchen and slammed the door.

They settled eventually. Then Ben had a sudden thought. 'You haven't said anything about yourself,' he accused Lisa. 'We have bared our souls, and you have just been drunk and disorderly.'

Lisa tapped the side of her nose. 'It'll keep,' she smiled. 'I've been a terrible mother and an unfaithful wife, but, as the senior member of this forum, I claim loss of memory, virtue and dignity.' She stood up again. 'Vodka and red wine?' she muttered. 'Never again.'

Ben picked up the bottle and poured dregs into his glass. 'Mother?'

'What?'

'You weren't that bad. You took us on holiday twice a year. I remember you met a lovely man in Crete.' He grinned impishly. 'You walked with us in the parks round here and we fed ducks. I remember you bringing down my temperature with ice when I was ill. So you've been a bit selfish. Haven't we all?'

Harrie agreed. 'Very true. But I declare this meeting closed, because our mother is inebriated.'

As Lisa climbed the stairs, she clung to two things. One was the banister rail; the other was the realization that she had just met two wonderful young people. They could be her friends now.

Seven

'Ooh, look what the wind blows in on a Thursday when you think everything's all right with the world.' Freda Nuttall stepped back and allowed her son to enter the bungalow. She couldn't believe her eyes. Where the hell had he been since ... since whenever she had last seen him? Yes, it had been when she had returned from holiday. How long ago was that? Another senior moment, she thought ruefully as she led the errant off-spring into her best room. 'Where've you been?' she asked when he showed no sign of opening the conversation.

'Here and there,' he answered. 'And it's Wednesday.'

She pursed her lips. 'Oh aye? Well, you look like nobody owns you. Get a bath. And look in my wardrobe – I think I've a shirt of your dad's in there.'

He didn't move. 'I've been helping a mate with a job.'

'Right. I hope it wasn't a bank job, and I hope it wasn't Barclays – they've got my few bob in there.'

He stared at her steadily. 'You've never had any time for me, have you, Mam?'

'Don't talk so Fairy Liquid – you're me son. I love you. But I can't stand the bloody sight of you at times. Times like this, when you've been helping a mate, when your wife's thrown you out for messing about, when your kids–'

'Shut up, Mam,' he begged. 'I've got a bad head.'

Freda closed her eyes. He had more than a bad head. She felt as if the years had been lined with a guard of honour, every member in blue, every one carrying truncheon and handcuffs. Jimmy had brought more trouble to her door than she really wanted to think about, so she changed the subject. 'Glad to see your Annie fell on her feet.'

'You what?'

'Your Annie. Getting a gradely job like that one, apprentice jeweller at Milne's. See, your bit on the side has a brain, and she spotted a good 'un in your Annie. She'll not go far wrong, that Lisa woman, if she sees Annie's got potential.'

Jimmy closed his gaping mouth with an audible snap. Bloody women. There was this one here, who had given birth to him, who was supposed to nurture and comfort him in all weathers; then Lisa Double-Barrel, who got frightened off by Annie, who made a friend of Annie, who employed Annie...

'I mind Daisy, and Annie's mother has the boys.'

He tried not to grind his teeth. He'd had a rough day of it, and no mistake. Sal was turning bolshie, and he had driven off in his van so that he would be out when she got home from a job she was absolutely useless at. The van had broken down, and he was now covered in oil, hence his unkempt appearance. Sal? Find the gun? She couldn't find the end of her own nose without ordinance survey and a couple of guide dogs. She

186

hadn't even managed to get to know that Annie was employed in one of those damned shops, and she worked in that big, fancy house. Some use she'd turned out to be.

'Where've you been today, then?' Freda asked.

'Looking for work.'

'Last time you had work, Clement Atlee was in charge.'

'Who?'

'Never mind. Even I wasn't alive when he was putting the boot in. At least, I think I wasn't. What sort of work, anyway? I could do with my garden clearing if you're at a loose end.'

He ignored her and gazed round the room. No, they wouldn't have brought the gun here, would they? Not to an old woman's bungalow. It would be up Weaver's Weft and hidden in Weaver's Warp, probably under some floorboards or up in the gods with the granny.

'Jimmy?'

'Aye?'

'What is it you want from life?'

'I want that flaming gun back, is what. Them Compton-Milnes have got me over a barrel – aye – a gun barrel. How do I know they won't give it to the police?'

Freda shrugged. 'You don't know. But you'd best steer clear of Annie, the kids and Lisa, or they might just hand you over to the coppers.'

'I never shot anyone.'

'So you said.'

'I need it back, Mam. I can't rest till it's in the sea or buried under a ton of concrete. I can't get on with me life while they hold that thing, can I?

187

If I go to my house, if I try to see my kids, if I drop me aitches – how can I start again when she has all my cash and she's sitting in my house? You have to help me, Mam.'

She leaned forward. 'If I could make you straight, Jimmy, I would lay down and die. Just to see you in a proper job with a wage and no stealing, I'd climb in my coffin here and now. But I know you, love. I can't help you. You'll not alter. I grieve for you, honest, I do. You were such a lovely baby.'

Jimmy stared down at her. She'd been a looker, had Mam. She'd worked damned hard all her life, and he had turned out to be her biggest disappointment. Something akin to guilt invaded his chest and he could scarcely breathe or swallow.

He would never be able to explain what he did next, not in a month of Sundays. Jimmy Nuttall bent and kissed his mother's grey, frizzled hair. 'Ta-ra, Mam,' he managed before leaving the house.

Freda sat still for a long time after her son had gone. She finally stirred herself to make a cup of tea before her soaps started. 'He's in a right state,' she told herself. And she wasn't referring to the oil smeared on clothes and face, the dirt edging his fingernails. Jimmy was desperate. Should she phone Annie and warn her? Warn her about what, tell her what? That Jimmy was wearing dirty clothes, that he had kissed his mother as if saying goodbye for the last time?

The *Emmerdale* music was playing when she

188

switched on her TV. Freda took a mouthful of tepid tea and stared at the screen. But if anyone were to ask her, later, what had happened in the Dales that night, she could not have answered.

At least twice a year, Sheila Barton made the trip to Tonge Cemetery in order to lay flowers on her parents' grave and on the final resting place of her husband. It was all she could do for them now, and, as a dutiful daughter and widow, she felt she had to go out of her way to mark the lives of the people who had created her. She also needed to leave a token on the monument of the man who had left her two houses and complete freedom from children.

There was a dilemma, however. Space in the family grave would feel more welcoming than that in her husband's. She hadn't wanted to lie down with him in life, so she would prefer not to spend eternity in his company. The problem reared its head on every visit and, as she grew older, the difficulty became more pressing. Dead was dead, yet she cared about where her bones would rest after life had deserted her. It wasn't right, and she knew it. A wife should join her husband from altar to grave and beyond, but she felt she simply could not be at peace with Sid.

She stood over him, read the wording etched in stone, remembered choosing the text – MUCH LOVED HUSBAND OF SHEILA. 'I never loved you,' she said dolefully. 'I'm sorry, Sid, but I'm going in with Mam and Dad. I knew them better, you see. Thirty-odd years is a long time, and I still miss them. You were good to me, I know that. But I couldn't rest, not here, not with you. Please, please forgive me.'

With moisture in her eyes, she crossed the cemetery and stood by the grave of Enid and Alan Armstrong. They had been the best mam and dad a person could ever have. She remembered Dad giving her the yolk of his egg, Mam brushing her hair and making her pretty. Sheila had never been pretty, but her parents had viewed her through rose-tinted lenses. She had owned a dolls' house with working lights, a beautiful dolls' pram, the best tricycle.

Perhaps those things were nothing compared to property, yet Sheila knew that Mam and Dad had denied themselves in order to furnish her with all she needed and much of what she wanted. This would be her last place on earth, then. People could talk all they liked, because she would not be around to hear the gossip.

As she rose, after placing a bunch of flowers in the pot, she noticed a man two rows away from her. She knew that figure. Even with his back turned towards her, he remained recognizable. What was he doing here? And why were his shoulders shaking? He hadn't said a word about anyone dying. She stood completely still and watched him for several seconds. It was plain that he was heartbroken. Professor Gustav Compton-Milne weeping? That cool, calm, brilliant man standing by a grave and allowing emotion to spill? Impossible.

Sheila bent down behind her parents' headstone and waited for him to leave the graveyard. She squatted for so long that cramp began to set in, but she didn't want him to see her. It was important that she should remain invisible, because she had seldom encroached on his private life and had merely been an ear when he had dropped snippets of information. He was a disappointed man, that was plain. Yet there he stood, head bent, shoulders moving, back shaking as he cried. Even from this distance, she could see that the plot over which he stood was not newly dug, so the deceased had not made his or her exit recently.

It occurred to her that she was some female version of a peeping Tom, as this was a personal moment to which she ought never have been privy. She stayed. She stayed until he had turned away and walked out through the main gates, then, after pulling herself up into a standing position and waiting for the cramp to subside, she walked over to the place where he had stood.

There were lilies on the grave. Just pure, white lilies from whose centres orange tongues reached as if in search of sunshine. Behind the flowers, a wreath of dark green leaves made a bed fit to support such simple, beautiful blooms. Sheila felt privileged, because she was now standing right at the centre of Gus's heart.

The words were simple, the message brief. In marble, the headstone stated: 'KATHERINA LOUISA BARFORD DIED 1 JUNE 1983.' Underneath, in lower case, the legend read: 'Greatly loved and sadly missed.' Sheila scratched her head. Sadly missed by whom? By him and only him? Where were her parents, sisters, brothers? Who had buried this woman? *I don't know who you are*, Sheila thought, *but you've a*

191

grand man visiting you. There was grief in him, she'd already known that. Sometimes, at the table, he would pause between mouthfuls and stare into the near distance – was the occupant of this grave the cause of his occasional absence from actuality?

Sheila shivered. It was a warm enough day, yet she suddenly felt chilled to the backbone. She wished that he would open up to her. Should she say that she had seen him here today? Or did he want to continue holding his unhappiness inside? He was a very private man – who seemed cold at times, who dealt with practicalities, who played with trains and got excited about cures for disease. But here, today, he had sobbed his heart out. Here, he had felt something very real and deeper than the grave.

Sheila left the cemetery without reaching a decision, but the sadness she felt for him remained with her for a very long time.

Hermione half-listened as Eileen prattled on. In the middle of a crossword, the old woman would have preferred to have been left to herself, but Eileen Eckersley was on her high horse, and nothing would bring her down until she fell at some impossible fence.

'Slow down,' ordered Hermione, putting down the newspaper with the air of one finally succumbing to divine intervention.

'She didn't see me. I was doing the creeping about like a mouse looking for cheese. And I saw her. I did. With my own two eyes, I saw her plain as day.'

Hermione bit back a quip about the impossibility of using any other eyes. 'Mrs Potter, I take it?'

'Right up the chimbley, she was.'

'What?'

'She was right up the chimbley, with just her hindquarters sticking out. She looked like a cow tethered ready for the visiting bull, so she did.'

Hermione ordered herself not to laugh. 'Did she see you?'

'Only if she has eyes in her nether areas. I mean, what is a woman doing with her head stuck up there?'

Hermione shrugged. 'Looking for Father Christmas?'

'It's near July!'

Hermione gritted her teeth. Eileen had got it into her head that the new woman was up to no good. This was probably because the cleaner had been hired to do all the jobs Eileen had been doing downstairs. Perhaps Eileen was feeling usurped, feeling her age, getting paranoid, even.

'You'll have to talk to her,' announced the carer. 'Because it's not my place to ask why she's emptying cupboards and pulling the kitchen to bits and poking about up chimbleys. She's had the contents of sideboards spread from here to Rivington Pike, and I even found her trying to take up the carpet.'

Hermione sighed. 'Everybody approaches cleaning differently. She goes into too much detail, takes the job too seriously.'

'Is she a chimbley sweep on top of all else? Because she's brought no special brushes along with her, I can tell you that for no money.

193

Normal people don't go prodding around in grates, do they? And you don't pick up fitted carpets to clean underneath. There's something very wrong about that woman, may the good Lord forgive me for saying so.'

Hermione, whose patience was thinning, tapped her pen on the table. 'Four down,' she said. 'Something used to strangle an Irishwoman? She looked up. 'Any ideas? Because garrotte doesn't fit.'

Eileen folded her arms. 'When all the silver's gone and–'

'But there's nothing missing. Eileen, if this carries on, I shall need a double dose of the pain pills. If I could walk, I'd be out of here in two shakes of that cow's tail – the one you have waiting for the bull. You've not a shred of evidence against Mrs Potter. Just because she does things differently – that doesn't mean she's a thief or a murderer. Does it?'

'No, but–'

'No, but nothing. I've had enough. Just find something to do and leave me in peace, woman.'

Eileen bustled off, words still emerging from beneath her breath. 'It'll be my fault when it all goes wrong,' she whispered to Hermione's kitchen sink. 'It'll be me who should have noticed, should have said something, should have–'

'Eileen? Come here.'

The Irishwoman entered, a tea towel twisting in her hands. 'What now?'

Hermione was standing at a window, a Zimmer frame keeping her steady. 'Look,' she ordered.

Eileen obeyed. In the garden below, Sal Potter was spreading soot between plants. 'Why is she doing that?'

'Because soot is good for the garden. Now, what do you have to say?'

'She must have heard me. With her head in the fireplace, she must still have known I was there. Prodding about among people's things – she's got no right.'

Hermione sighed wearily. 'If she's a thief and a chancer, what was she doing up a chimney? Did she think we had treasure up there? You're making no sense at all, woman. If she'd her hands in a till at the shop, I'd understand your attitude.'

'But I only wanted to draw your attention to–'

'She's doing a good job, and you don't like that. You thought you'd carry on for ever being in charge, didn't you? Well, you're getting no younger, and neither am I. So shut up about Sally Potter, for heaven's sake. And straighten your face.'

Eileen flounced out and carried on with the washing-up. She didn't care what Madam said. There was something wrong with Sal Potter, and time would prove it.

Hermione continued to stare through her dormer window. One thing she had learned over the years was that Eileen Eckersley was a person of strong instinct. She had a nose for things that were not quite right, was capable of summing up with a degree of accuracy most situations. She talked a lot of nonsense, got her words wrong, but she knew people. This was a gift bequeathed to but a few, and Hermione began to wonder, albeit reluctantly, about Mrs Sally Potter. The woman was too good. She stayed beyond her allotted hours and, according to Lisa, never claimed overtime. So what was she doing in the shed? Stanley Eckersley did the gardens. There was no need for a Sal Potter to potter about in the potting shed. Hermione grinned. Eileen always called that place the 'pottering' shed. She was right again, wasn't she?

'Why are you watching her?'

The older woman jumped. 'Good God, Eileen, you'll give me a stroke if you carry on like that. A person of my age can't take too many shocks.'

'Well, it's sorry I am about that, but you have to admit that Mrs Potter is not acting like a cleaner. She's been a plumber, a chimbley sweep, a carpet fitter and a gardener – and they're the jobs we know about. The good Lord alone knows what she gets up to when I am not looking. She'll be fetching one of those pewmatic drills if we don't shape up.'

Hermione turned and gazed into the unlovely face of her companion. 'And when, pray, are you not watching? It's like living with a hawk.'

'It's just my way, madam.'

Hermione allowed a deep breath to escape from deep in her lungs. 'I've told you to call me Iona. All my friends call me Iona.'

'I'm an employee. I know my place.'

The employer sat down and faced her single member of staff. 'Listen, birdbrain. That's not an insult, because you are a watchful hawk and, sometimes, you are right. Fetch out my best Cooper coffee set and make up a trolley for two. Some scones would be nice. Then get yourself downstairs and invite Mrs Sally Potter to join me for coffee.'

Eileen folded her arms. 'So Lisa's servant sits with you and I don't?'

'You'll be in the hall listening. For once in your life, will you simply do as you are told without question. Can you manage that for half an hour?'

'Of course I can, and well you know it.'

Downstairs, Sally Potter was at her wits' end. She couldn't find a safe anywhere, had searched cupboards, shelves and drawers, had even had a root round in the garden shed. It was a good job she'd heard the Irishwoman creeping about. With her head up a wide chimney and wearing a Sainsbury's bag to save her hair, she had been lucky to hear anything at all. Eileen Eckersley was suspicious, but Sal hadn't dared tell Jimmy about that. She was here to find a gun and, beyond that, there was–

'Mrs Potter?'

Sal turned from her current task of preparing vegetables.

'Yes?'

'Madam says would you care to come up and take coffee with her?'

'Why?'

Even Eileen was perplexed by that question. 'Oh ... it's the way she is. She sits alone a lot, you see, so you're someone for her to talk to.' She sniffed. 'And it's fortunate, you are, because she doesn't invite many for morning coffee. Or afternoon tea, come to that.'

Sal fiddled with the potato peeler. She didn't want to go up into what Jimmy described as the gods or the dress circle. She was quite happy peeling carrots and washing broccoli. 'I've a fair few things to do.' She had stuff to remember as well. There must be no mention of Jimmy, she was a widow, she was here to work and not to search – oh, God. 'Can we make it another day?' she asked.

'I think it's best you come when invited. She suffers from MS, so she sees people only on the good days. And we don't get many of those just lately.' That, at least, was the truth.

With a heart even heavier than her very tired feet, Sal followed Eileen up the stairs. She glanced at the lifts and wished that she could use them, but they were there for one person only, and Sal was not that person. She was quite winded when they finally reached the top storey, and she stopped for a few seconds, pretending to tie a shoelace while Eileen waited.

'Have you done?'

'Yes.' She entered Mrs Hermione Compton-Milne's apartment. It was beautifully furnished, understated and quite modern for a woman of such an age.

'How do you do?' said Hermione.

'Nicely, thanks.'

The handshake was limp, and the skin felt damp with fear. Hermione cleaned her own right hand on wipes kept for that purpose, as she was always spilling food and drink. By the time Sal had turned to place herself in a chair, the wipes and Sal's sweat had been disposed of discreetly.

Eileen poured the coffee.

'Lovely cups,' commented the guest.

'Wedding gift,' replied Hermione. 'Susie

198

Cooper. It has, so far, survived the ministrations of Eileen, but I don't hold out a great deal of hope in the long-term.'

Eileen glared at her employer, then left the scene.

Sal munched on a scone, though she didn't feel like eating. Both these women had X-ray eyes, of that she felt certain. Well, the Irish one had gone, but the person who held all the top trump cards was sitting opposite Sal and staring right through her.

'Have you done this type of work for a long time?' asked the hostess.

Sal nodded, noticing that a few crumbs fell down the front of her blouse. She wished she had worn something nicer, but it was too late to worry about that now. And what had Jimmy said? 'Dowdy but clean,' that was it.

'My carer says you are doing a very thorough job. I understand that you have even lifted carpets and moved boards in the kitchen in order to do a good clean.'

'Mice,' Sal managed after swallowing the last of her scone. 'I always look for them. We've been plagued in the past, me and my dad. Farm cottage, you see. Sometimes, there were rats, too.'

Hermione shook her head. 'Oh, dear. And is your father dead now?'

Sal nodded. 'Yes. I nursed him for a long time. I do like your glass tables.'

'Safety glass. I fall a lot.'

'Well, that's a shame. And the metal trees on the wall – very modern.'

'Linda Barker. I like to keep up with the times,

don't you?'

Sal smiled weakly. 'Never got much of a chance, Mrs Compton-Milne. Always too busy to know what the trends are. Before I came here, I worked in six different houses. Then, of course, there were the years I spent looking after Dad. He wasn't an easy man to please.'

Hermione allowed a few beats of time to pass. 'So you're alone now?'

'No ... I mean yes. Except for Barney. He's my cat.' She had no cat. Now she had to remember the name of a feline that didn't even exist. Barney. She had to remember Barney. 'I called him after Barney Rubble in *The Flintstones*. It's a cartoon.'

'Yes.'

There followed a silence during which Hermione learned much about her companion. She sweated when she was nervous; she touched an ear-lobe when lying; she had something sizeable to hide. 'And your husband?'

'Eh?'

'Your husband. What happened to him?'

'Heart attack. Right as rain one minute, dead on the floor the next.'

'Terrible business for you.'

'Oh, it was. I tried that mouth-to-mouth, but it didn't work.'

'And the paramedics tried, too, I suppose. Did they shock him?'

'Er ... what?'

'Did they use a machine to start his heart again? Like they do in *Casualty?*'

'Er ... yes, I think they did.'

It was time for a pause, decided Hermione. Like a boxer, she needed to retreat to her corner in order to calculate her next move. She stood and took hold of a nearby walking frame. 'I'm all right,' she told Sal when the woman went to rise from her chair. 'I can get to the bathroom, thank you.'

Alone, Sal gazed around the room. It was all cream except for the chimney wall, which was done in an amazing wallpaper with bronze in its pattern. It probably looked lovely in the evenings when the lamps were on. Everything was so modern and clean, lots of metalwork, square shades on the lights, a black sofa with fancy cushions thrown about, all different geometric shapes in the fabrics. This was posh. This was how the rich people lived.

The rich person returned. 'And when did your husband die, Mrs Potter?'

Sal squirmed. 'Two years come September.' She touched her left ear.

'Very sad,' said Hermione. 'No children?'

'No.'

'Just Barney.'

'That's right.'

There was definite justification for Eileen's misgivings, and Hermione told her so when Sally Potter had left the scene. It was difficult, though, to imagine why so many lies had been manufactured. Unless she was 'casing the joint' for some criminal, there could be little reason for such behaviour. 'Carry on watching,' advised Hermione.

'I wasn't wrong, then?'

201

'No.'

'So that means you were wrong, while I was right?'

'I suppose so.'

Eileen made her jubilant exit. Sometimes, Mrs Clever-Clogs wasn't as bright as she made herself out to be. When it came to people, Eileen Eckersley was the expert. And woe betide anyone who did not agree with that.

Hermione sat in silence for over half an hour, an achievement that would have been termed miraculous by all who knew her. There were brown mottles on the lower parts of Sal Potter's legs. They advertised a woman who had no central heating, who sat a great deal, who rested too close to an open fire in the winters. The scars were pale at present, but would deepen in colour towards the end of the year. There was no cat. Barney had been a quick touch-of-the-ear job, though the cleaner did not live alone at the present time.

Hermione picked up her crossword, but could not concentrate. The failure to remember the activities of paramedics was another clue. She had not been married. Most widows continued to wear a wedding ring, but the lack of a ring had not been the main pointer. The date of death probably belonged to Sally Potter's father. Most liars needed some truth to which they might cling, so she had used the real date of her father's death. Why was she here? Why did she tell lies that seemed meaningless and nonessential? It would be relatively easy to find out if anyone named Potter had died on the date provided. Had she changed her surname? Probably not. No imagination, no mental energy in the poor creature.

Hermione stood and hobbled across to the other dormer. Harrie's house was almost completed. It was quite pretty, too. 'She made all the doorways wide enough for me,' whispered the old lady. 'That is a good girl. I'll miss her when she goes to university.'

'Talking to yourself again?'

Hermione did not turn. 'This way, I am sure of an intelligent audience,' she answered smartly. 'And your scones were drier than usual.'

Getting used to being in love took some doing, though it proved immensely enjoyable. Suddenly possessed of enormous energy, Harrie set herself the task of nest-building in her new home. It had to be right – absolutely right. With a flair for colour and style, and as owner of three magazines on the subject of beautiful homes, she considered herself to be adequately qualified. Also, there was an urgency in her, almost as if everything should have been done yesterday.

Perched on a ladder, she painted a wall in her sitting room. Milly, who seemed to have moved in already, lay in a peaceful heap in the doorway. Will was asleep. Harrie laughed quietly. *Vive la différence?* she asked herself. The fact was that a woman, after making love, could probably do a week's washing, tile a floor and varnish five doors. Men slept. Or was it just Will? She giggled again. The making love was probably harder work for a man. Also, women were programmed differently. Like all female animals, they treated sex like a beginning, not as an end in itself. It was about making babies. She shivered. *Not yet, please God.* Was she painting a bloody nursery?

He staggered in from the bedroom, each hand rubbing sleep from an eye.

'Is there a war on?' she asked.

Will sighed. 'Don't go all clever on me, Hat. Not at this time of day.'

'It's ten o'clock and it's Saturday.'

'And?'

'And we are going into town to see my mother.'

'Right.'

She climbed down from her perch. 'No more sex in the morning, love. It clearly causes the gradual death of your brain cells, while it turns me into a decorator. See?' She spun round. 'I have done one and a half walls while you snored. I'll invent some brunch. Make yourself at home. Pull up a crate and put a cloth on the tea chest. We are going to eat in style.'

He smiled, ran a hand through tousled hair, then did as he had been told. She was the most wonderful, beautiful, troublesome part of his life, and he adored her. But he had always felt like this about her, whereas she had taken a longer and more measured route into love. He refused to imagine life without her. And her family – apart from her father – consisted of people who were merely eccentric, he told himself repeatedly.

Today, they were going to buy the ring – at cost, of course. Harrie, ever the watchful business-woman, had no intention of paying retail. Connections were there to be used, she said. So romantic, his Hat. A bowl of cornflakes was set down in front of him. 'No bacon?' he asked.

'No bacon.'

'Eggs?'

'Eggs is orf, sir,' she replied smartly.

'Why?'

Harrie carried a box of candles to the makeshift table. 'Here, dangle your bacon over a couple of those – it'll cook in about a week. No gas, no electricity, no breakfast.'

'I forgot.'

'Quite.' She sat and grinned while he ate his cereal. 'Just think, by next week we shall have a table and some chairs. Oh – thank your mother for the bits of furniture; I like an eclectic mix. There's milk on your chin.'

'And paint in your hair. Touché.' He finished and pushed away the bowl. 'Who's going to look after Milly? Our house is empty today, and I can't leave her there because she ate Mum's kitchen lino last time.'

'Keep her here, then?'

He shook his head. 'No. She'll chew all your paintbrushes and overdose on apple-white emulsion.'

Thus it happened. Hermione Compton-Milne met her new best friend that Saturday morning. She'd never owned a dog, never wanted one, thought they were best leading the blind or sniffing for drugs. Until she met Milly.

She glared at Harrie when the dog appeared. 'What's that?'

'German shepherd,' said Will.

Hermione liked Will. He was a good, sensible chap and was, therefore, fit to be joined in wedlock to her only granddaughter. 'Have you brought the sheep as well, then? Because she'll need something to masticate.'

'Old shoes,' Harrie suggested. 'And chicken. She'll do anything for chicken.'

Before negotiations reached breaking point, Harrie dragged Will out of the room and slammed the door.

'Will she be all right?' Will asked.

'As long as she has no more falls.'

'I meant the dog.'

'I know.' Harrie squeezed his hand. 'Gran has never eaten a whole one. Although a very small Yorkshire terrier did go missing a few years ago, and Gran was discovered standing at the window licking her lips.'

It was his turn to pull her out of the house.

Upstairs, a stand-off between dog and lady-of-the-upper-chamber was taking place. Eileen had gone to the shops, so just the canine and the almost-octogenarian were in residence. The dog blinked. Hermione did the same. Milly scratched an ear; Hermione followed suit, though she could not use a lower limb for such purpose.

It happened when she tried to stand. The walker was just out of reach and, as she leaned over to grab it, Milly rushed to her side, providing a warm, strong wall against which the old woman could steady herself. The dog remained beside her, though not as closely, as she walked to the bathroom. Together, they entered the room, Milly standing on guard while Hermione performed her ablutions. For several seconds, they studied each other – and fell head-over-heels in love.

'You're a clever girl, aren't you?'

The animal woofed politely.

'And so beautiful. God, you really are so beautiful.' Hermione sniffed. How could a young, healthy dog make her cry? It was the eyes, she decided. They were dark, warm and so wonderfully intelligent. 'You've a better brain than Eileen, but, now that I consider the statement I just made, you could scarcely fail.'

Back in the sitting room, they waited for Eileen, Hermione in her chair, the dog stretched out near her feet. Hermione told her all about the family, about Lisa's trouble, about the forthcoming wedding. 'You'll be a lovely bridesmaid,' she said. 'But not in pink or peach. You would look ridiculous.'

Eileen, complaining vociferously about the cost of beef, entered the room and stopped in her tracks. 'Is that Milly?'

'It is, indeed. She's my chambermaid.'

'She's a what?'

'A member of staff. Feed her.'

Milly, who gave the impression of one who understood English perfectly, followed Eileen into the kitchen. After a few minutes, the dog emerged.

'What did you give her?' Hermione asked.

'The leftover chicken and at least two of my fingers.'

'Good.' Hermione closed her eyes. With the dog beside her and Eileen in the house, she was safer than ever before.

Harrie had never before met Annie, and she was pleased to find that her mother was working in pleasant company. Simon, the deputy manager, was sweet, effeminate, and a very good friend to his employer, but Annie was amazing.

She took charge of the situation right from the start, since both Lisa and Simon were busy with customers. 'Come through,' she said. 'See what we have. Though you could have got it from your own shop.'

Harrie shook her head. 'Roger and his wife are looking after the place. They tend to get overenthusiastic when doing something special. Anyway, I know every item of stock in there – I want a surprise.'

Annie chuckled and took a seat at the desk. She eyed Will critically. 'Yes, nice looking bloke, Harriet. Your mother said he was handsome. When's the wedding? Only, I've got a pouf at home and–'

'I'm the only poof we need.' Simon's head was poking through the doorway.

'Bog off,' ordered Annie. 'It's not a poof, it's a pouf.'

Simon pulled a face. 'Oh. Well, I suppose that's all right, then.'

Annie explained her pouf. 'The colour's buttered toast, but it has all shades of brown and blonde going through it. You use it like a scrunchie, only it's made of hair. Well, not hair, but better than hair. Or you can figure-of-eight it round a chopstick – that looks nice.'

'Useful, too,' added Will. 'If we have a Chinese restaurant reception.'

Harrie dug Will in the ribs. 'I'll deal with you later,' she threatened.

'Promises,' he mumbled.

Annie continued to wax about her pouf. 'All the brides have them. You can put rhinestones in – they look like real hair – or hang a veil underneath if you want to make a bun of it.'

Will scratched his head and said he had never eaten a bun with chopsticks, but he was willing to give it a go. In receipt of withering glances from both women, he kept his counsel.

'I'm not wearing a veil,' Harrie said.

'Oh. A Juliet cap, then?' asked Annie.

'No. A gas mask.'

Lisa walked in to gales of laughter. 'Is she at it again?' She pointed at her daughter. 'Behave yourself, Harriet. Simon's in charge out there. I'll show you the rings.'

Annie was still mopping her face after the gas mask statement. She looked at the tray in Lisa's hands, put her head on one side and pursed her lips. 'Lisa?'

'What?'

'Remember that little Ceylon sapphire? Two diamonds each side? Look at your daughter's eyes. And it's got an uneven number – remember? That book you gave me says an even number is unlucky and it should be a solitaire, or three, or five and so on?'

Lisa nodded.

'One Ceylon, four diamonds. That makes five. And just look at this girl's eyes. Perfect with those eyes, that sapphire.'

The owner of the shop sighed deeply. 'There's

been no dealing with Annie since she read that book. She's still trying to get her head round platinum – aren't you?'

Annie smiled. 'If they melted down all the platinum found so far on this planet, it wouldn't fill an average room. Isn't that something?' She opened a drawer and picked out a box. 'Here it is.'

Harrie tried it on, picked up a jeweller's glass and examined the ring. The sapphire, palest blue and beautifully cut, had a good, solid heart and excellent refraction. 'These diamonds are quite fine – probably from one parent stone. Mother?'

Lisa took the glass. 'Amsterdam's best,' she declared. 'Annie, you have a good eye.'

The little trainee jeweller looked as pleased as Punch when Harrie eventually decided to choose the Ceylon. At the same time, she shed a few tears because these two people were so beautiful, and it was the beginning for them. Annie prayed that there would be no ending like her own had been. But there was little danger of that. Will was an educated man. He wouldn't fit alarms and then go back on the rob.

Across the road, a figure lingered. In overalls and Sal's father's flat cap, he looked like a working man on his way to a job. When Annie, Lisa and the young couple came to the door of Milne's, he tried not to stare. But it was clear that the daughter had taken after Lisa in the looks department. She was a stunner.

In that moment, the seed of an idea took root in his head. It was a dangerous thought, ambitious and frightening. He would use it only if all else failed. If Sal failed, he corrected himself inwardly. He didn't know how much longer Sal would stay up at Weaver's Warp, because the stress was getting to her. So, if nothing else worked, there was a way. Drastic? Yes, it was. But living in the knowledge that any one of three females could take the gun and grass him up was just as terrifying. Needs must when the devil drove. And the devil was a fast mover.

Ben knew only too well that he would not recover overnight, as most of his problems seemed to have been rooted in childhood, but he was determined to win. The Internet now became a learning tool via which he intended to hasten matters. He was different from other people; every person on earth was an individual, and he had to learn to accept and love himself exactly as he was before stepping forward. 'I must forgive me,' he told the screen. 'And my parents. They, too, have been in the wrong.' His father was still in the wrong. His father hadn't bothered to attend the meeting so carefully arranged by Harrie. Even so, both parents must be forgiven. Anyway, the meeting had turned silly, and Father didn't do silly. Mother was making a real effort. She was even likeable, so that was a huge bonus.

The diary had to be filled in every day. He did that on the computer, printing it out in duplicate – one copy for himself, one for Alan Browne, his Manchester-based therapist. Every event had to be listed and, alongside each account, he had to write his feelings and how he had dealt with them and with the situation in hand. Behaviour modification was the flavour of the month, and he worked hard at it.

He came to realize early on that he had begun his own treatment when he had learned to drive and bought the van, when he had gone into the woods in order to get dirty. Ben knew that he was fortunate. His excellent brain provided him with all he needed, because he was able to study the true meaning of cognitive behavioural therapy and could understand all that had been written about it.

University would be postponed for twelve months. During that time, he would do as Harrie had done – he would sell jewellery, meet people, touch them, assist them. In order to help himself, he needed to inter-react. Already, he had one real friend, because Will Carpenter had turned out to be a brilliant listener. 'I suppose I am gaining a brother,' Ben had told Harrie. 'He's a good bloke, sis. Very bright, too.'

'Too bright to be teaching in a comp?' had been her question.

Ben had shaken his head. 'I was wrong. I am happy to be wrong.'

There was a long road ahead of him, but he would take those baby-steps, would keep his diary, would survive. His mantra came from Popeye, that cartoon character who depended so heavily on spinach. 'I am what I am,' Ben told himself repeatedly.

He was what he was. And there was a great deal of room for improvement.

Lisa did not forsake all her friends. There were

some she had known for years, and she introduced several to Annie, who found that she truly enjoyed the company of the older women. Most were in retail, one owning a couple of market stalls, another having her own dress shop, a third running a dance school. Annie's life was opening up, and she loved it, loved Lisa's humour. 'Alice named her shop Veronica's Haute Couture, though her pronunciation's nothing like the French,' Lisa told Annie. 'She sells frocks with posh labels. To folk who fancy themselves as haughty culture, which sounds a bit like gardening, eh? Most of them are weeds, so it suits. Size six? They look like bloody Barbie dolls, according to Alice.'

Antoine's became a favourite haunt of Lisa and Annie, who dined occasionally with others, though for the most part, they were alone. When Lisa's Botox and facelift companions came in, she was polite, though never effusive. Her life had changed. She was closer to her daughter, was trying to make a breakthrough with her hermit son.

Annie had entered Lisa's life like a bright torch in the dark, and the older woman found it amusing when she noticed her bridge pals whispering behind menus in the restaurant. They would be commenting, no doubt, on the 'mistake' Annie had made on her first encounter with Lisa. 'They remember you ripping my hair out,' she whispered one lunchtime.

'Aye, I've got a good grip for a little 'un, eh?'

'You have indeed.'

Annie's fork clattered into her dish. 'Lisa?'

213

'What?'

'Don't look now, but see that bloke across the way?'

'How can I see if I don't look now?'

'You can be very annoying,' said Annie.

Lisa looked. 'Yes, that's him.'

'Buggeration,' cursed the small woman. 'He went to see his mam one night last week. We thought he'd gone away after that, but–'

Lisa stood up.

'No,' begged Annie. 'Don't go, don't–'

But Lisa was already out of the restaurant. She dashed across the road and collared him outside the bookmaker's. 'What do you want?' she asked.

He felt his cheeks burning. How had she found him? He was a long way from her shop, was just thinking of backing an outsider, had been doing no harm to anyone. 'It's a free country,' he snapped.

'Not for you, it isn't.'

'Is that a threat?'

Lisa swallowed. She had never before noticed that he had evil eyes. Or perhaps they hadn't been evil before he'd been pushed too far. 'It's a promise, Jimmy.'

He grabbed her arm. 'I need the gun. Nobody will believe it wasn't me, because the ones who did the shooting have all pissed off to God knows where. Get me that gun, Lisa, and I'll leave the north right away.'

She didn't believe him. 'You know what we want,' she stated coldly. 'Annie will feel safer with you out of the way. If you don't go, if you don't leave everyone alone, she'll have you dealt with.

As for me – well – if my name gets dragged into it, I'll survive. That gun is Annie's insurance. She doesn't want you near her children.'

'There are other ways,' he whispered menacingly.

'One foot wrong and you are inside,' she replied icily before crossing the road.

He watched her, saw her sitting down at a table near the window. Annie was with her. A couple of other women stopped to pass the time of day with Lisa. He recognized one of them from a stall in the market. Annie was staring right at him. She was clearly becoming one of the in-crowd, one of the ladies who lunched, the high and flaming mighty.

Jimmy Nuttall walked away. He was in danger, and he knew it. No matter what he said if he were arrested, the cops would send him down for the Birmingham job. Well, if he was going to jail, he'd make sure he went for something he had bloody well done.

It was time to get his thinking cap on. It was possibly time to ditch Sal, or to force her into a higher gear.

Eight

He woke in a sweat again, gasping for breath, head aching as soon as he switched on his bedside lamp. Alan Browne had helped him greatly, but Ben still had the nightmare at least once a week. The hanged man had probably saved Ben's sanity, because the enormity of the event had shaken him to the core. *It could have been me if I had carried on among those people*, he thought. Theirs was a special madness, but it was addictive, contagious, supremely dangerous. How many more would die or go insane through loneliness? Because isolation was the factor that drove men and women of all ages to seek contact via computer. He had to get out and mix, had to take hold of life and shake it.

It had been stated by several people over the years that the most successful kind of policeman was one with a criminal mind, that the best gamekeeper was an experienced poacher. Ben would turn gamekeeper. Whatever it entailed, wherever he must go to achieve his aim, he was determined to become an Internet spook. Dangerous sites needed to be closed; people who collected certain data via the web had to be jailed. There was too much power out there in the ether, too little control. So many kids sat in bedrooms at night, eyes glazed from staring constantly at screens, innocence stolen by predatory monsters. It would be a terrible job, a needle-in-a-haystack task, but Ben wanted it and intended to get it. What must a person study to achieve such an aim? Criminology, psychology – both?

But first, he had to deal with himself. It was three o'clock in the morning, and he was wide awake, thanks to that recurring dream. Both Mother and Harrie knew that he intended to go off somewhere in his van, so why not now? For too long, Ben had been guilty of over-planning; he had depended on rigid control of his environment, and everything had been done on his terms. It was time to begin making sudden decisions, even if the decision to make such decisions originated in his desire to be in charge.

He laughed out loud. 'That thought was Irish enough for Woebee,' he said to himself. Better to get on with living than to sit here wondering about his own sanity. Judged compos mentis by two experts, he now had to modify his behaviour. Easy? Probably not, but it would be done.

He threw belongings into a bag, had a shower, dressed. At half past three, he was making his way downstairs, map in one hand, luggage in the other. When he reached the hall, he stopped suddenly. There was someone skulking in a doorway.

'Benjamin?'

Oh, bugger. It was Father. 'Yes?'

'Where are you going?'

Ben bit his lower lip. 'Exams are over. Thought I'd go away for a few days. Are you still working at this hour?'

'Yes. Any idea where you are heading?'

'No. It doesn't particularly matter. Thirty years ago, I suppose I might have said that I am going

218

to find myself. Wasn't that the way with your generation, all flower power and self-discovery?'

Gus stared at the floor for a few seconds. Then he raised his head. 'And in the long-term?'

It was Ben's turn to ponder. 'After taking a year out – I'll help Mother and Harrie in the shops – I am going to attack disease. You've always said that it wouldn't be a hydrogen or neutron bomb that would finish the human race. You told me it would be the little people.'

Gus half-smiled. 'Microbes, yes. I am still convinced of it. Just by the way we all live, mankind has created its own means of self-destruction. The bacteria and viruses get stronger; we grow weaker by the day. Our immune systems are showing signs of flat-lining.'

Ben sat on the stairs. 'The diseases I want to attack also end in death. I saw a man die – I believe I told you that in temper. The Internet is a great carrier of germs. But they don't show on a slide, Father. I want to become a back-room boy for the police.' He waited for the onslaught. The problem with Father's responses was that they were quiet, infrequent, reasonable and potentially fatal. The man could kill an idea with a whisper, so Ben prepared himself for the inevitable. But it didn't happen.

Gus, hands deep in pockets, head bowed in thought, was nodding. 'Too much time alone, boy. You are more like me than you can ever know.' He raised his head and looked straight into his son's eyes. 'Take life by the throat and live it. I know how you have been. I ... I am not good with people. Someone ought to have helped you. I am not ... not in the slightest way gregarious.'

'I know.'

'That's why I stopped being a doctor of medicine.'

'Yes.'

Gus took a few steps forward and placed a hand on the shoulder of his son. 'If you have a calling, follow it. Be glad every morning when you wake, and do your best with that day. I really should have tried harder for you. There has been a reason. Not a good enough one, but nevertheless, a reason for the way I have been. Excuse is, perhaps, the better term for it.'

Ben thought the shock would steal his breath away, but it didn't.

'Take care of your mother and your sister. Harriet is to marry William Carpenter, I believe.'

'Yes.' Would he ever say more than 'yes'?

'I am not a bad man, Benjamin. I have been careless and too engrossed in my work. Don't spend all your time at a computer. The world may be diseased, but it remains worthy of your attention. Lose the fear.'

For at least five minutes after Gus had wandered off, his son remained on the stairs. What had all that been about? Was Father going away? Was he leaving Mother at last? 'Look after your mother and your sister'? Life in the middle lane was interesting, to say the least of it.

Halfway between the existence he had known and the world he was about to discover, Ben still feared the fast lane. Well, he would drive along it today in reality, if not yet metaphorically. On the M62, he would learn to overtake at speed.

Harrie polished off the rest of the liquorice allsorts.

Across the desk, an amused Miriam Goldberg watched a happy, almost carefree young woman who had burst from her shell completely in recent weeks. Harrie was in love. Her brother, too, was showing clear signs of climbing out of the deep pit into which he had fallen. 'How's your mother?'

'Fine. She's given up collagen and men. For now. But you never can tell with Mother. My father isn't exactly communicative, and she needs company. We talk now – the three of us.'

'You, Ben and Lisa?'

Harrie nodded. 'It's hilarious. The first time was the best, because my mother had to get herself completely plastered before facing the two of us. Father didn't come.'

'Shame.'

'Yup.' Harrie eyed her mentor. 'Do you think we're a crazy family, then?'

The psychologist laughed. 'Show me a completely sane family – if you can find one. That's a beautiful ring, by the way.'

Harrie breathed on it, then polished it with a tissue. 'You'd like Will – he's the real gem. But there is a situation, and he is not best pleased.'

'Oh?'

'His dog has divorced him.' Harrie went on to tell the tale of Hermione and Milly. As soon as any outer door to Weaver's Warp was left ajar, Milly was through it like a bullet. She would shoot upstairs, stand on her hind legs and open Hermione's door with her teeth. 'She adores my

221

grandmother and the feeling is reciprocated. Will is heartbroken.'

'Is your gran a lover of dogs?'

'No. Just Milly. We manage to get her out for a walk – Milly, I mean, but she is only truly contented when helping Gran. The help is not always helpful, if you get my drift. Milly decides what Gran wants to do, then arranges Gran's life accordingly. It's very amusing.'

Miriam leaned back in her chair.

'I have to sack you today,' Harrie said.

'Oh?'

Harrie smiled. 'I think I'm cured, Doctor.'

After saying goodbye to a woman who had helped without seeming to do a great deal, Harrie stood on the steps outside and looked across Bolton. It was a splendid view, marred, perhaps, by the blue fug of busyness that hung over the centre of a town easily large enough to be a city. She looked at the beautiful clock, at Trinity Church, at the school she had attended for seven years.

Then she looked right. Her father was making his way up the steep steps leading to a house further down the terrace. His lady friend and his trains were in there, then. On a sudden whim, she called to him.

Gus stopped, turned and waved to her, then disappeared into the house.

Harrie grinned to herself. He might have custard and gravy on his tie or shirt when he got home, but at least he could play with his trains. She hoped he was happy. It was important that everyone should be happy, because she was not the only person deserving of joy.

Back in her shop, she advised Roger that she had dismissed her head doctor.

'Good,' he replied smartly. 'Both Claire and I knew–' He broke off, peering through the window. 'There's a bloke out there. He keeps walking past – are we going to be burgled?'

'Where?' Harrie tried to look outside, but Roger was in her way.

'He's gone.'

'Well, that's all right, then. We can scarcely be burgled by a man who isn't there.'

'He could have been casing the joint, though.' Roger opened the door, stepped outside, and returned immediately. 'No sign.'

Claire, Roger's wife, came through from the back. 'It's been nothing but watch batteries all morning,' she complained. 'Can I go home now?'

'Yes,' answered Harrie. It suddenly occurred to her that Mother's ex-chap was something of a criminal. 'We did get the safe and alarms changed, didn't we?'

'Oh, yes,' replied Claire as she struggled into her lightweight summer coat. 'We're all up to date, Harrie. Anyone who breaks in here will get his eardrums burst. We've a real screamer inside now.'

Harrie made tea and sat in the office. Annie Nuttall's husband was not to be trusted. He had installed alarms, then had burgled the houses months later. Mother thought the police were after him. And there was something about Birmingham a few years earlier, a job that had gone disastrously wrong. 'I should bring Milly to work,' she said to Roger.

'From the sound of it, that would take surgery,' he answered. 'Is she still fastened to your grandmother?'

'With superglue, yes.'

There were few customers that afternoon. Harrie engaged in polishing and cleaning while Roger, who was still on pins, kept watch at the window. He didn't see the man again, but he still felt uneasy when he and Harrie left the shop, shutters down, valuables in the safe, alarms on, everything bolted.

'Stop worrying,' Harrie advised. 'You'll be old before your time.'

She drove home, her mind filled with plans for her new little house. It wasn't too little, she reminded herself. There was a second bedroom in case Gran wanted a change of viewpoint, and all doors had been widened to make room for a wheelchair.

She noticed, however, that every time she looked in her rearview mirror the same van was there. When she reached the ring road, she stopped near a row of shops, outside which people walked and chattered. The van drove off, and she immediately forgot about it. It was a mere coincidence. Roger had made her nervous, and she would deal with him tomorrow.

At home, she found a note from Ben. He had run away with the gypsies, apparently. She laughed at her absent brother, then ran upstairs to separate dog from old lady. Milly needed exercise, and it was Harrie's turn to take the miscreant out.

Jimmy was fast reaching the point of no return with Sal.

Satellite TV had been a mistake. Sal would come home from work, throw off her coat and shoes, switch on and watch all evening. She watched anything and everything, and he was fed up with it. 'When are you going to clean up?' he asked repeatedly.

She would look at him, sniff, and ask him the same question. 'I'm at work all day and looking for your bloody gun – what the hell do you expect? Can't you do something while I'm out? I'm too tired.'

He always had an excuse, of course. He had installed an alarm, gone to mend a faulty one, had helped a friend with some decorating. 'Can't we have a decent meal for once?' he asked, looking down at his microwaved Sainsbury's 'Peppered Beef with Vegetables'.

'If you want to cook, feel free,' she answered. She found it amazing how she had stopped loving him. All her life, since her mid-teens, she had been head-over-heels with Jimmy Nuttall. He made her laugh, caused her to feel special, stopped the loneliness. But now she wanted him gone.

He knelt on the floor beside her. For a silly moment, she imagined that he was about to propose, but that would be impossible because he was still legally married. 'What now?' she asked.

'Didn't you say the prof was going to New Zealand?'

'Yes.'

'Then you can search his office. That's the only place you haven't tried.'

Sal closed her eyes. 'You've no idea, have you? I was told to give it a miss unless he asked for something to be done. There's stuff to the ceiling in places. Some of it's been there that long, the bottom layers have gone all yellow.'

'Then don't touch anything that's gone yellow, because yellow means it hasn't been disturbed in years.' Didn't she have any sense at all? If an item had been hidden in that office, whatever hid it must have been moved.

Sal was getting annoyed now. 'Look, Jimmy. I am reaching the end of my rope here. I clean, I cook, I end up in daft places for your sake, and that Irishwoman keeps catching me at it. She's sly, tiptoes around in brothel-creeper shoes. They know I'm up to something. And I think they know that I know they know.'

Jimmy blinked just once. 'So? They can't prove anything except you're good at your job, eh?'

'I've had enough,' she said. 'I've had more than e-bloodynough, if I'm honest. I want me other jobs back. I was all right till you came.'

His eyes narrowed. 'All right? All right? You still had your father's teeth in a glass over there, and all his pills lined up. The place was a midden, and you know it. It's getting that way again – is this the thanks I get for buying you new furniture and a big telly?'

Sal scraped the last bit of gravy from the bottom of her plastic dish. 'If you want staff, you'd best hire them, Jimmy Nuttall, because I am not fettling all day up yon, then coming back here to wait hand and foot on you.'

He returned to his chair and sat. 'Just leave the office window slightly open,' he said. 'If it's alarmed, I'll just have to jump out quick.'

'And if they catch you?'

He scarcely heard her. The fact was that he felt as if he might be losing his grip altogether. If the gun reached the police, if Annie spoke up, he was done for. He would go to jail for something he had not done. It would be a long sentence, far longer than the punishment for housebreaking and burglary. If he got the gun back, he could be relatively safe. If he got caught trying to get the gun, Annie and the rest might well breathe a sigh of relief and leave him to serve the shorter sentence for the burglary of Weaver's Warp. But, with him captured and removed, they would still have the weapon. After he had done his time, he would continue in this mess.

The police were looking for him – or so the coven of witches had said. Already a hunted man, he needed to ensure that any prison time would be kept to a minimum. He was sick of all this turning in his mind all the time, felt as if his brain would burst if something didn't happen soon.

The old woman had ordered him to keep her family out of it. She was the one with all the power. If that gun showed its barrel, he would drag Lisa through the mud, would try to make her an accomplice, at least, in the alarm crimes. But Birmingham? He could not think past Birmingham. And Lisa Compton-Milne was res-pected: Chamber of Commerce, Association of

Bolton Traders, all that kind of stuff. Who would take his word against hers? He'd been in trouble off and on all his life, so...

'Jimmy?'

'What?'

'I'll leave that window a bit open if I can. After he's gone to New Zealand, like. Because I've heard the girl talking to her mam about the prof working in the night. He's like Maggie Thatcher – needs no sleep.'

'Aye, and she brought the country to its knees, didn't she? Businesses closing, folk losing their houses just so she could try and keep the bloody pound clean.' Sal was staring at him. 'What?' he asked.

'Are you in a bad mood?'

Was he in a bad mood? Where had Sal been for the last few weeks? He was always in a bad mood.

'I liked Mrs Thatcher,' Sal said. 'She was the best man in England at the time. We'll not see the likes of her in a hurry.'

Jimmy made no reply. He had seen her double only too recently. The name was Mrs Hermione Compton-Milne...

Sister Mary Magdalene began yet another decade of rosary. Mathilda was breathing on her own. This had happened before on several occasions, but this time she was having no trouble at all. Machines measured, clicked and beeped, all recording that the patient was maintaining a decent level of oxygen and a good heart rhythm.

Although she considered herself fully prepared for further developments, Magda almost fell off her chair when the finger moved. It was happening. The good Lord had answered all the prayers, and the princess in the tower was showing signs of mobility. Magda pressed a bell. After a minute or so, Mother Benedict put in an appearance. 'Yes?' she asked, breathless after dashing up the stairs.

'She moved the index finger of the right hand.'

'Are you sure?'

Magda nodded. 'Praise God,' she mumbled.

Mother Benedict did not quite share in Magda's joy. This had been a coma of great length and, when Mathilda had been a child, waking had meant sedation because of the fits. Many times, the sedation had been reduced and the patient had breathed unaided, but she always reverted to type: fitting, failing to breathe, coming very close to death.

'She's going to be all right, isn't she, Mother?' Magda asked.

Mother Benedict had no idea. This young girl had never walked, never spoken, had not responded to any stimulus. Could she hear the music that was played for her each day? Did she listen when someone read aloud to her? 'I don't know, Magda. Before you joined the order, we hoped on many occasions that she was going to recover. But there has to be something wrong with her wiring, or she would have woken properly a long time ago.'

'Where there's life, there's hope. Is that not right, Mother?'

The head of the convent agreed with a nod of her head. 'But we have all questioned our consciences on this matter, have we not?'

'Yes, I suppose so.'

'As Catholics, we are bred to believe in life at any price. But I have looked at this injured child of ours and I have wondered. What sort of life is this? Should we be keeping her alive with machinery? Would it not have been kinder to let her go when her breathing deteriorated?'

'Then you question the very core of our faith, Mother. And yes, I have done the same. There – see? The finger moved again.'

'Yes, I saw. But I won't contact her visitor. There is no point in raising hopes needlessly. It's far too cruel.' Mother leaned over the bed and kissed the pale forehead on its paler pillow. There was something so unbearably sad about Mathilda. She lingered somewhere between life and death, never truly living, never completely escaping the bonds of human flesh. 'Let me know if anything further develops, Magda.'

'Of course, Mother.'

The finger did not move again during Magda's shift. There was no flicker of an eyelid, no motion at all save for the steady movement of the girl's ribcage as she took in and expelled air. If she could do that, if she could move a finger and remember to breathe, surely there must be a chance of recovery?

The nun continued to count her beads until relief arrived and she was free to return to her depleted convent. She went reluctantly because she wanted to be there when Mathilda woke, wanted to share the adventure. Would she understand words, would she recognize Vivaldi,

Beethoven, Chopin?

Magda descended the stairs, finding herself wondering what would become of Mathilda when all the sisters were gone. There were no novices, no postulants, no young women willing to dedicate their lives to the service of man in the name of God. The world was changing, depreciating; mankind became more selfish with each passing year.

But there were carrots to peel, paying guests to feed. Worries had to be postponed for now. Yet Mary Magdalene's unease plagued her for the rest of the day. She would not be satisfied until she saw Mathilda again.

Annie was exhausted.

She had just got the twins bedded down, had acted as referee in a row about a computer game, and was ready to settle down with her jewellery books. Working with precious stones and metals was delicious. She loved the feel of gold and silver, the sight of a good, well-cut diamond with its deep, rich heart. Wearing a suit at work was great, too. In her previous job, it had been a sweaty nylon overall; even a bucketful of Chanel Number Five could never have eradicated the stench of cooking fat and vinegar. Now, all dressed up and somewhere to go, she was pleased when a customer asked a question, delighted when she was able to answer sensibly, but did not mind if she had to refer to Lisa or Simon.

She grinned. Simon was a card. During tea breaks, he would regale her with tales of Canal Street in Manchester, the wonderful restaurants,

231

the outrageous karaoke, the gays' molls who came along just for the fun of it all. 'Come and be my moll,' he would beg repeatedly. 'I can show a girl a good time, sweet. And my Derek would love you.' Except that Simon didn't say 'love'. He allowed the word to reach out far beyond its natural life, so that it became 'lo-o-o-ove'. He was a scream.

Annie grabbed her mug of Nescafé and placed it on a side table at the end of the sofa. Tonight, she intended to find out why a red sapphire was not a ruby, since both stones were basically corundum. She flicked through a few pages, went back to the index, sighed when World War Three broke out again upstairs. 'If you two don't shut up, there'll be no spending money come Friday,' she yelled from the bottom of the stairs.

Someone giggled, but silence ensued.

Annie turned to find herself staring into the familiar eyes of her departed husband. Except, he looked different. There was a wildness about him, a desperation that made her feel almost sorry for him. Almost, but not quite. 'What do you want?' she asked. 'You're supposed to stay away, because you upset Lisa something shocking with all your lies and your stealing. She thought you were going to give her the world, and all you gave her was trouble.'

He bared his teeth in a nasty, mirthless grin. 'Then she should have kept herself to herself, eh? She's a married woman, just as much to blame as I was.'

She led him away from the stairs because she did not want Billy and Craig to find out that their dad was here. They needed precious little excuse to spend more time downstairs, and she had taken her fill of their messing about for one night. 'Get in there and keep your voice down,' she whispered.

In the living room, he settled into his usual chair. 'Anything to eat?' he asked.

Annie laughed, though the sound was muted and hollow. 'It takes me all my time to feed the three kids. No. The chippy's open – go and get something.'

He looked her up and down. 'So. You've gone from dishing out mushy peas to flogging diamonds and pearls. How did you manage that? After all, you and madam should be sworn enemies.'

'Don't talk so wet,' she answered. 'You're not worth fighting over. We got on right from day one, me and Lisa–'

'Once you'd taken her hair off your hands and scraped her skin from under your fingernails.' He leaned forward. 'I want to come home when this is all sorted out,' he pleaded.

Annie's eyebrows shot upward. 'You what? You're going to jail, Jimmy Nuttall. All those houses burgled after you fitted the alarms – you're history, mate. Now go before I call the cops myself.'

He bared his teeth again. 'You won't do that, Annie. You don't want to be the one who put the kids' dad away, do you? Oh and by the way – go near the phone and I'll break your bloody neck.'

A short silence followed the threat. It was his eyes that betrayed him. They couldn't keep still.

He blinked a lot, while his gaze darted about like a wasp in a fury at the end of summer. She suddenly realized that she was frightened. If he didn't hurt her now, he could get her any time he chose. Worse than that, he could get her children. There was little point in reasoning with him. He was clearly past the point of sensible discussion. To her untrained eye, he looked as if he might be on the verge of lunacy. 'Why are you here?' she asked eventually. 'I thought you were long gone.'

He made no reply.

'Jimmy?'

'What?' He jumped, was startled as if he had been woken from deep sleep.

'I asked why you came here.'

He shrugged, but his shoulders remained rigid and tense. 'To get some more clothes and to ask you about that gun.'

Only the ticking of an old clock filled the next few seconds.

'Well?' he said.

'I haven't got it.'

'Then who has?' He stood up, crossed the room and grabbed her hair, lifting her out of her seat. 'Tell me,' he snarled.

She refused to scream. The lads would be down faster than sugar off a shiny shovel if she yelled. The pain was intense. She could feel strands of hair ripping out at the roots. 'Let me go,' she sobbed.

But Jimmy was in a world of his own, a place where reason did not dwell, where fear roamed like a large, black bear in the dead of night. It was fear that made him angry, made him hit her with the flat of his hand, then with his fist. He was beating her, his mother, Lisa and that old double-barrelled woman who probably had the gun. He was lashing out at Sal, too, because she was a lazy slob and she had taken his money for furniture and–

He stopped as suddenly as he had started. Where the hell had that come from? The idea had been to ask about the gun, to get some clothes, to plead and beg for help. Annie was his place of safety, his wife, mother to his kids. 'Oh, God,' he groaned. He had taken a chance by coming here, but he had blown that chance by losing his rag.

She dropped to the floor like a stone. But there was no blood in a stone, was there? The beige rug was stained, and a dark pool pouring from her head was spreading. 'Annie? Annie, love?'

She moaned, then lay very still.

Jimmy stood over her, felt the pain in his right hand, knew that he had hurt her badly. 'I didn't mean it,' he said, tears choking the words as they emerged. What must he do now? He needed an ambulance, but he would be arrested. The children might come down in the morning and find their mother dead on the floor. She could be dead already. He knelt, took her wrist, found a pulse.

He had no idea where to start. People died from head injuries; he could have killed her – or worse. She might be brain damaged. If he went to jail and Annie went crazy, what would happen to Billy and Craig and Daisy? He swallowed hard. A cloth. He needed a cloth to wipe her head so that he might see the extent of the damage he had done. But would he see? If there were injuries inside her head...

Minutes ticked by, each beat of time marking his lack of courage, his inability to make a decision, every second emphasizing the cowardice that prevented him from picking up the phone. Not the house phone. No, he wouldn't call from here because a 999 call was always traceable. He would definitely go down for this. Unless she died or woke up too puddled to remember, he would be imprisoned for this attack. Why the hell had he lost control so suddenly? It was living with Sal, he decided. Living with Sal and not being able to find the Birmingham gun. But this was his wife.

Overcome more by self-pity than by sorrow for Annie, he wept for a while. She still wasn't moving. The bleeding had slowed. He couldn't leave her here, dared not move her, didn't know where to take her. She was so still. Were it not for the blood, she might have been asleep, lips slightly parted, breathing even. That was a good sign, surely? He had to go, had to abandon her.

Jimmy left the house, closing the door quietly behind him. He jumped into the van, found that his legs were shaking so badly that he kangaroo-ed his way up the road. Phone box. He needed to find a phone. When he eventually called for an ambulance, he used a scarf in case he left prints, because the cops would be round this place like flies once the call had been traced. He spoke through the scarf, gave the address, said he had heard screaming and banging, thought someone had been attacked.

The operator asked for his name. 'Just a neighbour,' he replied. 'I don't want to get involved.' The second part was true, anyway. He couldn't afford to be associated with what had happened tonight. She would tell them. Once she woke, she would grass on him. Annie must not die, must not be brain damaged. But he would be punished – it was only a matter of time.

He drove very quickly away from the phone box, taking a chance by breaking speed limits. 'Get away,' he kept muttering under his breath. 'Get as far as you can and as quick as you can.'

Back at Sal's, he remained outside for a while. He could hear the television through the walls. She was watching Challenge TV, he decided, probably reruns of *Family Fortunes*. He had lost his family tonight, and he'd never had much of a fortune. No matter what happened from now, he was on his own. Except for Sal.

The phone woke Lisa at just before three in the morning.

She groaned, peeled off her eye-mask and grabbed the offending item from its cradle. 'Hello?'

It was the police. Mrs Anne Nuttall was in hospital after being discovered injured in her home. They had found Lisa's number in her address book. 'She came round long enough to tell the nurses not to phone her mother yet. Seems her mother's got angina, so we have to let the old lady sleep till morning. Mrs Nuttall kept telling the hospital staff to phone you, madam. The children are in the house with two constables.'

237

By now, Lisa was bolt upright and wide-eyed.

'She wants you to take the children, Mrs Compton-Milne. We don't know where their father is, so they should really go into care for the time being. You are Mrs Nuttall's employer?'

'Yes.' Lisa swallowed. She was hopeless with children. She'd been hopeless even with her own. But that didn't matter, not now, as this was clearly an emergency. 'How's Annie? What happened to her?

The policeman sighed heavily. 'She's been beaten about the face.'

Lisa, brought to her full senses by the shocking news, was suddenly furious. Annie? Poor little Annie who loved jewellery, worked damned hard and would help just about anyone if she could? 'Is she very ill?'

'Sorry, but you'd have to ask the hospital. As far as we know, she's still in theatre.'

Lisa leapt from her bed and pulled on a pair of jeans. She dragged off the nightdress over her head, found a sweater and rushed to the door. Keys. Car keys, house keys. She ran back, grabbed what she needed and dashed down the stairs. It had to be him. Should she phone the hospital now? No, no, Annie wanted her to get to the twins and Daisy, so that was exactly what she would do.

Lisa remembered nothing about the journey. When she reached Annie's terraced cottage, she was greeted by two members of the force, one male, one female. She was led through the narrow hail into the rear kitchen, since the living room was cordoned off as the scene of the crime.

Two ashen-faced boys sat at the table. The little girl was asleep on a small, two-seater sofa. 'God,' breathed Lisa. She looked over her shoulder and saw white-suited SOCOs padding about, shoes covered in fabric.

'Will Mam die?' asked the nearest boy.

Lisa gave him a weak smile. 'I shouldn't think so. I need her back at the shop as soon as possible, so she'd better buck up. Can they go upstairs for clothes and toys?' she asked the policewoman.

The woman constable nodded. 'I'll go with them. You stay with the little girl.'

Lisa, near to tears, sat at the kitchen table. This was very much Annie's house: vibrant curtains, children's paintings framed on the walls, coloured fairy lights surrounding the fireplace. In a glass-fronted cupboard, Annie's collection of dishes was displayed, a wonderful mixture of reds, oranges, greens and blues. She was a treasure, and she was in an operating theatre.

Oh, God. Jimmy had done this. It had to be him. The male constable came in and asked quietly, 'Have you any idea who did this to her, Mrs Compton-Milne?'

Lisa shook her head. She had to talk to Annie first. If Annie accused him that would be all well and good, but Lisa didn't want to make things any more difficult than they already were. Anyway, it could have been a burglary. She looked round the kitchen, saw little worth taking. 'Why would anybody do this?' she asked, almost of herself. Then she spoke to the PC. 'She's just a mum trying to bring up a family as best she can. This is a good woman, officer.'

He patted her shoulder. 'That's usually the case, Mrs Compton-Milne. Now, can you look after these kids until tomorrow? Then we'll decide what's to be done with them.'

She glared at him. 'What's to be done is that they will live with me, Constable. I have a grown-up daughter, an excellent housekeeper, plus cleaning staff. Milne's Jewellery has adequate cover. If Annie wants me to care for her children, then I shall.'

A police car followed Lisa home. Officers placed the twins and Daisy in their newly-allocated beds, and the female stayed with them while Lisa woke Harrie. Everything had to be explained all over again, and, by the time Harrie was in possession of all the facts, Lisa was flagging.

The police left. Harrie and her mother sat at the kitchen table. 'Cocoa?' Harrie asked.

'No, thanks. Anyway, your gran pinched the last of it – I don't know whether Eileen replaced it.'

'She did.' It was difficult to find words, but Harrie tried. 'Mum, she'll be all right.'

Lisa ran a hand through hair that had seen better condition. 'Phone the hospital, please. Tell them who you are and that we have the twins and Daisy. They should be able to tell you something.'

Harrie was gone for what felt like hours. She could have carried the handset into the kitchen, but she didn't. Beginning to fear the worst, Lisa lowered her head and wept.

'Mother?'

It was the full title; it wasn't Mum – it was

240

Mother. 'Yes?'

'In intensive care, but stable. They had to let some blood out of her head. She woke up once and cursed them, or so the ward sister said.'

Lisa smiled weakly. 'That's our Annie,' she wept. 'She'll have told them to eff off and leave her alone.'

'We'll manage,' promised Harrie.

Lisa dried her tears. 'We will. Get me a vodka, love. Double. Just a splash of orange.'

'OK.' Harrie stood up. 'Dutch courage?'

Lisa almost laughed. 'Daughter of mine, you have not had the pleasure of Craig and Billy, have you? Neither have I. But according to their mother, who does own a tendency towards exaggeration, those twins are little devils. She was thinking of shaving their heads to look for the three sixes.'

'Eighteen?'

Lisa shook her head. 'No. Much worse – thirty-six. Even poor old Gregory Peck never had to deal with so high a score.'

Harrie fetched the vodka. It looked as if life might be about to become interesting, so she poured a dose for herself.

Hermione woke to find a large, long-haired Alsatian staring at her. 'What big eyes you have, Mr Wolf,' she declared.

Milly was not impressed. She had already been chased half a dozen times round the copse by a couple of smaller humans. They carried less weight than adults, but they could certainly move. Sorely offended by this intrusion into her highly

241

organized life, the young bitch was more than slightly put out by the recent turn of events. 'Woof,' she said.

'I know how you feel,' replied Hermione. 'I feel a bit woof myself – mornings are not easy, you know. MS creeps up on a person during the night and–'

'Glory be to God, the Martians have landed.'

Hermione closed her eyes. She now had both carers in attendance, and the human variety was the louder of the pair. 'What now?'

'Creatures with green heads,' Eileen continued. 'Running all over the place, they are. I didn't know whether to go for the hills or for the Dublin ferry – it's a nightmare out there.'

'Help me sit up,' ordered the boss. 'They'll be from the estate.' Hermione had a habit of blaming everything in the vicinity on the short-sightedness of planners, and this clearly included intruders from other planets. 'Visitors from outer space are the last thing we need round here, Eileen. We've enough with this German shepherdess.'

'Hello?'

Two green faces attached to boys in pyjamas appeared in the doorway.

'Well, we now have a quorum,' said the woman in the bed. 'Who the dickens are you?'

They replied in unison. It appeared that they were a Billy and a Craig and they wanted to know how the stairlifts worked.

Eileen grabbed the boys by the scruffs of their necks. 'Where are you from?' she asked. 'And what on God's good earth are you doing here half

242

naked with green faces? Where's your mother?'

'In hospital,' replied the one to Eileen's left. 'And if you rip these pyjamas, she'll kill you. She'll be in a bad mood, anyway, because of the Black & Decker. We got brought here by the police.'

Hermione eyed them up and down. 'Eileen?'

'Yes?'

'Did I miss something in the night? Has Weaver's Warp been taken over by the government as an annexe? I know the prisons are full, but this is ridiculous. They should have taken them to Strangeways or Walton – they must have a spare broom cupboard. Or there's that supposedly secret place in America where they store aliens.'

Eileen dragged the miscreants to the bed. Milly, no longer keen on small boys, went to sit under the window.

'Is that your dog?' one asked. He removed his mask, then pulled off his brother's facial armour. 'We're from Bury Road, not space,' he said with the intention of clearing up one small matter. 'Is it yours?' he asked again.

'No,' replied Hermione with exaggerated patience. 'She is not my dog. I am her victim.'

The boys glanced at each other. 'Why have you got a wheelchair?'

'Because I am a cripple.'

'Why?'

'Because I have MS.'

'What's MS?' The last question was delivered in stereo.

'Murder schoolboys,' she replied quickly.

The twins were immediately riveted. They

wanted to know how many she'd killed, the manner in which she had dispatched them, and where the bodies were buried. She answered their questions. 'Too many to count, a variety of methods, and they were cremated by my Irish friend here.'

The boys looked at each other in wonderment. What a find the old lady was. She was lying, of course, but she was a sight more amusing than school teachers and playmates. They asked did she watch *Doctor Who*, what she thought of *Star Trek*, and had she had any operations, because some doctor had drilled a hole in their mother's head with a Black & Decker to let the bad out and make her well.

The old lady glanced quizzically at Eileen, then said she liked Dr Who's scarf and she was in charge of training Daleks for the BBC. Star Trek she judged to be rubbish and how did they know it was a Black & Decker.

'Lisa said,' they chorused. Craig continued. 'Mam bled in her head and the blood had no-where to go, so they made a hole with a drill and got rid of the blood. They could have left it. She's already got holes.'

It was Billy's turn to pick up the baton. 'There're two eyes, two ears, one mouth and two holes in your nose. The blood could have come out and no need for Black & Decker.'

'Lisa told you about the drill?'

'And Harrie,' Billy said. He was the taller of this pair of promising delinquents. 'Harrie said they use ordinary tools because these things happen all the time.'

244

'Said it to make us feel better,' Billy added. 'But she got beat up.'

'Your mother?'

They nodded as one man.

'By whom?'

'Me dad,' replied Craig. 'We heard him. Then we came down and found me mam and we rang for the ambulance. Police came and looked after us and Daisy, then they gave us to Lisa.'

Lisa and Harrie entered the equation, both gasping for breath after chasing Craig and Billy for what had felt like a half marathon.

'Oh, good,' said Hermione, smiling. 'The backbenchers have decided to attend. Is there a three-line whip on?'

A whip? The boys' eyes widened further.

The old woman carried on: 'We only need Tony Blair, then we can have *Gardeners' Question Time*.'

Lisa blinked. 'Don't you mean...?'

'I know what I'm talking about. There are more cauliflowers in the lower chamber than they sell in Morrisons. Organic produce? They should ditch the Brussels sprouts for a start, because we never needed Belgians. Who ever found a use for Belgians?'

'Agatha Christie?' offered Harrie. 'Hercule Poirot?'

But Hermione was on her high horse. 'European Community? What did the Bundesbank say on Black Monday? Or was it a Monday or a Wednesday? Anyway, what I am saying–'

'She's away,' shouted Eileen. 'And so am I. If she's gone political and vegetarian, I am putting the kettle on.' She stamped out to the kitchen.

245

Lisa sank into a chair. 'Harriet,' she said wearily. 'Take them away and feed them.'

'Can we borrow your whip?' Billy begged.

Harrie dragged the twins out of the room and closed the door.

Lisa cocked an ear. 'She's letting them use your stairlift. Oh, Mother.'

Hermione clucked her tongue. 'Annie's children?'

'Yes.'

'Lisa, they said their dad hit their mother. What on earth is going on?'

'The police have questioned them. They asked me, too, but I said nothing, though I am fairly sure he did it. I want to wait until Annie wakes.'

'How is she?'

Lisa sniffed back some moisture. 'She's been brutally attacked. Doing better. She's still wired up like a power station, I believe, but they have to be careful with brain bleeds. They seem confident that she will make a full recovery, because she's given them a few tellings off.'

'It's the gun, isn't it?'

Lisa sighed, stood up and walked to the rear dormer window. She looked out at her daughter's cabin and smiled sadly. 'She's playing house in there with Billy, Craig and Daisy. Daisy is going to sleep in Harrie's room, and the boys are to have the spare. She's a good girl – Harriet, I mean.'

'Lisa?'

'Yes, Mother?'

'Is he still out there?'

Lisa nodded. 'They've road blocks, packs of

dogs and all kinds of search parties, but he's gone to ground. Could be at Land's End for all we know.'

Eileen came in and began the business of getting Hermione out of bed. It was clearly a tiring process for both of them. They were going to need even more help, Lisa mused as she watched the two women. But, no matter what happened, Hermione would not go into a pending tray – that was the old woman's term for so-called care homes. Sometimes, she called them parking lots, dead ends or wheelie bins.

At last, Hermione was installed in her chair, breakfast in front of her, a towelling bib tied at the throat. Lisa swallowed. It was the loss of dignity that was most upsetting. This had been a great woman, an excellent jeweller, a public speaker, a person of some standing. Standing was a problem now. God, life was so sad.

The door opened. 'Hey, missus?'

Hermione put down her cup. 'Yes?'

'Can we have a lend of one of your wheelchairs?'

Lisa started to laugh. She laughed until she almost wept.

'Which one are you?' Hermione asked the boy.

'Billy,' came the reply.

'Billy, the answer is no.'

'Right.'

'Why did you want it?'

The boy shrugged. 'Have you seen a film called *Back to the Future?*'

'No.'

'Never mind, then.' Billy withdrew.

'They wanted to time travel,' explained Lisa, drying her eyes on a tissue.

The older woman thought about that. 'Oh, right. They'll need the motorized one, then. I'll plug it in, shall I?'

Nine

Gus's visits to the house on Wigan Road were becoming less frequent, and, as he was to travel to New Zealand in a few days, Sheila Barton had to make a decision about Katherina Louisa Barford. Why had he been in that graveyard? What had made him weep? He was a man who kept his emotions under lock and key; he probably had a Chubb fixed to his soul, because he seldom gave anything away. Should she ask about the cemetery? Could she?

There were many graves in Tonge Cemetery. Some had almost made Sheila sob when she had read endless lists on cheap sandstone memorials, whole families wiped out in the nineteenth century by influenza or some such bug. Nobody cried for them any more, since no one remembered them.

Should she ask? After all, they were close in a way, because she cooked for him, listened to him when he became excited about maggots, honey, broad-spectrum antibiotics, antiseptic hand-cleansers. Yet he never made much of the houses in which he tested domestic bleach: homes of the rich and famous, folk who were seen on TV. He was an extraordinary man, she reminded herself. He was even stranger than she had thought at the beginning, when he had first arrived to inspect the roof space for his trains. Katherina. Who had

249

she been? What had she meant to him?

He was eating roast beef, was delivering a lecture on why a person should not consume too much red meat. 'Inside the bowel of most dead American males,' he was saying now, 'there is often up to two pounds of undigested red meat.'

He was still eating. How could a person eat while producing a monologue on the subject of bowels?

'We're not made to digest the flesh of milk-fed animals. When we were apes, we ate all the time – except when sleeping, of course. It was a berry here, a root there...' He droned on.

Who was Katherina?

'Civilization gave us tables, chairs and language, so, in our less than infinite wisdom, we turned eating into a social occasion.' His sister, perhaps? A married sister?

'We have made ourselves ridiculous.' He wiped a drop of gravy from his lower lip.

Cousin, neighbour, lover? He was staring straight at her. Sometimes, she felt as if he could see through her, could hear what she was thinking. No. He was asking for the salt.

'Too much salt is another problem,' he continued after using the cruet. 'It can kill a small child.'

Sheila swallowed a mouthful of cranberry juice. On the few occasions when she had allowed herself to ask a simple question, he had not always given a straight answer. From time to time, he allowed some small detail to escape from his fortress, but it was usually eat, drink, go upstairs and play. It was as if he wore a 'KEEP OFF THE

GRASS' sign, or one that read 'TRESPASSERS WILL BE PROSECUTED'. Was he lonely? Did he miss having a proper family, one with whom he could share the unhealthy niceties he had just described? He was talking about sugar. She had heard it all before.

Gus stood up, patted his pockets in that mad professor way he seemed to have acquired. 'I'll just ... er...'

He left the room, presumably to 'just ... er'. A 'just ... er' could be a visit to the bathroom, three hours in the loft, or even a goodbye. Yes, he often left the house after a 'just ... er'.

Sheila carried the debris from the meal into her kitchen. He had gone upstairs. Often, he stayed until she had gone to bed, and she wondered how a man of such obvious intelligence could spend so much time watching little engines pulling little carriages over little lines. There were miniature bridges, trees, a few cows and houses, but it was still just a train set. Perhaps the monotony all-owed him space and time to think about the cultures he was growing in the lab. Or did he indulge in thoughts and memories about Katherina?

'I'll probably never find out,' she told the Fairy Liquid container.

After washing up, she returned to the living room and found him standing with his back to the empty grate. It was too warm for a fire, but he positioned himself just as her father once had, in the place from which heads of households delivered life's agenda.

'I thought you were upstairs,' she said, hoping

251

that he hadn't heard her talking to herself.

'I was,' he replied. 'But I came down again.'

Of course he had come down again, she told herself inwardly with an unusual degree of impatience. Sometimes, he treated her like a child.

'About New Zealand,' he began.

Excitement stirred. Did he want a travelling companion?

'I'm not going,' he said, his words measured, 'but all the members of my family believe that I am going.'

Sheila sat down and kept quiet for the moment.

'It is easiest if they think I am flying out of the country,' he continued. 'I am, in reality, going into hospital.'

A hand flew of its own accord to her throat. 'Why?' she managed.

'Oh, just for an exploratory procedure.'

Sheila swallowed nervously. Why was he telling her? Why not his family?

'I may need things while I am in there,' he said. 'Toiletries and so forth. I prefer to use my own towels, and I shall require a change of nightwear. Also some washing – if you don't mind.'

Her brain was racing. 'No, I don't mind. Not at all.' Exploratory? What were they exploring for? Not buried treasure, that was certain. 'The private hospital?' she asked.

He nodded. 'Though some of those can be filthy, you know. Still, I have to take the chance. Otherwise...'

'Otherwise?'

'I want to know what's wrong with me and whether it can be remedied.'

'Ah. Yes, of course.' She couldn't even ask him about the symptoms, let alone enquire about a woman in a grave. But what if anything happened to him? She would be the one with the bad news, wouldn't she? Although, knowing him as she did, he was likely to have told the hospital what to do in the event of... She didn't want to think about it. He was her only regular visitor, the only person in her life. To be completely alone again would be unbearable. But she mustn't think of herself. 'How long have you known?'

'About the operation? Oh, two or three weeks. New Zealand no longer expects me. Which is a pity, as I was getting somewhere with the monoflor bees.'

Dear God, the man was obsessed. Sheila thought for a moment about Lisa Compton-Milne, found herself beginning to understand the woman. She understood Gus, too. He wouldn't want strangers visiting his hospital room, because there would be nothing to say. The man had a family, but he didn't know them – and, by the same token, they didn't know him. 'Yes, I'll do all that,' she told him.

'Thank you.'

Sheila swallowed. 'Gus?' He had invited her to call him by his abbreviated Christian name, and she had finally found the courage to do it.

'Yes?'

She should have kept her mouth shut, should never have started this. 'Do you... Do you ever feel sad?'

'Yes.'

She thought he had decided to be monosyllabic

again and was surprised when he continued after a couple of seconds. 'When I see my son and can't help him. My daughter should have gone to Oxford, but she stayed with him. Sometimes, I look at Lisa and wish she could have been ... wish I could have... Things should have been better – different.'

Sheila nodded.

'My mother will soon be unable to walk. I wish I could have found a cure for that. They think I see nothing, but I am well aware of the situation at home. My wife has sought consolation elsewhere, and I cannot blame her. We are mere animals, and we have our needs.' He smiled at her. 'You are an excellent friend, Sheila. This has been a refuge for me.'

It felt as if he were saying goodbye. She swallowed hard again. 'Are you in pain?'

'Yes.'

'All the time?'

'No.'

He had reverted to words of one syllable. She watched as he took a small piece of paper from his wallet. 'The address and telephone number of the hospital. I shall be in room eleven. Don't tell anyone where I am. Please?' He placed the paper on the table. 'Nobody must know. I am in New Zealand.'

She nodded. When he walked to the door, she did not turn to look at him. His footsteps sounded hollow in the hall, as did the crash of the outer door as it closed behind him. Cold fingers wrapped themselves around her heart, and she gasped. Everything was so loud, so empty, so bloody lonely. She picked up the scrap of paper. On the reverse he had written an instruction – she was to sell the trains in the event of his death.

As quickly as she could, Sheila Barton ran to the front of her house. For some stupid reason, she was suddenly desperate to find out about Katherina. It was a foreign-sounding name, almost Russian. But when she reached the bottom of the stone steps that led up to her house from the pavement, she saw the Mini making its way towards town. Slowly, she turned and climbed back to her door.

'How did you know she had it?' Craig asked. 'How did she know?'

Harrie raised her eyes to heaven. Questions, questions. 'She saw two of everything.'

Billy chipped in. 'Like me dad when he's drunk? He once said he had four twins, not two. Said he'd never touch another drop. But he did.'

Harrie served up fish fingers, oven chips and peas.

'These aren't proper peas,' groaned Craig.

'Oh yes, they are,' replied Harrie. 'I shelled them myself.'

Forks clattered on to plates. 'Shelled? They're not nuts or cockles. They're peas. They're frozen in a bag, or they come in a tin called marrowfats.'

Harrie shook her head. 'They grow in pods. The freezer people take them out of their pods and put them in large refrigeration units. Or the canning factory shells them, cooks them and puts them in a tin. These are proper peas.'

Daisy didn't seem to mind. She was too busy

chasing peas across the floor every time they dropped off her fork. It didn't appear to bother her – she ate them, anyway. 'Playing marbles,' she said happily before popping another green orb into her pretty little mouth.

The boys had quietened a little. Harrie found that they behaved better if she kept them divorced from sweets and other sources of sucrose. She also bought food with fewer additives, so the twins had slowed down considerably since their arrival.

'But how did she know it was MFI?' asked Craig.

Here they came again – more queries. 'MS, not MFI, that's a chain of shops. The doctor told her. She had a special scan, and they said it was multiple sclerosis.'

'I like her,' Billy announced. 'She tells us some great stuff. Did you know that a duck's quack has no echo?'

Harrie hadn't known, and she admitted that immediately. 'And elephants have four knees, but they can't jump?'

'I knew that one,' she said.

Billy served up the opinion that it was a good job elephants couldn't jump because, if they *could* jump, Africa and India would fall to bits, especially if all the elephants jumped at the same time.

Harrie kept finding herself smiling. She smiled now because she had a mental picture of synchronized elephant-jumping choreographed by Walt Disney. There was probably a saleable story in Billy's head. He, Craig and Daisy had already provided her with an education, and the result was that she made the decision not to teach history. Instead, she would teach children. Primary school pupils had hungry minds, and she would not be confined to one subject. Yes, it was about teaching people, not history.

Daisy was making a circle of peas under the table. In the centre, she had placed two chips and a fish finger. Should a child be allowed to eat off the floor? Probably not. It was best to pretend not to have noticed.

Will entered. The fact that he seemed to have acquired a family overnight did not bother him. The boys loved him, though Hermione remained their favourite toy. Will had been deemed 'dead interesting' and 'safe'. Harrie asked about 'safe', and was told that it used to be 'sound'. 'Safe' was the new 'sound', then. She was learning all the time. Soon, she might acquire a fuller relationship with her native tongue.

The boys stuffed the rest of their dinner into their mouths, then rushed off to play football with Will. The dog was clearly on the tea break she had earned while looking after Hermione, so Harrie wrote 'FOOTBALL' at the top of her shopping list, since Alsatian and football did not make for a good marriage and the ball would no doubt be punctured in minutes.

She sat and watched Daisy who, after re-arranging her dinner on the floor, was playing with her dolls. The little girl's mother was recovering. Everyone knew she was recovering because she was reputed to be making radical changes to the National Health Service. These three wonderful, brilliant kids had come from a fabulous mother who fed them the wrong stuff, but who gave them guts, humour and imagination. Additives aside, Annie was doing a great job.

'I'm going to be a teacher,' she told Daisy.

'Teacher,' came the echo.

'I shall teach people like you, Billy and Craig.'

'BillyandCraig,' was returned as one word.

Harrie was happy. She had Will, her own little house, a lovely gran, a mother beginning to see the light, and a brother who had wandered off to mend himself in his own way. And that was the only method that really worked. Counsellors and psychologists were useful, but the day had to come when a person must stand up to be counted. Or sit behind the wheel of a geriatric camper van. 'I hope he's all right,' she mused.

'All right,' said Daisy.

The road ahead was clear for Harrie, and she hoped with all her heart that the brother she loved was coming to his senses. Ben was important. But Will was her world. For the present, so were Annie's children.

'Why aren't you at work? Jimmy Nuttall, still wearing pyjamas and dressing gown, stood in the living room doorway. Sal was sitting on the sofa watching morning TV. 'Are you ill?'

She turned, looked him up and down, then continued to stare at the screen.

'I asked you a question.'

'And I heard you. It's my house, my job, my choice, my aching feet. I'm having a day off. Oh, and the office window is open a bit, and he's gone to New Zealand, so do what you must. They know I'm having the day off. I told them I had a lot of dental work needing doing.' She had seen the piece in the newspaper and had watched the television. Mrs Annie Nuttall had been found seriously injured, and the police wanted to talk to her husband. Sal knew she should get the police, yet she didn't dare. If he got bail, if they couldn't prove anything – would she get the same treatment as Annie? He had to decide for himself to go. Sal didn't want to suffer the beating that might result from a direct attempt at eviction. She'd just have to give him a bit of a push.

'Any breakfast?' he asked.

'No idea. Go and look for yourself.'

'You'd have made my breakfast a few weeks ago,' he complained.

'Happen I was still daft a few weeks ago.' Loneliness, she decided, was emphasized all the more when the wrong person turned up. The most isolating condition on earth was probably that of a person locked into a bad marriage. She thanked God that Jimmy had never left his wife until now. Husbands, like cars, should be test-driven. She wanted her life back.

'How long are you staying here?' she asked, finally turning from the television to gaze at him. She couldn't tell him that his kids were with Lisa. If he wanted to go into the office in the middle of the night, that was OK by her. But he must not learn about his children. They were staying with the daughter in that little wooden house, and he wouldn't go near that unless she told him. Jimmy had lost the plot. His eyes weren't right. He was

259

jumpy, he looked even shiftier than usual, and his wife was in the hospital. 'Jimmy, I can't carry on.'

'Has it been on the news?' he asked.

Sal nodded.

'It wasn't me,' he said. 'I found her like that. I went for some of my stuff, and Annie was lying on the floor with her face all bloody.'

It was never him, Sal concluded. It wasn't him who'd acquired the gun, wasn't him who'd half-killed his wife. The whole world was guilty; he was the sole innocent member of the human race. 'I am – what's the word? Harbouring. I am harbouring you, and that's a crime in itself.'

'Not if I'm not guilty.'

'Maybe. But they're looking for you, so I should phone them, shouldn't I? The longer I leave it, the more trouble I'm in. They've half a dozen forces out looking for you. I'm surprised they haven't brought the army in.' She should stop digging, or he might well push her into a hole of her own making and would fill up said hole in a trice. Knowing that she ought to shut up, Sal clamped her lips together tightly. What if he kept her here? Nobody would find her till hell had frozen over. Oh, God, she should have gone to the police station.

He walked round the sofa and stood between her and her beloved plasma TV, his arms folded tightly across his chest. 'I never touched her, Sal.'

'So you said.' She could not keep her mouth shut, and she cursed herself inwardly. 'If that's the case, why don't you go to the police and tell them you found her like that?'

He hesitated for a fraction of a second. 'See,

there's the burglaries. Some of the lads under me installed several alarms, but I was the gaffer. I don't know which one of them robbed those people, but it–'

'It wasn't you.' She had noticed the pause before the explanation.

'That's right.'

'Well, it's up to you, Jimmy. I know I have to keep my mouth shut, because I'm frightened of you.' There, it was said. 'I'm afraid you might go berserk if I grass you up. But they're looking.'

'Nobody comes out here.'

Sal shivered because that was the truth. The gas and electricity men visited every few months, but no one else called. She was off the beaten path, so her postman was glad that she seldom got mail. 'They'll find you.'

'How?'

She shrugged. 'They will. They just do, don't they?'

'Not always. If folk keep their mouths shut, I might be all right.'

'Then you'd best stop away from Weaver's Warp, because that van of yours might be seen. You could be seen. They're all over the shop looking for you.'

'Sal, you haven't *said* anything to the Compton-Milnes, have you?'

She pursed her lips before speaking. 'Look, what do you take me for – a bloody duck egg? Why would I talk to them about you? And, if I had talked to them, why aren't the police swarming all over these fields? Sometimes, I wonder whether you've sent your brain to Johnson's for dry-cleaning. Jimmy, I've said nothing and I will say nothing. I am already an accessory after the whatever, aren't I?'

'I never touched her. I never owned a gun.'

'Right.'

'Do you believe me?'

'Yes.' She didn't believe a single word that came out of his mouth, but she had to play it his way. Annie was getting better; his next target could end up on a slab with a ticket tied to one of its big toes. 'On my own life, I swear I won't grass on you. OK?'

'Thanks.'

'Put the kettle on,' she said. 'And I could murder a bacon butty.'

He hesitated for a split second. 'Brown sauce or ketchup?' he asked.

'Brown, ta. And sweeteners instead of sugar.'

On the third day, Sheila visited Gus in hospital.

She found him sitting up in bed, no drips or wires, no machinery in the room, nothing complicated. It was a pleasant place, apparently clean, with en-suite bathroom, a large TV and a view across large gardens and a lake. What a silly person she was. After his last visit to her house, she had almost known that she would not see him again – so much for female intuition.

She placed a package on his bedside cabinet. 'Towels, pyjamas and a few other bits and pieces,' she told him. 'All boiled and disinfected and wrapped as you asked. How are you?'

'I am doing quite well at the moment,' he replied.

At the moment. She wondered what that meant, but decided that he would speak when he was ready. He was, as usual, more interested in clinical matters. He made her rub gel into her hands before sitting down, advised her not to touch any surfaces in the room or on her way out of the building, and begged her to buy some gel to take home. 'It's everywhere now, you see,' he explained. 'Go to the chemist and buy this one. I had a small part to play in its manufacture.'

'Right.' She folded her hands in her lap and sat as still as possible.

'The situation should all have been remedied, or at least curtailed long ago,' he said angrily. 'If surgeons would listen, if health authorities would stop doling out cleaning contracts to the great unwashed, if...' He ran out of steam.

'If pigs could fly?' she suggested.

He almost smiled. 'Quite. Months before it all got out of hand, I advised the government, but would they listen? No. They happily spend millions on bombs to drop in a totally illegal war and leave their own citizens to sit and watch while the flesh falls away from their bones.'

Sheila wondered whether he had a temperature, because he was very animated, so she decided to allow him a rest by contributing to the conversation. 'I remember my mother telling me about when she worked in the infirmary,' she said. 'The surgeons, nurses and cleaners were all members of staff. It wasn't unknown for them to pass the time of day in a corridor. They had loyalty, Gus. Mam was a cleaner. I remember she used to stink of carbolic and pine disinfectant

263

when she came home, but the wards were clean. She took pride, you see. Just as much pride as the surgeons did.'

He nodded. Here was someone who agreed with him – yet another who knew some of the facts. But anecdotal matters were of no interest to the powers in London – people were dying because hospitals were filthy.

'At least this place is clean,' she said.

Gus tutted. 'No, my dear. This place is unlikely to be truly clean. Remember the footballer's wife who almost died after a procedure in a private clinic? That was because of dirt, the kind of debris that is invisible to the naked eye. She contracted MRSA. Nowhere is clean. The microbes are in our houses because we have brought them home with us. They are in the curtains around ward beds; they are on the surgeon's hands. He is busy, he forgets to gel, or something on his cuff makes a short journey south while he's on his rounds and – whoops! Another patient dies.'

The visitor shivered. 'You'd better get out of here as soon as possible, then,' she said.

He agreed and asked her to prepare a room for him. 'Am I imposing?' he asked.

Was he imposing? Almost overcome by joy, she told him that she could prepare a room and that he was not imposing.

'I am, of course, still in New Zealand.'

'How's the weather down there?' she asked.

'Wintry,' was the terse reply. He went on to instruct her in minute detail of the preparation required. It would take a while to prepare his ultra-clean environment, and he apologized for

264

that. 'I have a wound,' he said. 'And I need to be careful.'

'Yes, of course. I understand.'

'Good,' he said.

According to Gus, anyone with the slightest cut on a finger was in jeopardy. She remembered something he had prepared for *The Lancet*. It had been entitled 'No Hiding Place'. Was he right when he said there was no need for terrorism because biological warfare was already under way? Or was he that special kind of crackers that happened only to people of superior intellect?

'I brought your laptop, the one you keep at my house. Are you going to disinfect it?'

That half-smile reappeared. 'Sheila, even I have my limits.'

She left and hurried home to get on with the sterilization of her second largest bedroom. It was going to be a big job, so she thanked God that schools had closed for the summer. There were cleaning materials to buy, and her washing machine would be on a boil programme for some time to come. It was worth it. At last she understood where Gus's place was in her life. He was the brother she had never had. Until now.

The twins were running about outside. Daisy, as placid as they were noisy, was sticking pasta shapes on to a bit of cardboard. She was an unusual child whose vocabulary was increasing at a rate of knots. She had declared her breakfast to be delicious, and, after spinning Will's globe of the earth for a while, had pronounced the item a 'planet' before moving on to pasta and glue. She was bright. Harrie wanted to keep her for ever.

The shopping list grew by the minute. Billy and Craig were eating everyone out of house and home. At this rate, Harrie might need a mortgage, and she said so.

'Mortgage,' repeated Daisy, who was now covered in glue.

'Nearly-three going on thirty, aren't you?'

'Yes. Three. Birt'day.'

Annie would be out of hospital before Daisy's September birthday, surely?

Harrie's mobile sounded. She clicked, read the message and grinned.

Hi sis dont laff. Am living with travellers outside Rochdale. Pretty here. Got fortune told, have big future in communications but must never wear red. Cya soon. Ben xxx

She laughed, of course. It was beyond the bounds of her imagination to picture her brother living among folk who had possibly never been to school, people who lived hand-to-mouth and by poaching and begging. Could Ben sell lucky heather? Did travellers do lucky heather and pegs these days?

'Stuck.' Daisy, who had just arrived at Harrie's side, was smiling broadly. Her hands were covered in glue, and there was even some in her pretty hair. 'Stuck,' she repeated pleasantly.

'Worry not,' Harrie advised. 'It isn't poisonous, I checked.'

'Have a bath,' suggested the child.

'Good idea.'

Harrie picked up the little girl. 'My brother is going to be all right,' she said.

'Ben.'

Where the heck had the child heard his name? She had never met him, yet she had absorbed and retained his name. It was plain that Daisy was a listener, that she soaked up information like blotting paper absorbed ink. The child was capable of grasping concepts, however abstract or absent they might be. And she probably wasn't alone. There were other special kids like Daisy, children who should be encouraged and helped. 'It's not just the disabled who need our attention, is it?'

'No,' replied Daisy.

The cream should come off the top. The cream deserved attention, or it might curdle in the pot. 'I wonder whether the cream causes the trouble out there? Nowhere to go with their brains, so they fight.'

'BillyandCraig.'

Nothing wrong with the old grammar school system? It hadn't been wonderful, but the top four per cent had got their chance, Harrie supposed. While she filled the bath, she found herself thinking about Ben, who was probably top two per cent. He had been creamed off, yet he had gone astray for a while. Perhaps the bright ones had to go through something because their emotional development was impeded by their intellectual difference from the norm. It was worth studying, certainly.

While Daisy splashed, the twins dashed in. 'It's stuck,' gasped Billy-The-Taller.

'What's stuck? Daisy's been stuck to a bit of cardboard, but other th–'

'No,' shouted Craig. 'Stairlift. And Mrs Iona's sitting in it.'

Harrie sank to the floor and started to laugh. Life was certainly interesting these days. She pictured Gran, heard the words she was probably using, hoped the lads hadn't learned any new language. She dried her eyes. 'Is Woebee with her?'

They nodded in unison. 'Said it's our fault.'

'Is it?'

They hung their heads. 'It was his idea,' they said, each pointing to the other.

Billy kicked his twin. 'We seen it on the telly. A fat man stuck halfway up the stairs. It was funny – everybody was laughing. He was there all night. So me brother shoved some cloth in the underneath bit.' He jerked his thumb in the direction of Craig. 'It was him, not me.'

Craig puffed up his cheeks and expelled a huge amount of air. 'It was both of us.'

Harrie attacked the problem. 'You seen it on the telly?'

They nodded.

'No. You saw it on the telly.'

'That's what we said.'

Harrie sighed. Perhaps teaching was not going to be an easy option. As far as the Nuttall family went, Daisy was clearly in a class of her own. 'Go and tell Gran I'll be there when I've dried Daisy. Gran needs to be lifted out of the chair – she can get downstairs on her bottom.'

'Can she?'

'Yes.'

'So she doesn't need her stairlifts really, does she?'

Explanations would take too much time, and there was no point, anyway, because Billyand-Craig would carry on as before. She shooed them out and got on with the task in hand.

'Daddy can mend it,' Daisy offered.

This was heartbreaking. One concept that Daisy was happily unable to understand was that her daddy was a criminal. Her daddy had put her mummy in hospital. 'We'll see,' she said, remembering how adults had often used those very words when she was a child. 'We'll see' meant no. But Daisy couldn't grasp that. Yet.

Annie was sitting up in bed. She waved as Lisa entered the ward. 'Oi,' she yelled. 'I've been promoted.'

Lisa chuckled. Promotion was a move higher up the ward away from the sister's office. Annie was too much of a troublemaker to be kept near the staff. But while she was now at a safe distance from the nurses, she was in a position from which she might energize patients who were well enough to give a damn. Since most of the upper end were well enough, Annie was halfway to forming a trade union with a massive charter and an agenda longer than the Bolton ring road.

When she had sat down, Lisa passed a small package to her new-found friend and colleague. 'That's for you from Harrie, Simon and me.'

'You what? It's me should be sending life support for Harrie – how's she managing? What have they broken so far?'

Lisa thought for a moment. 'Three mugs, a bed, some branches off a listed oak tree – quite a few of our trees are protected – oh, and a stairlift.'

'Buggeration.'

'Quite.'

'What did your ma-in-law say?'

'I wasn't there, but I understand that much of it would not bear repetition. But she saw the funny side. She usually does.'

'How's Daisy?'

Lisa smiled broadly. 'You'll have trouble there, because Harrie's fallen in love with her and won't want to give her back. It seems that your daughter is unusually gifted.'

'Like yours.'

'Yes.'

Annie opened her package and burst into tears. 'Aw, God,' she moaned. 'You knew I liked it. And I know how much it's worth.'

'No. You know how much I was selling it for. Stop it, now. You'll get another headache.'

Annie, who had lost a lot of hair in the operating theatre, was still heavily bandaged. 'In case my brain cell falls out,' was her usual explanation.

'You're worth it, girl. Every penny,' Lisa said.

'It's Italian.'

'Yes. Like they sell on the Ponte Vecchio over the Arno. I went there with Harrie. Florence is the most amazing place on earth. See Rome and die? OK, but see Firenze as well. It's gorgeous. I'll take you there. At night, the priests plug in amplifiers and so forth so that the kids can dance in the street. I loved it, loved the people.'

But Annie was mesmerized by her bracelet.

Never in her life had she allowed herself to imagine that she might own a piece of good, Italian gold. 'Is it fourteen?' she asked, drying her tears on the sheet.

'Yes. Eighteen carat would be too soft, and nine is too heavily alloyed to keep colour. You can be lucky with nine, but fourteen's safer.'

Annie nodded. 'So white gold is alloyed with silver, and rose is with copper.'

'You're a fast learner.'

'I am.' She closed her eyes and leaned back on an Everest of pillows. 'How much to mend the stairlift?' she asked.

'Nothing,' came the reply. 'It's under guarantee, and my mother-in-law is an accomplished liar. She was trained well – jewellery trade.' She paused. 'Are you feeling tired?'

'A bit.' The eyes opened. 'Where is he, Lisa?' The bottom lip quivered. 'God, where is the bugger?'

'No idea, love. Not since he was seen in town weeks ago. He's disappeared.'

'He'll be back.' She closed her eyes again. 'I hate admitting this, Lisa, but I'm scared to death. More for the kids than for me. I've got used to being in here, as well. I hate hospitals, but every-thing's done for me, no kids to worry about.'

'You'll be all right, because you'll be staying with us until you're sorted out. I'll get you a wig from Ideal World shopping channel – they do some great ones. We could turn you into Marilyn Monroe. Hermione is completing the research as we speak. You'll be a beautiful blonde. Or a brunette.'

The eyes were wide again. 'Oh, yeah? Silk purses and sows' ears?'

'Don't be silly.'

Annie sat up. 'You know all this patients' charter stuff?'

'Yes.'

'It's just to make me feel normal.'

'I know.' The staff did, too – as did most of the patients. 'But, Lisa, there is one valid thing. It's the fat police.'

'Oh?'

Annie nodded. 'My consultant – Mr Simpson – he looks like a long stick of Blackpool rock. Sugar-free, of course. We're all too fat in here. He wants to put us on diets. We're getting thrown off the operating table and on to the Ryvita. I just want to kick his head in.'

'Don't. You've seen and felt the results.'

Annie pondered for a few seconds. 'Are you sure? About me stopping up yon with you and your lot? You've already got the kids.'

'I know.'

'It's a lot of trouble.'

'I know.'

The woman in the bed laughed. 'Aw – hey – we're not that bad, are we?'

'Yes, you are. And that makes me happy. Don't worry about a thing and do everything you're told in here. Except for the Ryvita.' Lisa planted a kiss on top of a white bandaged head. She wanted to weep for this brave little person, but she couldn't, not yet.

She sat in her car and thought, not for the first time, about the cruelties of mankind. Sometimes, she saw more sense in Will's dog than she did in her fellows. Annie would have struggled on without help from Lisa and the shop. She would have claimed support, would have broken the law by doing little cash-in-hand jobs like Sal Potter did. It wasn't right. There was still a poverty trap where people were forced to break the law just to feed a family. 'I should go into politics,' she told her rear view mirror. But she hadn't the time, and she hated London, anyway...

Mathilda's eyes opened and remained open. She seldom blinked and did not seem to react when items were moved inches from her face.

'Could she be blind?' Sister Mary Magdalene asked. 'Or might it be that the messages aren't getting through to her brain? She hears. I know she hears music, because her hands move. She hears me reading, too.'

'I shall try him again.' Mother Benedict had been phoning Mr Earnshaw repeatedly. Mr Earnshaw was Mathilda's sole visitor. But his mobile phone had remained switched off for several days, and his voicemail was not activated.

'Send him an email,' suggested Magda. 'Perhaps that will get to him more quickly. He needs to know that she is awake.' Was she awake? Did open eyes mean wakefulness? 'And she's on no sedation,' the nun added. 'We all know what happened last time.'

Mother Benedict went downstairs to use the computer. Time might well be running out for Mathilda. And Mr Earnshaw had to be told.

Jimmy found an ancient and filthy rucksack at the back of Sal's shed. He cleaned it up as best he could, got his hands on some food containers, a torch, Stanley knife and a few tools of his own questionable trade. Something to eat and a Thermos of tea were a necessity, as he did not know how long he would be away. Sal was back at work and had promised to keep the office window ajar. Preparations had taken longer than Jimmy had expected, as the canvas rucksack took ages to dry.

He sat in the living room and completed his plans. He'd already hidden the van, driving it further along the path to the left of the cottage and covering its rear with a piece of old carpet from Sal's shed. He'd have to make his way to Weaver's Warp on foot. If he moved in a westerly direction across the moors, then took a circuitous route through farmland, he could get to the area in an hour or so. No one on the new estate near Weaver's knew him. Walking, he could be as quiet as he needed to be. It had to be tonight, before somebody noticed a slight gap in the office window. According to Sal, no one but the master of the house ever went in there, and he would be on his way to the other side of the world by now.

If he couldn't get the gun, the other method would need to be employed. It was a terrifying idea, yet there was no alternative. Focused solely on the retrieval of the weapon used in the Birmingham raid, he deliberately tidied away recent events, including burglaries and the attack on his wife. The fact that he might have to break the law again was of no consequence – he would do whatever it took to achieve the most important of his goals. The weather had turned unpredictable, so he needed to wait for a dry night. It would be soon, he hoped.

According to Sal, the girl had moved into a wooden bungalow in the rear garden of Weaver's Warp. She was isolated. If he failed to find the gun in the office, he would remove her from the scene. They had something he needed; it did not take much of a brain to work out that the daughter would be precious, as vital to the Compton-Milnes as the gun was to him. There could be a straight swap; the plan was simple, dangerous and essential. Nothing else mattered. Jimmy was going to save himself. And to hell with everybody else.

*

Freda Nuttall was very impressed by Hermione's apartment. 'It's lovely,' she exclaimed after entering. 'Modern. Makes my place look like Pot Bailey's stall down Bolton market when I was a kiddy.' She sat down. 'But why do you live up here, Hermione? Wouldn't it be easier for you downstairs? That's why I have a bungalow – no stairs.'

'Call me Iona – it's easier. I live up here because I can see everything and everybody. I like to take an overview, you see.'

'She's nosy,' offered Eileen. 'Nosier than a herd of elephants.'

Hermione awarded the carer one of her harder stares. 'Make the tea,' she said. 'And I hope you produced a decent cake this time.' She winked at Freda. 'Can't get the staff these days, you see. This one thinks she's in charge and I am supposed to do as I am told.'

The visitor was still trying to recover from the shock resulting from her first encounter with Eileen Eckersley. It was easy for the Compton-Milnes because they were used to her, but a new arrival often took a few minutes to absorb the vision. It was the hair. No, it wasn't, it was the eyes. No, it was definitely the teeth. Whatever, Eileen took some digesting at the first sitting. Freda cleared her throat behind a well-mannered hand.

'The children are fine,' said Hermione reassuringly. But she continued, 'We, however, are not. The twins are ... adventurous.'

'You're telling me?' Freda sighed. 'I've lost more figurines through them two than I have in thirty-odd years. It's like letting a pair of bulls loose on Pot Bailey's stall – I mentioned him before. Do you remember how he used to juggle plates? Clever man, he was. Never dropped a plate. Craig and Billy drop everything.'

Eileen reappeared with a tray. She dumped it on a low table between them, sat in a third chair, began to pour tea and cut slices of cake.

Freda glanced at her hostess. Was it normal for a servant to sit down with her boss? Then she watched while Eileen guided a shaking hand, while she fixed a napkin around Hermione's neck and helped her with a bit of cake. It was a damned shame. But it was difficult to feel pity for very long, because the old woman was more than feisty.

'What did you use to clean this silver? Sand-paper?' she asked. 'I've seen a better shine on

276

fitted carpet.'

'No, I used a nail file. Now drink up and shut up, because I can't be doing with all the complaining and the whatevering while you're spilling tea.' Eileen spoke to Freda. 'She does half of it on purpose, I swear to God. There's no reasoning with her some days. My mammy warned me that life would be hard, but she never mentioned impossible. I suppose we all have a burden in life, and madam's mine.'

Freda smiled uncertainly. It was strange, because the second time she had a good look at Eileen, the woman looked ... well ... normal. It was not a face that might launch a thousand ships, and it owned a voice that could sink the same thousand, but she was kind and humorous. 'You can only do your best, love,' she replied.

Hermione chuckled. 'Whose side are you on?' she asked her guest.

'My own,' was the fast reply. 'I've learned to duck while there's low-flying objects. With my husband and my Jimmy, I had to fettle fast.'

Hermione gave her cup to Eileen. 'He's not visited you since that night.'

'No.'

'Any phone calls, letters, postcards, pigeons with notes fastened to their feet?'

'Not a dicky bird,' replied Freda deliberately. 'Not even a budgie in a cage. I can't think where the bloody hell he's got to.' She lowered her chin. 'I'm ashamed,' she said. 'Annie always said if he clouted her, she'd get him while he was asleep, but she never got chance, did she? Cos she slept for a couple of days, nearly in a coma, holes bored in her head and I feel so guilty; because he's–'

'Don't upset yourself,' ordered Eileen. 'Children can be a blessing or mortallious troublesome – often both. I'd a brother with a limp – one leg a smidge shorter than the other. So Mammy goes down to the market one Tuesday, and there he is, bold as brass and twice as ugly as sin, playing the mouth organ while people threw pennies in his cap. He couldn't play a tune to save his life. He'd a notice in front of him that read "look what the English did to me". Mammy clobbered him good and hard with her basket, and that was an end to his game. She never forgave him, and it was ages before she showed her face at the market again.'

Hermione and Freda were both doubled over with laughter.

Eileen scowled at both of them and asked why they found so tragic a tale in the least way funny, then she joined in the merriment.

The door opened. In walked Milly like the leader of the band. Behind her, both looking suspiciously clean, Craig and Billy each held a hand of their little sister. Harrie brought up the rear. 'I followed them so they wouldn't get filthy on the way,' she explained.

They kissed their grandmother, and Daisy climbed on to her knee. 'When Mummy coming?' she asked.

'Very soon,' promised Freda.

'With new hair,' added Hermione. 'She knew more about wigs than I did. So we got two. She can have a split personality for as long as she likes.'

'Have they took her hair off?' Craig asked.

Billy dug him in the ribs. 'Course they have, you div. You can't use a Black & Decker on hair. All the hair would go through to your brain.'

In Harrie's opinion, this was rather too much information for Daisy, so she changed the subject by displaying the child's works of art. 'That's Princess Diana's castle, and this is Princess Beatrice's palace.'

Everyone made the right noises until pasta started to drop off. There was an immediate scuffle, and the children retrieved all except for two pieces, both of which were consumed by the dog.

'You see?' said Eileen to no one in particular. 'It's always complicated. Still, as long as they don't start playing the mouth organ and begging, you should come out of it with no shame.'

Enlivened by the idea of mouth organs and begging, the twins bombarded Eileen with questions. 'My lips are sealed she said.

'And so they should be,' remarked Hermione. 'Get that super-glue, Harriet.'

Ten

The children were in bed at last. The battle had been fought, and Harrie, who had emerged triumphant from the field of battle, was exhausted. She tidied away debris and thought about motherhood, wondering how on earth women coped with kids and a full-time job. Most had a kid before they gave birth, since few men she knew had really achieved full adulthood. Will probably had. It was nothing to do with the 'new man' thing, it was about inner maturation. He had it. She hoped with all her heart that her little brother was finding it. It wasn't enough for her own life to be sorted; Ben had to get a sense of direction, and it seemed to be happening.

Texts from him came thicker and faster, though they grew shorter. 'OK n still alive', and 'how ya doin? Rode a horse today'. That last one was brilliant, because horses had to be dirty. Equines certainly didn't keep their CDs in order and never worried about a scratch on a kettle. They didn't take three showers a day, either, so Ben's chances of recovery looked good.

She finished her tasks, lay down on the sofa and wondered about normality. Mother had been running all her life from an apparently cold husband who was buried in microbiology. Why was Father so embedded in his work? God alone knew the answer to that one. Ben's obsession with

281

cleanliness had possibly come from the mad prof who was his dad. But Ben had found refuge in a bad place, a bolt-hole that had turned out to be the catalyst that began the mending. Was Father a bad man? Probably not. Mother was definitely not bad; she had been lonely to the point of desperation.

Gran was becoming forgetful – just a symptom of old age. She had always been eccentric and was travelling in splendid disgrace through the winter of her life. Woebee was wise, but wonderfully daft. Will, though sensible on the whole, was madly in love. The twins were enjoying and employing the lunacy of youth.

But true insanity rested with the man who had beaten the mother of his three children. Jimmy Nuttall was the one who had truly lost it. She shivered. No one knew where he was. He could be outside now, might be preparing to take away Daisy, Billy and Craig. 'He'd have to get past me first,' she said. All the same, she was glad that Will was on his way. They had to sleep on the sofa bed, since the children filled two divans, but she and Will would be together if the ogre appeared.

'And I was the one with the psychologist,' she said. 'I was the one who needed treatment? Sheesh!'

'Talking to yourself again?' Will leaned over and kissed her. 'An early warning of madness.'

'It's the only way I can be sure of an appreciative reception,' she replied. 'I didn't hear you come in. Did you see any mad men skulking around outside? Anyone with a chainsaw or an axe? Perhaps a black-hatted bloke carrying a violin case?'

'No. Just a mad woman in here.' He went into the kitchen and clattered things.

It was amazing, she thought, how the sound of plates and cups could be such a comfort. Rattling kept the world sane, somehow. He appeared with drinking chocolate and a rose in a jam jar. It was a beautiful yellow flower, but it didn't seem too happy in its Sainsbury's 'Reduced Sugar Strawberry Jam' pot. Harrie rescued it and placed it in a tiny vase. 'Men,' she said sweetly. 'No idea.'

He sat down. 'Harrie?'

'What?'

'Can we get married now?'

She glanced round the room. 'Well, I see no vicars or registrars. We could use the twins, I suppose. Daisy's a bit young.' She laughed. 'What's the rush? Are you pregnant?'

'No. Just scared.'

That was it, she decided. The fact that he could admit his fear was a symptom of adulthood. He wasn't concerned about his masculinity, couldn't care less if people thought him weak. That was his strength. 'Why?' she asked. 'If there's no rush, things are fine as they are. We are almost living together.'

'You might meet someone else at uni.'

'And a certificate would prevent that?'

Will shrugged.

Harrie clouted him with a cushion. 'And here was I, congratulating myself on having found a grown-up man. Marriage changes nothing. No, that's not true, because it often ruins a relationship. And children don't mend it. If the cracks are

283

there, offspring will make the building tumble. Let's make sure we have good foundations before we start bricking ourselves in.'

He rubbed his head. 'I only asked,' he said. 'No need to give me brain damage. Or a property surveyor's report, come to that. Anyway, our marriage will be fine. I've loved you since I was a mere boy.'

'Will?'

'What?'

'Shut up.'

He drew a hand across his mouth as if closing a zip fastener, then sat still and held her hand. Each knew that life without the other would not be bearable. Married or not, they were welded together. But she could not resist a final dig. 'You could get me an ASBO and one of those ankle things – a tag. I'd have to be inside by seven p.m. every evening. But-' she grinned mischievously – 'would I be alone? Would I?'

Sheila never once complained about the tedium. Happy to do Gus's bidding, she planned her day around his needs: cooking, cleaning, boiling bed linen and pyjamas, shopping for whatever he fancied. He never said much, yet she knew she was appreciated. They were like brother and sister; it felt as if they had been together for ever.

It was during an expedition to Bolton that she happened to wander past Lisa Compton-Milne's jewellery shop. Deep down, she knew that this was no accident, that she had followed her instincts without allowing the knowledge to seep through completely. She stood at the window and looked past displays all set out on dark-blue

284

velvet. Lisa Compton-Milne was just about visible. She was a pretty enough woman and was probably very well-dressed, though Sheila could see only head and shoulders.

While she lingered as if planning on choosing an item, a younger version of Gus's wife arrived at the shop. So this was his daughter. She, too, was remarkably pretty. Sheila had seen her before, but not closely. This was a lovely girl. Yet he didn't seem to be involved with these beautiful people. He chose instead to spend time with Sheila, because she allowed him to be himself.

The pair emerged from the shop. They were arm in arm as they went to the pavement's edge to prepare for crossing the road. The younger one was speaking about children being minded by ... Woebee? What kind of a name was that? They crossed and entered an elegant coffee shop across the way. Sheila followed suit and chose a table next to theirs.

The girl had blue eyes. They were similar in shape to her father's, although the rest of her face seemed to have been borrowed from her mother. Conversation at this point related to blends of coffee: skinny latte, cappuccino and espresso. Sheila guessed that they also knew about fine wines, designer clothes and good shoes, but she was still better than they were. In her house, a good man lay trying to hide from hospital infections. He was at war with germs, was the very embodiment of hope for the future, and here they sat deciding about coffee.

Lisa was not as uninformed as she pretended. She knew all about Gus's friend, had made a note of the address he visited, and had immediately recognized the woman skulking outside the shop. So. Gus's chosen companion had followed them here, presumably to look at the competition. There was no competition. However, some devil in Lisa made her play the situation for all it was worth. 'I wonder how your father's getting along in New Zealand?' she asked.

Harrie wiped off her frothy moustache. 'As long as he has an audience, he'll be happy. I do hope he wears a new shirt to his lectures. Frankly, most of the germs in the world are probably attached to that suit of his. He's had it since Noah emptied the ark.'

'Oh, I bought him a new one,' said Lisa. 'Marks and Spencer – two pairs of trousers with it. If he remembered to pack it.'

Sheila stirred her coffee. He wasn't wearing a suit. He was in her back bedroom reading books and making notes on his laptop. It wasn't worth her getting an Internet provider, he had said. All the work he needed to send electronically could wait until he got home. Or back from New Zealand, because that was where the family believed him to be.

'Such a brilliant mind,' said Lisa loudly. 'I hope he gets the recognition he deserves at the end of his search for hospital safety.'

Harrie stared at her mother. What the heck was she going on about?

'Just a minute,' Lisa went on. 'I'll finish this list, then you can see if you have anything to add.' She scribbled for a while, then tore the sheet from her notebook.

Harrie read the note: 'The woman to our right is your father's friend. She lives near the psycho you were visiting. DON'T STARE AT HER.' Harrie passed it back. 'No, that's fine, Mother. Though you must remember to get some single malt before Father comes home. You know how much he loves a good scotch.'

Lisa managed not to choke on her drink. Gus hated alcohol. Apart from the odd glass of red wine with a meal, he was almost teetotal. Happy that her daughter was partaking in the naughtiness, she dabbed her mouth with a napkin and told Harrie to add whisky to the list. 'And chocolate mousse. He enjoys that, as well.' Gus never ate chocolate mousse. Would the woman go and buy the items they had listed? Was she so desperate to impress him that she would follow such ill-advice?

Sheila drank her coffee. They were beautifully dressed, these Compton-Milne females. The younger wore a suit of blue-grey, the elder a dress and coat in milk-chocolate silk. Chocolate mousse. She must remember that. They were talking now about furnishing a bungalow, about a melee of modern and traditional, some bunk beds in case Annie's children wanted to stay. Oh well. Let them get on with their empty little lives.

She stood at the bus stop. In her bag, she had a bottle of Cream of the Barley and some chocolate mousse from the food hall at Marks and Spencer. She would keep him happy. Perhaps he would not want to go home ever again.

Meanwhile, Lisa and Harrie were giggling about their own delinquency. The thought of Gus returning from the Antipodes to a diet of scotch and mousse was too funny for words.

'Were we cruel?' gasped Harrie eventually.

'Probably.' Lisa dried her eyes. 'But she isn't his lover, I am sure. She thinks the relationship is pure and beautiful. Wait till she serves him a shot of single malt – he'll be so polite, yet forceful. She'll get the lecture on liver disease–'

'And the mousse will attract a homily on type-two diabetes.'

They ordered a second coffee and talked about Annie. That subject led them into territory that was occupied by fear. James Nuttall. 'We haven't seen the last of him,' Lisa predicted. 'But let's hope the next time we catch sight, he'll be under arrest and on the six o'clock news.'

Harrie shivered. She was in nominal charge of his children, and she hoped that he would not discover where they were living. If he was vindictive enough to batter a small woman halfway to death, he'd be well capable of trying to take her children from her.

They left to return to their respective shops. Harrie found herself hoping against hope that the twins were behaving themselves for Woebee; Lisa's mind was more happily occupied. How was Gus's woman going to explain away her odd purchases? Or had he told her about his aversion to hard liquor and over-sweet puddings? She imagined him on his first visit after his return, pictured him kneeling among his precious trains, then going into the dining room to be greeted with scotch and rich, sweet stuff.

When she entered the shop, Simon was grinning like the Cheshire cat. 'They're letting Annie out,' he cried.

Lisa grinned. 'Throwing her out, more likely. Simon, put the kettle on. Coffee leaves me so thirsty. Bring on the Earl Grey.'

Ben had locked himself in the van. He needed space not for the usual reason, but because he had something to do. Solitude had become a sudden necessity. After a quick dip in a stream, he was not in a state of real cleanliness, yet that scarcely mattered any more. There was no longer a need for such rigid control in small day-to-day details, but he wanted to be alone for a couple of hours from time to time. For now, he had to be totally in charge, because he had discovered a project.

The first chapter – if it was a chapter – had been written. It was in longhand and in pencil, because pencil was easier to erase. And there had been a fair amount of erasing. Starting a story was difficult. He knew the ending, had a rough idea of the middle, but a beginning was where the reader started, of course. 'Not that it will sell,' he told his grubby fingernails. It was therapy. It had grown from the diary he had kept, but the start altered from day to day, so his tale had an open opening. He'd heard of open endings, but open openings? That would never do.

Compromise was a necessity. He would write down the performers, choose names for them, describe them, then give an account of them. Names would have to be changed to protect the guilty; but that was probably normal. Normal.

He gazed round his living space, saw that it was a mess, though hardly filthy. *That* was normal. Bathing in a stream into which fish had defecated was all right, too. There was no need to worry; he was learning to live and share space with humans and other creatures.

A title had invented itself right from the start. *A Head over my Roof* might seem odd, but he knew what he meant. He was controlling his need to control. He was the head, while the roof was a cap worn by the life he had known thus far. There had been too many ceilings, too many no-go areas.

What was it Mr Martin said? Mr Martin was reputed to be the best teacher of English and creative writing this side of the moon. 'Speak as you find, write as you speak, and never fear language.' Yes, that was it. So the way to write this ... whatever it was, must be as if Ben were speaking it. Gran had what she called a talking-into-it machine, a voice-activated recorder that helped her remember lists.

Thinking of Gran, Ben found himself grinning. She was useless with lists. Woebee's opinion was that Gran wrote the lists then ate them, as she believed they were top-secret documents. He could hear Woebee, too. 'She's never got over reading about Burgess and MacLean – they were spies for the Russians.' Were Woebee and Gran suitable material? Because truth was very strange indeed, a great deal less credible than manufactured stories.

He looked out, saw Josh leading out a mare recently acquired at the Appleby Fair, watched children at play, noticed one of the women hanging out washing. Berated and vilified wherever they went, the travellers held on to their corporate temper for the most part, lived from hand to mouth, loved each other, loved their animals. Their homes were, on the whole, ramshackle wrecks that could be driven or towed at short notice, since moving on was a part of everyday life. Nobody wanted them. Yet they retained a remarkable sense of identity.

They had taken him into their camp without the slightest hesitation. He ate some strange foods and was set to chop wood or fish the stream in return for being fed. It was a barter system seasoned with kindness; it was a way of living he had come not just to endure, but also to enjoy. He'd ridden a horse and had his fortune told; he had experienced more real – and surreal – life in a few weeks than in the previous ten years.

Was he a writer? Writers were meant to be a bit weird, he supposed. But he had been more than a bit weird; he had been off the bloody radar altogether. However, writing was a channel and a challenge. Even if the exercise proved to have no more use than to empty his soul of debris, it would have done its job.

When Annie left the hospital, she behaved in the manner of the Queen Mother, waving from her wheelchair with a slight movement of the hand, almost as if bestowing a blessing on her people. She had so many flowers and planted baskets that she was likened to a trolley emerging from some garden centre after a massive sale.

Outside, she turned, sneezed when a fern inter-

291

fered with her a nostril, then looked at her pilot. 'James,' she said. 'Take me home.'

'I'm Simon.'

'Who's counting?'

Lisa helped Simon to install Annie in the back of the car. Floral attachments were removed from her: some stowed quickly in the boot, others left to chance in the spare rear-seat. Annie, with a colourful turban covering her dignity, chattered almost all the way to Weaver's Warp. Her list of grievances against the hospital was long. The beds were uncomfortable, and no one should be expected to sleep on plastic. 'I've never wet the bed since I was two,' she said. 'And why they have central heating on at the end of July – God only knows. It's like living in a Turkish baths.'

Simon and Lisa exchanged sideways glances.

'No air-conditioning. Food like chipboard and blotting paper. They must have boiled that cauli for a month before serving it up. As for bedside manners – they should all get a refund from whichever charm school they went to.'

Lisa hid a giggle behind her hand.

'It's all right you laughing, missus. That bloke from the fat police is lucky to be alive – I nearly crowned him with me bedpan. There again, bedpans aren't what they were. Fancy having to wee in cardboard. Re-bloody-cycled cardboard at that. Say everybody in the ward did a lot of wee and they had overflow and leakage, it would've been like the streets of Venice after a storm. They used to have enamel bedpans– What's so funny?'

'You are,' answered Simon.

'Oh, aye? You want to try it some time, love.

292

They start sticking bits of cameras up people's dooh-dahs without so much as a by-your-bypass. And every one of them's a flaming Dracula. They want blood for this, blood for that – liver function, kidney function, probably even for social functions. Well, it's free, isn't it? Another way of making a Bloody Mary without the blinking tomato juice. I'm running on empty here.'

Lisa giggled. For somebody running on empty, Annie was getting up a fair head of steam.

'Old woman opposite me – a hundred and three, she looked. They brought her teeth with her breakfast, and when she put the teeth in, they were some other bugger's. She looked like a horse winded after Becher's Brook – it was awful.'

'Be careful,' Simon suggested to their driver. 'She'll have you off the road.'

Lisa slowed down. Tears of laughter were impeding her vision, but Annie was on a roll. 'Annie, will you be quiet so that I can get us all home in one piece?'

'All right.'

Silence reigned for about ten seconds, then was forced into abdication by the Queen Mother in the back seat. 'And her catheter leaked.'

Simon turned round. 'What? Whose catheter?'

Annie sighed in an exaggerated fashion. 'Her with the teeth. Red Rum, we called her after they gave her the wrong ones, but it didn't matter because she was as deaf as a post. She sprung a leak. If the pancreas in the bed next to mine hadn't spoken up, we'd have had to swim out of there. Never mind a bloody wheelchair – it would have taken a life raft.'

Lisa gave up and parked the car. 'Stop it, Annie,' she said. Then, overcome by curiosity, she asked, 'What do you mean by the pancreas in the next bed?'

Annie thought for a moment. 'Oh yes. Her. We called each other by our diseases and accidents, so's we would remember why we were there. She had a pancreas with an I-T-I-S on the end. She nearly died.'

'Then there was Red Rum,' added Simon helpfully.

'Ah, she was different because she had everything wrong.'

'And you were?' Lisa turned and raised her eyebrows.

'I was brains. Obviously.'

Lisa nodded. 'Now, Annie. There are two ways of tackling this. Are you listening?'

'I am.'

'We can call a taxi – I have my mobile here. You may ride home in splendid isolation. Or you can shut up properly. Because if you carry on making me laugh, we'll crash. All right?'

'OK.'

All was quiet until they pulled into Weaver's Weft. The gate to the house swung inward when Lisa used her remote control. 'That was clever,' commented Annie. 'If I'd had one of them at the hospital, no bloody doctor would have got near me.'

'You'd have died,' said Simon.

'Happen I would. But there'd be air-conditioning in heaven, wouldn't there? And no blinking plastic mattresses.'

To that final comment, neither found an answer. There was going to be some fun, Lisa thought ruefully. With Annie, Hermione, Eileen, Craig, Billy and the dog, Weaver's Warp was about to become a national institution. Its name would be Bedlam.

Sheila opened her front door and walked up the hall into the kitchen. After placing her purchases on a counter, she removed her coat, then went upstairs to enquire about the state of her patient. She hadn't yet offered him chocolate mousse or single malt, as he had not seemed well enough. His appetite, which ought to have picked up after he left hospital, continued poor. He was fast reaching the soup followed by rice pudding stage, so she didn't want to tempt fate by offering the goodies advertised by his neglectful wife.

He wasn't in the bedroom. The bathroom door stood wide, and she could see that the space was empty. Looking up, she confirmed that the trap-door into the loft remained in its closed position, so he was not playing with trains. She didn't really expect him to play with trains, not yet. Sutures had already been removed, so he would not be visiting the doctor or the hospital...

Panic struck. Was he worse? Had he been taken in an ambulance? Was he too ill to leave a note? Had he gone home? 'Gus?' she called. 'Gus, where are you?'

No answer was forthcoming. Sheila Barton descended the stairs on leaden feet. His mobile phone. Damn – why had she never asked for the number? There was no point in telephoning any of the labs in which he worked because there were far too many and she didn't know how many people believed he was out of the country. It was all too complicated. Telephoning his wife was out of the question, since she definitely thought he had gone to New Zealand to look at some bees or tea tree oil mixed with something or other – oh, God. What was she going to do?

Downstairs, she sat while dusk arrived, remained where she was until the light had completely gone. Then, feeling stupid, she ran back upstairs to look at his clothes. His lightweight jacket had gone, and his pyjamas were on the floor at the far side of his bed. Slippers sat under a small easy chair – why hadn't she seen all this before? But, no matter how hard she thought, she failed to imagine where he might have gone. His wound was healed and clean, and he had been sitting out his New Zealand time and recharging his batteries – those had been his exact words.

Feeling guilty, she opened the top drawer of the bedside cabinet, gasping when she saw its contents. Pills. At least half a dozen bottles, some with names almost too long to fit on a label. He'd never mentioned any medication...

Shivering, Sheila went into the kitchen and made tea. It wasn't like him. He always left a note. Gus was too precise a man for such careless behaviour. Something had happened. The phone did not ring. She sat next to it, almost on top of it, and it still refused to ring. He had a mobile; he could call from just about anywhere.

The hands of her mother's clock crawled slowly

over its face. Nine o'clock, ten. Darkness came to claim all the space around her, so she switched on a table lamp and watched the television news. Nothing was said about accidents to brilliant professors. Midnight found her in the same position, her head nodding towards sleep. Every time her chin dropped, she came to with a start, heart pounding, ears straining for a sound – any sound.

It had to be something extraordinarily unusual. Gus would not have gone without letting her know, not unless something had happened very suddenly. Heart attack? Ambulance? It was too late now to ask the neighbours, and she didn't mix with them, anyway.

She toyed with the idea of telephoning hospitals – even the police. But he might think her foolish if she did anything so rash. The police would contact his family, and that would do no good.

Finally, she lost her fight against sleep and dozed fitfully in a chair not designed for such purpose. When she woke at dawn, she had a crick in her neck. And he still had not come home.

Mr Earnshaw entered the tower room in which the girl had lain for more than two decades. He saw the violent finale of her fit, watched monitors as they went haywire, heard doctors shouting out orders regarding defibrillation. When the spasms ended, someone looked at the EEG result and declared brain activity to be minimal. The paddles were out, pads on the patient's thorax, the unit charged to two hundred. Everyone was ordered to stand back so that electricity might be fired through the now motionless figure on the bed.

'Shock,' ordered the man in charge.

'Stop,' commanded the newly-arrived visitor.

A nun turned to face him. 'Mr Earnshaw – she was doing so well until this fit. I swear to God she was beginning to see me. Can we not try again?'

'No.'

'But–'

'No. I am her guardian, and the stupidity and the money keeping her here are both mine. This has not been a life. Suspended animation is no longer an option. Let her go. I shall sit with her while she dies.'

None of the lay medics argued with him. Many had held for some time the opinion that the princess in the tower should be allowed to die. But Sister Mary Magdalene was on her knees. 'Please, please,' she begged.

The man shook his head slowly. 'I shall not always be here to pay the bills. The electro-encephalograph shows huge damage. I am a doctor, and I know the implications. Please, clear the room. I need to be with her.'

They left.

He sat for many hours holding the hand of this beloved and beautiful creature who had never truly lived. He told her stories about his life, about the nuns who had cared for her, about the siblings who had never known her, who would never meet her. He described the home she might have had, the mother who had not once held this baby in her arms. Finally, he fell asleep in the armchair.

He woke with a stiff neck, his body rigid and strangely cold. The temperature in the room had been maintained at a constant level for a long time, yet he felt as if he had been to the North Pole. Mary Magdalene was sitting next to Mathilda at the other side of the bed. 'Has she gone?' he asked.

'Soon,' was the broken reply.

'I'm sorry, Sister. I know that you have loved her. We never knew her personality, but she looks like one of your saints, doesn't she?'

'Indeed, she does. She is. We baptized her – I hope you don't mind – so there will be no Limbo for her, no Purgatory.'

'Just straight to Heaven, do not pass go, do not collect your money?'

'You don't believe.'

'It makes no sense to me. I subscribe to the belief that we are animals like the rest and that the end is the end. We may have acquired the means to communicate in a superior manner, together with the ability to kill with ease and without conscience, but I expect no afterlife. In fact, I should prefer it so.' He looked at Mathilda. 'She will never walk, talk, marry, work, have children. I cannot continue with such cruelty.'

The nun cleared her throat. 'Why did you bring her here in the first place?'

He didn't know, and he said that.

Magda left the room to attend Chapel. The man sat again and held the hand of the only piece of love he had carried with him for as long as he cared to remember. His chest hurt, his neck was sore, while his spine, made stiff by a night in the armchair, ached from skull to coccyx. 'Go,' he whispered. 'Go where there is no pain and no worry.' She would never have another fit. The decision to sedate would not need to be made ever again.

When she expelled carbon dioxide for the last time, he stood, kissed the alabaster forehead, felt for pulses in order to make sure that she was safely on her way. The silence was deafening. No beeps, no ticks, no respirator. So beautiful. Perfect child in a room of virginal white. Appropriate.

Mr Earnshaw turned to leave the room. He had to tell the nuns that their beloved Mathilda had gone. Mr Earnshaw had entered the tower, but Gustav Compton-Milne left it.

He had to interrupt Mass. Mother Benedict followed him into a corridor lined with statues and small coloured vases in which tea lights flickered. 'We know who you are,' she told him. 'We have seen you on television.'

'Yes.' He paused. Had Gus not turned on his mobile phone, Mathilda would probably still be alive in the technical sense. He cleared his throat. 'We shall give her a Catholic funeral. I shall, of course, attend if my health allows it. She will be buried with her mother, who was Catholic. Please phone a taxi for me. I was not well enough to drive here yesterday.' He'd had no car, anyway. His Mini was still up at Weaver's Warp. 'And thank you – all of you. She was hope. At the bottom of Pandora's box, only hope remained.' He burst into tears, sobbing so fiercely that Mother led him into her office. 'There now,' she said, patting his shoulder. 'You'll be all right.'

He shook his head. He would not be all right. That was an absolute certainty. 'She's gone again,' he sobbed. 'Gone from me twice over.'

Mother Benedict could not guess what he was talking about, yet she recognized truth born of real, deep anguish. 'God bless you,' she said. And, whether or not he believed in the Deity, she meant it. His grief was profound, and she pitied him for it.

It rained. It rained in a professional manner, persistently, deliberately, taking just short breaths between heavy showers. Jimmy was fed up. When Gustav Wotsisface came back from New Zealand, the office window would be closed, and there would be no chance of the room getting searched. The attacks of panic were closer together now. He could not concentrate to read, listen to the radio, watch TV.

He asked Sal when the master of the house was expected back. 'They said he'd gone for about three weeks,' she answered. 'But he's one of them folk who just does as he wants. He might be back tomorrow, or he could stay till Christmas. Anyway, nobody misses him.'

'And the boy?'

'Still away. I heard Harrie saying something about him writing a book.'

'She carrying on living in that wooden shack?'

Sal nodded. She nodded because she didn't know what else to do. The fact was that Harrie had moved back into her old room, while Jimmy's wife and kids were occupying the new bungalow. 'People come and go up yon,' she told him. 'They move about. I don't know who's where and what's what because I don't live in.'

Jimmy was already preparing for plan B. He had removed from Sal's shed a pre-war heater and enough paraffin to keep it going for several days. Even if the weather warmed up again, nights in that empty farmhouse might be cold. He had made a couple of careful journeys for tinned food, and he was almost ready to make a move, an action he would take only if it became absolutely necessary. He thanked his lucky stars that Cotters Farm was derelict. It was far enough away from Sal's cottage to be safe, near enough if he needed any help from her.

But he wasn't sure of Sal any more. She had become grumpy, sometimes almost ill-tempered. Meals were thrown together in haste, and she made no effort in the house or with her appearance. They slept now in separate rooms because she rose early and didn't want to disturb him. That was her excuse for it, anyway. He knew the truth; she wanted rid of him as soon as possible.

'I'll be going when I get the gun back,' he said.

She didn't even turn her head, as she was engrossed in an antiquated drama series on Sky. 'OK,' was all the reply she offered. Then, when the commercials interrupted her programme, she added, 'What if you don't find it? What if it's not in the office?'

He had to tell her. If he didn't prepare her, there was a chance she might crack wide open once plan B came into operation. While the Compton-Milnes would soon be made aware of the identity of the kidnapper, he needed a couple of days during which they might worry. 'I'm going to kidnap the daughter,' he said. Jimmy was amazed when she jumped from her seat with an alacrity he had not seen in weeks.

'You what?' Her face glowed with heat. 'What did you say?'

'You heard.'

'You can't do that.' His children were in the bungalow! 'You never know where she is. Sometimes, she sleeps in the house in her old room, sometimes she stays in the bungalow with her boyfriend.'

'I won't be taking her from the house,' he said. 'I'll take her from the shop she works in, and then I'll have two things to barter – the girl and her diamonds. So when she does disappear, you know nothing. Do you hear me?'

Sal nodded mutely.

'If they catch on, I'll know it was you who gave them the nod. If I have to take the girl, I will.'

Jimmy walked out of the house and sat in his van. He sat in his van quite often these days. Hanging around in an old wreck covered in carpet was infinitely preferable to staying in with Sal Potter. He had to trust her, had to depend on the fact that she feared him. A couple of months ago, she would have protected him for love, a bit of furniture and a plasma TV. Now, she kept her mouth shut for two reasons. Firstly, she knew he would batter her if she spoke up; secondly, she was involved. Not only had she harboured a criminal, but she had also gone to work for the very family he was targeting.

The route map was ready. Because of the rain

and the need to save energy, he had worked out a way of taking the van along country lanes and hiding it before doing the final mile or so on foot. If he found what he needed, there would be no kidnap; if not... What if they told the police? What if they didn't tell the police until they had the daughter returned to them, only to inform them after the event?

He had to admit that he didn't really know what he was doing. The Compton-Milnes could take the gun to the police whenever – just on a whim. He might be too late. Was there any sense in the plan? Lisa and her family could tell the cops about the gun when everything was over. He couldn't win. But, by God, he would go down fighting. Because he hadn't done the Birmingham job. To that single truth, he clung like a leech. It wasn't fair; he would try to redress the balance. And he realized that he was rocking back and forth again...

Sheila almost jumped out of her skin when she heard the key turning. She looked in the mirror, tidied her hair, then stood waiting for him to come to her. But he didn't come. She heard his heavy, slow footfalls as he made his way up the stairs. The door to his bedroom closed. Sheila blinked and scratched her head. Even for Gustav Compton-Milne, this behaviour was excessively eccentric.

After a few minutes, she began to set a tray for him. She knew he liked ham salad sandwiches and a sliced, cored apple accompanied by a chunk of Lancashire cheese. With a nice cloth on

304

the tray and a pot of tea, she crept up the stairs. He was sobbing. As quiet as any mouse, she placed the tray on a landing table, then knocked on his door. 'Gus?' She paused. 'Gus, are you all right? I've brought a sandwich and a bit of fruit. Some hot tea, too.'

Inside, Gus dried his eyes. It occurred to him that he had scarcely eaten for twenty-four hours, and his strength was failing. 'Come in,' he said, his voice wavering.

She placed the food on a bedside cabinet, poured tea and milk into his cup. It seemed impolite to look at him. Men did not weep. If they did, they probably preferred to shed tears without an audience in attendance.

'Sit down,' he told her.

She sat.

Gus took a mouthful of tea, but did not begin to eat. 'Sheila, my daughter died early this morning.'

A hand flew to her throat. Not that pretty girl in the gorgeous grey suit. She was so lively, so beautiful, so—

'Not Harriet,' he told her. 'This one was older, and she had a different mother. This one was Mathilda.'

There was nothing to say except, 'I'm so sorry.'

'Her mother died giving birth. Mathilda was frail. I took her to the nuns, and they fought time and time again to save her. And I allowed that, even though I knew that brain damage could increase with every fit. But the machinery told us she was viable, even if she did need ventilation because of varying levels of necessary sedation.'

305

He drank more tea. 'I decided to let her go.'

'Oh, Gus.'

He sighed. 'It's been a long night. Thank you for the food. Thank you, Sheila, for everything.'

Knowing she had been dismissed, Sheila left the room. She now knew who Katherina was and why Gus visited the grave. Like many males, he hugged the most precious of truths close to his chest, living life as if now was all that mattered. Buried in research, he had seldom allowed grief to interfere with his regime. She admired him more than ever before. This was, indeed, one of the greatest of men.

Sheila did her chores, prepared an upside-down cake for the oven, tidied away dishes and pans.

'Sheila?'

He was in the doorway. 'Oh, hello,' she said.

'I need your help. I want you to go to the lab in Manchester – I'll give you a letter and I'll phone them – and you must ask for the Mathilda file. No one will think that odd because we often give female names to lines of research. The deeds for the grave are in there. Mathilda's body will be brought to a Bolton undertaker. Please come to the funeral with me.'

'Of course I will.'

'There will be just us and a handful of nuns. But she has to go back to her mother. She should have gone with her in the first...' His voice died. 'I did wrong, didn't I?'

She had never before heard him expressing self-doubt. 'Who can say? Mathilda might have made it, Gus. Only God knew the outcome.'

306

He nodded. 'But I played God, you see. I played a being whose existence I have never acknowledged. I kept her alive. Who was I to make a decision of that magnitude?'

'But–'

'But she should have been allowed to die at birth or soon after. The fight began there and then, and I could see that it was potentially futile. Once the baby was stable enough to travel, I took her to the nuns. It cost money and time, yet I was fool enough to let it happen – to make it happen. I feel so ashamed of myself.'

Sheila was lost for words. She opened her mouth to offer a grain of comfort, but nothing emerged.

'Be there for me. My family – my real family – knows nothing.'

'I'll be there. I'll get your deeds. Telephone the lab.'

'Yes.' He turned to leave.

'Gus?'

'You did nothing wrong. Being an eminent scientist doesn't mean you are not human. Mistakes are human.'

He smiled wanly, then left the doorway.

Lisa was a light sleeper. She had to have complete quiet, and, even if her bedroom was absolutely dark, she needed the eye mask. The slightest sound, the smallest chink of light, and she was wide awake and annoyed.

It was just after two thirty when she heard the first noise. She knew the house off by heart, was used to its aged creakings and groanings when

307

water pipes cooled, when the wind blew, when a door wasn't closed properly. Weaver's Warp had a lot to say for itself, but it wasn't speaking tonight. Whatever she had heard was a wrong sound, a different noise.

She sat up, peeled off her mask, switched on a forty-watt lamp and reached for her dressing gown. It was cold. Nights were developing an edge, as if preparing England for the coming of autumn. Gus was away. Gus would not have been much use, anyway. Had he been here, she might well have blamed him for the disturbance, as he had a disconcerting habit of working well into the night. Lisa wondered whether Harrie was up and about. Or had Will arrived?

She got out of bed and pushed her feet into a pair of mules. Even Ben was away. She could not imagine Ben as a protector, but there were no men at all in the house. The very sight of a man might put off a burglar. Had Will's dog found a way in yet again? Her dedication to Hermione was commendable, but rather a nuisance.

It was no good. She would have to go and see what was going on, or she would never get back to sleep. Another little sound – a quiet thud this time. And none of the disturbance was coming from above, so Hermione was not having another of her accidents. Hermione's misfortunes were different in nature; they were loud and accompanied by a great deal of cursing.

She opened her bedroom door and stood on the landing. There was someone downstairs. These were not kitchen sounds; no water tumbled into a kettle, no cups or plates clattered. It was the study. Lisa's hearing had been likened to that of a bat, especially when the children had been young and up to mischief. There had been no midnight feasts for Harrie and Ben, because Mother had radar.

Feeling a little foolish, she crept down the stairs and saw a light under the study door. Gus's office was often lit in the night, but this light was mobile. It was a torch. Should she wake Harrie? Should she phone for police? It was probably nothing; she would make a complete idiot of herself if she sent for help and it wasn't needed. Perhaps it was Harrie in the study. If the lights in there had fused, a torch would be needed. It could be Gus. He often turned up when least expected.

At the study door, she stopped. She could hear the thud of her heart; she swore she could hear breathing. The breathing was not her own. She was suddenly terrified. As she turned to run, she overturned a Victorian sewing stand. The sturdy item made loud contact with parquet floor. As she righted herself, an arm reached out from behind and covered her mouth. Fighting and kicking, she was dragged into her husband's office.

Thrown into a chair, she blinked hard. The torch was shining right into her eyes.

'Where is it?'

Lisa bit the hand that tried to stop her breathing. When he drew back, she made a supreme effort to compose herself. 'Where is what?' She remembered how poor Annie had looked in hospital, knew what this man had done. He was probably capable of murder.

'The gun.'

She had no idea. 'I don't know.' But she could not tell the truth, dared not say that Hermione had taken charge of the thing. The old woman had enough problems without being beaten senseless by this thug.

'Then you'd better find out. Because I am not going down for Birmingham. All right? What did I just say?'

'You are not going down for Birmingham.'

He laughed, but there was no humour in the sound. 'Get the gun,' he said.

She blew out her cheeks. 'It'll be in a safety deposit box at the bank. Or with our lawyers. It's not here.'

He looked round the dimly lit room. 'You wouldn't know what's here and what isn't. Bloody dump.'

She offered no further comment.

'Right,' he said. 'I've got your mobile number. I'll phone you tomorrow, and you can tell me where I can find the gun. Otherwise, there'll be real trouble.'

'You'd better go. I'm not alone here.'

He smirked. 'I know more about this house than you can imagine. This isn't my first time in your home. And someone has been helping me to watch. Oh yes, I've been keeping eyes and ears open. There's nobody here except the old witch upstairs.'

Lisa had reached the end of her rope, but she held in all she wanted to say. It was important that she stayed alive. It was vital that she should

310

ring the police.

'You used to love me,' he said, a nasty edge to his voice.

'Mistake,' she replied.

He pushed his face close to hers. 'Phone the police and I'll make sure you suffer. They'll not find me in a hurry. Plenty of time for me to make sure that you and yours suffer. And I mean suffer. Get me that gun. After that, I'll bugger off and take my chances.'

He left the way he had entered – through an open window.

Lisa breathed deeply. Harrie was one of the fortunate people because she slept through most things. Lisa thanked God because her daughter was safe. What was to be done now? What would any sane person do? Firstly, she locked the window. There was no alarm in here because Gus set the things off with monotonous frequency.

She picked up the phone and dialled the three nines. Before the connection had been made, she slammed the receiver back into its cradle. 'I know more about this house...' he had said. 'This is not the first time...' Think, think. 'Someone has been helping me to watch...'

Eileen. Eileen had been following Sal Potter for weeks now. 'If you ask me, she's a burglar in disguise. She's up chimneys and pulling kick boards off in the kitchen, says she's after mice. There's something funny going on, and I don't mean funny ha-ha. Now, she's rattling about in both sideboards...' Why did people not listen properly to Eileen? In a nonsensical way, the woman made sense.

Lisa sank into Gus's leather chair. She would wait until morning. Tomorrow, there was going to be an extraordinary general meeting. Now, where was that address?

Eleven

Lisa was in what she judged to be the daftest position ever. Across from Sal Potter's house, she had secreted herself behind a ragged hawthorn hedge that had probably never been manicured, and she was lying flat on a couple of black rubbish bags. It was extraordinarily cold. The leaves and branches were prickly, she was getting cramp, and she was a fool.

What the heck was she doing here in the chill of dawn? Why hadn't she simply picked up the phone again and had him arrested? She shifted position in order to achieve a degree of comfort, failed miserably, took a sip of tepid coffee from a Thermos jug lid, hid as best she could, and lit a cigarette. It was about five o'clock and the sun was threatening to rise. All around her, pasture was sodden from recent heavy rain, and her shoes were ruined. Decent shoes, too, she mused as she waited.

Quarter past five. She sat up. It was too early to be completely flattened in the cause of safe concealment, and the hedge was thick enough. 'I'm not here,' she told the distant Friesian cows. 'I am a product of your collective imagination.'

She bet herself a new pair of shoes that Jimmy Nuttall was living with Sal Potter, that he had sent her to spy. The bet didn't really count because she would be buying new shoes anyway, but there

313

were shoes and there were shoes. If she won, it would be serious shoes with a serious matching handbag. She could wander into Jenkinsons and see if her old collagen friend could kit her out.

Hugging her knees, she kept her eyes glued to Sal Potter's windows. The next couple of hours were going to be the longest week of her life. There was a big hole in the right leg of her tights. She should have worn old jogging pants, but she couldn't because she didn't have any. 'Could have, would have, should have.' Twenty-five to six.

Think. Think. Keep occupied. Ben's going to be OK. That was what Harriet had said, and Harriet was the cleverest person known to Lisa. Except for Ben himself, who was off the graph in most directions. He was living with travelling folk, was washing his clothes in a stream, was writing a book. It was time somebody in this family did something vaguely interesting.

A quarter to six.

I am lucky, Lisa thought. This bloody gun business had been to protect her, to prevent Jimmy from naming her as accomplice in his burglaries. But she didn't care any more. He was going to be locked up. Had it not been for her inquisitiveness, he would have been in a cell already. She was here to prove Eileen right. Wasn't she?

The sun announced its arrival, brilliance stretching across a promising sky just before the true light appeared. Perhaps she should go home. This was a stupid place to be. What on earth would customers think if they saw her in such a state? Six o'clock. Clever people were still in bed;

314

only lunatics hung around in damp grass just to prove an Irishwoman right.

A door slammed, and Lisa thought she might have a heart attack on the spot. He was there. She peered through gaps in the hawthorn and drew breath sharply. Large as life and twice as ugly, Jimmy Nuttall had emerged from Sal's house. It had to be her house because it was the only one in sight. Eileen had been right. Sal Potter was looking for the Birmingham gun. 'Hell's bells and buckets of whitewash,' she whispered. 'Conniving cow.'

He dragged carpet from the back end of his van, got into the driver's seat and reversed off Sal's land. So he wanted his gun back today, did he? He'd be getting more than a gun, a lot more. Arrested, was what he would be getting. She stayed for a few minutes, then edged out of the field gate and began the walk back towards her car. She had proved Eileen right. And the danger was still out there. He had to be caught. Today.

'I know this may sound terrible,' said the dark brown voice at the other end of the line, 'but people do play tricks. I am sorry to tell you that this would not be the first time. We haven't yet had the death certificate, and the person who called about the funeral could have been a nasty prankster. It was a mobile number, you see. It's currently switched off, and we haven't been able to ask for the necessary paperwork. So I found Dr Compton-Milne's home number because I need to speak to him.'

Harrie held the phone away from her ear and

315

examined the item, as if there might be something wrong with it. The man with the graveyard voice had just told her that she was dead. Symptoms to prove that she was adhering to life were manifold, and not the least among them was the fact that she was able to speak. 'I am Gustav Compton-Milne's only daughter,' she informed the invisible entity, 'and I remain in the land of the living.'

'You are Mathilda?'

'No, I am Harriet.'

'What about Mathilda?'

A flippant response about Australian folk songs was deleted from the agenda before it saw the light of day because the man was so very serious. 'There is no Mathilda,' she replied. 'There's just Harriet and Benjamin.'

'Died in Nazareth House in Didsbury? Aged twenty-seven? Interment at Tonge Cemetery after a requiem Mass? We have to pick up the deceased, and we have never dealt with a Nazareth House before. It would not be the first time such nastiness has happened, which is why we seek confirmation in this case.'

Harrie sat on a stool. If she hadn't sat, she might have fallen, as she suddenly felt dizzy. 'Who phoned you?' she asked.

'Dr Gustav Compton-Milne, professor of microbiology. It could have been one of his students, you see. There are some nasty people about. Sorry to have–'

'He's in New Zealand. My father is working in Auckland – he's an expert in the field of hospital super-bugs.'

There followed a short pause. 'I have no

316

number for Nazareth House, and I have never heard of the place, but I shall find it if it exists. It's outside our normal area, you see. We usually bury people from Bolton and the surrounding district. Yes. That would be the sensible thing to do if your father is abroad. I shall look for a number. Thank you for your time.'

The line went dead. Harrie continued to hold the phone, her fingers curling tightly around it until she felt pain in her knuckles. The world had gone mad, and her mother had gone missing. Mathilda was dead, and Father was abroad and...

Did people really make hoax calls to undertakers? If it was a hoax, why Mathilda? Who picked such an unusual name?

Lisa rushed in while Harrie was still perched open-mouthed on her stool, phone clutched to her chest. 'Crisis,' Lisa yelled. 'Upstairs. Now. We need to get together – you, me, your gran and Eileen. Annie, too.'

Harrie blinked a few times. 'What?'

'We have to have a meeting.'

'Who's Mathilda?' Harrie asked.

Lisa tutted. 'No time for who's who, sweetie. I've been under a hedge watching – oh, never mind. Then I went and arranged for Simon to supervise your shop and Roger to run mine. It's the gun, you see.' She ran out of the kitchen.

Harrie felt very strange. She dug into a chemist's bag and pulled out the article she had purchased the previous day. 'Might as well go the whole nine yards,' she said to the package. 'It's a mad day, so let's try to make a royal flush of it.'

Several minutes later, the flush was performed

317

in the downstairs loo. It was game, set, match and bull's eye. So many mixed metaphors. Harrie was pregnant.

He would be in possession of the missing gun today. Lisa wouldn't dare talk to the police – she would be implicated in the burglar-alarm scam. She hadn't the guts. Now, he needed to go to the twenty-four hour garage for a few more supplies. He knew all the back lanes. The only vehicle he might meet would be a tractor.

List. Had he forgotten anything? He had to stop this rocking. His mind was busy all the time, inventing scenarios and imagining outcomes, fearing prison, thinking, thinking. List. A fridge would have been good, but he couldn't carry one, and there was no electricity at Cotters Farm. His brain was working, yet it wasn't. There was something wrong with his legs. They weren't steady; nor were his hands. Gun, gun, gun. It was all he ever thought about.

Kidnap was a big deal. But the only thing that mattered was the truth. For once, he was not guilty. Birmingham was just a place halfway between here and London. He scarcely remembered being there. But he would carry the can for it if the cops got the weapon used on that guard. God, he wished he could stop shaking. Get the stuff, take it to the farm, phone Lisa, go for the gun.

Or. Get the stuff, take it to the farm, phone Lisa, pick up her daughter. Risky. 'But it wasn't my gun. I never had a gun, never shot anybody,' he told the windscreen. Birmingham. It was nothing to do with him. That was his truth, his one truth. If only his hands and legs would calm down...

Gus wasn't at all well. Sheila did her best, but she wanted to call her doctor. 'You'll be classed as a temporary resident,' she told him. 'You can't go on like this, can you?' His hair was thinner. She'd found some of it floating in the lavatory. 'Gus?'

'Yes?'

She swallowed hard. 'Are you on chemotherapy?'

He turned to face the wall. There was a gap in that lovely head of hair.

'You've the funeral to see to, haven't you?'

He managed to sit up. 'I go for more tests this afternoon. Yes, it is chemotherapy, and I may need radiotherapy as well. There's also a possibility of further surgery.'

Gus had never been a highly animated person, but the life seemed to be draining out of him before her very eyes. He was giving up. 'You have to fight this,' she told him.

'I am fighting. My immune system is depleted, and that is why you're still boiling everything. But a patient can live too long in a bubble. I have to get out. And I have to go home after the funeral.'

He had no home. He had a wife, a daughter and a son at the other side of Bolton, but his life was here and in the laboratories. The family didn't care about him. She knew now that he hated whisky and chocolate mousse, was fully aware that Lisa and Harriet had put on a show

319

for her. They knew who she was, all right. Nasty, nasty women. 'I can look after you properly,' she said.

'Like you did for your husband? Why should you go through all that again?'

'This is different. I didn't love him.' She clapped a hand to her mouth for a split second. 'You're like a brother to me.'

'I know, and I'm grateful. But there are things I need to deal with. Most of my personal notes are at Weaver's Warp, as is my blood family. I have a mother there. There's a will to amend, the office to go through, and I must, must talk to my wife and to Harriet and Benjamin.'

'Right.' She was more than disappointed – she was devastated. What if he died? What if she never saw him again? This was a big house for one woman. Perhaps it was time for her to go the way of all flesh, put one foot in the grave and buy a two-bedroomed bungalow in Harwood. She could certainly afford it if she sold these two properties. Or she could keep one. The rent she charged was enough to live on.

'Sheila?'

'What?'

'You'll be all right. I know you will. You have more strength than you realize. You're still relatively young, and you should develop some interests. Go to evening classes, make friends.' That's what he should have done, he mused. Perhaps not the evening classes, but a few close companions might have helped to make the next six months more palatable. Chemotherapy was no fun. He fell back on to the pillows. 'Let me rest for an hour,' he begged.

Downstairs, Sheila decided to be practical. Being practical had brought her back from the edge many times when she had nursed her dying husband. She went out to the small shed and pulled out a wheelchair. Gus would get to Mathilda's funeral even if she had to push him all the way from here and up Bury Road to the cemetery. She would not let him down.

She cleaned the chair thoroughly before parking it in the front room. No, she would not forsake him. She wasn't like those two women in their perfectly cut blue-grey and chocolate suits. Sheila Barton was a real woman, and a real woman stood by her brother.

'Harrie? Where on earth are you?' Lisa's voice floated down two stairways until it reached the hall. 'What are you doing?'

'I'm on the phone.' She was using a portable instrument, and she carried it out into the garden. Pregnant. Bloody hell. And who the heck was Mathilda, and what was the matter with Mother?

'Hello, Nazareth House, Sister Marie Claire speaking. How can I help you?'

Harrie swallowed hard. 'My name is Susan Watkins and I am calling from Rushton's Funeral Services in Bolton. We have the first name of the deceased, but no surname. Mr Rushton left that part blank – sorry.'

'Ah. You're meaning Mathilda?'

Harrie's heart skipped a beat. 'Yes. We need a death certificate.'

'I think Dr Compton-Milne has that. We

321

already spoke to one of the Mr Rushtons a few minutes ago. Perhaps he didn't tell you yet? Mr Compton-Milne will bring in the certificate later today. We have a copy, so we can release the body when the undertaker arrives.'

He was in New Zealand and–

'Hi, Harrie.' BillyandCraig flew towards her. The whole household now lumped them together, no space between the names, because where one was, the other was almost always by his side and up to the same mischief.

Harrie put a finger to her lips.

They stood and stared at her.

She didn't know what else to say. The twins started jumping up and down and were pulling funny faces at her. The poor Irish nun at the other end said 'Hello?' several times.

Harrie pulled herself together. 'Sorry about that, Sister. Some children have come to say goodbye to their grandfather.'

'You what?' Billy asked.

'God bless them,' said the sister.

'So Mr Compton-Milne has been to Nazareth House and has the death certificate?' Harrie asked.

'Oh, yes. He'll give it to you later on today. He was with her when she passed, poor man.'

'Thank you. Goodbye.' Harrie switched off the phone.

A tousled Annie was on her way to the house. It seemed that she, too, had been invited to the conference. 'You coming?' she asked.

'Er ... yes. What are you going to do with those two?' Harrie said.

'They're off to Mrs Eckersley's house. Her husband is going to watch them and Daisy. Mrs Eckersley took Daisy across earlier.'

God would need to be on Stanley Eckersley's side today, Harrie decided. Now, there was to be a meeting with Gran and Mother and goodness alone knew how many others. Mother had been missing earlier; Father was not where he was supposed to be. There were many mad people in the world, and most of them were related to Harrie.

Annie disappeared up the side of the house, each arm clinging to one twin. She was blonde today. Well, a dirty sort of blonde, but it suited her. The wigs kept her feeling human until her hair grew back, Harrie supposed. Pregnant.

Will was walking towards the bungalow. He was carrying supermarket bags loaded with groceries. 'I don't know where they put it all.' He was referring to the twins and their capacity for food. 'Hello, you,' he said. 'I've finished Annie's shopping.'

Right, he needed to be the first to know. It was hardly the right time and place, but it had to be done and–

'Harriet!'

Oh, well. Mother meant business. She had descended two flights of stairs in order to capture the attention of her wayward daughter. And she was using Harrie's full name, so there was something deadly serious afoot. As well as all the other stuff...

'Sorry, Will. Talk later. Oh – dump that lot, then get across the road and help Stanley Eckersley.

He's got the kids.' She, also, had a kid. It would be about the size of a millet seed, she supposed...

'Harriet?' yelled Lisa again.

'Coming! See you later,' she said to Will before going off to do her mother's bidding. She wouldn't be much use. There was a dead Mathilda, a missing father and a cluster of cells – it wasn't going to be easy to concentrate. But Mother was flustered, so the meeting was bound to have almost as much significance as a G8. 'Onward, Christian soldiers,' she muttered before walking resignedly into the house. Mother was rattling on about cows, shoes and guns. The world was insane, and it promised to get worse.

Stanley and Eileen had never been blessed with children, and both had been sad about it. But Stanley was having second – and third – thoughts. Daisy was lovely, yet the other two could start a war in a monastery – no doubt about that. They were in the garden. He had hidden most implements and was hoping that he would still have a garden at the end of the day. Daisy, happily established at the kitchen table with crayons and paper, was a saint.

Craig ran in. 'Can we water the garden for you?'

There had been enough rain to provide water for half a century. 'No.'

'Even a little bit?'

'No. And no means no, mister.'

Craig left the scene. Stanley watched while Annie made her way back to the big house. She'd hardly been away twenty seconds, and they were already playing up. Would they survive to the age of nine? How old had Bonnie and Clyde been when they'd blown the kick-off whistle?

It was Billy's turn. Billy was the taller one, Stanley reminded himself. And he owned the cheekier grin.

'Do you want any weeding done?' the boy asked.

'Not at the moment, thanks,' replied the man of the house. 'I do my own weeding regular as clockwork.' That was an apt remark, thought Stanley, because these two were winding him up something shocking.

'We only charge two quid. And we know the difference between weeds and flowers.'

'So do I.' Stanley comforted himself by gazing at Daisy at the table. She was a lovely little flower, whereas these two weeds... He turned to look at Billy, but there was just an empty doorway. As quickly as age allowed, Stanley went to the back window. There was no sign of either boy in the rear garden. He ran to the front window – no joy there, either.

'Cat,' said Daisy.

'What, love?'

'BillyandCraig have a cat. They ran with it.'

'To the big house?'

Daisy nodded. Not yet three, she had already learned that she was required as a second pair of eyes in the service of her mother. 'They found it outside that door.'

'Bugger,' said Stanley.

'Bugger.' Daisy lined up her crayons in an orderly fashion, got down from her chair and took

Stanley's hand. 'Find them,' she said. She was used to this. She and Mam often went on long walks in search of the twins. 'Find BillyandCraig,' she insisted.

They walked hand in hand out of the house, only to find that Will was halfway across the lane and moving in their direction. 'Did they get away already?' he asked cheerfully.

'They did.' Stanley's mouth was set for a moment in a grim, tight line. 'Daisy says they've got a cat. Did you not see them coming across? With a cat?'

Will shook his head. 'They could have gone down the other side of the house. All the gates are open. We'd better find them, because there's some sort of summit conference going on in the roof. Harrie's mother is not in the best of moods.'

On the brink of saying 'bugger' again, Stanley bit his tongue. Daisy was too quick a learner, and he must not curse in front of her. She could already count to twenteen, and Stanley had been teaching her, with a degree of success, that it was really twenty. Counting that far at such an age meant that 'bugger' would be just another *bon mot* to add to her increasing collection.

They entered the house and mayhem was advertised immediately by Eileen, who stood half-way up the first flight, arms folded, expression far from inviting and hugely less than pretty. 'What are you at?' she asked her husband. 'Three children we gave you. Just three kiddies for you to tend. The twins arrived just seconds ago at our house across the way. Can you not keep an eye on Annie's lot for a short time?'

326

'They disappeared,' he said. 'I can't keep up with them.'

'Well,' she said. 'You can get yourself up here now and see the mess you made of it all. I've never come across the likes in all me born days, may the Mother of God be my witness. They're here. With a cat that has no patience and no sense of humour at all.'

Daisy climbed on to the stairlift. 'Ride,' she demanded.

Stanley pressed the switch and the ascent began.

'Get up here now, the both of you. Will, you're a tall lad. We need a tall lad.' Eileen lifted Daisy off her throne and sat her on the second stairlift.

Stanley was fed up. He was falling behind with his gardening jobs, which paid better in the summer months. And why was he falling behind? Because of two kids and a cat. A thought struck. 'Oh, no,' he muttered.

'What?' Will was right behind Stanley in more ways than one. The twins were driving just about everyone to drink, distraction, or both.

'Your dog!' Stanley shouted.

Will stood in the doorway of Hermione's living room and wondered why a person never had a camera at moments like this. The cat was up the curtains, was clinging to the pelmet like a desperate survivor of the *Titanic*. Milly, acting as jailer, was at the hem of the curtains. She was whining because she had lost her new toy. Her new toy began to spit and yowl. Annie, who was not long out of hospital, was standing precariously on the window seat. Even on the window seat, she

327

was too tiny for the job, though the dormer was relatively shallow.

'Get down,' shouted Hermione.

Annie got down.

Stanley, muttering oaths under his breath, dragged the Alsatian from the room. Will reached up to rescue the cat and was repaid for his trouble by the removal of skin from his left arm and the pain that accompanied this attack.

'It's lost,' said Billy sadly.

'Out,' yelled Will. 'And take the other one with you. And don't let the dog in.' Said dog was now barking furiously.

'Lost,' repeated the twins in unison.

Will glared at the twins. 'The cat is not lost – it's too well fed to be lost. Didn't I tell you to get out? Well?'

Harrie watched as the twins slunk from the room. Will was probably good at his job in a concrete jungle populated by ASBOs and delinquent parents. He had presence.

So did the cat.

It took about twenty minutes and several towels before the feline was captured. The dog was still barking, but Stanley had shown enough sense to drag her out into the gardens. Blinded by the towels, Puss was placed in an upside-down bird cage on to which the bottom – now the top – was attached at speed. 'Good God,' breathed Will. 'That was nearly as much trouble as year nine.' Sweating profusely, he faced an appreciative audience. 'You can carry on now.' He winked at Harrie, then left the room, a screaming caged cat in his arms.

Lisa was open-mouthed. The day had developed a surreal character that was not enjoyable. Everyone else was laughing fit to burst, but she was deadly serious. 'Shut up,' she yelled. 'Sal Potter will be here shortly. So be quiet and listen.'

'Bugger,' announced Daisy as she left the room.

More gales of laughter bounced off the walls.

'Will you all stop and listen?'

They shut up. Lisa meant business, and they had best take heed before she started tearing out her hair.

Milly returned and sat beside her beloved friend. They weren't going to remove Hermione, not while Milly lived. A cat was one thing, but–

'Ah, there you are,' said the old woman as she patted the dog's head. 'We can start now because we are a full committee.' Thus was the meeting announced as officially begun.

He had to get to the undertaker's to pass on the death certificate. There was a copy, but the nuns needed that for their records. There was also a requiem Mass to be booked – the undertaker would deal with that and with the local newspaper. In the end, Gus settled for a simple statement mentioning only Mathilda's mother, already deceased.

He was beyond tired. Walking was a chore. Even eating was an exhausting business, while dressing himself took several minutes. But he had to keep going. For Mathilda, for Katherina, he needed to do as Henry V had advised via Shakespeare – stiffen sinew and summon up blood. Which was very good advice except when meted out to a chap whose blood was useless due to chemo-therapy.

Sheila was a great help. She now understood the tablets, knew what had to be taken before or after meals, before sleep, after waking. She was a pragmatic, down-to-earth woman, the sort he should have married instead of poor Lisa. Poor Lisa had fitted the bill. She had been an experienced jeweller and in good health. After Katherina, there had been no point in looking for love; he had given it all away to her, and she had taken it to the grave in Tonge Cemetery.

Sheila had just posed a question.

'Sorry? I wasn't paying attention.'

'Shall we take my husband's wheelchair? It's lightweight, and you...' She looked at him. He was becoming smaller by the day. 'You're not heavy,' she added.

'Five kilos,' he answered. 'That's how much I have lost. Nothing fits me any more.'

She had a suit upstairs that might just do for the funeral, she thought. He was now about the size her husband had been when that last suit had been bought. She must remember to give it to Gus before he went home. He had no home. He should remain here, where he would be looked after and properly medicated, where his absent-mindedness would not interfere with the strict regime dictated by doctors. It wasn't simple forgetfulness any more; his condition was worsened by the terrible tiredness and its accompanying apathy. He was depressed.

'You'll come to the undertaker's as well?' he asked.

'Of course. Now. What about this wheelchair?'

He looked at her for several seconds before replying, 'Not yet, Sheila. We'll take taxis and stop to buy flowers.'

'For Mathilda?'

'No. For her mother.' Whilst he didn't believe in an afterlife, some force compelled him to go to Katherina's resting place before it was opened up by gravediggers. He had to ... not quite tell her, yet he needed to put in a short appearance before the funeral.

'All right. Now, shall we go? The taxi's waiting outside.'

He nodded. 'Yes. Let's get the unpalatable business over. I'd take you for a good lunch, but I can't seem to settle in the vicinity of food. It will be better once the course of medication is over.'

She wondered about that. 'Will you be all right?' she asked. 'Will this one lot of pills do it?'

'I don't know.' He had postponed his appointment at the hospital because there was so much to do, so little time, and he had a marked lack of physical energy. Always a strong and healthy man, Gus felt as if he had been hit by an overcrowded bus. 'I'll know more once the tests are done.'

She would have to be satisfied with that, and she asked no more questions. His wife didn't even know he was ill. Sheila was probably the only person on earth who had an inkling about his condition. The medics would be aware, of course, but his family believed him to be in New Zealand. They didn't deserve him.

When they reached the funeral parlour, Sheila

331

remained in reception while Gus, the paying client, was taken through to the inner sanctum where he had to choose a coffin, its lining, the pillow and the furnishings, including handles for the casket and a plaque for the lid.

Mr Philip Rushton Senior invited Gus into his office. 'There's been a slight faux pas,' he began. He went on to explain company policy regarding mobile phones and to give a reason for telephoning Gus's domestic line. 'You were distressed when you spoke to us after the death, and we didn't get all the information we required.' He continued to tell tales of nasty neighbours who had asked for a hearse to pick up the dead next door. 'Bestial behaviour, Dr Compton-Milne, because no one has died, you see. We thought someone with a grudge might be trying to make you suffer by imitating you, because the mobile was turned off and we could not reach you.'

'I was ill.'

'Ah.' Mr Rushton Senior dabbed a handkerchief against a hooked nose. With such over-exaggerated features and miserable black clothing, the man looked positively Dickensian. Yes, he would have done well as Scrooge or an evil schoolmaster. 'The young lady seemed confused,' the man added.

'Yes, she would.'

'And while we do our utmost to maintain high standards of confidentiality, the unusual nature of your circumstances led to the unfortunate disclosure of your business with us.'

Gus nodded. This man even spoke in nineteenth century English. Perhaps he was one of

332

the undead? He was very pale, terribly ugly, and his voice might have been used to commentate for Hammer House of Horror films. 'Please don't worry. None of this is your fault. Did you speak to Harriet?'

The man in black nodded.

'She's a sensible girl. Yes, these circumstances are odd, but don't worry. It's just another of life's twists and turns.' Gus thought for a moment. 'I want Mathilda all in white. The coffin must be lined in white, too. White lilies on a bed of dark green. Just the one spray, but let it cover the whole top of the casket.'

'Ah. À la Princess Diana?'

'No. À la Princess Mathilda. She never did a wrong thing, never spoke a wrong word. Mathilda is truly pure.'

'Quite.' The senior partner shuffled brochures on his desk. Some of them advertised what might best be described as a pay-now-die-later scheme. The room was perfumed, and soft music drifted in via hidden speakers. This was the sepulchre described in the Bible, all sin hidden behind grand facade and pretty decor, because the nuts and bolts lay beyond the scenes: where faces were straightened after strokes, where the dead were washed and made pretty for their relatives, where the quick prepared the deceased for that last journey. Gus shivered.

'Are you still unwell, sir?'

'Chemotherapy.' He rose from his chair. 'Thank you, Mr Rushton. The certificate is with your receptionist. Good day.'

He went with Sheila to the graveyard after picking up lilies from a florist. While his companion stayed in the taxi, he walked the last few yards and placed his tribute on the grave. He didn't weep. He lacked the energy required. He simply stood and remembered a girl who had run barefoot through buttercups, who had abandoned a husband for him, who had loved him with a heart bigger than the revolution her elders had fled. Katherina had been a White Russian, born to a family whose members had deserted Hungary in the face of encroaching communism.

They had not liked Gus; they had blamed him for her betrayal of her husband, for enticing her away. 'I did not do the enticing,' he whispered. He closed his eyes, pictured her in folk costume, watched her dancing to music from a country that should have been her own. She had cooked borscht, had spilled beetroot juice all over the tiny kitchen of the flat in which he had kept her. 'I am mistress of all I survey – you included, Gustav.'

Dancing, always dancing. Laughter like tinkling bells; neck, long and white; dark hair tumbling over soft breasts when she released it from its braids. The sexual act had been glorious, since it had been accompanied by love so overpowering that Gus had been lost in her.

No God would have taken her. No infinite power based in love and goodness could have dragged the life from her in so cruel a fashion. There was no God.

'Mathilda' had been her last word. Baby in a box, a plastic box heated and fed with measured oxygen. Running, running with that final piece of

334

Katherina. Pleading for Mathilda to be saved, for hope to remain. Selfish, always so selfish. 'I am sorry,' he said.

'Gus?'

He turned and looked at Sheila.

'What are you doing down there?'

He had not realized that he was on his knees. 'Sheila?'

'Yes?'

'Make sure they heed my will. My remains go in here with theirs. I shall explain, of course. But I beg you. Make sure.'

Sheila nodded mutely before helping him to his feet. The sun shone, but this remained the greyest of days.

Sal Potter arrived at her place of work, mind filled by worries because Jimmy seemed to be preparing to leave. Stuff had gone missing. He hadn't found her building society pass book, so that was one thing less to ponder. She had never been a big spender, and she had salted away several thousand against the day when the peppercorn rent cottage would be taken from her by the developers who now owned Cotters Farm.

There was a lot less food than normal. Salmon, tuna, baked beans and soup had disappeared overnight. Lavvy paper, kitchen rolls and the wet wipes she used to clean her face were also in short supply. He owed her nothing, she supposed. The new furniture and TV had cost much more than he had stolen, so she was keeping quiet about the problem. But she was afraid. In fact, scared to death would be nearer the mark.

She changed her shoes, put on a tabard and went to fetch her tranklements, a word employed by her long-dead mother when describing a box filled with a variety of items. Armed with said tranklements, she picked out kitchen cleaners and began the wet work. Somebody had been over-enthusiastic on the stove, so she set to in order to rid the top of various burnt offerings that covered two of the four gas rings.

Sal was suddenly aware that she was not alone. Turning, she saw the unhappy face of the spy from upstairs. It was the kind of face described by some as a bag of spanners, but a bag of spanners didn't ask questions in a foreign language when a person was trying to do the work for which she was paid. 'Hello,' said Sal nervously.

'Yes,' replied Eileen. 'You're wanted.'

'Eh?'

'You're wanted by madam upstairs. Mrs Hermione.'

Oh, God. Not more tea and scones. 'I've a lot to do, Mrs Eckersley. I fell behind with my day off.'

Eileen sniffed and folded her arms. 'It's not a request, Mrs Potter. It's an order.'

'Oh. Right.'

'And whose is the cat?' The intruder pointed to the open kitchen door. 'Have you been feeding that?'

'No.' Sal banged her implements back into their box. 'No, I haven't fed it. I've never even seen it before.'

'Right. Up with you now till we see the missus.'

Sal's heart pounded in her ears all the way up

336

two flights of stairs. She didn't know what was coming, but she hoped it was only the sack. There were a lot of things worse than getting the sack, and she had been living with one of them. He'd even stolen her toothpaste and some of the old towels, so he was definitely–

She entered Hermione's domain and found herself facing not only the old woman, but also her daughter, granddaughter and – she gulped hard – Jimmy's wife. Even close to, it was plain that Annie hadn't changed much; she still looked too young and tiny to be the mother of three kids.

'Sit over there,' commanded Hermione.

Sal obeyed without hesitation. It was the only option when Hermione was in charge. Feeling like the prisoner in the dock, Sal faced the four women. Three were on a sofa; the fourth was in her wheelchair. Next to Hermione sat the large dog that was responsible for deterioration both inside and outside Weaver's Warp. The Irish-woman, probably clerk of court, hovered behind the four seated females.

Lisa opened for the prosecution. 'According to my friend Mrs Nuttall, you have never been married, yet you gave your identity as Mrs Potter, widow.'

Sal hung her head.

Lisa carried on. 'I won't go into too many details – we leave all that to Mrs Eckersley – but you have been searching this house repeatedly. For this?' She held up a mangled article. 'We took a photograph of it before Mrs Eckersley's husband flattened it in his vice. There's already one life ruined because of the damned thing, and

337

we wanted to make sure it could never be used again. Right. What have you got to say for yourself?'

Harrie chipped in. She was clearly present to offer some kind of mitigating defence. 'Mother, she's afraid of him. Look what he did to Annie.'

Annie put in her ten-pence worth. 'Sal? I'm not your enemy, girl. We all know what Jimmy is. I don't want my kids' dad in jail, but what's the alternative? He made a hole in my head – you've every right to be scared.'

Sal burst into tears.

Hermione joined the self-elected magistrates. 'No time for tears, Mrs Potter. The man has clearly parted company with any sense he might have had. He needs to be separated from the children for their sake.'

Sal dried her eyes, opened her mouth to speak, but found no words.

'It's all right,' said Harrie quietly. 'Believe it or not, we're on your side.'

Lisa grinned ruefully. 'I was on my side in a field full of cows this morning, and I got no sympathy from this lot. Look at me. Look at me, Sal.'

Sal managed to make eye contact with her employer.

'You can help.' Lisa tried to smile reassuringly. 'We women have to stick together. Come on, now. Tell us what's happening. Did he get you to apply for this job?'

It poured from her in a stream that seemed never-ending. Filled with plasma screen, misplaced love, new furniture, depression involving her dead dad's teeth, Sky TV, boredom and separate bedrooms, the story flooded out of her. She returned to teenage years and the loss of her virginity, told how he had visited her over the years, how he had been nice to her poor, dying father, how nasty he was becoming now. 'He's dangerous,' she concluded.

'In what way?' Hermione asked.

'I seen it on the telly.' Sal mopped her face again. 'Saw it, I mean.'

'Saw what?' Hermione leaned forward.

'About loonies. He can't keep still. He rocks and shakes and talks to himself. Then there's his eyes – they're not right. Stares a lot, then starts blinking all the while. Sometimes, I think there's two of him. Or more. Mood swings, they called it.'

Harrie stood up, walked across the space and placed a hand on Sal's shoulder. 'We'll look after you,' she said.

The sobbing began again. 'Don't be nice to me,' Sal begged. 'You'll only go and make me worse.'

'But we *will* look after you.'

The seated woman took a deep breath and looked into Harrie's eyes. 'It's you needs looking after, girl. If he doesn't get that gun back today, he's going to kidnap you and rob the shop. He says the Compton-Milnes would swap the gun for you and a few diamonds.'

Harrie blinked. Was that the bloke seen skulking outside, the one Roger had mentioned? 'Stop worrying, Sal. I'll stay away from the shop until he's caught. Are you safe at home? Are you sure

339

he won't hurt you?'

Sal nodded.

Harrie pulled Sal to her feet. 'Look. Go to Gran's bathroom and sort yourself out – wash your face. Don't go home yet. Stay for the usual length of time. You don't need to do any work. Then carry that blessed gun home with you and let him do as he wishes with it. My mother will take her chances if he accuses her of involvement with his burglaries. She can stand up for herself, because this town knows and respects her. She's been daft, but no more than that. There's no danger of her being thrown out of office like poor President Clinton–'

'And look what they replaced him with.' Hermione was in the saddle again. 'An ape with the brains of a–'

'Be quiet,' Harrie shouted. 'Get off your high horse, Gran. This poor woman's had enough.'

Hermione muttered about not being able to say her piece in her own house. She threatened to leave all her property to a home for sick donkeys, but nobody listened. Eileen, however, eyes and ears of the world, found the temerity to put a hand on her boss's shoulder. 'Enough,' she said. Hermione stopped talking immediately.

'Shall I say you gave it to me?' Sal was asking, in reference to the mangled gun.

'No!' chorused five females. 'Say you found it in the garage with the photo,' Annie advised. 'Then he won't phone Lisa this afternoon. If he does phone her, she can say that it's gone. It would be the truth.'

Sal went out to wash away her tears.

'Can we trust her?' Hermione asked.

'Course we can,' replied Annie. 'She's one of us. She's another female who's been stood on by a bloke. His mam said he wasn't right the last time he visited her. She thought he looked wild – like a tiger kept too long in a cage. She's scared of him and scared for him. She *is* his mother, so she must have mixed feelings over it all.'

'Well, he'll be in a cage soon enough,' promised Lisa.

Annie sighed. 'He was always wild. And I've got two of his sons to tame. God help me.'

The door had been left ajar by Sal. A face appeared low down, very near to the floor. It was black, fluffy, and had recently travelled, together with the rest of its person, in a skyward direction via Hermione's summer-weight curtains. The room seemed to hold its breath. Hermione placed a hand on Milly's neck.

Milly remained where she was. The cat, having looked from a distance into the face of its natural enemy, walked straight in and placed itself between the Alsatian's huge front paws. There was no clawing or hissing this time. The animal had done its research and reached a decision.

'Is this a suicide mission?' Harrie asked. 'Are we in the presence of a kamikaze cat?'

Lisa smiled. 'In a fight between a cat and a dog, there's only one winner. And it ain't the dog.'

A pink-faced Will appeared. 'Sorry to interrupt,' he panted. 'She got away from me. I found out her owner died a few days ago – lived on the estate – Beech Gardens. They used to have a dog as well – their son's taken it, but he can't have the cat because his wife's allergic to them.' He paused for breath. 'Bella's used to big dogs. See?' He pointed to the animals. The cat had curled into a ball at Milly's feet. 'Can we keep her?' he asked.

'Bloody hell,' laughed Annie. 'You sound like Billy or Craig. They even brought an old tramp home once – he stank of booze and was covered in sick. "Can we keep him, Mam?" Will, you proved my theory – males never grow up.'

Harrie's eyes filled with moisture. He was a good man, and she would have his child. He would want her to have his child. University needed to be managed, and it would be managed. She stood up. 'I'll look after Sal till it's time for her to go home. Then, I have a few things to do.'

'If you're going out, take Will with you,' ordered Lisa.

Yes, she would take Will. Firstly, she had to share news with him. Secondly, he might help with the mystery of Mathilda.

Twelve

The hammock was slung between a pair of apple trees that seemed old enough to have figured in Genesis. Will, who had fallen off the thing twice, was now balanced precariously between comfort and broken bones, Bella purring contentedly on his chest. She had fallen to the ground with him, but she seemed to have accepted such events as examples of the vagaries of the life she had chosen for herself.

In a nearby upholstered swing made for two, Harrie was perfectly composed. The air of contentment was a mere cloak, however, as it concealed a great deal of inner turmoil. Firstly, there was the blob created by herself and the idiot in the hammock. As occupier of an unstable item of leisure furniture, he was, perhaps, not in the best of positions when it came to discussing blobs. She would deal with that in a minute, as he was sure to come crashing down fairly soon.

Ben wasn't answering his phone. She knew he had experienced trouble when it came to recharging, but she so badly wanted to talk to him. About Father and Mathilda, about Will and the blob – though Ben had to be placed in the bronze position on the podium regarding her pregnancy. Will must take gold; Mother, Father – if he could be found – and Gran shared silver; while Ben would be forced into third position. In reality, she knew that her brother was all the gold in the world, because, in accordance with his instructions, she had opened a certain letter on his behalf. He had gained four A-stars in his A-level exams. She could tell him that, at least, before informing anyone else.

'I have never understood hammocks,' said Will sadly. 'All those sailors hung up like that on heavy seas. It must have been dreadful – one big wave, and they'd be crippled.'

Harrie sniffed. 'It was the only way to keep them all in there. They couldn't fit everybody on the floor. Poor sailors would have been laid like sardines from helm to poop.'

'What is a poop?' asked Will just before he tumbled down to earth yet again. From his new position in life, he asked how the meeting had gone.

'Meeting? More like a fracas. I am confined to barracks, and you can stay where you are,' ordered his fiancée. 'Leave the hammock alone for a minute. The meeting was interesting, and I have something to tell you.'

The cat shook herself, stiffened her tail as if raising a finger to the world, then stalked off. In her opinion, dogs and old ladies made more sense than these two clowns.

Will was not one who gave up easily. Ignoring the order to the contrary, he struggled to climb back into his hammock. When he heard Harrie's next words, he performed the classic full turn and re-deposited himself on the grass. 'What? A baby?' He scratched his head.

Harrie shook hers. 'Parenthood is not to be

undertaken lightly. You will have to learn to comport yourself in a sensible and upright manner, and you have less than eight months to improve. Close your mouth – you look like a goldfish in a dry tank.'

'You mean we can keep it?' he asked.

She remembered Annie's remark about her twins. 'Men never grow up,' she had said. 'Either keep it or put it to auction on eBay,' Harrie replied. 'Stop it, stop it. Put me down!' She was suddenly airborne. He ran in circles, whooping and shouting like a cowboy who had just reined a heifer. But she wasn't a heifer – not any more – she was twenty-one and a bit. 'Put me down,' she repeated.

He put her down. 'Are you pleased?' he asked.

'Are you?'

'I asked first.'

'Yes, but I'm hormonal. I'm pleased if you are.'

'I'm pleased.'

'Are you sure?'

'Shut up.' He kissed her, and that shut her up. 'We can get married now,' he said, a grin stretching almost from ear to ear. 'Can't we?'

She didn't want the fuss, and she said so. 'We shall elope to the Bolton Registry,' she suggested. 'Witnesses are easy to find. Give a couple of tramps a fiver each – sorted.' She further decreed that they should live in the shed. It was a beautiful shed with all mod cons and double glazing, but they'd have to wait until Annie and the children felt safe enough to go home. 'Then we can do a bit more painting and decorating and stuff.'

'OK,' he said. 'But won't our mothers be upset if we get married without telling them? Mothers can be very strange.'

Harrie told him the rest of the story. Her father was not in New Zealand and someone named Mathilda was in Rushton's Funeral Parlour, established 1871. She didn't know who Mathilda was, but she thought they could track down Father with a bit of careful research. 'He's with his train woman, I bet. Sheila. On Wigan Road. There's something strange going on.'

Will thought that there would be something strange about Weaver's Warp if nothing strange was happening, but he didn't want to upset the mother of his child. 'So you need to find your dad?'

'Yes. I also need not to get kidnapped, and we are closing my shop until Jimmy Nuttall is safely behind bars. That should happen some time today or tomorrow, if our luck holds.'

'Kidnapped?' he shouted. 'Kidnapped?' He would not leave her side for a second. He listened open-mouthed while she outlined recent history about the gun, about Birmingham and some raid that had left a man paraplegic. 'Annie's husband has become dangerous. He's been staying with our cleaner, Mrs Potter. She loved him to bits, but now even she is scared to death of him. He's started talking to himself.'

'We all do that.' Good Lord, what was he getting himself into?

'Yes, but not like this. He's gone loopy.'

They sat together on the swing, then a thought crawled into a small gap in Will's overcrowded brain. 'The paper,' he said before running into the house.

Harrie closed her eyes and concentrated on blood pressure. She must not get worked up, or her passenger might suffer. She realized in that moment how much she wanted the child -Will's child. When he returned, she told him how dearly she needed to be a family with him and the blob.

He said he was pleased, then carried on with the result of his earlier thought. 'It's in,' he said. 'Her mother's name was Katherina Barford. Mathilda's death is announced.'

'What time is it now?' she asked.

'Ten to three.'

Harrie stood up. 'Come on. We're going to meet Mathilda.'

'But shouldn't you stay here?'

'Be my knight in shining armour. Come and protect me.'

They left the garden hand in hand. During the drive to town, they spoke quietly about the future, about Harrie's determination to attend university, about crèches and mothers-in-law and the old bats in the belfry of Weaver's Warp. With joy seasoned with not a little trepidation, they planned their future.

Then they saw Mathilda.

In spite of bright sunshine and a temperature that had made her sweat on her journey home, Sal shivered when she entered the cottage. It felt deadly cold and empty. Her footfalls in the little hallway echoed loudly throughout the place, and she knew right away that Jimmy had gone. It was

347

amazing how the presence of just one other person's effects could soak up sound, how the absence of that same body and its belongings served only to magnify the isolation of someone who lived alone.

Retracing her steps, she confirmed that the van was not there, but she needed to find out whether he had gone for good. Relief was mixed with fear. She had what he wanted, had been told to say that she had found it in the garage. The photograph should confirm that the squashed item had been a gun, but how could she pass it and her lies on to a man who was no longer here?

What would he do? Where might he be?

Upstairs, she looked in the wardrobe and a chest of drawers in which he had kept his clothing. Apart from a holey sock and its intact twin, there was no trace of the man she had once adored. The top pillow still bore the shape of his head. Weeks ago, she might have lifted that just to smell him again, but love had died, had been murdered by him. She, too, had helped in the killing, because she had become depressed and anxious once more. 'No bloody wonder,' she grumbled quietly.

There was no longer a working phone. Sal had never found the need for one since she had no friends, and a short bicycle ride would take her to a public telephone in any one of three nearby villages. Had Jimmy needed to communicate, he had been free to pay the bill for reconnection. Lisa had given her a mobile. Sal recalled listening carefully to instructions, but could she remember how to use it? After calming down through controlled breathing, she found that it was easy. She just keyed in the numbers and pressed green.

But telling Lisa was far from easy.

'Are you sure?' Lisa asked.

'Oh, yes. There's nothing left here. He's even taken a few quid I kept behind the clock for emergencies.'

'And the van?'

'Gone. What shall I do?' She waited for what seemed an age for the answer.

'Just put what's left of his gun somewhere safe. The police are already on their way.'

'What?'

'I got them in case he hurt you, Sal. Once he had what he needed from you, he might have wanted to tidy you away.'

'But he's not here! He could be near enough to be watching me, or he could be in town getting ready to kidnap Harrie. When he sees her shop closed, he'll know I've told you he was going to take her.'

'Calm down,' ordered Lisa. 'We've put a refurbishment notice in the shop window. He won't know you've said a word against him.'

But Sal was not convinced. She turned off the phone, sat and waited for Armageddon. It arrived within minutes and with a magnificent flourish, just like something out of a film. Two police cars and one unmarked vehicle screeched to a halt in the lane. She felt surrounded, vulnerable and terribly alone. A female officer in uniform took her to one side, and Sal spilled out the whole truth. While she spoke, men ran up and downstairs, into the garden, into the shed. The ruined gun was handed over, together with a rough explanation about its provenance.

'And he was involved in that incident?' asked the constable.

'He drove. I believe him when he says he just drove and knew nothing about the crime till it was too late. That's why he feels so strongly about it. The pair that did it disappeared abroad, and they left the gun in his car. He hid it, but his wife found it and took it away.' Should she mention the Compton-Milnes? 'He's not right, you know. In his head, I mean, because he's not thinking straight. There's more to the story, but I don't want to—'

'We know the rest,' said the policewoman. 'You were too afraid to come to us — that's under-standable, since he seems to have given his wife a hiding. Mrs Compton-Milne has been very open with us, and she is anxious to protect you. She wants us to take you back to her house.'

Sal bit her lip; she would not cry, not now. 'They're already looking after Jimmy's wife and kids. The house is going to be bursting at the seams.' Mind, they did have about eight bed-rooms...

'So we understand. Strength in numbers, Mrs Potter.'

'Miss.'

The woman patted Sal's arm. 'Come on. Let's take you up there. We shall keep watch around here, so don't worry.'

Sal collected clean underwear, a change of cloth-ing and a few toiletries from her little bathroom. She was going back to where all the eggs sat in one basket. It would not feel completely safe, but anything was better than staying here alone. Once again, she felt chilled to the bone. With all his perceived enemies in one place, Jimmy needed only a can of petrol and a match. She would not dare to sleep that night.

Using binoculars stolen from Sal Potter's shed, Jimmy watched the scenario as it unfolded down the lane. He was furious. So this was how she paid him back for all he had done? He had furnished her house, for goodness' sake. They were all in it together, the women ganging up to plot against him – even his own mother was not to be trusted completely.

He descended from the tall tree and walked. He strode back and forth, all the time cursing Sal, Lisa and Annie under his breath. The van. Where had he put it? Remember, remember! Third beech along, small gap, covered in branches. All his stuff was in the vehicle, so there was nothing here to advertise his presence. 'Except me,' he muttered. 'I'm here.' Could he stay?

He climbed the tree again. The cars had gone, and Sal's house seemed deserted. Were the cops in there? Were they waiting for him? Did they have the gun? Anger overwhelmed him, and he fell. Fortunately, a lower branch managed to hold his weight, and he waited for his lungs to get back to normal. Normal? He couldn't even remember bloody normal.

He paced about, unable to settle, incapable of ordered thought. The van. She would have given the police the number; Jimmy thanked his stars that he had taken her bike in the back of his van. He could travel under the cover of darkness, at least. Those false number plates had been a good idea, too. Good ideas were few now. He had collected the number plates when he had been thinking sensibly. Remember, remember. His mind was like a colander.

Where could he go, though? She might have found the gun, might not have found it. She could be in league with the Compton-Milne family. And Annie. Yes, Annie would be at the back of all this. He had hit her, and Annie was not renowned for her forgiving nature whenever she allowed herself to feel righteous indignation.

'Go and see Annie,' he told himself aloud. 'Get the truth out of her.'

He advised himself over and over to see Annie. It became the mantra of the day. Annie had to be his next port of call. But would the police be there as well?

Will knocked at the door. It was black and shiny, and its leaded lights gleamed to advertise recent polishing. The house looked well-maintained, as did the tiered front garden. This part of Wigan Road was blessed with lovely views across the valley that contained Bolton. 'It's all right round here, isn't it, Hat?'

Harrie made no reply – she simply stared at the door behind which her father was possibly hidden.

A woman answered. She was a plain person, not particularly ugly, not pretty – the sort of woman nobody noticed, really. There was sadness in her eyes, and not a little fear. 'Yes?'

Harrie recognized her from the day in the coffee shop when she and Mother had played tricks. Had they but known the truth... 'Mrs Barton?'

Sheila nodded.

'Is my father here?'

'No. But please come in.' She led them through to her middle room, the one in which she lived and ate for the most part. 'Your dad isn't here, Harriet. But he has been staying here – he is still staying here. And...' She broke down and began to weep. 'Does your mother know he never went to New Zealand?'

'Not yet.' Harrie looked at Will. 'Find the kitchen and go and make a cuppa, love.'

He left the two women together. 'What is it?' Harrie asked.

Sheila shook her head, then mopped at her face with a tissue. 'He's gone for more tests.'

'More tests? What kind of tests?'

'The usual. Blood and stuff, then some sort of scan. He's been quite poorly, lots of tablets, very tired and nauseous. He hasn't been near his trains for a long time. That's why he comes here, you see. The trains. My husband was a collector, and your dad needed somewhere...' She grabbed Harrie's hand. 'I am so glad you're here. I've come close enough to getting on a bus up to your house, but he might not have liked that.'

Harrie swallowed hard. 'What's wrong with him?' she asked.

Breath left Sheila's body in a long sigh. 'Well, he had a biopsy, and they gave him tablets that make him fit for nothing. He says they compromise his

353

immune system, then he starts going on about doctors being too free and easy with antibiotics and destroying the world. Sometimes, it sounds as if he's not thinking straight, and that's a shame. Such a clever man, your dad. Those tablets do damage. His hair's coming out in clumps.'

The younger woman gulped again. 'Cancer?' she asked.

Sheila shook her head. 'Well, that's the conclusion I came to, but he's not a great talker, is he? Very private sort of man. He's never said the word cancer. Not in my hearing, anyway. He's inside himself and doesn't often reach out. Too quiet, if you ask me.'

'Yes. Yes, he is.'

Sheila wrung her hands. 'I don't know what to do. He eats next to nothing, and I try to stay on top of the medication, but it's not easy.'

Harrie stared through the window into an imaginative rear garden with arches, trellises, pebbled areas and a bit of lawn. Pots of flowers provided a riot of colour, and roses bowed their weighty heads. The woman was a nest-maker, but she couldn't manage her cuckoo. 'Do you know who Mathilda is?' she asked.

Sheila paused before replying. 'There are some questions I will answer for the sake of his health. But there are other areas where I daren't tread. It has to come from him, Harriet. I'm just a friend. He has treated me well in return for the use of my attics – always brought trout or salmon or a good cut of meat. We've been close, but there's been nothing ... personal. He's become a brother, yet not a brother, because I'd expect a close

354

relative to confide in me.'

'He confides in no one,' said Harrie sadly.

'He needs to go home, love. If anything happens to him, he should be with his own family.'

Harrie nodded. 'I know. Look, tell him we have been – he knows who Will is. And tell him if he doesn't come home, I'll dig him out of here with a shovel. We may not be close, Father and I, but he knows my threats are never empty.'

They left Sheila with a full pot of tea. Harrie did not want to encroach any further, and the whole afternoon had been distressing for her. How big did a blob have to be before it suffered via its carrier's emotions? She sat in Will's car and held his hand tightly. 'That was scary,' she said.

He knew she didn't mean the meeting with Sheila Barton. The big shock had happened earlier in the day, when Harrie had stood in the chapel of rest at Rushton's.

Because today, Harrie had seen herself in a coffin.

'What worries me,' said Hermione, 'is the idea of them finishing up in borstal or whatever they call such places these days. They're not bad boys – they're just temporarily impossible. I'm sure they can be cured.'

Eileen wasn't so sure. 'They took my washing line and several personal items of clothing. They folded up the clothes very neatly, sure enough, and placed them in the laundry basket, but that's not the point. The washing line was used to swing from tree to tree in the manner of Tarzan. They were lucky not to break their necks, so they were.'

Hermione expressed the hope that they would not destroy Harrie's little wooden bungalow. 'I know she doesn't say much on the subject, but Harrie's going to be an excellent homemaker. The sooner that man is arrested, the sooner Annie and her children can go home.'

Lisa ran in. 'He's disappeared,' she said breathlessly. 'Sal phoned me. She's on her way back here in a police car. They stopped off while she made a proper statement at the central police station. She can't go back to her own place. She'll have to stay here.'

'You should change the name of the house,' suggested Eileen. 'It's becoming a home for waifs and strays who bring back cats and steal a person's washing line and–'

'Oh, be quiet,' Hermione ordered.

Eileen stopped. There was an edge to her employer's tone that spoke volumes to all who knew her well. Hermione was not pleased – and that was putting it mildly.

'I couldn't send her back up there, Mum. You know I couldn't do that. It's very isolated. Except for the blinking cows.' She smiled ruefully.

The old woman nodded. 'You did right, Lisa. If he'd done to her what he did to poor Annie, we would never have forgiven ourselves. Have you space for her?'

'Of course. One thing we've never been short of in this house is space.' She touched her mother-in-law's arm. 'You've looked after us all well. Try not to worry.'

Hermione wondered whether they would feel looked after when she was dead, because she had

356

decided to leave everything to the one person she trusted to act fairly – Harriet. Gus would be too engrossed in his work, Lisa might become addicted to cosmetic procedures again, while Ben was simply too self-absorbed. 'I do my best,' she replied absently. Though she might have been better pleased had she not needed to sell off so much of the land. That housing estate was a damned nuisance.

'The cat's settled, then,' said Lisa to Eileen in an effort to lighten the mood.

Hermione looked at both her animals. Neither was hers in reality, yet both had chosen her. She had never had pets. Harrie and Ben used to own cockatiels, but no dogs or cats. Bella and Milly were content; they had decided what they wanted, and had gone for it. The dog needed Hermione, while the cat needed the dog. Had it not been for the housing estate, perhaps Hermione would have gone to the grave without having been privy to such an excellent relationship between natural enemies. Humans could learn a lot from certain quarters, she concluded.

'We had better batten down the hatches tonight, then,' she told Lisa. 'Since our police force could scarcely catch a cold, we shall be forced to look after ourselves.'

'They'll send someone to keep watch if we ask.' Lisa suggested.

But Hermione had seen practically every episode of *The Bill,* and she knew the stories off by heart. A pair went on watch. One fell asleep in the car, while the other relieved himself behind some poor soul's privet hedge. 'Forget it,' she said. 'While one's nodding off and the other's emptying his bladder, the crook gets in and does the dirty deed. If we want guards, we'll pay our own.'

Sal tapped at the door, then put her head into the room. 'I'm back, and thank you.' She smiled nervously. 'Shall I cook?' she asked Lisa.

'No. Glad you got here, Sal. Don't worry about a meal – there's loads of salad stuff – I'll do it. Come along and I'll show you your room. Try not to get upset again – we've all made mistakes.'

'Especially with my washing line,' Eileen grumbled.

'Be quiet,' chorused Hermione and Lisa.

The Irishwoman stalked off to feed her husband, close on the heels of Sal and Lisa. On her way downstairs, she advised Sal not to get into a state and smiled reassuringly.

Sal nodded. Eileen Eckersley wearing a smile made this witness think of a heavyweight boxer in a tutu. Some things just didn't seem right together.

She wasn't there. Find Annie, find Annie – those repeated words had rattled round his skull all day. The van was hidden and he was on a push-bike. He was pretty sure there were no police around; he was certain there was no one at all around because the house looked dead.

Locks had been changed. He broke in through the living-room window at the rear of the building, switched on no lights, simply sat in a corner until his eyes adjusted. There were bits and pieces all over the place. While Annie was not

358

the tidiest of housewives, she did have her standards. Someone had left here in a hurry. Yes, of course – Annie had been taken to hospital. But she wasn't in hospital any longer, because a report in the newspaper had announced her discharge. Hadn't it? Was he right?

Where were his kids? Had they been taken to his mother and mother-in-law, or were they in care? He walked up the stairs as quietly as he could. It wasn't easy, because toys were strewn around like large pieces of lumpy confetti. It wasn't at all like Annie, this mess.

In Daisy's room, he found Dilly-Dolly. It was a soft rag toy, and Daisy had seldom been separated from it since Annie had made it for her. Daisy was growing up fast, faster than the lads. If he missed anyone at all, it was this precious little girl, his flower, his ray of sunshine. She had brains enough to change the world, a world of which he would soon cease to be a part.

It was almost midnight, and he was bone-weary. They wouldn't look for him here, surely? Not after all these weeks. There was a gun somewhere. Hadn't he been looking for a gun? Yes. Who had it and did it matter? His ruination had come via Lisa Compton-Milne – oh, he remembered her, all right. She had broken ... things. Somewhere, she had broken – yes – she had broken his mother's ornaments. Where was Annie? Where was Sal?

He sang the song invented by Annie. 'Dilly-Dolly licked a lolly, dropped it on the floor. Asked her mummy for another, Mummy said no more.' Things had been all right, hadn't they? Here. They'd been all right here. He picked up

Dilly-Dolly and left the house. With the doll inside his jacket, he rode off on a bike without lights, cutting through alleys, pushing the vehicle along pavements when forced to use the main routes. He had to find ... not Annie. He had to find Lisa, because Lisa had broken things.

Sal didn't sleep. It wasn't the change of bed that made her wakeful; it was the watching, the waiting and the listening. Weaver's Warp was a creaky sort of house. She could hear it falling asleep – floor-boards relaxing, treads on stairs breathing out because they were glad of a rest, windows settling as if relieved that no one would move them in the night.

He would. Any room in which there was no anti-burglar alarm could be entered as and when he pleased. The system had been renewed, but he was clever, far too astute for Sal to rest easy. Yet he wasn't as clever as he used to be, was he? His mind had changed a gear, had moved to an area that was either too fast or too slow – sometimes both. She could not explain to herself what she meant, yet she had seen him, heard him moving his thoughts along at the speed of light while, at the same time, unable to process the simplest of questions. He needed doctors, not prison warders.

It was a long night. She slept when dawn arrived, only to be woken just after seven by noises from upstairs. A dog was scuttling about; she and her feline friend would be celebrating another day's living. These daily sessions had been designated by Hermione as 'o joy, o joy, the morning'. Animals

360

celebrated life; humans sometimes feared it. Sal feared it. She feared it even more when she went downstairs to be greeted by Annie, who had all three children in tow.

'Dilly-Dolly,' sang the little girl.

'He's been in our empty house, then he's been here. We found Daisy's Dilly-Dolly in the hammock. The doll was at home. He's fetched it here. It has to be him – no one else would do this.'

'I never told him you were here, honest,' said Sal.

'I believe you. But other people notice things, you see. He might still be around – there's a lot of land, a lot of trees.' She dragged the children upstairs because she needed to talk to Hermione.

Sal sat on the third step up. A rail ran all the way to the top so that Hermione could move about the house. The poor woman would be better off without all these lodgers, but what was to be done? That doll hadn't walked here by itself. She remembered the creakings and groanings in the night, wondered whether she had misdiagnosed their origins. Because he was here. She could feel him, could almost smell him.

Annie came down again at speed, the two boys behind her, Daisy in her arms. 'Stay in all day, Sal,' she ordered. 'Missus upstairs is getting a couple of security men to come for the night. She doesn't trust the cops unless they're Frost or Morse. We'll be bedding down in the big house as well, you see. That wooden bungalow's too easy for him.' She went off to feed the children in the kitchen.

Lisa came down. 'Are you all right?'

Sal shook her head. She told Lisa about the doll, about the security men and about the Nuttalls having to come into the main house. 'He was here in the night, Lisa. I don't know what's going through his head – neither does he, half the time. Annie's scared half to death – finding that toy really upset her.'

Lisa was doing a mental bed-count. 'Yes, we can manage.' Right. What must she do next? She turned and went back upstairs, knocked frantically on Harrie's door. Will opened it. He was a fine-looking boy, Lisa mused. Especially in nothing more than his boxers. She blurted out the tale. 'So we stay in. All of us sit tight here until he's caught.'

'We're going to a funeral.' He turned and looked at Harrie. She was sitting up in bed, rubbing sleep from her eyes. 'It's your mother,' he said.

'Come in,' Harrie called.

Lisa stepped inside and was invited to sit on the bed.

'Don't flip your lid,' Harrie warned, 'but you are going to be a granny. I haven't told Gran yet.'

Lisa didn't know how to feel or what to say. Harrie was so young, and she and Will were just getting to know each other. Perhaps if the house had been in less turmoil, she would have found the words. As things were, she simply burst into tears.

'Don't worry,' smiled Harrie. 'As long as the child has my looks, everything will be OK.'

'I don't know how to act or react any more,' sobbed Lisa. 'Too much going on. But, as long as

362

you love each other...'

'We do,' they said simultaneously.

'That's all right, then.' She dried her eyes. A grandmother? That was truly frightening. 'What's this about a funeral?' she asked.

Will came to the rescue. A girl had died very young – that much was truth, at least. And they had to go because she was sort of related to his family. Well, he was nearly married to Harrie, so if Mathilda really was Harrie's half-sister, the rest hadn't been too much of a lie, either. 'It can't be avoided,' he finished.

Harrie smiled at him. She was not going to allow her father to go through this day on his own. Sheila would be there, but Sheila was the one who kept Father on the rails – in more ways than one, she suspected. Because Sheila was ordinary and he needed ordinary. Will understood so well... He was perfect. Almost.

'Then stick together,' ordered Lisa. 'Stay close to the rest of the funeral party. Remember Jimmy Nuttall threatened to kidnap you, Harrie. Both shops are now closed. Gran is getting in some guards for the house. No one sleeps in the bungalow – not until all this is resolved.' She smiled at her daughter and left the room.

'Black doesn't suit me,' said Harrie, apropos of nothing at all.

'Then wear dark blue or something. Come on, it's not a fashion show. It's for your dad, and he's ill.'

Once again, she knew why she was marrying him. He was sensible and daft – exactly what she needed.

Harrie and Will waited at the graveyard. The requiem had been held at the church of Sts Peter and Paul, and they had decided not to intrude there. It was a fine day, too pretty a morning for the burial of one as young as Mathilda had been. They found the open grave in the Catholic part of Tonge Cemetery, saw Katherina's name on a temporarily moved headstone, watched as the cortège moved slowly towards them. 'He might not want us here,' said Harrie at the last minute. 'If he'd wanted us, he would have asked.'

'You're more like your father than you think. Too late, anyway,' replied Will. 'He's probably seen us by now. Stay strong.'

Father looked so thin, and his shoulders were bent just as they always had been when he had curled into the Mini. He was standing unrestricted now, yet he looked frail, old and shrunken, almost as if he had folded his body in readiness for packing away somewhere. Harrie drew in breath sharply. Parents were an institution she had taken for granted. They had always been there, had not been ideal, but they were her own. She had never imagined that either would die while young. 'Oh, Will,' she gasped, 'look at him.'

He squeezed her hand. 'As I said, stand firm, lass. Your being here is already a shock for him. Be strong, Hat. Today's word is strong.'

'Thanks, Will.'

'For what?'

She blinked rapidly. 'For being Will.'

Gus made a beeline for his daughter. 'Harriet,' he said. 'Thank you for coming. I didn't... I couldn't...' He inhaled deeply. 'She was your sister. I wanted to spare you, but–'

'It's all right, Father,' she whispered. 'I went to visit her in the chapel of rest. I knew she was related to me. Finding out wasn't difficult – a few phone calls, a bit of impersonation. Here she comes now.' She clung tightly to her father's arm, while Sheila propped him up from the other side. 'We're here for you, Father,' said Harrie.

Will stood back. These minutes and seconds belonged to a family of which he was almost, yet not quite, a member. Birds stopped singing. It felt as if the whole planet had ground to a sudden halt. As the sombre procession approached the grave, a cloud covered the sun's shame.

The coffin was carried by four men, a priest leading the way. Prayers were droned, the casket was lowered into the ground, then bearers and priest left the scene. Gus gazed down into the gaping hole. Mathilda's earthly remains were with her mother now, and, although he had no faith in a hereafter, he had needed to be here when mother and child were reunited. This was, for him, the last of Mathilda, and yet... He opened his mouth, and a whisper emerged. '*Istenhozzad*,' he breathed. '*Kedvenc*.'

Then he turned to his daughter. 'She was beautiful like you. But she never woke properly, you see. I kept her, and it was cruel, because without sedation she fitted. Now, as I approach my own end, I have let her go. It was time to let her go.' There was a hysterical edge to his voice. 'Katherina died the day Mathilda was born. Mathilda was Katherina's only child.'

A man approached. He was dressed in black, and he carried a single cream rose. 'Gustav?' he asked.

'Yes.'

'I am John Barford.' They shook hands.

'Yes, I remember you.' Gus's eyes filled with saline. 'She bewitched us, didn't she? I hurt you. I am sorry I hurt you.'

This was not the father Harrie had known. Had she known him at all? He was crying in the arms of the man whose wife he had stolen. Gustav Compton-Milne had feelings. As if agreeing with her, the sun broke through in that moment.

The two men whispered to each other, spoke of a past they had shared, of a young woman they had loved to distraction. Knowing their weaknesses, they separated, yet still their hands clung together.

The widower finally drew away from his old adversary and threw the rose into the grave. He raised his hat, said his goodbye, then left the cemetery.

They had been so dignified, thought Harrie. And men, too, were capable of huge forgiveness – that was plain.

Katherina must have owned a power given to very few. Absolute beauty was extraordinarily dangerous because it swept before it all in its path. Would Katherina have stayed with Father, would she have returned to John Barford, would she have moved on? She noticed at the base of the headstone some smaller words. The inscription read 'Daughter Of Hungary'. So that was the language Father had used when talking to those he had loved and lost.

Gus and Sheila climbed into a black car and left the cemetery.

'She was of Hungarian origin,' Harrie told Will.

'Yes, I noticed. Let's follow them, shall we?'

At Sheila's house, the small cortège stopped. 'Look,' said Harrie. 'She has to help him up the steps. So ill in so short a time. It's frightening.'

The four of them sat in Sheila's living room. It occurred to Harrie that, while Gus must come home, she needed to prepare her mother and to empty the house. She could not imagine her father coping with the twins, with Annie's enthusiasms, Sal's misery, Daisy's happiness, with a crazed man lurking in the shadows. 'There are things happening at Weaver's Warp,' she told him. 'They are beyond our control.'

Gus smiled weakly. 'Another of the indiscretions for which my wife must never be blamed? Lisa is a good woman, Harriet. Remember that. She had a difficult husband.'

'Yes. Are you very ill, Father?'

He shrugged. 'I am ill, yes.'

'How ill?'

'They are thinking of removing something from my abdomen next. It will supposedly improve the quality of my life for a while. But the tumour in my brain will be the worst. Perhaps the chemo and radiotherapies may help. I am at the mercy of doctors and am therefore not safe. They are killing us, have been killing us for years with unnecessary antibiotics. Now, we pay the price. Filth in theatres doesn't help, either. My own ailment does not arise from overprescription, but it is one whose grip on the world is tightening. It's man-made. Of that I have little doubt.'

Father had cancer. Sheila was heartbroken. Harrie was suddenly terrified. 'Father?'

'What?'

'Try to stay alive until my baby comes.' That was vitally important. He had to see hope before he left the world. If she had a daughter, she would name her Hope – as long as Will agreed, of course.

Gus smiled. The lines in his face were deep, the skin grey. 'All our tomorrows,' he said. 'I wish I had–'

'It doesn't matter now, Father. I don't believe in blame.' Although she had to admit to blaming Jimmy Nuttall for a lot of things. But this man had provided for his family, had worked hard, had hidden a heart as unsteady as the San Andreas Fault. 'Stay here for a few days longer. Is that all right with you, Sheila?'

The woman nodded. She had plodded her way through the morning like someone on automatic pilot: no words, no tears, just going through the motions. Would the Compton-Milnes allow her to visit him after he had gone home? Judging by the attitude of Harriet, the answer was probably positive. 'I'll make some tea.' These were the first words she had spoken.

When Sheila had left the room, Harrie asked the big question. 'Does Mother know about Katherina or Mathilda?'

'No. There was no need. But there is need now because I wish to be buried with them. Lisa must be told, and I have not the energy.'

Harrie agreed. 'I'll do it. My mother has a generous soul. She's acted selfishly, and she's aware of that, but I think she's a sensitive spirit deep down.'

'And needy,' said Gus. 'She must remarry. I have been an unfit husband.' He stared hard at his daughter. 'You are so like Mathilda. May I give you some advice? Not that it will work...'

'Of course.'

He turned to Will. 'You, too. Never let the love take over. Never let the love become a burden you can't carry.'

Harrie swallowed hard. 'So you loved Katherina too much?'

Gus shrugged. 'She took everything in that department, yes. But I allowed that. Perhaps I am weak, or perhaps there was only one woman in the world for me. I stopped feeling, started working. You must love and work. The two are not mutually exclusive.'

They drank tea and talked about nothing in particular. It was clear that Sheila felt excluded in her own house, so Will and Harrie left.

Only then did Sheila speak. 'Are you definitely dying?'

'We are all dying. But yes. It will not take very long. The surgery may buy some time during which I may work, but it all depends on Humphrey.' He tapped his skull. 'That's the name of my chief tormentor.'

Sheila excused herself and went to the bathroom. The world was losing a brilliant man; the world had not deserved him.

369

The Warburton brothers arrived at one o'clock. Smartly dressed in dark-grey suits, they climbed out of a black, shiny car and walked towards the house while Lisa operated the gates. Weaver's Warp was now battened down. Annie, standing next to Lisa, dug her in the ribs. 'Well,' she whispered, 'mine's all right, but I don't think much to yours.'

'Behave yourself.'

'You're no fun.'

The men introduced themselves and were sent up to meet their true employer in the attic. Annie was blushing. As soon as the guards disappeared, Lisa rounded on her. 'Listen, birdbrain. They're here to look after us – all of us.'

Annie sighed. 'Matthew can look after me any time he likes. I'm going to put my face on. And the other wig. Don't you think the other wig suits me better? Oh, you can have Luke Warburton. He's the older one.'

Lisa clipped her friend lightly across the ear. 'If they were the bread Warburtons, I'd understand you. The bread lot are millionaires, at least. You've no idea, have you? Brain damage. Definitely. Not even a birdbrain. And,' she looked over her shoulder, 'Luke has the bigger feet. Do you know about bigger feet?'

'Aye, but I'm daintier than you are. So there.'

Lunch that day was in shifts. Although the kitchen was the size of the whole ground floor of one of the original weavers' cottages, it was still a push to feed so many. Harrie and Will were forced to eat with Daisy and the twins. Their agenda for the day had been mapped out – they were to eat with the children, then play with them until bedtime. 'My cup runneth over,' commented Will as he sat down with Annie's children.

When the first shift was over, Sal had to take her place with Lisa and Annie. The latter was making eyes at the younger of the security men, who had both been invited to partake. The men did not sit down, choosing instead to walk about the house and get their bearings while eating sandwiches. Lisa kicked Annie under the table several times, but Annie took no notice. Matthew Warburton reminded her of Brad Pitt; Lisa nominated him Bottomless Pitt, because his trousers were not quite as well filled when observed from the rear. 'Luke has the better bum,' she whispered.

Annie was ready, as ever. 'Trust you to go for the biggest arse,' she whispered.

Sal simply smiled. Surely, he would be arrested today? She was safer here in company. It was better not to think about how wild Jimmy had become; she was among decent folk, and that should be enough.

Will popped his head round the door when the second sitting was almost finished. 'Mrs Compton-Milne?'

'Yes, dear? Oh, and call me Lisa.'

'I'll mind the kids. Harrie needs a word with you.'

'Are you sure about the twins?' asked Annie. 'You've my permission to tie them up if necessary. And I'll help you entertain them in a minute.'

Lisa made her excuses and prepared to leave

371

the room. For someone expecting a happy event, Harrie had been quiet since her return from that funeral. Yes, it was sad when someone young died, but Harrie had never met Will's cousin, had she? She would have said so.

'Excuse me,' she begged again as she stood up. 'Annie, make sure you do help Will. Those boys of yours are ready for straitjackets.'

Annie scarcely heard. She was too busy keeping an eye on Matthew-Brad Pitt-Warburton. Could he tell she was wearing a wig? Did these jeans do her justice? Should she have worn a frock and her best gold sandals?

'I'll be back,' Lisa threatened.

'See you later, then,' Annie answered absently.

Lisa followed her daughter into Gus's office. This was the one place in which they were unlikely to be disturbed.

'Mother,' Harrie began, hands twisting nervously in her lap. 'It's not easy, but he isn't fit to tell you himself.'

'Who isn't?'

'My father.'

Harrie allowed the whole truth to make contact with the air. She said her piece slowly, trying hard to keep the emotion from her voice. 'So,' she concluded. 'There you have it, Mother. No New Zealand, treatment for cancer, and now you know the rest of it.'

Lisa sat in silence for at least ten seconds. Emotion moved across her face, but she did not open her mouth until she had risen and gone to stand at the window. 'I'm glad,' she said.

'Mother?!?'

Without turning to look at Harrie, she carried on. 'There was something – always something. I don't mean I'm glad about cancer – you must believe that. But – what did you say her name was? The mother, I mean.'

'Katherina. The family came from Hungary when the trouble started with communists. He fell absolutely head over heels. She left her husband for him. Then she died giving birth to their daughter.'

'And he kept Mathilda alive.'

'Yes. She was a piece of Katherina.'

Lisa's back began to shake. 'Thank God,' she wept. 'He loved somebody, Harrie. He really, really loved somebody. He married me because I was there – I married him because he showed promise as an earner. Though, I have to admit, I was fascinated by him. A clever man, you see. I had a rough upbringing, and Hermione and Gus carried me out of the gutter.'

'You carried yourself, Mother. You are a master jeweller.'

'Yes, I am.' She faced her daughter. Tears streamed freely down her cheeks. 'He loved. Don't you see? He is capable of that all-consuming passion. That means he is human after all.'

'Yes. My father is a human being. Sheila Barton – there's nothing going on. She just has a vast attic full of trains, and he uses it.'

'We must bring him home, Harrie.'

'Not yet. Not until the house is back to normal.'

Lisa smiled grimly. 'Normal? When were we that?'

Harrie nodded pensively. 'I was thinking, at the

beginning of summer, that mine was a life lived in parallel with everyone here. But hers was the real parallel life, wasn't it? Just lying there, not truly with us. We're all alone, I suppose, because we're locked in our own heads. Things get shared, but we're little islands, since a person can never absolutely know anyone apart from him or her self. Mathilda was denied even communication. Life without communication? Doesn't bear thinking of.'

'Poor girl,' said Lisa.

'I wonder if she heard? I wonder if she listened, Mother?'

'We'll never know.' Lisa wiped her face. 'And neither will he. God help Gus.' She disposed of her tissue. 'They have to get hold of Jimmy Nuttall so that your father can get back here when he's had that next operation. I shall talk to him on the phone. It will be easier now because I feel as if I know him. Pity he has so short a time.'

Harrie remained in her father's office for a while. She looked at the tomes he had published, books used by students of biomedical sciences all over the world. Loose papers filed under MRSA, folders marked with words too long to read, essays on antibiotic warfare against killer bugs. He had given his whole life to cleanliness, to safety. His son had developed the same fixation to a degree that had proved unhealthy. 'But Ben will come good,' she told the empty room.

Outside, a brilliant sun shone on a garden filled with people. Even Hermione and Woebee had come down from their higher realm to watch the twins and Will playing football with two large security men. It was all so wonderfully normal – fresh lemonade in icy jugs, kids screaming, their elders looking on and smiling at the antics.

Harrie sat on the grass. Soon, the sun would move to shed light elsewhere, and he would have the darkness he required. Sal, Lisa, Annie and herself were in the most danger – but what about his children? If he knew they were here... How much did he know?

So they had brought in some big boys, had they? From just below the highest canopy of a tall oak, Jimmy Nuttall watched the al fresco party, twisting controls on the binoculars until he could almost count the raisins in a scone. Tea, lemonade and scones. His children playing. 'Mine,' he growled. Annie was there, as was Sal. Lisa and her daughter sat to one side; they were plainly engaged in conversation of a private nature.

Bouncers. Two of them. Great big men with sleeves rolled up. Annie laughing at one of them. His wife.

Third tree along, covered in branches. Not here, no. Up at Cotters Farm, there was a van and ... and stuff. Stuff. What was it he had to do? There was something he must find and, if he didn't find it, he had to kidnap Daisy. No, not Daisy. Where was Dilly-Dolly? Had he lost her?

Daylight was dangerous, but there was plenty of cover. It couldn't be a fire, not if his children were here. He would burn the rest of them without a care, but not Daisy, not Craig and Billy. Lisa had broken things... He looked at her. She seemed sad, so that was some kind of justice, he supposed. Annie laughing again, laughing at one of the big men. Daisy skipping.

The games ended. A thin, ugly woman pushed a wheelchair into the house. Sal just sat. She was good at sitting. Now, she lived ... she lived in a cottage that had once been tied to Cotters. Dad. Teeth in a glass, pills lined up. Why was she here? Why were they all here together?

He climbed down and ran further into the woods. Chocolate had melted in his pocket, but he licked it from the wrapper. Calories were needed when a man had to think, had to remember why he was here and who his target was. Better to sleep for a while. If he could wake refreshed, he might remember what the hell he was supposed to be doing.

The Warburton brothers took their job seriously, so Annie got no chance to show her feathers to Matthew that evening. She bathed her children, put them to bed, threatened the twins with all kinds of deprivation if they moved a single toe out of line. Daisy was no trouble. She clung to Dilly-Dolly and fell asleep the moment her head hit the pillow.

Annie stood for a while and gazed at the doll. It looked as if Sal Potter might be right – Jimmy was losing his grip. He wasn't the type to leave evidence all over the place, was too keen on saving his skin to put himself in the limelight. The Jimmy she had known would not even stand under a forty-watt bulb if it endangered him, so he certainly wouldn't be leaving a blazing trail unless he had mislaid the plot. Sal reckoned

Jimmy needed doctors, not jailers. It looked as if Sal might be right. Poor Sal. So down in the mouth, she looked.

Hermione had been funny about the police. She couldn't stand them, wouldn't trust them to crack an egg, let alone a case. 'Let them root around at your house,' she had said. 'I'll get some real men here.' Well, Annie had enjoyed that bit of fun with Matthew Warburton. It took her mind of the main issue, made her remember that she was still relatively young. But, upstairs in Weaver's Warp, she looked at her children and felt as if her chest had been run through by a sword. Without distraction and the company of other adults, she was frightened to death.

In the kitchen, Lisa, Harrie, Will and Sal were playing cards for money. Annie bucked up and joined them, noisy as ever. She was no good at it, couldn't hide her joy when she got a good hand, her disappointment when the cards were poor.

But Sal was miraculously successful. Each time she won, she beamed at everyone and came to life.

'You're pretty when you smile,' Lisa told her.

Sal blushed. 'I learned my poker face from a good master,' she told them. 'It was me dad. Oh, he was a bugger for cards, darts, dominoes, crown-green bowls, even cricket when he was young. Good enough for Lancashire, we all thought.'

Annie started the argument. 'Just a cotton-picking minute,' she said. 'Somebody keeps changing all the rules. Is a flush better than two pairs and a few crumbs off my butty?'

'Yes,' chorused the assembly.

'Oh.' Annie was also the one who stopped the argument, since she had forgotten the hand over which she had decided to quarrel. 'Please your bloody selves, then,' she pretended to snap. 'You're only taking bread out of my kids' mouths.'

The noisesome group scarcely noticed sounds from outside until Matthew and Luke Warburton appeared at the door, a scruffy-looking individual in their grip. 'We found this outside,' announced Luke. 'Fiddling with a van. Didn't you say Nuttall has a van?'

Harrie stared at the miscreant. The miscreant stared at Harrie. 'That's not Jimmy Nuttall,' she said.

Everyone agreed. Lisa opined that Nuttall was never as dirty as this creature, while Annie said the captive was too good-looking to be mistaken for the bag of manure she had married. The prisoner said not a word until Sal asked the men to take their prey and give it a good wash, because it was scarcely recognizable as human.

At last, the captured man spoke. 'Back into the arms of my loving family. I was mending my engine.' He shook off his captors and said a few short words that did not bear repeating. 'Mending my van, causing no trouble, then these two apes pounced. I am Benjamin Compton-Milne, and I am going for a shower.'

Luke scratched his head. 'Eh?' he murmured.

Harrie leapt up. 'Four A-stars!' she shrieked before throwing herself into her brother's arms. 'The world's your oyster, babe. Or your lobster, as Woebee would put it.' She was then forced to explain to the uninitiated that Woebee was Eileen

378

and why Eileen was Woebee.

'What's going on?' Ben asked. 'Have we been invaded?'

Harrie linked her arm through his. 'Come on, ratbag. I'll tell you what you've missed while you clean up your act.'

Lisa smiled tentatively. 'We're in a bit of a mess, son. But welcome home, and congratulations on your exam results. If anyone deserves it, you do.'

'Thanks, Ma.' Brother and sister left the room.

Annie busied herself making tea for the Warburtons. She found some Bourbons in a tin. Matthew liked Bourbons – she had heard him saying so earlier in the day.

Upstairs, a cleaner version of Ben sat with his sister. He had just returned from the rim of life, an area in which the unacceptable endured the scathing attitude of those who existed behind hedges and triple-glazing. And he had come home to this. 'Our half-sister?' Tears threatened.

'I wish you'd charged your phone. But I understand the difficulties, babe.'

He learned that he was about to enter a state of uncle-hood, that Jimmy Nuttall had lost his marbles, that Gran had brought in security. He lowered his head. 'And on top of all that, our dad has cancer.'

'Yes.'

'Can't imagine Father as a Romeo.'

'Well, he was. Emotionally, he died the day he buried Katherina. Our dad's been through hell, and we never noticed. Mind, it happened before he married Mother. Even so, he's been so ... stoical.'

'Remind me never to be that,' said Ben. 'Poor Father. Poor, poor man. Stoicism is never a good idea.'

Things were jumping off the edge of his mind, deserting him like rats diving from a sinking ship. Jimmy Nuttall was entering an area of confusion from which he needed to escape as quickly as possible, because he was fighting for his life and his freedom. He remembered that much, at least. Places were all melding into one – where was his van, where was Cotters Farm, where was Sal's cottage?

Something was after him. They were after him. No. They were all in the one house, a big place made out of four cottages knocked together. Old woman in a wheelchair. Gun. Lisa with a safe under the shop floor, Sal and her plasma screen, leather sofa, Dilly-Dolly. Where had he left that toy? Teeth in a glass – bottles – tablets – policemen. Up a tree, looking at cops – no – looking at all the women, all except his mother.

He found himself walking across the front of Bolton Town Hall, and he didn't know how he had got there, couldn't remember where he had travelled from or to. It was brightly lit. Tea and scones on the lawn, people playing, lemonade in a jug. Thirsty. He was so dry. Daisy. Little face looking up at him, hospital blanket, Annie with her hair wet through after the exertion of birthing. There was a gun somewhere...

He walked past the open market – it was deserted now, of course. Mam used to bring him here. So colourful. Asian men and women selling

380

bright silks and bangles, sheets of finest Indian cotton. There was a shop somewhere that used to be a mill. All the spices of the orient were in there. Annie used them for curries, said they were authentic.

He should go home. Annie would make a brew and a bit of toast. He was starving, and his throat felt like sandpaper. All this walking. Why was he doing all this bloody walking? St Patrick's. Would a priest help him? Was there a priest? Someone had said there weren't enough priests to go round. He remembered that, all right.

Bradshawgate. There were a lot of gates – Deansgate, Moses Gate, Churchgate. But there were no gates any more – except in the names. He leaned against a column erected to the memory of ... of some Earl or other who had been beheaded here under the rule of ... that chap who was Protector rather than monarch. Bolton didn't like the monarchy – he recalled that, too.

His legs didn't work any more. It was the knees. They didn't seem to want to take his weight. As for the backbone – it was aching all the way down. He sank to the base of the column and waited. Whatever he waited for didn't matter any more. As long as there was a glass of water at the end of it, he couldn't have cared less.

When they picked him up, he answered the question – yes – he was James Nuttall. They cautioned him, asked if he had anything to say, warned that whatever he did say would be used, that whatever he didn't say, he'd wish he had said. All he managed was a request for water.

Before they locked him up, they gave him a huge plastic cup and he took the lot in one draught. 'More,' he begged.

A doctor arrived and asked questions. They were daft questions, and Jimmy was too tired. At the end of the session, he heard himself declared unfit to plead. He wasn't unfit, just tired. And he hoped he'd get a proper breakfast in the morning.

Epilogue

9 May, 2008

Summer came early. It was strange, because winter seemed to have lingered well into April, yet this first week in May had brought sunshine tempered by a slight breeze that kept thick-blooded Northern-Englanders from frying on the spot. The area now known as Greater Manchester was famous for its rainfall and for its complainers. It was always too cold, too windy, too wet, too hot, too cloudy. But today was just right.

It is almost impossible to suit a determined Lancastrian. Hermione, who refused to accept the change of boundaries, would not allow the words 'Greater Manchester' to be included on her stationery. She was Lancastrian, as was everybody else right across to Liverpool. Her Majesty the Queen was Duke of Lancaster, and that was an end to the argument, as loyalty lay with the crown and with the Duchy. Government and opposition were great puddles of acid rain, she would no longer vote for any of them, and she complained the whole afternoon while Eileen Eckersley prepared her for a vital expedition. 'Would you ever keep still for only a minute?' asked the Irishwoman.

'I have the shakes, you dreadful moan. Part and

383

parcel of my condition, don't you know?'

Eileen knew the difference between MS shakes and naughtiness. This was definitely naughtiness. 'The whole town hall will have its eyes on you – the Mayor and all. Do you want to arrive looking like a badly-cut privet with a birds' nest on top?'

'Why should I care? No one looks at a wheel-chair. Everyone speaks to the person behind me, the one with the power to steer. If anyone asks you am I all right, I shall stand up and punch that person.'

'Aye, you will and all. Think of Harrie. Think of what she has to do tonight. She's worked herself to the bone with all this – and she has Hope to care for. On top of all of which she's doing the university as well – can you not appreciate what you have in your life, Iona?'

The older woman's lower lip quivered, but she sat her ground and didn't weep. Until Harrie had explained it all, she hadn't known her son, hadn't realized what Gus had gone through, how hard he had worked, how serious his research had been. 'I know I'm blessed,' she said softly. 'My granddaughter is a star.'

Lisa dashed in with two outfits on hangers. 'Green or blue, Mum?' she asked. 'I need to know because the make-up girl will go with the colours. And Annie needs to know, too, as we don't want to match. She has to choose between green and blue as well. Come on!' They were both staring hard at her.

'Green,' said Eileen.

'She's Irish,' pronounced Hermione unneces-sarily. 'Take no notice of her. Blue. Definitely the

384

blue. But, before you go, what have you done to your hair?'

'I am "sweating in" the oil,' replied Lisa haughtily. 'And you beggars are no use.' She dashed off to ask Harrie.

'"Sweating in" the oil?' the two women repeated simultaneously. Lisa with her head wrapped in yards of towelling had not been an impressive sight. 'Never mind,' added Hermione. 'It'll be all right on the night, as they say.' It had better be all right, because it had been all wrong for too long a time.

Milly rushed in with Bella hot on her back paws. They did three rounds of the room, stopped for half-time, then scuttled out and rattled down the stairs. There was nothing quite so inelegant as an Alsatian and a black half-Persian pretending to be enemies. 'Do they improve with age?' Hermione asked.

'I doubt it very much,' was Eileen's reply. She continued, just as she often did, with a tale. 'We'd a calf back home with its mother dead. Another took her for a while, but got fed up with it, so we had it in the house. All very well and good, you might say, but they pull so hard on the bottle teat, you've your shoulder out of socket. And it grew.'

'The shoulder?'

'The cow. But it didn't know it had grown until it got stuck in the doorway. We'd half the local lads round cursing and swearing and trying to shift the cow with oil.'

'Like Lisa with her hair?'

'No comment. At the finish, we lost the door

385

frame. They learn only the hard way. When Bella finds herself flattened under three or four stones of dog, she may change the way she votes. Until then, be sure to remain seated, or they'll have you spread out from here to Manchester.'

'I don't like Manchester.'

'Aye. Then keep yourself still, but.'

Eileen was now full-time carer for Hermione. Sometimes, when alone, she wept buckets, because the illness had taken so much from a proud and independent woman who should have gone far. She should have gone to London for a start. The Tory and Labour parties might both have run for the hills had Hermione got to them. She said some daft things, but Hermione Compton-Milne was a wonderful, if somewhat eclectic, mix. Left wing to the core, she remained a landowner and lady of the manor. She had hated selling all those acres for housing, yet she recognized the right of every Briton to shelter and care for a family. As far as Eileen was concerned, her employer was everything good rolled up into one frail person.

'What are you trying to do to my hair?' asked the good, frail person. 'Don't you need planning permission and a decent architect?'

Eileen smiled. As long as the old lady had her humour, there was hope for the world.

Annie phoned Lisa. Lisa was wearing the blue, so Annie could sport her new designer-labelled emerald green three-piece with the diamanté flower on the clasp of its edge-to-edge jacket. It had come from Oxfam, but it was brilliant. She even had shoes to match, so she sang happily through her housework while Daisy washed dishes. The lads were up Wigan Road with their blessed train sets. Sheila had almost tamed them. Almost, but not quite. With their energy channelled, they now spent hours reading railway books. They also continued to annoy most of the neighbours, but a woman couldn't have everything.

She seated herself with a cup of tea and thought for a few minutes about Jimmy. Declared fit to plead after a month of treatment, Annie's husband had hanged himself in his cell. In spite of fifteen-minute checks, James Nuttall had rendered himself terminally unfit to plead, and he now rested with his mother. It had all been too much for poor Freda; Jimmy had killed her, too. Annie glanced at her mantelpiece where some of Freda's treasures sat. She hadn't been able to throw away all the figurines. Those bits and pieces were Daisy's now; she made up stories about them, just as she had with her paternal grandmother. 'Sad, sad time,' Annie murmured.

But it hadn't all been sad. Matthew Warburton of Warboys Security Services was now living with Annie and her children. He would be a good influence on Billy and Craig, she told herself repeatedly. His brother, Luke, was trying to court Lisa, but Lisa had declared herself to be a recycled virgin and an excellent grandmother. Luke would wear her down – of that, Annie was certain. He would be there tonight as Lisa's escort. They looked beautiful together. 'And together is what they should and will be,' whispered the determined little woman.

Daisy stepped down from her stool. She was four years old – but going on forty, as her mother often told her. 'Mam?'

'Yes?'

'Can I not come tonight? I'd be good.'

'No, love. It's just for grown-ups. There'll be no little girls or boys there.'

'But I'm clever.'

She was. Annie wondered where little Daisy had come from because she seemed to have brains and common sense. 'I know you're clever, babe, but we'd have to take the twins as well. To the Town Hall. The Albert Hall. They'd wreck it.'

'Yes. Yes, they would.' Daisy moved on happily to her next task. They were tidying up for Mrs Mason. Mrs Mason was the fiercest of baby-sitters, and she would keep BillyandCraig quiet. Mam was too gentle with them, and she always laughed at her twins. They were funny, but they were naughty. Did she want her mam to be more like Mrs Mason? No. Daisy hugged her mother. This was the best mam ever.

After the death of Gus, Sheila Barton had been a wreck. She had given up on life, on herself, on her appearance – even her beloved home had suffered. After one of her visits to Weaver's Warp, Hermione had decided to take Sheila in hand. Being taken in hand by a woman like Hermione Compton-Milne was an unforgettable experience. In fact, Iona was probably a one-off in this day and age, when folk seemed to care nothing for each other.

Sheila remembered the scene vividly. It had been populated by the lady of the house, her Irish carer, a lunatic dog and a cat with attitude. Looking back now, it was easy to laugh, but laughter had not come easily at the time.

'Sit down,' Mrs Compton-Milne had ordered.

Sheila grinned. Accidentally sitting on a cat was not a situation that was easy to forget. The cat had taken the huff, and Sheila's scars had lasted for a week. Eileen had bathed and dressed the hand. Such kindness, so well hidden behind that gargoyle face – bless her.

Sheila closed her eyes and went back to that day. 'Is it hurting now?' asked Eileen.

'Yes. But thank you.'

'Do you like living alone?' the old woman asked.

'No. But I don't want another husband.'

'One is enough for anyone,' replied Hermione.

'One is one too many when he leaves screws and nails all over the path for me to step on,' interspersed Eileen.

Hermione cast a withering eye in the direction of her carer. 'Tea, please,' she said.

Sheila found herself almost grinning.

'I know another woman who needs not to be by herself,' Hermione continued. 'Cottage tied to an estate that no longer functions – she'll be out on her ear when the developers move in.'

'Oh?'

'Yes. Needs a bit of encouragement, a little company from time to time. Like you, she nursed an older man – her father – until he died. There is something to be said for a mutual support system. Your house is big enough, I take it?'

Sheila nodded.

'Then I suggest you get together with Sal Potter and discuss the matter. She works here in this house. She could live here – there's sufficient room – but I think she'd be happier with you.'

Sal and Sheila had shared for some time now. They each had a sitting room and a bedroom, and the other facilities were communal. Pleasant evenings were spent walking in the nearby park, or, when daylight hours were shorter, they would sit in one room and read, the shared silence comfortable and appreciated. They bought dictionaries and learned to cheat at Scrabble, went to the cinema, sometimes to Manchester for shopping and an evening at the theatre. They were content.

Sal was going to wear dove grey tonight. She had gone on for months about a well-cut suit and, in the end, a seamstress had produced exactly what Sal had craved. Sheila had chosen navy because she already had an outfit in that colour. Gus wouldn't have needed her to dress up specially, and the whole evening was about him.

They had been to the hairdresser. Sheila's hair was its usual sensible self, but Sal, who had discovered the Internet, had bought some Hot Hair and it was added in at the back like a French pleat. She wanted to be elegant and, having lost some weight, was looking just about as elegant as she would ever manage. The country girl had come to town, and she wanted the town to notice her.

'Are we eating?' shouted Sal from the kitchen.

'We're having supper up at Weaver's after the do.'

Sal dashed in. 'And we're invited? I'm invited?'

'Of course we are. It wasn't your fault, any of it. God knows they've told you that often enough. You were not responsible for the behaviour of Jimmy Nuttall.'

Sal stared blankly for a moment. 'What? Oh, I know that. It's just going to feel odd because I'm the cook and cleaner – tonight, I'll be a guest.'

'Then make the most of it,' Sheila said, laughing. 'Remember – a cat can look at a king. And their cat is a force to be reckoned with.'

Sal stood in the doorway, a question in her eyes. 'Sheila?'

'What?'

'Do you think she didn't really mind when he got buried with that other woman?'

'Lisa Compton-Milne?' Sheila pondered for a moment. 'There's something ... big about her. As if she can put up with just about everything. It was more important that she did as Gus asked. If the world wants to talk about her, she won't listen.'

'A great woman, then?'

Sheila nodded. 'Oh yes. A very great woman. All three of them are exceptional – the Grandma, the mother and the daughter. I think the best is yet to come, though. When Harrie comes into her own, the rest of us will sit up very straight and listen.'

Annie Nuttall's boys clattered their way downstairs. They had spent an hour with Gus's favourite trains and were due to be picked up shortly by their mother. 'Thanks for the biscuits,' said the taller one.

'You're welcome, Billy,' replied Sheila.

'And the orange juice with no additives.' Craig grinned. He and his brother knew that they could blame almost anything on additives. If they were naughty, they used the excuse that someone had given them the wrong food.

Sheila was fit for them, though. She had taken their measure right from the start. 'No trouble tonight. That new babysitter of yours knows full well that your diet's controlled. Don't spoil things for your poor mother. She deserves a bit of fun.'

They stood there, a picture of innocence. For the chance to play with the trains, they would have promised the earth on a bed of lettuce. 'No, Mrs Barton,' they chorused. There would be no chance, anyway. They had been working for weeks to create a situation that might flummox Mrs Mason, but Mrs Mason was not an easy target. For a start, she moved too fast and owned a tongue that lashed like whipcord.

Sheila smiled inwardly. These two precious souls reminded her each time they visited that she was, indeed, a fortunate woman. She had not been blessed with children; nor had she been cursed by them. They made her laugh, but so did Joe Pasquale. Best of all, she could send them away when the laughter stopped. Life was good.

Harrie had named her wooden bungalow The Carding Shed. It was almost an annexe to a house that paid tribute to the art of cotton-weaving, so her little place was a nod in the direction of labourers from the bottom of the pile, low-paid

392

carders who combed the cotton once bales were broken. Like her grandmother, she was deliberately eccentric and immovably left wing.

She, Will and Hope lived happily in their hut. It was a very nice hut, big enough, well insulated and beautifully furnished in bright, happy colours. Sometimes, Harrie stayed in Liverpool with other students, but she managed to get home most of the time, as she had no difficulty in maintaining a decent standard without attending every available lecture.

'What are you wearing?' called Will from the bedroom. 'Probably clothes,' was her reply. She followed it with, 'Be quiet – I am making a few last minute adjustments.'

Hope was playing on the floor. She was now fifteen months old and walking, though she preferred to be carried. Harrie was all for leaving the child to get on with it, but Hope only had to reach up her arms and say, 'High,' and her dad couldn't resist picking her up. He did that now, then came to lean over his wife's shoulder.

'The frightening thing is that I understand most of that now,' he told her.

'The frightening thing is that it's a frightening thing,' she answered. 'Go and give Hope a bath. She is to be carried in at the end. Father would have liked that.'

Will went off to clean up Hope's act. She was still at the getting-into-everything stage, and much of what she got into clung to her person. The child had made such a wonderful difference to their lives. It was early days, but the marriage looked strong enough to support Hope and, perhaps, one or two more. Harrie wanted 'heaps' of children, and Will would be happy to oblige. But the hut would need extending. That was the beauty of these section homes – another child meant sticking on an extra room – it was no big deal.

'Why can't they give these bloody antibiotics pronounceable names?' Harrie yelled from the other room.

Will placed his daughter in the bath and didn't bother to reply. When it came to her subject, Harrie's questions were, for the most part, rhetorical. He was proud of his Hat. She had taken up the cause, was on her way to a first-class degree, and she was determined.

As was her daughter. 'Duck,' shouted Hope before throwing the yellow plastic object. Will smiled. The word had been appropriate as noun and verb, though he had not heeded the latter.

'If I have a black eye tonight, it will be your fault,' he told his daughter.

Hope smiled prettily. Then she threw the second duck.

Ben was on his way up the M6. Studying maths and computer science at St Anne's College, Oxford, his intention was to gain an MSc before moving into a job involving the police, the government and, almost certainly, the Official Secrets Act. Like several others on the course, he was determined to make some contribution towards stemming Internet crime, and the road ahead promised not to provide easy travelling. Nor did the M6, since the world and his wife had decided to come out and enjoy a weekend of decent weather.

But Internet highways were a lot worse than he had first imagined, because fraud, pornography, paedophilia and many other diseases thrived healthily in the ether. Like hospitals, the Internet housed some very ill patients and some extremely robust bacteria, which trawled, hacked into and ate people's lives on a daily basis. He was more like his father than he had imagined, since he, too, was fighting the almost invisible and the potentially invincible.

On the positive side, he had discovered that it was possible to live in close contact with others and for that, he thanked Angelina. Angelina was the battered camper he now drove homeward, because tonight was Harrie's night. His sister remained the one person in the world who was truly deserving of admiration, though several others vied for second place. Ben had discovered girls. Like the first man to top Everest, he wanted to plant a flag to mark the spot, because he was turning out to be what most would term normal. He accepted now the concept that he had taken a long time to grow up, that his intellect had been a burden which could soon be put to good use in his career.

Angelina had started to struggle of late. As he intended to keep her for the rest of his life, Ben would have her hospitalized in Bolton under the care of a master mechanic on whom his family had depended for at least two generations. She required careful handling and was deserving of only the best.

As he drove, he remembered the momentous summer of 2006, when he had literally taken his life into his own hands after watching that webcam suicide. Living with travelling folk? Fishing, chopping wood, helping to settle a horse after a traumatic journey down from Appleby? He remembered feeling truly alive for the first time ever, remembered with great affection Josh, his close friend, face tanned and lined, hands strong enough to defy the excesses of the most unbroken of stallions. Ben had fought, that summer, for his very existence, as he had determined to use as little money as possible. So, it had been Ben versus the elements, and he could not have succeeded alone.

He thanked God for Gran and her generosity, as it was she who had provided the cash for Angelina and, indirectly, for the travellers. How reluctant Josh had been when receiving the money from Ben. Travellers' pride was beyond measure, but Ben had won in the end – they would have been more comfortable for several months after his exit from their lives.

How far he had come, thanks to Harrie. It was she who had watched over him, she who had tried to understand, she who had walked away. Like an alcoholic, Ben had been left to come to terms with his own misbehaviours, and the miracle had happened. He tried and failed to remember how it felt to worry about a scratched kettle, ordered shelves, sanitized kitchen. The house he currently inhabited would have driven his father wild, as it had probably not been cleaned for months. It didn't matter. Only the bigger picture mattered now.

He wished he'd known his father better, wished he could remember more than a few occasions on which they had talked. The man had been intuitive; when he had indulged in conversation, it was clear that he understood and took an interest in whatever was going on around him, that he cared enough to give advice. Too late now. 'No, no,' Ben told himself. 'Never too late, and never give up hope.'

Hope. He was an uncle. The minute those tiny fingers had closed around his thumb, the child had clutched at his heart like a steel vice. So small, so perfect. Unfortunately, she would deteriorate into a human adult, but he would never stop loving her. He had found her first tooth, had been present for the inevitable 'da-da' that was always presumed to be a baby's first word.

Ben found himself grinning. It was he who had sung to her, and, at eight weeks of age, she had joined in with 'All Things Bright and Beautiful'. She sang some of the right notes, but not necessarily in the right order, putting him in mind of a famous Morecambe and Wise sketch involving Andre Previn, a piano concerto, and a lot of jumping about. Soon, he would see Hope again. She was walking now, so perhaps she could do the jumping about bit as well.

He drove into his home town, wondering whether he would ever live here again. The job he wanted might take him just about anywhere – even across the Atlantic. But Bolton would always be home. It was a great town, a proud town in which his family had established mills, then shops. It had given birth to several notable people among which number his father was counted.

They had watched their father die alone, behind the glass, because he would not allow them to enter his room. In the end, the cancer was not his murderer; he was killed by *Clostridium difficile*, an antibiotic-resistant bacterium that spreads in dirty hospitals. It was an ironic death, for a man whose whole life had been devoted to cleanliness, who'd been an expert on superbugs and how to combat them.

Tonight, in the Albert Hall, the Gustav Compton-Milne Memorial Lecture was to be delivered by Harrie. She had given up the idea of becoming a teacher and had decided to pick up the baton dropped by her father in August 2006. It seemed inevitable that she would gain a first from Liverpool, that she would go on to PhD level, that she would study for the rest of her life, just as Father had. She had decided, Ben thought, to see that no one else would die, as their father had, of an infection that should have been preventable.

There had been no religious ceremony for Gus, as he had not believed in anything that was not completely proven. Had he been able to find God under a microscope, perhaps he might have relaxed his view. Father would have approved of the lecture. Harrie was not yet the professional her male parent had been, but she had fire in her belly and faith in her subject. Tonight, Harrie would burn bright.

The publishers hope that this book has given you enjoyable reading. Large Print Books are especially designed to be as easy to see and hold as possible. If you wish a complete list of our books please ask at your local library or write directly to:

Magna Large Print Books
Magna House, Long Preston,
Skipton, North Yorkshire.
BD23 4ND

This Large Print Book for the partially sighted, who cannot read normal print, is published under the auspices of

THE ULVERSCROFT FOUNDATION